Maisie Thomas was born and brought up in Manchester, which provides the location for her Railway Girls novels. She loves writing stories with strong female characters, set in times when women needed determination and vision to make their mark. The Railway Girls series is inspired by her great-aunt Jessie, who worked as a railway clerk during the First World War.

Maisie now lives on the beautiful North Wales coast with her railway enthusiast husband, Kevin, and their two rescue cats. They often enjoy holidays chugging up and down the UK's heritage steam railways.

Also by Maisie Thomas

The Railway Girls
Secrets of the Railway Girls
The Railway Girls in Love
Christmas with the Railway Girls

Hope
for the
Railway Girls

MAISIE THOMAS

PENGUIN BOOKS

PENGUIN BOOKS

UK | USA | Canada | Ireland | Australia
India | New Zealand | South Africa

Penguin Books is part of the Penguin Random House group
of companies whose addresses can be found at
global.penguinrandomhouse.com

Penguin
Random House
UK

Published by Penguin Books 2022
001

Copyright © Maisie Thomas, 2022

The moral right of the author has been asserted

Typeset in 10.75/13.5 pt Palatino LT Std
by Integra Software Services Pvt. Ltd, Pondicherry

Printed and bound in Great Britain by Clays Ltd, Elcograf S.p.A.

The authorised representative in the EEA is Penguin Random House
Ireland, Morrison Chambers, 32 Nassau Street, Dublin D02 YH68

A CIP catalogue record for this book is available from
the British Library

ISBN: 978–1–529–15694–2

www.greenpenguin.co.uk

*To the memory of Able Seaman Horace 'Horrie' John Walker
(1925–1944) and his brother Ivan Clive Walker (1936–1972) who
was the camp photographer at Bovington Camp during his
National Service.*

*And to Margaret Cowlan, for her kindness at a difficult time in
my life; and Oliver Campbell, grandson of Margaret and Ivan.
Oliver, you have grown into a remarkable man – hard-working,
considerate and full of affection. Kevin and I love you dearly and
are so proud of you.*

Acknowledgements

I am grateful to Laura Longrigg, Katie Loughnane and Rose Waddilove, who ensured this book was polished until it gleamed. Also to Caroline Johnson, my copy-editor, whose keen eye and extensive knowledge of the series ensured I didn't fall into any heffalump traps.

Huge thanks to Catherine Boardman for choosing the perfect name for the dog in this story. To find out more, please read my short article, *Brizo, the Railway Dog*, in the back of the book.

When writing acknowledgements, the word 'support' crops up time and again. To avoid that, I'd like to thank all these people for their support, as well as …

Deborah Smith for befriending and encouraging me from the start;

Zoe Morton for the book-reveal videos;

Jane Cable for being the friend every writer needs;

Beverley Ann Hopper for her generosity;

Jen Gilroy for sharing all the ups and downs.

And much love to Jacquie Campbell, who allowed me the honour of dedicating this book to her darling Daddy and Uncle Horrie.

CHAPTER ONE

Friday, 2 January 1942

With the oily smell of the rag making her nostrils itch, Margaret rubbed hard at her allocated section of the locomotive's enormous body. Polishing the loco sounded like an easy job, but it wasn't, not if you did it properly. It called for loads of elbow grease – 'good old Mark 1 elbow grease', as it was known – but the effort was more than worth it, she had discovered.

It was funny how things worked out. She had sat the tests in English, maths and geography to work on the railways simply as a means of escaping from her old job, a job she had loved ever since she had started at Ingleby's the day after she left school, aged fourteen. But she had ended up dreading going to work in case one of her old neighbours appeared. You couldn't run away and hide, not when you were an assistant in a successful and highly regarded shop.

Margaret smiled to herself. You were supposed to run away and join the circus, weren't you? Well, she had run away and joined the London, Midland and Scottish Railway. She had even been desperate enough to write a letter, asking if she could please have a job that didn't involve working with the public. She had no idea whether anyone had paid attention to her request, or whether she would have been assigned to engine-cleaning anyway, but it didn't matter. She was here now and she loved it.

1

There was something deeply satisfying about giving a loco a jolly good clean. Everyone depended on the railways. They were an essential part of the war effort and Margaret believed all the way down to her toes that the war couldn't be won without them. Troops, munitions, food and fuel were all transported around the country by rail. As a railway worker, Margaret was aware that dummy tanks were moved about on the back of huge flat-bed wagons, just to keep Jerry guessing when he flew over in his spy planes. And then there were the ordinary passengers, of course, who put up with all sorts of delays because they were at the bottom of the pecking order these days when it came to deciding which trains were given priority; but folk took it on the chin, because everybody knew the importance of transporting soldiers, coal, weapons, food and other essentials.

Margaret stopped for a moment to roll her shoulders inside her boiler suit. All the women in the engine sheds wore boiler suits or else heavy-duty dungarees with old blouses underneath or, in some cases, old shirts that had previously belonged to their husbands. Although Margaret preferred dungarees in warm weather, she was in a boiler suit now, because this January was proving to be colder than usual.

'Let's hope it's even colder in Russia,' Alison had said a couple of evenings ago at home in Wilton Close when Mrs Cooper was busy preparing hot-water bottles for her, Margaret and Mabel. 'That'd freeze Jerry in his tracks.'

Wilton Close. A warm feeling crept into Margaret's heart as she pictured it. Even now, after living there for a few weeks, she still sometimes felt like pinching herself to make sure it was real. Imagine her, Margaret Darrell, having such good luck. It wasn't just that she appreciated having a clean and comfy billet after the frankly shoddy bedsit she had lived in previously. It was the *feeling* of home that permeated the house, thanks to the kindly good nature of Mrs Cooper, her landlady, and also of Mrs Grayson, who was really another lodger but who did all the cooking and was a wizard at producing tasty meals in spite of shortages and rationing. Mabel joked that Mrs Grayson possessed a magic wooden spoon, and she wasn't far wrong.

'Forget Elsie and Doris Waters and Freddie Grisewood and *The Kitchen Front* on the wireless,' Mabel had declared. 'Mrs Grayson should have her own programme. It could be called *Meals by Magic*. How does that sound?'

'Get away with you,' Mrs Grayson had said, but she hadn't been able to hide how pleased she was.

Margaret shared a bedroom with Mabel, and Mrs Cooper had turned the old box room into a little bedroom for Alison. Living with the other two girls had helped Margaret to feel very much a part of the group of friends she had been drawn into last summer. It had been daunting, to say the least, to join a group of such established friends. Margaret had Joan to thank for her inclusion. They had known one another back at Ingleby's, though it hadn't been until they were put on fire-watching duty together that they had become friendly. Truth be told, it was because Joan had left Ingleby's in a state of such pride and excitement to join the railways that Margaret had decided to do the same when she had been in need of a bolt-hole.

And how glad she was that she'd done it. Thanks to that decision, she now had a cosy billet with the loveliest landlady in the kingdom, and she had a group of chums to whom she felt closer than she had to anybody else in a long time.

Life was looking up and sometimes the past didn't matter quite so much any more.

Sometimes.

At the end of her shift, Margaret hurried to the changing room, which, in spite of the staggered shift patterns, wasn't big enough for the number of women needing to get changed at any one time. Peeling off her boiler suit, Margaret put on an oyster-coloured faux-silk blouse and a tartan wool skirt that, along with some other items, had been given to her by the women running the local rest centre after her house had been bombed and she had lost nearly everything. Back when she had worked at Ingleby's, she had always dressed nicely with everything properly co-ordinated, thanks to her staff discount, though when you'd been bombed out, swish clothes never seemed as important afterwards. You weren't supposed to use your staff discount for anyone other than yourself, but sometimes Margaret had been unable to resist treating her sister to something special. Anna was kind-hearted and generous, as well as being pretty, and she deserved to have lovely things.

A pang smote Margaret. She hadn't seen Anna for such a long time. In some ways, it was worse missing Anna than missing William, their brother. You sort of accepted that your menfolk had to be away because of the war. Not that that made their absence easier to bear, but at least it felt necessary.

Anna had had a baby on the way – twins, as it turned out – when war was declared, so she had been evacuated along with all the children and the other mothers-to-be. That had been in the September of 1939 and now it was the start of 1942 – and the country was still at war. To think she hadn't seen the older sister she had always looked up to in

4

all that time. It would have been unthinkable before the war, but now these things, these separations, were normal. Anna's twins, one of each, would be two this month. Two! Strewth, but war was a cruel business.

Over the top of her blouse, Margaret put on her new jumper, which was mainly a warm russet-brown with a three-inch stripe in cream about four inches above the hem. Anna had knitted it for her for Christmas and she was dying to show it off to those of her friends who hadn't yet seen it. It might not be the best match for her blouse, but Margaret didn't have so many clothes that she could afford to be choosy. Besides, she would have loved anything her sister made for her and wore it as much as she could.

She removed the turban she wore all day long to protect her hair and keep it out of the way. Lots of the girls and women wore curlers under their turbans. Margaret hadn't to begin with, because she had seemed to hear her dear late mum's voice inside her head. Mum would have seen it as setting foot out of doors improperly dressed, but she had passed away several years ago and things were different now. It was normal for women in factories and other mucky jobs to wear curlers under their turbans. Margaret, declining to do so when she started in the engine sheds, had ended each shift with flattened hair while all the others had been busy fluffing up their curls and waves. These days, Margaret was very much part of the fluffing-up brigade. As for Mum – well, Margaret had done a lot worse than wear her curlers outdoors.

When her dark brown page-boy cut hung loose and uncurled, it sat on Margaret's shoulders. She styled it so that full curls waved away from her face and she had let the fringe grow so that it too could be curled and sit in a froth at her temples. She shrugged into her coat, winding her scarf around her neck, paying attention to her brimless felt hat and making sure it didn't muss up her hair.

Calling cheerful goodbyes, she set off to walk to Victoria Station, where she was going to meet up with her friends in the buffet. As she entered the station, she was greeted by the mingled aromas of smoke and steam. The sound of a train pulling in lifted up into the arched canopy that covered the station platforms and echoed around the enormous building. Margaret glanced up at the metal and glass canopy. As one of Victoria Station's fire-watchers, she regularly spent the night up there – not on the canopy, of course, but on the roof.

The concourse was packed, as always at this time of day, with people going home after work. It was a bit early for the 'funk express' crowd, those folk who legged it out of Manchester to spend the night elsewhere in case the city was bombed. One or two people looked impatient as they made their way through all the passengers standing about smoking, chatting or reading newspapers as they waited, but Margaret didn't care how busy it was. She enjoyed feeling that she was a part of it. She relished her position as a railway girl and loved the thought of joining her friends for a cuppa and a good natter before heading for home. It was to be their first get-together since Christmas Eve. Her heart delivered a bump. Christmas Eve. Oh, Colette. They had all shared their memories and feelings about their dear friend. It had been a deeply emotional experience, but also the beginning of healing.

The buffet was busy, but Dot had already bagged a table near the fireplace – and with her was Cordelia, one arm in her coat sleeve, the other hidden beneath her coat. Margaret went straight to them.

'Cordelia!' she exclaimed, only to become aware of eyebrows raised in surprise and disapproval at neighbouring

6

tables at her use of her friend's first name. 'I mean, Mrs Masters,' she corrected herself, feeling heat in her cheeks. For a girl in her twenties to address a lady in her forties by her first name simply wasn't the done thing and the group of friends were flouting convention by allowing it, so it was important to maintain the proprieties in front of outsiders.

Margaret sank onto a chair, leaning towards Cordelia, her delight at seeing her washing away her moment of embarrassment. 'I wasn't expecting you to be here today.'

Cordelia smiled. 'I wasn't going to miss the chance of seeing you all.'

'How's the collarbone?' asked Margaret.

'Mending, thank you. It doesn't ache anything like so much as it did. I'll be back at work in no time.'

'Well, it's lovely to see you,' said Margaret.

She went to join the queue, her gaze drawn back to her friends as she waited. Cordelia wore her wine-coloured coat with the fancy topstitched collar and her grey hat with the upswept brim that showed off her fine features, ash-blonde hair and discreet pearl earrings. Dot wore a rather good navy coat with patch pockets and wide lapels – the reason it was rather good being that it had once been Cordelia's, and that was a mark of their friendship, if anything was. Cordelia had passed on the coat out of pure friendship, not out of concern or charity, as might have been expected by anybody who didn't know them, given their social differences.

Those two were great friends. Margaret knew that Mum would have been baffled by their friendship, but that was the war for you. Pre-war, Mrs Kenneth Masters, wife of a solicitor and not just middle class but upper middle class, would never have crossed paths with working-class Dot

Green, but thanks to their work on the railways, they had met and become firm friends.

In fact, so Margaret had been told, it had been Miss Emery, the assistant welfare supervisor for women and girls, who had advised the friends to stick together and overlook all the things, such as background and class, that would normally have separated them in society. Margaret hadn't been there on everyone else's first day, but even so, she was grateful to Miss Emery, because she had benefited from the advice as much as any of them.

When Margaret reached the front of the queue, Mrs Jessop poured her a cup of tea without her needing to ask. Picking up the teaspoon that was tied to a block of wood, Margaret stirred her drink. With cutlery now being in short supply, and certain to remain so for the duration, it was normal for cafés and suchlike to take precautions so that their precious items stayed put.

Margaret made her way to the table and sat down. Soon they were joined by the others – Mabel, Joan, Persephone and Alison.

After the first smiling greetings, they all fell silent, looking at one another.

'We're all thinking it,' said Dot, 'so I'm going to say it. Colette.'

Margaret swallowed a lump in her throat. Colette, their dear friend, had been killed doing fire-watching duty one night the week before Christmas. It was still hard to believe. Being all together like this made it both harder to believe and yet at the same time more real.

'It must have been a pretty awful Christmas for her husband,' said Persephone.

'He must be lost without her,' said Mabel. 'He could hardly bear to let her out of his sight.'

'I've been wondering,' said Dot. 'Ought we to do something for him, like we did for Mrs Cooper after Lizzie died?'

'That was before your time, Margaret,' said Alison. 'We gave Mrs Cooper the notebook we all write in to make arrangements to meet here, and we all wrote our memories of Lizzie in the back.'

'Do you mean us to do that for Tony?' Joan asked Dot.

Glances were exchanged around the table.

'It's one thing to do it for Mrs Cooper,' said Cordelia, 'but she's a woman and a mother. It's different for a man.'

'It was just a thought,' said Dot, 'but happen you're right.' She laughed. 'If I cop it, I can tell you now that my Reg wouldn't thank you for giving him our notebook.'

'It was a kind thought, Dot,' said Persephone, 'but perhaps not appropriate in this instance.'

'Tony needs to rely on his family and friends to see him through,' said Mabel.

'Does he have family?' asked Joan. 'I know Colette was an only child and she'd lost both her parents.'

'I know Tony still has his mum and dad,' said Mabel, 'because Colette occasionally mentioned going to her in-laws' for Sunday lunch, but I don't know if Tony has brothers and sisters.'

'He's in the Home Guard as well as being a fire-watcher,' Margaret added, 'so he'll know a lot of people. I'm sure they'll all be keeping an eye on him.'

Cordelia shook her head. 'Such a tragedy.'

'Aye, well, there are plenty of tragedies about these days,' said Dot, 'though perhaps not as many as there used to be, since the air raids have tailed off. Let's hope they fade away altogether.'

'America's in the war now,' Mabel reminded them, 'and that's good news. The first American troops should arrive at the end of the month.'

'That's summat to look forward to.' Dot pressed Joan's hand. 'Talking of things to look forward to, how are you keeping, our little mother-to-be?'

'I'm fine, thanks,' said Joan. 'The morning sickness seems to have passed now.'

'Bad, was it?' asked Dot.

'To put it bluntly, I practically heaved my heart out every morning. Jimmy heard me a time or two, so Bob told him I have a sensitive tummy and it wouldn't be polite to mention it to anyone.'

'I bet that kept him quiet,' said Mabel. 'From what I gather, Jimmy thinks the world of Bob.'

'Aye, he does,' confirmed Dot.

Margaret looked at Dot. Was it hard for her to have her young grandson hero-worshipping Joan's husband in the absence of his father, who was away fighting? Joan and Bob lodged with Dot's daughter-in-law, Sheila, near where Dot lived in Withington, and young Jimmy Green, Sheila's son, sounded like a bit of a handful.

'I need to see Miss Emery about my condition,' said Joan.

'Shouldn't you tell the head porter?' asked Alison.

'I'd rather speak to a woman.'

'Are you going to arrange to be evacuated?' asked Margaret, thinking of Anna.

'No. I don't want to leave home.'

'I can understand that,' said Cordelia.

'And it means you'll have all of us buzzing about, keeping an eye on you,' said Mabel.

The conversation turned to descriptions of everyone's Christmas.

'I saved each of my lads a mince pie and a slice of Christmas cake,' said Dot, 'and posted them on Boxing Day.'

'So they know you were thinking of them on Christmas Day,' said Cordelia.

'I must thank Mrs Cooper,' said Dot. 'She was the one who suggested it. It was a lovely thing to do.'

'Sad, though, I should think,' said Cordelia.

'Very sad,' Dot admitted, 'but in a meaningful way.'

'I'm sure Harry and Archie will appreciate the parcels,' said Persephone.

Dot laughed. 'As long as the pastry hasn't gone mouldy by the time they receive them. What about you, Persephone? You went to see your folks after Christmas, didn't you?'

'It was wonderful,' said Persephone. 'Of course, it's all very different at home now, because it's become an air force billet, so the family has been relegated to a few rooms.'

'A few rooms?' said Dot with a wry smile.

'I know.' Persephone took the teasing on her perfectly sculpted chin. 'Shocking, isn't it? When I say "family", Pa isn't there most of the time, because he's in London at the War Office.'

'Your mother must miss him,' said Alison.

A thoughtful look came into Persephone's beautiful violet eyes. 'I'm honestly not sure. That is, I'm certain she must, natch, but she's just so frightfully busy all the time. I don't know if you're aware, but at the outbreak of war, every village had to appoint a headman. With Pa due to be away so much, Ma decided she would be the headman and she's . . . well, embraced the role, shall we say? The first thing she decided was that if the invasion happened, she would plunder the gunroom to help arm the village. She said she personally would die with a shotgun in her hands.'

'Crikey,' said Dot.

'I think I'd like to meet your mother,' said Cordelia.

'She says the war is a lot more interesting than taking my sister and me to London in search of suitable husbands ever was.' Persephone turned to Mabel. 'You went to see your family, too, didn't you?'

'Yes, I did, and it was perfect. I hadn't seen Mumsy and Pops for ages. My mother organised a dance for everyone who works in Pops' factory and their families.'

'What a shame Harry couldn't have gone with you,' said Joan.

'Yes, it was, but Mumsy said that didn't let me off the hook. As the boss's daughter, it was my duty to dance with whoever asked me – and I did.'

Margaret quickly moved the subject along. She unfastened her coat. 'Do you mind if I show off my new jumper? My sister knitted it for me for Christmas.'

'Let's see,' said Dot. 'Oh, isn't it lovely?'

'She wrote in her card to me that the cream stripe is a patriotic stripe, because she couldn't get hold of enough of this reddy-brown.'

Everyone admired her jumper and Margaret lapped up the praise on Anna's behalf, but she had also wanted to divert the conversation away from family visits and she had succeeded in that. All she had done in that line was put a card for Dad through the letter box of the house where he had been billeted since their own had taken a direct hit. It sounded such a simple thing to do, to walk down the road where she used to live and pop a card in, but her stomach had started churning the moment she stepped off the bus and hadn't stopped until after she'd posted the card and walked rapidly to the corner to make her escape. Even in the blackout, she had been frightened of being seen by the neighbours.

At Wilton Close, she had made it clear quite early on after moving in that she didn't want to talk about her family and everyone respected her wishes. Even so, deep inside, part of her ached to talk and be understood, but that was just her being silly and unrealistic. Some things could never be discussed, especially not when you were clinging to the remnants of your self-respect.

But hearing Persephone and Mabel talk about their mothers had made her miss Mum more than ever. Mum was long gone, but Anna wasn't, and suddenly Margaret's heart ached with the need to see her beloved sister.

CHAPTER TWO

Alison spent Saturday morning standing at an office desk, putting a stack of files in order, ready for her to put them in the filing cabinet. It wasn't a job the other office girls were keen on, and Alison might not have been normally, but today she had volunteered because it was a straightforward task and she knew she could do it without mistakes while allowing her mind to dwell on other, far more compelling matters.

'It'll be my parting gift to you,' she had told her fellow workers with a smile.

Everyone knew today was her last day here. Alison was something of an oddity in terms of railway work. Back in September, she had been appointed to a new role in which she was to work in all kinds of different jobs in order to gain a wide knowledge of the railways and how they worked, though what this was to prepare her for, she didn't know. Miss Emery hadn't told her. All the assistant welfare supervisor had said was, 'I saw something in you when you first came to work here,' and she'd left it at that. Since there was resistance in some quarters to women being placed in jobs that traditionally belonged to men, Alison could only assume she was being groomed to take on a responsible role that women previously hadn't been trusted with. Although many of the male railway workers were polite and supportive to their new – well, not so new now, this far into the war – female counterparts, there were still plenty who thought women had no business being here, especially because they were being thrust into jobs that in former times had taken men years to achieve.

But it wasn't her work Alison was thinking about as she sorted out the files. It was Joel – Dr Joel Maitland. Her new boyfriend. Her heart did a happy little pitter-patter. When her long-time boyfriend, Paul, had dumped her last year for another girl completely out of the blue, she had never imagined she would recover from the terrible heartbreak she had endured. Losing her position as one half of the perfect couple had been a very dark time in her life, but then she had met Joel. She had been deeply reluctant to get to know him, but he had courted her with gentle persistence until she had accepted that she had feelings for him.

He was still something of a secret, though. Mabel and Margaret knew about him because Alison had confided her fear of getting involved for the wrong reasons, worrying that her growing feeling for Joel was a knee-jerk response to the news that Paul had got engaged. Margaret and Mabel had been wonderful about it, pointing out that all relationships involved an element of risk and that Joel was clearly willing to take that chance on Alison and the only question was, did Alison want to take a chance on him? Guided by their support and common sense, Alison had found that she did, very much, and her heart had filled with gratitude for her friends' kindness and concern.

Even so, Alison wasn't ready to tell her other friends yet about her fledgling relationship. Part of her felt bad about that, but she knew that her family must come first. Paul had been a member of the Lambert family in every way except for putting his ring on Alison's finger, and after the shock and distress that Mum, Dad and Lydia had all suffered when he had abandoned her, they deserved to be the first to know that she had now found the possibility of a new happiness with someone else. They would be taken aback,

Alison knew, because it had all happened in a matter of months, but they would be happy for her. Having spent her weeks of heartbreak being self-centred in a way she was now ashamed of, Alison was looking forward to giving her family the reassurance that she was going to be all right.

And today was the day.

At the end of her Saturday half-day, Joel was waiting for her outside. Alison quickened her pace at the sight of him. His blue eyes crinkled as he smiled at her, making her heart melt. He raised his trilby to her.

'Good afternoon, Miss de Havilland.'

'Idiot.' She swatted at his arm, enjoying the private joke that had come about because, to begin with, she had declined to tell him her name.

'Are you still happy for me to meet your family?' Joel asked, offering her his arm as they started walking.

'Definitely.' Excitement rushed through her, making her feel tingly all over. 'I want them to know. Well, actually, they already do know. Normally when I go home, I drop Mum a postcard so she knows when to expect me, but I couldn't put you on a postcard.'

'I wouldn't fit.'

Alison smiled. She smiled a lot when she was with Joel. 'So I telephoned my sister at work and told her. I gave her the job of paving the way for you. I hope you don't mind.'

'It's better than your mum seeing me on the doorstep and thinking I'm a door-to-door encyclopaedia salesman.' That was typical Joel. He had a breezy sense of humour that drew people to him and put them at ease, but he had a serious side too, and Alison was starting to feel that she would never tire of his conversation.

Now that she was no longer jealous and despairing because her younger sister had beaten her to the altar, it had been exciting to share her good news. Moreover, letting Lydia tell Mum and Dad meant they would have had time to get the surprise out of their systems and there should be no awkwardness, meaning no dropped jaws, when Joel was introduced.

They walked to the bus stop and queued up, not having to wait long. The bus was quite full, but they got seats together.

'How was your final day in the office?' Joel asked.

'Fine, thanks, but I'm not sorry it's over.'

'Didn't you enjoy it?'

'It's funny,' said Alison. 'I had only ever done office work until recently, and been perfectly happy, but now that I've had a taste of doing other things, it's made me realise that there's more to work than I used to think.'

All the time she had been with Paul, work had been nothing more than something she did in the time before she got married. This new job had come along at precisely the right moment. Not that she had recognised it as such to start with. It had taken her a while to realise that there was real interest to be found in the workplace.

'What are you due to do next?' Joel asked.

'I don't know. I'm seeing Miss Emery on Monday.' She looked up at him as she asked seriously, 'Do you think it would be in order for me to offer to take on Colette's job for a spell until they can replace her? Do you think that would be macabre?'

'Absolutely not,' Joel said at once. 'It sounds to me like a generous and sensible suggestion. It also,' he added gently, 'sounds like a good way to honour your friend's memory.'

'One last thing that I can do for her, you mean?' she asked, touched by his understanding.

'When someone is wrenched away from you like that, it can be difficult to come to terms with it.'

Was Joel thinking of the brother he had lost when they were children? Alison squeezed his arm.

17

'Maybe I'll suggest it.' Wanting to lighten the mood, she asked, 'Shall I tell you what my dream job would be?'

Joel laughed. 'Go on, though I have to say, I can't see you shovelling coal off the heap into the tender.'

'I'd love to be a station announcer,' Alison confessed. 'They're letting women do that now.'

'Oh, I don't think you'd be much good,' said Joel, straight-faced. 'Your voice is far too clear. You need to sound like you've got your head stuffed inside a bucket full of frogs to be an announcer.'

Alison laughed. Oh, she was going to enjoy introducing him to her family. She gave his arm a squeeze.

'What was that for?' Joel asked. 'Not that I'm complaining.'

'It's because you're going to meet my family and . . .'

'And?'

'It's the right thing to do,' said Alison. 'I want them to know I'm . . .' Again her voice trailed off.

'To know you're happy?' Joel suggested.

'They had a lot to worry about last year where I was concerned.'

She had told Joel about Paul and how he had let her down. She hadn't made a big thing out of it, but it was important that Joel understood what had happened to her, because it explained why she had initially held him at arm's length.

They got off the bus outside the local shops Mum used. Alison felt fluttery inside. This was her home turf and it was likely she would be seen with Joel by people who knew her. There had been gossip after Paul dumped her, and no doubt further gossip after he got engaged to Katie, though Alison had moved to Wilton Close by then – thank goodness. Now here she was on the arm of a new man and no doubt the gossip would start all over again. At least Mum

18

would be able to spread a little happiness among the neighbours this time. After all the anguish Mum had gone through last year on Alison's behalf, it was the least she deserved.

Alison slipped her hand into the crook of Joel's elbow, settling it lightly. When she had been with Paul, she had always disapproved of girls who clung. She had looked down on them, imagining that she and Paul would be together for ever. Now she still didn't cling, but not because she felt superior to those who did. Gone were the days of her being so self-satisfied and she held Joel's arm with a feather-light touch simply because that was the well-bred thing to do. And she no longer noticed how other girls held their chaps' arms. It was none of her business.

It didn't take long to walk home, especially not on a chilly afternoon like this when no one wanted to hang about. Dad answered the door, which was unusual, because normally it was Mum's job. Good old Dad. He wanted to get the first look at his little girl's new beau.

Alison performed the introductions. 'Dad, this is Joel Maitland. Joel, this is my dad, John Lambert.'

The two men shook hands. As she and Joel shed their outdoor things, Alison could see Dad sizing Joel up, but she didn't mind. It made her feel protected.

They went into the front parlour, where Mum and Lydia leapt to their feet and gave Alison what could only be described as a cursory embrace, their gazes already locked on the newcomer. Alison smothered a smile. It was exciting to bring home a new boyfriend.

The afternoon went well. They had a simple but tasty meal of vegetable fritters and mashed carrot and swede, followed by raisin pudding with a warm sauce made from jam. As was normal these days when going to someone's house for a meal, Joel had brought a contribution in the form of a bag of cheese straws made by his landlady, as well as a jar of chutney. Conversation flowed without trouble. Joel was easy to get along with – as Alison had discovered before Christmas when she had been trying to find reasons not to want to see him again.

When Mum went out to the kitchen, Alison went with her.

'Well, what do you think?' she asked, closing the door, only for Lydia to burst through it a moment later.

'I hope you weren't thinking of leaving me out,' Lydia said.

'Leaving you out of what?' Alison asked innocently.

'The big discussion about the new boyfriend, of course.'

'Isn't he charming?' said Mum.

'And good-looking,' said Lydia.

'Never mind what we think,' said Mum. 'The main question is, what do you think of him, Alison?'

Alison laughed, pleased and a little embarrassed.

Stepping forward, Mum took her shoulders and looked into her face. 'I'm gladder than I can tell you to see you looking bright-eyed again. I know how devastating it was for you when Paul left you.'

'I really don't want to talk about Paul,' said Alison.

'My only concern is that you might have met this Joel on the rebound,' said Mum.

Alison gently disengaged herself from Mum's hands, turning so that Lydia was included when she said, 'Can I say to you what two dear friends said to me? Every relationship is a risk. I like Joel and he likes me and for now, that's fine. That's all it needs to be.'

'I think what Alison means,' Lydia said to Mum, 'is that we shouldn't rush down to the milliner's quite yet.'

That made Alison laugh. 'I'm just so glad and grateful, not to mention amazed, that I feel happy again after things were so bad and so bleak. That's why I wanted to bring Joel here to meet you. I want you to know that I've recovered from all that unhappiness.'

Mum blinked furiously, but failed to hold back a few tears. Alison started to put her arms round her, then took a step back so that she could draw Lydia into the hug as well. Oh, it felt good. Her heartbreak had made her into a spiky, difficult person, but now she was at peace with herself and she wanted her family to be a part of that feeling. After the months of self-absorption, it felt good to want to be in harmony with others.

The little group separated and Mum turned away so she could pretend not to be wiping her eyes.

'I'll put the kettle on or the tea will never get made,' she said.

'I'll nip upstairs and dig out a couple of sweaters,' said Alison. 'If the weather continues this cold, I'll certainly need them.'

Lydia followed her upstairs and sat on the bed, watching while Alison rummaged through the drawer in the bottom of the hanging cupboard.

'Come to see what you can borrow, have you?' Alison teased.

'Who, me? Never! I've come to talk about Dr Joel. He's gorgeous.'

Alison was proud to receive the praise, but she bit her lip. 'You don't think it's too soon? After Paul, I mean.'

'You can't control when these things happen and surely it's better for it to happen soon, rather than making you wait for years.'

'That's true.' Alison pulled out a midnight-blue knitted sweater with cabling up the front.

'You're lucky to have met someone who's in a reserved occupation.'

Alison stopped rifling through the woollies and looked at her sister. 'You must miss Alec dreadfully.'

'More than I can say.' Lydia hesitated before adding, 'I was hoping that I'd fallen for a honeymoon baby, but I haven't.'

Alison reached out to cover Lydia's hand with hers. 'Are you disappointed?'

'I honestly don't know the answer to that. Lots of girls think it's terribly important to have a baby when their husband goes to war, so they have a part of him with them to love and take care of – and I feel like that too, of course. But there's another part of me that imagines bringing up a child all alone, with no father in the picture probably for several years yet. It hardly seems fair on the child.'

'That's how it is for nearly all children these days.'

'Anyway,' Lydia withdrew her hand, 'I'm not expecting, so that's that, and we aren't meant to be talking about me anyway. I want to hear more about the gorgeous Dr Joel.'

Alison laughed. She had never had a conversation like this before. Lydia had once accused her of being middle-aged in her attitudes and behaviour while she was Paul's girlfriend, because she had always helped the wives make the cricket teas, as well as helping with the church flowers and jumble sales – all the things that long-established wives did, not carefree single girls. Alison had certainly never had a giggly conversation about Paul, not even when they'd first met. There was something liberating about giggling with her sister about Joel – and it helped her make up her mind that it was time now for her friends to meet him. She couldn't wait.

CHAPTER THREE

Joan loved going to the Hubbles' house. She always had. From the time she had first met Bob, his family had welcomed her and made her feel they cared about her for herself, not just because she was Bob's girl. They lived in a two-up two-down in Stretford, Mum and Dad in one bedroom, the three girls crammed into the other. When Bob had lived at home, he had slept in a narrow bed under the stairs. Sometimes he kidded Joan that the best thing about being married was having shares in a double bed and being able to turn over without falling out.

They headed over to Stretford for tea on Sunday, both of them a bit giddy with excitement, because they were going to tell Bob's family about the baby.

Bob had briefly felt put out on Christmas Eve when Joan had got home from spending the evening with her friends and confessed she had shared her news with them.

'I'm sorry,' she had said.

Bob had hugged her. 'Don't be. It was being caught up in the emotion of Colette's death that made you do it and that's understandable, but we mustn't tell anyone else before we've told my folks.'

'And Gran.'

'Yes, and your gran.'

A short silence had followed these words, filled with all the difficulties of Joan's relationship with her grandmother. Such a strict, judgemental woman – but it turned out that she had brought up her granddaughters to believe a terrible lie that Joan had got to the bottom of last year. Even so, it had felt right to have Gran give her away at her wedding last June. It had been a spur-of-the-moment decision, made when Gran appeared unexpectedly at the church, but Joan had never doubted its rightness. Since then, she and Bob had paid duty visits to Gran and they were all polite to one another, but that was as far as it went. Bob's mum had said she would invite Gran to tea if Joan wanted her to, but Joan had never taken up the offer.

Now, as she and Bob arrived at the Hubbles', there was movement at the front window behind the anti-blast tape that the family, with typical Hubble high spirits, had made look like a game of noughts and crosses. A moment later, before they could reach the door, Petal, Bob's middle sister, opened it. She was a lovely-looking girl, and the one blonde in the family, with greeny eyes that added to her attractiveness. Maureen, the oldest, was a brown-eyed beauty, with shining chestnut-brown hair and good cheekbones. The youngest, Glad, with her mid-brown hair and hazel eyes, was ordinary in comparison and Joan liked her because of it. She knew what it was like to have a stunning-looking sister who turned heads wherever she went. Glad had no jealousy of her sisters, just like Joan had never felt jealous of Letitia.

As Joan and Bob entered the house, there were hugs and kisses all round. Joan loved being part of an affectionate family. She handed over the eggless sponge cake she had made from a recipe shared by Mrs Grayson, and followed Mum into the kitchen to help prepare the sandwiches. Bob's parents had asked her to call them Mum and Dad, a request she was more than happy to comply with, and they treated her as one of their own.

Back in the autumn, Bob's dad had bought second-hand an old Brownie camera, the sort with a drop-down front from which, when it was opened, the camera more or less unfolded itself.

'I'd like one of all the kids,' Mum had said.

With mock protests at having to pose, the four young Hubbles had sorted themselves out, while Joan hung back, smiling at their antics.

Dad looked at her over his shoulder. 'You an' all, Joan.'

'I'm just an in-law.'

'An in-law? What's one of them when it's at home? I'll tell you what you are, lass. You're one of our daughters – isn't she, Bernice?'

'No such thing as in-laws in this house,' said Mum.

'Now get yourself over there with the rest of 'em,' said Dad. 'I expect my children to do as they're told!'

In that moment, Joan had fallen in love with Bob's family all over again. Now the two of them were to have the huge pleasure of announcing their wonderful news.

'Hush up, everyone,' said Bob when they were all squeezed into the parlour. He was sitting on the arm of Joan's chair, his arm casually resting along its back. 'We've got something to tell you.' He looked down into Joan's eyes. 'Who's going to say?'

'You do it,' said Joan.

'It's always been a bit crowded in this parlour,' said Bob, 'but I'm afraid you're all going to have to budge up and make room for one more, because Joan and I will be having an addition to the family.'

There was a moment of deep silence, then the room erupted with joy as everyone jumped up, wanting to congratulate them in true Hubble fashion with hugs and kisses. Dad pumped Bob's hand up and down and slapped him on the shoulder.

'Well!' Dad exclaimed. 'A grandchild. Won't that be grand?'

'Of course it will,' teased Maureen. 'What else would a grandchild be other than grand?'

'You know what I mean.' Dad looked puffed up with pride.

'When?' the girls wanted to know.

'June,' Joan told them.

'I hope you have it on your anniversary,' said Glad.

'Will you be giving up work?' asked Maureen.

'Not right away,' said Joan.

'End of February, beginning of March,' Bob said decisively. 'That's about six months. Joan needs to be at home after that.'

'What about the war effort?' Joan teased.

'Part of the war effort is protecting children and taking care of mothers-to-be,' said Dad.

Mum drew Joan into her arms. 'It's the best start to the New Year we could possibly have had,' she murmured, the words for Joan alone. 'Thank you.'

Joan hugged her back. Oh, how lucky she was to be part of this family.

When she and Bob left Stretford, all Joan wanted was to get home as soon as possible, put her feet up and think about the wonderful time they'd just enjoyed, but there was something important they had to do before returning to Withington. Stopping off in Chorlton, they walked the short distance to Torbay Road.

Bob rang the bell and they waited, knowing all too well the palaver that went into answering the door in the blackout. Gran would be clicking shut the parlour door behind her and switching off the hall light before swishing aside the floor-length curtain that covered the front door because of the circular stained-glass window it contained.

The door opened a fraction.

'It's us, Gran,' said Joan.

'I wasn't expecting you.'

'We're on our way home from Stretford,' said Bob, 'so we thought we'd drop in, if that's all right.'

'Come in.'

Gran stood aside for them to pass. Closing the door, she reinstated the blackout curtain and switched on the light so they could hang up their things.

In the parlour, Joan's gaze went automatically to the sideboard. She always used to look over there to see the posed photograph of her handsome father. Now she still looked. She couldn't help it. The picture was no longer there. Gran had moved it into the back room, which was the dining room. She had never said why and Joan hadn't asked. She wanted it to be a sign of shame on Gran's part, but surely that would have meant removing the picture from view altogether.

Joan held out her hands to the fire, a smaller fire than Gran would have had in days gone by, as everyone was eking out their fuel now.

'It's jolly cold out there,' said Joan.

'It's January,' said Gran. 'What do you expect?'

'This is cold even for January,' said Bob.

The wireless was on. Gran had been listening to the news. She went to switch it off.

'What's on next?' asked Bob. 'Leave it on if it's going to be a concert. It's nice to have music in the background.'

'The news in Norwegian comes next,' said Gran, switching it off.

She sat in her customary armchair. Bob and Joan sat together on the sofa.

'How is your family?' Gran asked Bob.

'Very well, thank you. In fact, better than ever, because,' Bob added with a glance at Joan, 'it's going to get bigger.'

'Is one of your sisters engaged?'

Joan laughed. Visits to Gran involved fielding all sorts of emotional reservations, but right this minute she felt happy and confident. 'Closer to home than that.' She smiled at Bob as he took her hand. 'You're going to be a great-grandmother.'

Gran drew in a breath. 'A great—' She pressed a hand to her chest. 'I don't know why I should be surprised. It's only natural. A great-grandmother.' Her eyes went distant and thoughtful, but only for a moment. 'Thank you for telling me. When is the baby due?'

'The beginning of June,' said Bob. 'A summer baby.'

'Letitia and Joan were both winter babies,' said Gran.

'Birthday parties are better in the summer,' said Bob. 'Lots of outdoor games.'

Joan and Gran glanced at one another. Joan and Letitia hadn't had birthday parties. Gran had never encouraged friendliness of that sort with outsiders. Her life after she came to Manchester had been dominated by the family secret – and by the lie she had told her granddaughters. Oh, Gran had done terrible wrongs, there was no doubt about that.

'I hope—' Gran said and stopped. 'That is, am I to be a part of the child's life?'

Joan closed her eyes. This was so hard. Everything about her relationship with Gran was hard. She opened her eyes, preparing to answer, but Bob spoke first.

'Mrs Foster, you had the job of bringing up your grand-daughters from when they were babies. You never had the opportunity to be just a grandmother because you had to be the parent. But come the summer, you'll have the chance to be a great-grandma, and Joan and I both hope you'll enjoy it.'

What would Letitia do? She had always known the right thing to say to Gran, the way to get round her and even make her smile. Joan, the second-best granddaughter, had never been able to do that.

She found herself kneeling in front of Gran, taking her hands. 'It's a crossroads, Gran. We've talked about cross-roads before. My big crossroads was when I married Bob. This baby is another one and, yes, I admit I've thought about whether you deserve a place in its life. The truth is, I don't know what to think. But Bob knows. He's a Hubble and they have the biggest hearts of anyone I've ever met. This baby isn't about the past. It's about the future. You'll be the only great-grandmother the baby has and it isn't right to deprive him or her of that. We want to give our baby everything and that includes a great-grandmother. That's what we want, Bob and me. Is it what you want too?'

The front room in Sheila Green's house was Joan and Bob's sitting room. The cream and green wallpaper had retained its smart appearance, as, before she took in lodgers, Sheila had kept the room for best, so there was no faint yellowing caused by nicotine from her never-ending smoking. The floor was stained wood, which Mrs Cooper, who acted as Joan's cleaner, buffed up once a week, and the fireplace had a surround of brown tiles. When they had moved in, the room had contained a sideboard, a couple of chairs and a small table. To this, Bob had soon added a sofa, courtesy of his auntie Florrie, who had been bombed out and had moved in with Auntie Marie, taking with her what pieces of furniture were still intact. There hadn't been room for her sofa in Auntie Marie's house, though, so she had given it to Bob and Joan.

Joan sat on the sofa now, with her legs curled round and her feet up. Bob was in the kitchen, making tea, bless him. Most men wouldn't be caught dead doing that and Joan loved him for it, because it made her feel spoiled. Sheila, however, had other ideas and had tried to get Bob to stop doing it, because of setting a bad example to Jimmy.

'I don't want him to grow up to be a sissy,' she had declared.

'If putting the kettle on to make a fuss of his wife makes a man a sissy,' Bob had replied, 'then I'm the biggest sissy going.'

It had made Joan feel a bit uncomfortable. Having grown up under Gran's rigid thumb, it was in her nature to respect rules.

'We shouldn't undermine Jimmy's upbringing,' she had said privately to Bob, 'not when we're living under his mum's roof.'

'Leave it to me.'

They'd had this conversation on a Saturday afternoon. Bob had thrown up the sash window and called to Jimmy, who was playing marbles in the gutter with his mates. Jimmy had come running inside and knocked on their door.

'We need to talk man to man, Jimmy,' said Bob and Jimmy's chest had swelled with pride. 'It's about me sometimes making a cup of tea for Auntie Joan. Now then, there are folks who'll tell you I shouldn't do it, but I want you to know my mum dropped me on my head when I was a baby and I've never been the same since, so don't think badly of me, will you? There's a good chap.'

Now Joan lounged on the sofa, smiling at the memory. The door opened and Bob appeared with two mugs. He passed one to her, then poked the fire before sitting next to her, putting his arm around her. She snuggled up to him.

'How are you feeling?' asked Bob. 'Not too tired?'

Joan laughed. 'I'm fine. Having a baby isn't an illness. Your family were lovely, weren't they? They were so excited.'

'They're your family too,' Bob reminded her gently.

'I know.' She released a sigh of utter contentment. 'Baby Hubble. We should start thinking about names. Probably because of growing up with a sister, I always wanted two little girls of my own. I was going to call them Hebe and Sybil.'

Bob nodded. 'Hebe and Sybil. I like both of those.'

Joan dug her elbow into his ribs. 'You haven't thought it through. Hebe Hubble.'

'Well, perhaps not.'

'And Sybil Hubble is nearly as bad.'

Bob laughed. 'I'll take it as a sign of how much you love me that you married me even though my surname dashed your hopes of being mum to Hebe and Sybil.'

'Don't mock.' Joan pretended to be offended. 'We'll have to come up with more names.'

'I thought you might like Letitia,' Bob said quietly. 'Letitia Hubble has a nice ring.'

'It does, and thank you for suggesting it, but I think Letitia would be the middle name, not the first name. And I know I shouldn't say this after I've just said I want Letitia for a girl's middle name, but I don't want to use any family names – any other ones, I mean. If your parents were hoping that we'd name the baby after one of them, that really wouldn't be possible.'

'I understand. A boy couldn't be Dennis after my dad without folk asking what your dad's name was, and we can't have that.'

'You don't mind, do you?'

'Mind something that makes my wife feel better about things? Why would I mind that? This baby is a fresh start and we want a name no one on either side has had before.'

'Apart from Letitia in the middle.'

'Letitia-in-the-middle Hubble,' said Bob. 'There's something else we should consider too. I'd like us to look for somewhere else to live. Don't get me wrong. I like it here and Jimmy is a card, but it would be good to have a home of our own.'

'Us and all the hundreds of bombed-out families,' said Joan.

'I know. I don't mean we should have a whole house to ourselves. That would be too much to hope for. Just a place that feels more like ours.'

'I know what you mean,' said Joan, 'though I've loved this as our first home together. We're lucky to have two rooms, but maybe if we could have two rooms next to one another instead of one upstairs and one downstairs, it might feel more – well, more contained, more like our little piece of the world.'

'Our own kitchen would be ideal,' said Bob.

'So you can bring me lots of tea?'

'You never know. I might even run to toast.'

'Anyway, there's no chance of our own kitchen unless we can find a flat, and they're rarer than hen's teeth. We're almost bound to have to share.' Joan thought for a moment. 'Is it selfish of us to want somewhere else when we've already got this billet with Sheila?'

'No,' Bob said decisively. 'It's natural for us to want the very best for our baby.'

'Bob Hubble, you're going to be the best father ever.'

'Now there's a coincidence, because you're going to be the best mother.'

'I don't know about the best,' said Joan, 'but I'm certainly going to be the luckiest.'

CHAPTER FOUR

The problem with starting a new job without knowing in advance what it was going to be was deciding what to wear. Skirt or slacks? As a rule, Alison would automatically wear a skirt for preference, but some jobs required trousers – such as when she had been in the marshalling yard. This morning, trousers might be the safe option, were it not that Alison basically felt that skirts were the proper, smart attire for girls at work – and when they weren't at work, for that matter. Or was that attitude becoming old-fashioned? More suited, perhaps, to the 'middle-aged' Alison who had focused her every waking breath on her future marriage, rather than the new, rather dashing Alison she now felt herself to be, with her special job packed with variety and her handsome new boyfriend.

And why was she dithering over the question when her small bedroom was so chilly? Pulling on her dressing gown over her undies and her blouse, she padded along the landing to Mabel and Margaret's bedroom.

'Wear a skirt and take a pair of trousers in a bag, just in case,' suggested Mabel, brushing her long hair and clipping it away from her face. 'It's easy for Margaret and me in our unglamorous jobs.'

'You never know your luck,' said Margaret, sitting on the edge of her bed and bending over to pull on woolly socks that Mrs Grayson had knitted for her. 'You might end up working alongside one of us.'

'I'm hoping for something a bit warmer than that,' said Alison.

She liked it when the three of them worked similar shifts and got up at the same time. Yes, it made the bathroom seem like a busy railway junction, but she loved the feeling of being young and in a billet and doing war work.

'While we're all here,' she added, 'keep Friday evening free, will you?' Excitement bubbled up inside her.

Margaret sat up and looked at her. 'Are we going to meet the man of the moment?'

'I took him to meet my family on Saturday, so now I want to introduce him to my friends.'

'About time too,' said Mabel. 'I hope you're going to give us the credit for the relationship. We're the ones who encouraged you, remember.'

'I'm so glad you did,' said Alison. 'You made me look at things differently – both of you. Thank you for keeping quiet about Joel and me in front of everyone else.'

'Of course we did,' said Margaret. 'It's your news to share, not ours. I'm glad things have worked out happily for you.'

Oh yes, very happily. Alison hurried back to her room to finish dressing. The disadvantage of wearing a skirt in the winter was the lisle stockings. Serviceable and warm they might be, but who cared about that, compared to the beauty and elegance of legs clad in sheer silk stockings, which were impossible to buy these days, though Alison still had one precious pair squirrelled away.

She wore her hair in the same sort of style as Mabel and Margaret, but all three girls had different lengths, Alison's being the middle one. Mind you, if she had such gloriously thick and glossy hair as Mabel, she would probably grow it longer.

Downstairs, Mrs Grayson was busy making breakfast and Mabel had an arm around her shoulder as she leaned over to look in the frying pan.

'What have we got this morning, Mrs G?'

'Potato pancakes. We need to eat less bread because of wheat taking up so much space on the merchant ships, so I thought we'd try these for a change.'

'They look nice and crisp,' said Margaret. 'What's in them?'

'It said on the wireless that we should let people eat first, then tell them afterwards – not talking about these specifically, you understand, but as a general rule.'

'You've got to tell now,' said Mabel, 'or we'll think we're eating diced slugs.'

'Mabel!' Mrs Cooper chided. 'Really.'

'Potato, carrot and a little milk,' said Mrs Grayson.

'It'll fill you up,' said Mrs Cooper, 'which is important when it's cold, especially with you two doing such hard work, Mabel and Margaret.'

'Alison finds out her new job today, don't you, dear?' said Mrs Grayson. 'I wonder what it'll be.'

'Steam-hammer operator,' teased Mabel.

'Bridge painter,' said Margaret.

'Or I might get a lovely indoor job that involves sitting near a fireplace,' Alison retorted. As if!

After breakfast, the three girls dashed off to catch the bus into town, going their separate ways when they reached Victoria Station's handsome building, the clock tower topping one elegantly curved end, with the words LANCASHIRE & YORKSHIRE RAILWAY carved into the stonework beneath. That had been the name of the railway company before LMS had come along. Alison peeled off from the others and headed for Hunts Bank, the row of buildings in which all the administrative work was done.

She went upstairs to Miss Emery's office. Not that it really was an office as such, rather a large alcove that contained all the necessary furniture and accoutrements – desk, typewriter, cupboard, hatstand – but without having what Alison now considered to be the most important feature, namely a wall with a door. Often, Miss Emery had to arrange to use a proper office for the sake of privacy when she had to speak to someone, but this wasn't always possible.

When Alison arrived, Miss Emery was removing her coat and hat, revealing a smart skirt and jacket with a cream blouse underneath. Her top button was fastened and the short string of pearls she wore under the collar of her blouse peeped out at the front. There was evidently a mirror on the wall on the other side of the hatstand, because Miss Emery took a moment to pat her hair.

'Come in, Miss Lambert. How are you? Would you like to hang up your things?'

They exchanged pleasantries. Although Alison now met with Miss Emery on a fairly regular basis, the assistant supervisor was always perfectly professional and never attempted to move onto a less formal footing. Alison occasionally wondered what she was like beneath her kindly but correct façade.

'How did you get on?' Miss Emery asked. 'That was your first taste of office work since you took on this role.'

Alison tilted her head from side to side as if weighing things up. 'It felt familiar and I soon got the hang of the routines, but now I'm looking forward to doing something different.'

'Different? That's good. That exactly describes what I have arranged.'

What was it? Working alongside a stationmaster? Or would they teach her to drive a van so she could work on deliveries? . . . Might she have the chance to be a station announcer?

'You shall be working in a canteen,' said Miss Emery.

'But that's not railway work,' Alison blurted out. She could have kicked herself, but even so – a canteen. Surprise and dismay fought to be uppermost.

'You think not?' Miss Emery asked quietly, but with steel in her eyes.

'Yes, of course it is.'

The railways employed heaps of people in jobs that at first glance weren't railway jobs. Crane drivers. Welders. Blacksmiths and stable lads to take care of the horses that pulled the delivery carts in places where there weren't sufficient vans. And, yes, canteen workers.

'I'm sure it'll be fine,' said Alison. Trying to redeem herself, she made light of it, wanting to look as if she had taken it on the chin. 'After all, if it doesn't suit, at least it won't be for long.'

'On the contrary,' said Miss Emery, 'it will last some weeks.'

Alison braced herself. 'I've eaten in the staff canteen. Now I'll find out what goes on behind the scenes.'

'It won't be here,' said Miss Emery. 'You'll be required to go over to Leeds for the time being. Don't worry about accommodation. That will be arranged for you. Because of the bombing, new canteens are needed at both Leeds Central Station and the hospital. They aren't far apart and a suitable building has been found between them in a place called Park Square, which is to house a canteen for the railway and hospital workers and the girls from the nurses' home.'

Distress swelled inside Alison. Miss Emery was speaking so calmly, but Alison's life was here in Manchester. She didn't want to go to Leeds.

'This is a good opportunity for you, Miss Lambert, and I hope you'll welcome it as such.'

'I don't know the first thing about canteen work.' Alison tried not to sound as if she was protesting.

'Don't worry. You shan't be expected to produce a choice of meals for two hundred on your first day.' Miss Emery smiled, but it was her pleasant, professional smile, not an encouraging or sympathetic one – not the smile of someone who was going to give in and change her mind. 'So far you have shown yourself to be a quick learner. Now it's time to show you can put that aptitude into practice. You'll start in Leeds on Monday of next week. In the meantime, you'll spend a few days in the canteen here, so you won't be a complete novice. Do you have any questions?'

Oh yes, she had questions. Must she go to Leeds? And if she absolutely had to, couldn't it just be for a week, two at the most? If she had to work in a canteen, couldn't she stay here and do it?

But she didn't have a single question she could ask out loud.

Joan had arranged to see Mabel in the buffet before they went home on Monday. The two of them had grown close during the time they had shared a bedroom before Joan left Mrs Cooper's to get married, and she didn't want that special friendship to falter now, especially because, as a married woman, she was now generally expected by society to stay at home in the evenings unless her husband took her out. Not that Bob would ever mind if she wanted to go out with her friends, but she didn't want anyone pointing the finger and criticising her for not being a good wife.

Joan arrived first and nabbed a table that a couple was just leaving. Wrinkling her nose, she pushed the full ashtray over to one side. She had never been keen on the smell of tobacco and now that she was expecting, she cared for it even less. Of all the things to take against! Everywhere you went smelled strongly of tobacco.

Mabel came through the door and queued up for her cuppa. No one seeing her in her lengthman's clobber would ever guess she came from a moneyed background. She was wearing a wool overcoat, slacks and boots, with a felt hat jammed down on her head, her luxuriant dark curls scooped away from her face and tied with a bootlace. When she sat down, she unfastened her coat, revealing a navy blue jumper.

'That looks thick and warm,' said Joan.

Mabel laughed and lifted the hem to show another jumper underneath. 'It's freezing out there on the permanent way.'

'I don't envy you being out there all day in these temperatures.'

'The job keeps us warm enough,' said Mabel.

She did hard physical work as a lengthman, resetting the ballast under the sleepers out on the railway tracks. She was one of a gang of four women, who worked in pairs. One lifted the edge of the sleeper with a pickaxe or a crowbar while the other shovelled the stones back under. Mabel's gang was led by Bob's mum, Bernice Hubble.

'Anyway, never mind me,' said Mabel cheerfully. She leaned away for a moment so that Mrs Jessop's assistant could clear away the full ashtray, replacing it with a clean one. 'How did you get on with Miss Emery this morning?'

Joan spread her hands as if showing off something. 'Behold the newest recruit to Lost Property.'

'Do you mind being given another job?' asked Mabel. 'Would you rather leave and be at home?'

'I'm happy to stay for as long as they'll let me or for as long as I'm comfortable, at any rate.'

'I thought mums-to-be wanted to stay at home, nest-building.'

'Maybe I'd feel like that if we had a home of our own,' said Joan. 'Don't misunderstand. We're lucky that Sheila took us in.'

'But it's not the same as a place of your own.' Mabel nodded. 'I can see that.'

'We're going to have a look round for somewhere else. Not that we've much chance of finding a place, but you never know.'

'It's worth a try, if that's what you want,' said Mabel.

'Did you have a good weekend?' asked Joan.

'Harry came over and we went dancing at the Ritz.'

'Lovely,' said Joan. She had a soft spot for that particular ballroom, with its pillars and its balcony and the famous revolving stage, because that was where she and Bob had met – well, no, they had already met before that, but it was where they had finally got together.

'And I don't need to read your tea leaves to know you told Bob's family the happy news yesterday,' said Mabel.

'How do you know that?' Joan asked before answering her own question. 'Bob's mum.'

'She's thrilled to bits and couldn't stop talking about it all day.'

Joan felt a flicker of anxiety. 'You didn't let on you already knew?'

'Don't be daft. Of course I didn't.'

'It's wonderful to think of Bob's family being so pleased for us.'

'What about your gran?' asked Mabel.

'You know how things are. She was never going to throw her arms around me and burst into tears, but we want her to be a great-grandmother, and that's what she wants too.'

Mabel raised her cup. 'Let's drink to happier times ahead. You deserve things to go well.'

'Thank you,' said Joan. 'How's Mrs Cooper getting along with Magic Mop?' She couldn't help smiling as she asked. The name of her old landlady's one-woman cleaning business always had that effect on her.

'She's very busy,' said Mabel. 'Too busy sometimes. I'm concerned about her doing too much, but she's loath to turn away potential clients because she needs the money. I think it's time for Magic Mop to expand.'

'What does she say to that?'

'To be honest, I haven't mentioned it. Rather than just saying it as a general idea, I'm going to see if I can find her another cleaner. That way, she'll have something practical to think about and she'll be less likely to wave it aside.'

'Have you anyone in mind?' asked Joan. It was difficult to imagine privately educated Mabel having a list of cleaning women up her sleeve.

'I have, actually.' Mabel leaned closer, dropping her voice. 'Do you remember Louise Wadden?'

'Yes. Well, I remember her brother.' Joan shuddered. At the beginning of last year, the friends had ganged together to thwart a thief. The thief had turned out to be two thieves, one of whom was Rob Wadden, Louise's violent brother, who had escaped and hadn't been seen since.

'Rob Wadden was a bad lot,' said Mabel, 'but Lou's not like that.'

Joan was puzzled. Louise was a member of Mabel's gang of lengthmen. 'Surely she wouldn't want extra work as a cleaner?'

'No, but her mother might. I gather money is tight. Mrs Wadden does a few hours in a local shop, apparently. I've asked Louise to find out whether she'd be interested in some cleaning work. Don't worry. I haven't mentioned

41

Mrs Cooper's name and I shan't if she decides she doesn't want any help. D'you think I've done the right thing, or have I just stuck my nose in?'

Joan smiled. 'I think Mrs Cooper will be touched that you've gone to this trouble for her.'

But Mabel wasn't listening. She was looking over Joan's shoulder and then she stood up, an expression of disquiet on her face. Turning, Joan saw Alison coming towards them, looking pale and distressed. Mabel scooted out from her place and went to Alison, putting an arm around her shoulder and drawing her over to join them.

Exchanging glances of concern with Mabel, Joan leaned towards Alison as she subsided into a seat. 'Alison, what is it?'

'I'm sorry to dump myself on you like this,' said Alison, 'but I knew you were going to be here.'

'Don't be daft,' said Mabel. 'You're not dumping yourself. If you're upset, we want to help.'

Alison's chin wobbled and she swallowed. 'I went to see Miss Emery today.'

'About your next posting,' Mabel finished for her when she stopped.

Alison nodded. 'It's in *Leeds*,' she burst out. 'I've got to go to Leeds.'

'A week or so in Leeds doesn't sound so bad,' Joan said kindly.

'It's for longer than that. I don't know how long exactly, but it won't be just a week or two. It'll be . . .' Alison's voice trailed away and she swiped a hand across her eyes.

'Months?' asked Mabel, dismayed.

'Don't say that!' Alison exclaimed. 'It won't be for that long – please don't let it be that long. Miss Emery said it wasn't definite yet, but it could be several weeks.'

'Oh, sweetheart.' Mabel stroked Alison's shoulder.

'I don't want to go away,' said Alison, 'but I've got no choice.'

'No one has in wartime,' said Joan.

'I know that,' said Alison, 'but it's such a shock. I really don't want to go. I feel as if I've only just moved in with Mrs Cooper and got over Paul.'

'And met Joel,' Mabel added.

'I've just got my life sorted out,' said Alison, 'and now it feels as if it's being wrenched away from me. Sorry, I know that sounds dramatic.'

'Maybe a tad,' Mabel said with a kind smile. 'It's beastly that you have to go, but—'

'But I have to,' Alison finished. 'I know. I'll have to grin and bear it. I'm going to miss you all – and I'm going to miss Joel so much. I wasted time in the beginning not letting him get close to me, and now that I've seen sense and admitted I have feelings for him – this feels like a punishment. I'm sorry.' She glanced at them from beneath wet lashes. 'I'm being dramatic again. I've been feeling upset and wretched ever since Miss Emery told me, and I tried to contain it, but when I saw the pair of you . . .'

'It all came tumbling out,' said Mabel.

'We'll miss you and we'll all keep in touch, you'll see,' Joan promised. 'You're one of us and that won't change.'

She wanted to say something along the lines of a few weeks not being such a long time, but Alison wasn't in the mood to hear that, not just yet. Poor girl. What a blow for her, especially after everything she'd had to go through in the latter half of last year. Now it seemed she was about to be tested again.

CHAPTER FIVE

Carrying her steel rod, Margaret climbed up onto the side of the locomotive and walked round to the front, where the smokebox was. The huge circular door was already open, displaying the ends of the many tubes that filled the long boiler, stretching all the way back to the firebox. Lifting the rod, Margaret inserted it into the first tube and started pushing it down. Coming up against a clinker blockage, she shoved hard. Clinker could be a right so-and-so to shift and she put her back into it. Every tube had to be fully cleared, then it was the next girl's job to steam-blow the tubes one by one. After that, their supervisor would inspect their work and woe betide anybody who hadn't done a first-rate job.

It was dirty work – everything to do with cleaning engines was dirty – and Margaret gave her hands and face a thorough wash when she stopped for her midday break and went to the canteen, where she had arranged to meet Joan, whom she found standing outside near the doors. Dot was with her.

Margaret smiled at Dot. 'I wasn't expecting to see you.'

'Just passing the time of day with Joan while she waited for you.'

'You'll come in and eat with us, won't you?' said Margaret.

'If I'm not pushing in.'

'Don't be daft,' said Margaret. 'Of course you aren't. It's lovely to see you.'

'You've got a smut on your cheek.' Dot pulled out a hanky. 'Here – spit.'

Margaret did as she was told and Dot wiped off the offending mark.

'Is it still lovely to see me,' she asked, 'with me treating you like a nipper?'

'I don't think anyone has done that to me since I lost my mum,' said Margaret with a smile. She didn't mind. She'd had a lonely time before getting together with Joan and the rest and she felt as if she would never stop appreciating every tiny act of kindness.

'If you're not careful, you'll be getting a lot more of it off Dot starting next month when soap rationing comes in,' said Joan.

They entered the noisy canteen and joined the queue. Margaret opted for devilled fish – there was no indication of what kind of fish it was and she didn't ask – followed by coconut pudding. She had developed quite a taste for coconut over the past year, which was just as well, as desiccated coconut now appeared in a lot of cakes and puds.

'I thought Alison might be serving,' said Joan as the three of them sat down, 'but there was no sign of her.'

'Apparently, she spent her first couple of days peeling and chopping veg,' said Margaret. 'She wasn't best pleased when she got home.'

'She's just upset at the thought of going away,' said Dot. 'It's a big thing to do, but she'll be all right. If she'd been sent away when Paul left her, it might not have seemed so bad.'

'It might have felt like she was escaping,' said Joan.

'But she's settled now and she's got her new chap,' said Margaret. 'It's bad timing.'

'All you young 'uns are meeting up on Friday, I hear,' said Dot.

'Yes,' said Joan. 'We're all going to the flicks in Chorlton.'

'This Joel is coming to Wilton Close,' said Margaret, 'so Mrs Cooper and Mrs Grayson are looking forward to meeting him. Afterwards, he'll walk Alison, Mabel and me to the cinema.'

'Bob and me and Persephone will meet them there,' Joan told Dot. 'After that, we'll have to arrange for him to meet you and Cordelia.'

Dot laughed. 'It's a good plan for him to meet us all a bit at a time. It'll ease him in gently. Seriously, though, I'm very pleased for Alison. She had such a hard time last year.' She turned to Joan. 'How about you, chick? How's your new job?'

'It's very different to being a porter. There's a lot of clerical work to be done, labelling and listing all the items. I reunited a lady with her umbrella and a gentleman with his bird-spotting book today. People are so relieved and grateful to get their things back.'

'Just you make sure you take care of yourself,' said Dot, before turning to Margaret. 'How are things with you?'

'Same old, same old. There is one thing. It's not exciting news like Alison's or Joan's with their new jobs, but it's important to me.'

Joan leaned forward. 'What is it?'

'I'm going to sort out some holiday so I can visit my sister.'

'I didn't know you had a sister,' said Dot.

'She went away at the time of the big evacuation, because she was in the family way. I haven't seen her since.'

'And you've never seen her baby?' asked Dot sympathetically.

Margaret smiled. 'Babies – plural. Twins. Their second birthday is coming up and it's high time they were introduced to their auntie Margaret.'

'Well, that's summat to look forward to,' said Dot.

Margaret felt a tingle of anticipation. 'Not seeing her for so long might make it sound like we don't get on, but we do. We write every week.'

'What are the twins called?' Dot asked.

'Tommy and Anne-Marie.'

'Anne-Marie is a pretty name,' said Joan.

'My sister is Anna, and our mum was Mary Thomas before she got married.'

'That's nice, using your mum's name,' said Dot. To Joan, she said, 'Are you and Bob considering family names?'

'We haven't really thought about names yet,' Joan answered. 'There's plenty of time.'

'It'll fly by,' said Dot.

'Until I'm as big as a house,' said Joan, 'and then I'm sure it'll slow right down.'

'If you see Alison, Dot,' said Margaret, 'make sure you tell her about time flying.'

'I'll be too busy pumping her for information about the new boyfriend,' said Dot. 'What do you know about him?'

'Nothing, really,' said Margaret. 'Just his first name – Joel. I haven't really seen Alison since the weekend, to tell you the truth, not to have a good chinwag. To be allowed to have Friday evening off, she's having to work extra hours Monday to Thursday.'

'So we've got to wait for Friday,' said Joan, adding in a dramatic voice, 'when all shall be revealed.'

'You daft ha'p'orth,' said Dot, laughing. 'He'll be every bit as lovely as Bob and Harry. Just you wait and see.'

On Friday, Margaret was late finishing. One of the other girls, Alice, was taken away by the supervisor and afterwards word went round that Alice's sister had turned up at Victoria Station in a right old state, because their mum had received the telegram that every family dreaded. Everybody was shocked to hear it, then they had to press on with their work. Margaret and another girl had volunteered to finish Alice's cleaning.

47

A huge sorrow took up residence inside Margaret's chest. This always happened to her when someone she knew had bad news. From time to time, she wondered what would happen should Dad get a telegram about William. The Christmas card she had put through Dad's door had elicited no response. If Dad ever turned up on Mrs Cooper's doorstep, Margaret was sure it wouldn't be to make amends with the daughter who had let him down so badly. She knew that the moment she clapped eyes on him, she would know that William, her beloved brother, had copped it.

When Alice's work was all done, Margaret quickly washed and changed and headed for home. She might just about be in time to meet the others as they left the house to go to the flicks. It was a pity, because Mabel had brought a couple of really good dresses back from her parents' house and had said with characteristic generosity that she and Margaret could each wear one tonight. Both were long-sleeved with padded shoulders. One was silk in lavender and cream stripes, with a knife-pleated skirt, the other peacock-blue linen with patch pockets.

'You choose,' Mabel had offered.

'You ought to choose,' Margaret replied, 'as they're your dresses,' but she had rather hoped she would end up with the stripes.

'Fine,' said Mabel. 'I'll wear this one.'

She had indicated the linen, leaving Margaret wondering if it was a stroke of luck or if Mabel had read her wish in her expression.

At last she alighted from the bus at Chorlton terminus and hurried along Beech Road, turning the corner opposite the rec to make her way to Wilton Close. She slipped quietly into the house, careful not to disturb the blackout. She heard voices in the front room, so she wasn't too late after all. The door was half-open and she could hear Mrs Grayson in the kitchen. If Mrs Grayson was about to produce good-ies, Margaret would have time to change if she was quick about it.

She approached the door to the front room. Not wanting to disturb the conversation, she stepped softly into the doorway.

And stopped dead.

She couldn't believe her eyes. It was an expression she had heard many times before. She had used it herself, too, but she had never imagined it could be the literal truth. Shock roared in her ears and she distinctly felt every ounce of blood in her body crash into her feet. Dear heaven, she wasn't about to pass out, was she? No, she couldn't, she mustn't. She took a huge step backwards and left the room.

Left the house.

Walked and walked.

Oh my godfathers.

Joel.

CHAPTER SIX

Joan was at home on Saturday afternoon. She had dusted her sitting room and bedroom and swept the hall, landing and stair carpets as a contribution towards keeping the house's common areas spick and span, but the truth was there was very little housework for her to do. Cordelia's wedding present to her and Bob had been two hours of Magic Mop per week for eighteen weeks. The eighteen weeks had finished back in October, but Bob, thoughtful and generous as always, had carried on employing Mrs Cooper and Joan hadn't liked to say that, much as she appreciated coming home to clean rooms, she would actually quite like the chance to tackle her own housework. Yes, it would be tricky fitting it in alongside her working hours at Victoria, but she would still like to have a go at it, because it was part of being married, the same as the endless hours spent queuing up at the butcher's and the fishmonger's and the grocer's.

Anyway, she would be stopping work in a few weeks and that would be the time to stop having a cleaner too. Mrs Cooper would understand. Joan just hoped she would find another client, so she wouldn't lose out. Mrs Cooper didn't have much money and Joan suspected that she had to make every penny do the work of thruppence. Losing the two and fourpence a week from Bob could make a big difference to her.

It was quiet in the house. Sheila was out at work in the munitions factory, leaving Joan to keep an eye on Jimmy, who was out playing with his friends. Joan had a small fire in the sitting room. Rather than add more coal to it, she went upstairs to add an extra layer, smiling to herself as she chose a sweater belonging to Bob, loving the fact that it was too big for her.

As she settled herself beside the fire to do some knitting for the baby, she heard the key being pulled through the letter box on its string.

'Only me,' Dot called.

'In here,' Joan replied.

Dot popped her head round the door.

'Sheila's at work,' Joan told her.

'I know.' Dot entered the room, shutting the door to keep the warm in. 'It's you I've come to see, chick. I thought you might fancy a spot of company.'

'Oh aye?' Joan laughed. 'And if you should happen to find out about Joel while you're here . . .'

Dot laughed too. 'A bit of both.'

'I'll put the kettle on.'

'Nay, lass, you stay put. You look comfy there. I'll make us some tea, then you can tell me everything.'

Before Dot could leave the room, the front door opened again and Jimmy called, 'Auntie Joan! Auntie Joan! You'll never guess what.' He threw open the sitting-room door, then belatedly remembered his manners and, with one hand hanging on to the doorknob, knocked with the other. She should probably reprimand him, but Joan couldn't help smiling.

'Nan.' Jimmy beamed. 'You're here an' all. That's good. I can tell you too.'

'And hello to you an' all, our Jimmy,' said Dot.

'Oh – yes. Hello, Nan. Sorry.' Jimmy looked abashed.

'What's so important that you had to come crashing in here?' Dot asked severely.

Instantly, Jimmy perked up. 'They found an unexploded bomb and me and Alf and Benny have been to see it.'

'You never!' Dot exclaimed.

'We didn't actually *see* it,' Jimmy was forced to concede. 'They've put up a DANGER: UNEXPLODED BOMB sign and there's an ARP warden guarding it – the bomb, not the sign,' he added helpfully.

'Where is it?' Joan asked.

Jimmy mumbled something.

'Where?' Dot's eyes narrowed.

'Near the girls' school in Whalley Range.'

'You've been all the way over there?' Dot exclaimed. 'By, your grandpa says we should keep you on a length of string, and he's right. Don't go so far without asking in future. Supposing summat had happened.'

'But nowt did.'

'That's not the point – and don't answer back, young man. Think of your auntie Joan. She's meant to keep an eye on you while your mum's out at work and how can she do that if you go piking off without a by your leave? You don't want to get her into trouble, do you?'

'No, Nan. Sorry, Auntie Joan.'

'Anyroad,' said Dot, 'since you're here, you might as well make yourself useful.' Delving in her handbag for her purse, she produced some coppers. 'Nip to the shop and get Grandpa his Woodbines, there's a good lad.'

Jimmy raced for the front door, then dashed back to shut the sitting-room door before hurtling from the house. Shaking her head, Dot went to the kitchen, returning presently with tea.

'I'm sorry I didn't keep a better eye on Jimmy,' said Joan.

'It's not your fault, chick.' Dot settled herself on the sofa. 'Now then, tell me all about last evening. What's he like, yon chap of Alison's? What does he look like, for starters?'

The corners of Joan's lips twitched. 'I don't think you'll be disappointed.'

'Good-looking, then?'

Joan settled in for a good natter. 'Not film-star handsome like Harry, but well worth a second look, and he has a nice manner, rather breezy but not shallow.'

'What did Mrs Cooper and Mrs Grayson make of him? Wait, I'm getting mixed up. You wouldn't know.'

'Actually, I do,' said Joan. 'Mabel had a quiet word with me when we went to the Ladies. Apparently, when they were leaving to come to the pictures, Joel said to Mrs Cooper and Mrs Grayson that he hoped he'd made a favourable impression, because Alison had told him how important they are to her.'

Dot pulled a face. 'A bit smarmy, perhaps?'

'That's what I thought,' said Joan, 'but Mabel said not. According to her, he said it in a light-hearted kind of way, but you could tell he meant it.'

'A bit of a charmer, then.'

Joan laughed. 'Not in the same league as Harry, but, yes, you could say that.'

'It sounds like you and Mabel both liked him, so I assume Margaret did an' all.'

'She wasn't there. She must have been kept late at work. Such a shame. It was a really good evening.'

'I'm sure she'll get to meet him soon – or maybe not, with Alison going away. When does she leave?'

'Tomorrow, and she starts work on Monday. Mabel says she's been a bit moody at home.'

'Fear of the unknown,' Dot said wisely. 'She'll be all right once she gets there and settles in.'

The front door opened and they heard Jimmy talking quietly to someone. There was no knock on Joan's door.

'He's brought a friend home.' Joan felt pleased. It was a big improvement on roaming the streets in search of UXBs.

'Haven't you learned yet?' Dot asked. 'When our Jimmy goes quiet, there's summat up.'

She left the room and a moment later, Joan heard an exclamation.

'Jimmy! What d'you think you're playing at? And what's that doing here?'

Joan jumped up and hurried to the kitchen, where Jimmy was clutching a tin of luncheon meat. At his feet, gazing up hopefully, was a bedraggled-looking dog with floppy ears and a shaggy coat that, where it wasn't dirty, showed itself to be a gingery golden brown. A length of tatty skipping rope was doing the job of a lead.

'It's a dog, Nan.'

'I can see that, thank you. What's it doing here?'

'He's a stray. He's hungry. He needs feeding.'

'Not with your mum's luncheon meat, it doesn't.'

'He *does*, Nan. I found him tied to a fence. Someone's abandoned him.'

'Don't be daft,' said Dot. 'They left it there while they went to the shops, that's all.'

'They'll be upset to come back and find him gone,' Joan added, though a little voice inside her was whispering that whoever they were, they didn't deserve a dog. Leaving it tied up outdoors on a cold day like today! The words 'poor thing' were on the tip of her tongue, but she knew she had to support Dot. Anyone dealing with Jimmy Green needed all the support they could get.

'But he's cold,' said Jimmy. 'He were shivering all over when I found him. He could have frozen to death.'

'Not in the time it takes for its owner to do the shopping,' Dot stated firmly. 'You've got to take it back where you found it.'

'He's hungry an' all,' Jimmy persisted. 'Probably starving.'

'Jimmy.' There was a warning note in Dot's voice.

'He's really thin. He doesn't look it because he's all hairy, but you can feel his bones.'

Moving forward, Joan let the dog sniff her hand before she felt along his side. Even though her touch was gentle, the dog flinched.

She nodded at Dot. 'Skinny.'

'Now don't you start going all soft on me,' Dot chided. 'That dog's going back where Jimmy got it from.'

'We could perhaps give him something to eat before he goes?' Joan suggested.

'Well, it's not having Sheila's luncheon meat,' said Dot. 'She'd have my guts for garters and string Jimmy up by his toes. Put that tin away, Jimmy.'

'But he's seen it now,' said Jimmy.

'Don't push your luck,' said Dot.

'I've got some meat paste,' said Joan.

'Are you sure you want to waste it on someone else's dog?' asked Dot. 'Righty-ho. Let's do it properly, then. Jimmy, put the kettle on. We'll make some Bovril pobs.'

'Bovril pobs?' Jimmy asked, interested.

'A bowl of weak Bovril drink with bits of bread in. My old mam – your great-nan, Jimmy – used to give us bowls of Bovril pobs to fill us up when she couldn't afford owt else when we were nippers.'

'Don't forget the meat paste,' said Jimmy. 'You said he could have the meat paste.'

'Aye.' Dot sighed. 'You do know you can't keep him – it?'

'Yes, Nan.'

'But you'll have done a kind thing by giving him a snack to tide him over,' said Joan.

'Oi,' said Dot. 'Don't tell him that or he'll end up fetching home every dog and cat he can lay hands on. His mum will have kittens.'

'Kittens?' Jimmy's ears pricked up.

'Not those sort of kittens,' said Dot. 'I mean, she'll be vexed. Let's get this animal fed and then you can take it back.'

Joan prepared the Bovril and Jimmy had to be restrained from putting half the loaf in it.

'Are you sure about the meat paste, love?' Dot asked.

Joan nodded. Bob would understand. He was a softy.

'Don't give it him all at once, Jimmy,' said Dot. 'A bit at a time.'

Jimmy was right about the dog being hungry. It gulped down what it was offered.

'I've got Grandpa's cigarettes,' said Jimmy. 'Shall I give them to you in Auntie Joan's sitting room, Nan? It's where your handbag is.'

'It's also where there happens to be a fire,' said Dot. 'Don't get visions of the dog stretching out on the hearth-rug, Jimmy. He's not stopping.'

'No, but he could have a bit of a warm before he has to go out again, couldn't he?' said Jimmy. 'So could I.' He shivered theatrically. 'It's blinking freezing out there.'

'Five minutes,' said Joan.

Dot nudged her. 'You're as bad as he is. Two minutes and that's your lot.'

Jimmy led the dog on its rope to the fireside, kneeling beside it. Dot and Joan resumed their places.

'They've got tins of tapioca and macaroni in the grocer's,' said Jimmy.

'If this is your idea of distracting me from watching the clock . . .' said Dot.

'No, Nan, honest. Mum said I had to look at what's in the shops and let her know now that there's points on food as well as rationing. She says she wants to use her points wisely, so I have to be like Tonto in *The Lone Ranger*, so I can make sure she gets the best use out of her points.'

'Good for you,' said Joan. 'That's very helpful.'

'I tell you what would be better, though,' said Dot. 'Don't hog the information to yourself for your mum. You should let the neighbours know an' all. They'd appreciate it and it's always nice to do a good turn for other people.'

'All right, Nan,' Jimmy said virtuously. 'I'll remember.'

'Good lad,' said Dot. She slapped her hands down on her knees. 'Time's up, Jimmy.' She held up a warning finger as he started to speak and he subsided. 'That dog needs to go back to where its owner will find it. Come on, love. I'll go with you and make sure you tie it up properly. I'm not having you coming home with Fido here just happening to be padding along behind you.'

'Are we calling him Fido?' asked Jimmy.

'We aren't calling him anything. He's already got a name.'

'He hasn't, Nan. He's not wearing a name tag. He hasn't even got a collar.'

Dot exchanged glances with Joan. 'I bet his owner hasn't even got a dog licence.'

'Does that mean they're not a proper owner?' Jimmy asked.

'It means it's time for us to take it back where it came from. Come on.'

Joan got up. 'I'll go with him. I've got to take a lemonade bottle back and Jimmy can have the tuppence deposit.'

'Bribery?' Dot asked softly.

Joan shrugged. 'If it helps.'

She went upstairs to put on her outdoor things. They all left the house together. Dot headed for home and Joan, Jimmy and the dog went in the opposite direction. There was a sharp edge to the chilly air and Joan felt awful as she stood by, watching as Jimmy tied the dog to a bit of fence sticking out beside a privet hedge, and she felt even worse as the two of them walked away. At the corner, they looked back and saw the dog had walked as far as the skipping rope permitted and was now staring after them.

'Come on, Jimmy.' Joan set off. 'Don't worry. His owner will be back to collect him.'

'Will they?' asked Jimmy.

CHAPTER SEVEN

Even now, twenty-four hours later, Margaret was still appalled. She had barely slept last night. She had gone to bed in good time before the others arrived home from the cinema and had pretended to be asleep when Mabel crept into their bedroom. Inside, she was shaking. Throughout the night, great surges of shock had washed over her, making her want to sob her heart out, but she didn't dare so much as whimper for fear of disturbing Mabel. She couldn't have faced the inevitable questions. No one must ever know.

Joel. *Joel.* After all this time – and just when she had finally got her life back on track – Joel.

This morning, Mrs Cooper, Mrs Grayson and Mabel had practically fallen over themselves in their eagerness to tell her how likeable he was, how good-looking, how amusing. With the blood thrashing about in her ears, she had smiled and nodded and agreed that it had indeed been rotten luck that she hadn't made it home in time to go to the pictures.

Alison had kissed her cheek – actually kissed her! 'Thanks, Margaret. Going out with Joel is absolutely the right thing for me and I've got you and Mabel to thank for making me see it.'

Ye gods. Margaret had encouraged Alison to go out with Joel, actively encouraged her.

This could be your chance to be happy, Alison. For what it's worth, I hope you'll take it.

That was what she'd said. Oh, if she'd known then what she knew now . . .

Today had been a heck of a long day. Long? Endless. If Margaret could have got away with claiming she was due at work, she would have. As it was, she had volunteered to do the shopping for Mrs Grayson in the hope of queuing for ages, but she hadn't allowed for what chatty places queues could be. What a misery she must have appeared to everyone else. Later, she had gone for a long walk, anything to be on her own while thoughts swirled around inside her head. This evening, she had concocted a story about meeting an old friend before she went on fire-watching duty, so she could scarper early.

'You're going to miss seeing Joel again,' said Mabel. 'He's coming to collect Alison – just the two of them this time instead of a posse. What a shame.'

Shame. Margaret knew all there was to know about shame. It had dogged her and come close to crushing her. And just when she thought she'd managed to put it behind her . . .

Joel.

In her thoughts, she relived the conversation she and Mabel had had with Alison before Christmas when Alison had been in two minds as to whether she should pursue this new relationship so soon after the heartbreak of being dumped by Paul. All through the conversation, the new boyfriend had been referred to merely as Joel, never Joel Maitland, and there had been no telltale mention of his being a doctor. Just – Joel. Mabel had joked about a Joel from her past who had been a spotty herbert, and while Alison had said her Joel was definitely not one of those, Margaret had had to look away for a moment, suddenly breathless at the reminder of her own Joel.

Except that he had never been *her* Joel, had he? Not really. He was nothing more than the fly-by-night boyfriend who had been out for one thing and, having got it, had vanished, leaving her feeling small and cheap. It had been nearly two years ago now and she still felt like damaged goods. Her only consolation at the time had been that you couldn't get pregnant the first time. Everybody said so.

Oh, how wrong everybody had been.

It was nearly half ten when Bob arrived home that evening. Joan was ready for bed, in her nightdress, dressing gown and, because it was another cold night, socks. Not very glamorous, perhaps, for a girl who was a wife of less than a year, but she could shed them in double-quick time if things took a romantic turn.

As Bob came through the front door, Joan went straight to him for a big chilly hug. He made a half-hearted attempt to fend her off.

'I don't want to make you cold.'

'I don't care,' she mumbled into his chest. 'I've got socks on.'

She quickly prepared cheese on toast with home-made carrot chutney. Where would they be without the humble carrot? It was in everything these days. It was even being made into jam.

Having shed his outdoor things, Bob came into the kitchen. 'I love the smell of toast. I was expecting a sandwich.'

Joan explained the fate of the meat paste. 'I hope you don't mind.'

'Mind?' Bob feigned outrage. 'She feeds my supper to a mangy animal and asks if I mind.'

'Poor Jimmy,' said Joan. 'For a short while, he really thought he'd acquired a pet.'

'I can't see Sheila agreeing to that.'

'I hope the dog didn't have to wait too long in the cold for its owner to come back for it.'

'Where did Jimmy come across it?' asked Bob.

Joan finally said what she really meant. 'That's just it. It wasn't outside the shops. It was tied to a fence near the park.'

With his fork halfway to his mouth, Bob paused. 'And you're worried it might have been abandoned.'

'Well – yes.'

'Just because someone left it in a place that doesn't fit in with the story you made up about it, doesn't mean it was abandoned.'

'I know. I'm just being silly.'

'It's not silly. It's warm-hearted. It's why you're going to be such a wonderful mum.'

'Flatterer.'

'It isn't flattery. It's the simple truth,' said Bob. 'You shouldn't have waited up for me.'

'It's my wifely duty,' teased Joan.

'And your railway duty involves the early shift in the morning. At least we won't have to worry about being on different shifts once you give up work.'

'We'll have the baby to keep us awake instead,' said Joan, picking up the empty plate and mug. 'You go on up. I'll clear away and be up in a minute.'

She took the pots to the scullery, using soda crystals and hot water from the kettle to wash up, then she dried and put the things away in her cupboard. Sheila was inclined to leave things on the wooden draining board to dry. She hadn't always – or rather, she must have always done it as a matter of routine in the past, before Bob and Joan came to lodge with her – but after they moved in, Sheila had for the first three or four months been meticulous about drying up straight away. Joan didn't know for certain, but she strongly suspected that Dot must have had a word with her daughter-in-law about keeping the kitchen in good order to please her lodgers. Apparently, however, Sheila had found that too much of a chore long-term. Reverting to type, Gran would have called it, had she known. Joan was careful not to provide Gran with anything to criticise.

Switching off the light, she went upstairs, where Bob was putting on his blue-and-white-striped pyjama top over his vest. They had hardly got into bed before the siren sounded and they rolled out again, pulling on thick jumpers and dressing gowns.

'It'll be freezing in the Andy,' said Bob.

Joan produced a couple of the knitted 'tea cosy' hats that Mrs Grayson had been churning out recently because of the temperature.

'Just in case bedsocks aren't glamorous enough,' she said.

The four of them had been through enough air raids together to have got their own system worked out and they quickly did all the jobs that needed doing before leaving the house. The blackout had to be taken down and all the curtains, upstairs and down, had to be left open, so that should an incendiary come through the roof, the flames inside the house could be seen outside. The water and gas were switched off and the buckets of water and sand that stood in the hall overnight were placed outside the front door. Bob carried his and Joan's strongbox of important papers under his arm and Sheila grabbed hers. Jimmy carried the biscuit tin and a flask of tea.

As they went into the back garden, the sound of aircraft engines filled the night and strong beams of lights swung this way and that, searching the skies.

'Don't hang about, Jimmy,' Sheila ordered as her son paused to stare upwards.

One by one, they climbed down the steep steps into the Anderson shelter, breathing in the musty aroma of damp earth. Bob lit the paraffin heater.

'Margaret's fire-watching tonight,' said Joan, and was grateful that Bob didn't try to fob her off with platitudes. Joan hoped with all her heart that Margaret would be all right, but there was no getting away from the fact that on the night of the last air raid, their lovely Colette had been killed and Cordelia had been buried alive.

'Bed, Jimmy,' said Sheila. In the glow of the light bulb, her face was shiny with cold cream.

'What about the dog?' Jimmy asked in a small voice.

'What dog?' There was a note of obstinacy in Sheila's voice.

'I told you. The dog that Nan and Auntie Joan made me take back.'

'Oh aye,' replied his mother. 'The dog that I told you – and Nan and Auntie Joan told you – hadn't been abandoned. It had just been left to sit and stay. That's what dogs are trained to do.'

'What if it's still sitting and staying?'

'It won't be,' said Sheila. 'It will have been fetched hours ago.'

'How do you know?' asked Jimmy, followed by 'Ow!' as his mum gave him a clip round the ear for answering back. 'Well, he might still be there,' the lad continued determinedly. 'He'll be scared stiff.'

Frozen stiff, too, thought Joan. She bit her lip, torn as to what to do.

But Bob wasn't.

'Where did you leave it?' he asked Jimmy.

'You're never going out to look for it?' Sheila asked incredulously.

'It's what—' Bob started to say.

'What Jimmy wants,' Sheila finished waspishly. 'Too soft by half. You can't give in to him or he'll be impossible to live with. Even more impossible.'

64

Bob said quietly, 'If you'll let me finish. It's what Joan wants.'

Joan thought her heart would burst with love and pride. Marrying this man was the best thing she had ever done. He wasn't a charming RAF hero like Harry Knatchbull, and he wasn't a clever, highly educated doctor like Joel, but in her eyes, he was better than both of them rolled together. He was Bob and he was the best, most considerate husband any girl could wish for, and he was hers.

'Tell me exactly where,' said Bob.

'I'll come with you,' Joan said at once.

'No, you're staying put.'

'It'll be quicker, honestly. There's a whole row of fences and hedges and I can go straight to the right place.'

Bob thought for a moment. 'All right.' To Jimmy, who was already on the step, he said, 'Your job is to stay here and look after your mum. No arguments, lad. Come on, Joan. Shut the door behind us, Jimmy.'

They made a dash for the house and went upstairs, fumbling about in the dark for warm clothes. Then off they went, armed with torches, the lenses covered with layers of tissue paper to dim the beams. They ran through the empty streets towards Fog Lane Park. A high-pitched whistling sound warned of a string of high explosives on their way to earth. Bob pushed Joan to the ground beside a wall and threw himself on top of her. There was a series of explosions and the ground trembled, but even though the noise was almost enough to stun them, the damage had happened elsewhere.

Bob hauled Joan to her feet and they ran on. Joan found the line of houses with the hedges at the front interspersed with old fencing. Was it this fence or that one? Everything looked different in the dark. There was no sign of the dog. Joan released a breath of pure relief. The owner had returned after all.

'Over here,' said Bob.

Joan hurried to his side and there was the dog. It had forced itself bodily inside the hedge, pulling the rope to its fullest extent to get there.

Bob hunkered down. 'Come here, boy. Come here, fella. Can you untie the rope and give it to me?' he asked Joan.

Without taking his eyes off the dog, Bob stood up and removed his coat. Taking the rope from Joan, he wound the end firmly round his wrist a couple of times before he reached into the hedge and drew the dog out, holding it snugly in his arms.

'Wrap my coat around him,' he told Joan. 'Cover his head. There we go, little fella,' he soothed the terrified animal. 'We'll soon have you home.'

'Home?' Joan asked.

'Well, if someone does own him, they don't deserve to keep him after this.'

'Sheila won't be pleased.'

'Sheila won't mind,' Bob predicted. 'It's only Jimmy who's not allowed to have a dog. She won't mind one bit if *we* do.'

CHAPTER EIGHT

As the train drew closer to Leeds, Alison felt tired and edgy. It must be nerves – and that wasn't like her. How many different places had she worked in since starting her new job last autumn? And she hadn't been nervous about any of them, certainly not like this, with her tummy not so much full of butterflies as full of stampeding elephants. The other placements Miss Emery had organised for her had lasted a week or a fortnight. The most recent had been longer, probably because of Christmas. If she'd only had to face a week or a fortnight in Leeds, she could have sailed through, regarding it as little more than a nuisance, but she was to be stuck here for . . . well, she didn't know how long.

'Several weeks,' Miss Emery had told her. 'I can't be more specific, because it will depend on how things go.'

It had been hard to keep her spirits up all last week with the move to Leeds looming. If she was honest, she didn't think she'd managed it a lot of the time, in spite of her friends' encouragement. After Paul had left her, she had spent a long time holding her friends at arm's length, but before Christmas she had come to her senses and realised how much she needed them and appreciated their support, as well as how much she enjoyed being with them – and now, having vowed to turn over a new leaf and be a better member of the group, she was doomed to spend goodness only knew how long on her own in Leeds.

Leaving Joel had been hard too. Being sent to Leeds had happened just when, after a slow start to their relationship that was entirely her fault for not knowing her own mind, she was eager to spend time getting to know him properly.

'I'll come home every chance I get,' she had promised.

'And I'll come over to Leeds too,' Joel had said.

It was upsetting to be separated from one another, but Alison wasn't worried about it as such because they were happy together and that meant being apart wouldn't shake their relationship. Then again, she had felt that sort of confidence when she was with Paul, and look where that had led. She tried hard not to think of it that way, but she couldn't help it. It wasn't that she didn't trust Joel or the relationship they shared, but she had learned the hard way not to take anything for granted.

Left to her own devices, Alison would have travelled later in the day, anything to delay the evil moment, but Mrs Cooper had suggested going earlier – 'so that you arrive in daylight, chuck. Getting there in the blackout and trying to find your digs wouldn't exactly feel welcoming now, would it?'

Alison took a taxi to the address Miss Emery had given her. It wasn't far from the station; it felt like a reasonable walking distance. Since the Park Square canteen was apparently near the station, she should be able to walk there and back. That was good, she told herself. It would make her working days that bit easier. It would give her more time at home too. Home. This tall, narrow house with soot-blackened bricks was her home for the time being.

If she had imagined that all landladies were as warm-hearted as dear Mrs Cooper, she was in for a disappointment. The front door was opened by a stout, keen-eyed woman in a wrap-around pinny – on a Sunday! Mum would sniff with disdain at that.

'Miss Lambert? I'm Mrs Freeman. Come in. I'll tell you right away I don't normally take girls. I prefer men. Much less trouble. But I've always took in railway workers and when I was asked to take you, well, it's my duty in wartime, isn't it? I'll expect you to provide me each week with a list of your work shifts, so I know when you'll be in and out. Depending on your rota, I can do you a breakfast or a hot supper each day for an extra three shillings a week. Your rent is eleven and six a week. The bathroom is on the first floor and there's a list on the wall outside for lodgers to book their slots. Please don't overstay your allocated time: one reason I don't like lady lodgers. No male visitors in your room, no noise. Everyone works shifts and everyone needs their sleep. Your room is on the top floor. You can find your own way up, can't you?'

Alison nodded. Grasping the handle of her suitcase, a smart leather one loaned by Mabel, she headed upstairs. On the first floor, there were two doors, both shut, though one had the promised list outside. Alison took a quick look. With luck, she would be able to have a slot that had a couple of empty ones either side and thereby not run into any men when she was in her dressing gown. There were two more closed doors on the second floor. The final staircase was narrower and was boxed in by walls on either side. At the top was a small square landing with a single door that opened into a narrow room in which the ceiling sloped steeply on both of the room's long sides. Alison didn't mind that. She had a sloping ceiling in Wilton Close and had soon got used to it.

Beneath the highest part of the ceiling was the bed, with a mat beside it – 'rug' would have been too polite a word for it. Tucked in beneath the slope were a chest of drawers, a cupboard and an old-fashioned washstand, which was good, really, because it meant she wouldn't be reliant on the bathroom if all she needed was a quick wash. There was a single skylight over which a blackout board had been nailed. Alison touched it and found it was cold, which gave her an ominous sinking feeling. There was a table, roughly the size of a card table, together with a ladderback chair in a dormer window. Alison looked across at the houses opposite and down at the road below. Further along the street, a house had suffered a direct hit. Its façade was missing and its roof sagged, but the bomb that had clipped the front of the building had also left a crater into which the resulting rubble had poured.

'Very tidy,' Alison said to herself. 'Thank you, Herr Hitler, I don't think.'

Turning round, she surveyed the room again – her room. That was how she must think of it from now on. Her room. And she must feel positive and cheerful when she did. There was nothing wrong with it. It was clean and it had the necessary furniture. Alison's keen nose caught a faint whiff of turps, linseed oil and vinegar, which said that Mrs Freeman, in true wartime style, had taken to making her own furniture cream. No, there was nothing wrong with the room at all. But . . .

But when she had moved into the old box room in Wilton Close, Mrs Cooper had put a cut-glass vase of golden chrysanths on the bedside cupboard and Mrs Grayson had left a gift of a knitted pyjama case on her pillow, and she had instantly felt fussed over and welcome.

For a moment, tears welled, but she forced them down. She wouldn't be here for ever, just for a few weeks, and she was going to make the best of it, which would make the time pass more quickly. She would unpack and then ask Mrs Freeman for directions and go for a walk to find where she had to present herself in the morning. Then she would come back and . . . and face a long evening alone. Oh, glory.

Determined to be sensible, she hoisted her suitcase onto the bed, undid the leather straps and used the little key

Mabel had given her to unfasten the lock. Then she clicked aside the metal knobs that made the keys flick open, allowing her to lift the lid. She frowned as she saw a pillowcase on top of her packing. She hadn't put that in there.

She took it out. There were things inside it. A warm feeling started to glow inside her chest. She sat on the bed and explored the contents.

The first thing that came out was a hot-water bottle with a note from Mrs Cooper. *An extra bottle to make sure you get into a warm bed every night.* Oh, bless her. Wasn't she kind? Next came a knitted scarf and mittens from Mrs Grayson. Then there was a Bertie Wooster novel from Mabel – *To make you smile, with lots of love xxx*

Next there was a small packet wrapped in brown paper from Persephone. *Emergency present to be opened when you need cheering up.* Alison laughed, intrigued. The packet felt squidgy, but was there something hard at its centre? She would put it in a drawer and open it if things got really dire.

Cordelia had given her what her note said was the last of her good stationery and Dot had provided some stamps. Cordelia's note ended: *Dot says, 'Make sure you write to your mother.'* And Joan had sent her an old envelope that had been used several times, judging by what was written and crossed out, inside which – Alison drew in a huge breath as she gazed at the photograph. It was one of Joan's wedding pictures. Bob's family had paid for a proper photographer and this picture was of the bride flanked by her bridesmaids – Alison, Mabel, Margaret and Persephone, with Colette as the matron of honour. Oh, Colette, dear Colette. Alison touched the photo with her fingertips. All those happy smiles, and the lace boleros made from, of all things, Joan's gran's net curtains, and those knitted white flowers Mrs Grayson had made for them to attach to their hats.

What a special day that had been, with the wedding reception being held in the buffet at Victoria Station because the church-hall kitchen had flooded.

How lucky she was to have such wonderful, caring friends. They knew how hard this was for her and their consideration drove away her reservations and misgivings – for now, anyway. There was more than one way to feel at home and the best way of all was to feel cared for.

At some unearthly hour of the morning, Alison dragged herself out of bed to find the air in her room was cold enough for her breath to appear in little puffs of cloud in front of her face. Her clothes were chilled too; she would take her underwear to bed with her tonight. Thank goodness she had added her name to the bathroom rota, because there was a thin film of ice on top of the water in the ewer on her washstand.

Breakfast was porridge – unsweetened, but a nice consistency – and toast. She was alone in the dining room.

'The others left ages ago,' Mrs Freeman informed her in a tone that suggested this was another reason why men made better lodgers.

So Alison sat in solitary splendour at the table. All the furniture was of dark wood – table, chairs, sideboard and the bookcase that was used for displaying ornaments. The fire surround was of brown tiles, as was the hearth. By contrast, the walls were a rather pretty hyacinth blue, which made all the brown look sharp-edged and dingy.

Afterwards, glad that she'd had the good sense to seek it out yesterday, Alison set off for Park Square. The air was chilly enough to make her feel as if tiny razor blades were cutting her cheeks and she pulled up her scarf, her new one from Mrs Grayson, over her nose.

The buildings surrounding Park Square were a handsome lot. 'Gracious' was the word that sprang to mind. Not fussy and Gothic like big Victorian places; more elegant, with cleaner lines. Georgian? Alison ran up the steps and entered a large hall with a wide staircase opposite the front doors. The hall's proportions were spoiled by the addition of a box-like office in one corner just inside the doors, which looked thoroughly out of place amid the stucco and tall sash windows.

Alison approached the office's hatch and asked for directions to the canteen. She soon found her way into a spacious room crammed with tables and chairs, many of which were occupied by men and girls in railway uniforms or boiler suits, and also by nurses, which took her by surprise before she recalled that this facility was being shared. A group had just finished. Stubbing out their cigarettes, they pushed back their chairs and carried their trays of used crockery over to where wheeled sets of shelves stood. Down one side of the room was a long serving-counter with shelves and metal hot cupboards behind. The staff were doling out porridge with what looked like but couldn't possibly be honey. It must be mock honey. All the best things were 'mock' these days. Further along, sausages and beans were being served, along with tinned tomatoes and toast. Further down again were huge urns beside cups stacked inside one another, while lines of mugs occupied the shelves behind. There were also trays offering masses of sandwiches. As Alison watched, the men who had tidied away their trays walked down the counter and selected sandwiches for later.

Alison hovered, waiting for a quieter moment so she could speak to one of the women serving, but she soon found there was no such thing as a quiet moment. Was she really going to have to queue up to ask her question? That would make her look a proper clot.

Several women of varying ages in wrap-around pinnies and turbans were moving about the room, wiping tables as

73

people left them and removing used dishes where breakfasters had failed to do so. Alison approached one of them, a motherly-looking individual with a strawberry birthmark on her cheek, who was leaning over a table to clean its other side.

'Excuse me,' Alison began. 'I'm new here.'

The woman straightened. 'Fetch yourself a tray from over there and choose what you want from the counter. Oh, and it helps if you put your tray on one of those trolleys when you're done.'

'I'm not here to eat. I'm here to work.'

'Oh.' The woman looked round. 'Well, I suppose you'd best go to the kitchen.'

Alison peered round in search of likely-looking doors. Last week, in the Victoria Station canteen, it had been obvious where the kitchen was situated.

'That door there, love, at the far end, and down the stairs.'

Downstairs? Did that mean all the food had to be carried up? Alison didn't want to think about that. She threaded her way through the length of the room and headed for the door.

'You can't go through there. That's for staff only. Where are you trying to get to?'

Alison faced a burly man. 'I'm looking for the kitchen. I start work today.'

The man nodded. 'Welcome aboard.'

Alison went downstairs into a cavernous kitchen with a massive range and long shelves of canisters and jars. A line of three pine tables placed end to end appeared to be where the main preparations were done. At one end, on a floured surface, a dumpy little woman was rolling out pastry. Across most of the surface, veg was being chopped at astonishing speed – carrots, swede and winter greens. And at the end nearest to Alison, two girls were piling cooked macaroni and tinned tomatoes in several large dishes.

Alison stood for a moment, taking it all in. No one seemed to notice her, or if they did, they didn't stop what they were doing. Alison approached a thin lass, who looked young enough to have left school that Christmas.

'Excuse me. I'm looking for the person in charge. I'm reporting for work.'

The girl gawped at her. 'D'you mean the cook? Mrs Bertram's the head cook this shift. Here she is now. Mrs Bertram, this lady says she's to work here.'

Mrs Bertram was an energetic-looking woman with non-descript colouring. She had come bustling in, but now she stopped dead and looked Alison up and down. She didn't smile.

'Good morning,' said Alison. 'My name is Alison Lambert.'

'You're late.'

Alison looked at the clock on the wall. 'It's not quite seven.'

'Then you're not quite two hours late.'

'I was told to report for the early shift. When I worked in the canteen at Manchester Victoria last week, the early shift started at seven.'

'Oh aye?' Mrs Bertram replied. 'Well, they may give the early lot a lie-in over in Manchester, but here in Leeds we know the meaning of hard work and the early shift starts at five. You're late, so you'll have your pay docked.'

'I'm sorry. I didn't know.'

'You should have made it your business to find out. Well, you're no good to me now. I expected four new girls this morning and I got three. They've had the grand tour and the talk and they were put to work an hour since. I can't be doing with you swanning in halfway through the morning.'

Alison didn't know what to say. Was she about to be dismissed before she had started?

'Through there.' Mrs Bertram indicated with a jerk of her chin. 'Potatoes. Get washing.'

'Wash the potatoes?'

'Are you deaf as well as late? Yes – wash the potatoes. Thoroughly, mind. We cook 'em with their skins on to preserve the goodness and nobody wants to find mud on their spud.' Mrs Bertram delivered the rhyme without cracking a smile.

Alison entered a chilly tiled room. On one wall were deep sinks with long wooden draining boards. Stacked against the opposite wall were more sacks of potatoes than she cared to count. Two girls were already at work. They looked round, greeting her with smiles. Alison was relieved, then she realised the girls were actually grinning at what must be her horrified expression. She quickly rearranged her features and introduced herself. The two girls were Betty and Eddie, short for Edna. They pointed out the rough aprons hanging on the back of the door – 'Best wear two, love. It's ever such a wet job, this' – and Eddie moved sinks so Alison could go in the middle.

'Someone said you'd come here from Manchester,' Betty said to Alison. 'What brings you to Leeds?'

'I work for LMS,' Alison explained. She hesitated. 'It's difficult to say this without sounding big-headed, but I'm being trained up for a special job.'

To her surprise, Betty and Eddie looked at one another and then burst out laughing.

'What sort of special job requires you to wash spuds as part of your training?' chortled Eddie.

Alison wasn't daft enough to take offence. She smiled at them, taking the ribbing in good part. 'I don't know what the job will be, to be honest. All I know is that I've done all kinds of different things in the past few weeks. I was told it'll be useful for me to have a good general knowledge of the workings of the railways. And as we all know, how to wash potatoes is an essential part of that,' she added, making the other two laugh all over again.

After an hour or so, a message came that Alison was to go to the private room at half past ten.

'That's a little room they take you to when they have to give you bad news,' Betty explained. 'Sorry, love. I didn't mean you should expect bad news. It's just as the name says – it's when someone needs to speak to you in private.'

'It'll be the dragon lady,' said Eddie. 'She'll want to give you a roasting for fetching up late on your first day.'

'She's already done that,' said Alison. 'In public, too.'

'Not Mrs Bertram. She isn't the dragon lady,' said Betty. 'She's not a bad old stick, Mrs Bertram. It's because she's on earlies this week. That always makes her ratty. She's a different person when she's on afternoons or nights.'

'Honestly, you'll love her,' said Eddie, 'even if you don't like her now.'

Alison had taken off her wristwatch and put it on a shelf before she started washing the potatoes. Now she kept picking it up to keep an eye on the time.

'You'd best get gone,' Betty said at quarter past ten. 'The dragon lady won't be pleased if you keep her waiting. She's in overall charge of this place and she likes us all to know that she does this on top of her proper job.'

Memorising the directions they gave her, Alison removed her aprons with hands so cold her fingers could barely undo the bows at the back of her waist. She made her way upstairs to find the private room, which was a small room with a couple of mismatched armchairs and a table between them. On the mantelpiece over a boarded-up fireplace was a carriage clock. Ten twenty. Good. She was ten minutes early.

One wall was mostly taken up by a window criss-crossed with tape, under which was an ancient sofa. A girl sat there.

She wore a smart jacket over a black dress with a simple round neckline. On one lapel, she wore a discreet brooch. Her dark brown hair was beautifully curled and styled to sweep back from her face. She wore spectacles and was pencilling notes onto a sheet of typing. Looking up as Alison entered, she removed her specs. Her eyes were dark, her eyebrows perfectly arched.

Something inside Alison relaxed. At least she wasn't the only one here to be carpeted.

'Hello,' said Alison. 'Are you here for a wigging too?'

'I beg your pardon?' said the beauty.

'I'm here for a carpeting from the dragon lady who runs the Park Square canteen on top of doing another job. It looks like she's very efficiently doing two carpetings in one go.'

'The dragon lady, did you say? How . . . interesting. I was unaware of that. I assume you must be Alison Lambert from Manchester Victoria. Late on your first day – and insolent to boot. Not a good start.'

Alison stared at her in dawning horror. 'I'm so sorry . . .' she began.

'I imagine you are,' replied the dragon lady.

'I never thought someone like you . . . I mean, I pictured someone a lot older.'

'You think that a young woman isn't capable of coping with a responsible job?' The dragon lady kept her voice low and measured, which somehow made her words even more stinging. 'That's the kind of attitude one expects from a certain type of man, not from another woman.'

'I didn't meant to suggest—'

'Not another word. Believe me, there is nothing you could say at this point that would redeem you. I feel like walking out of here, but, unlike you, I am professional in my attitude to my work. For example, I was here before five this morning so that I could deliver my introductory talk to the new canteen staff. Because you missed my talk through your lateness, here I am once more to fit you in, despite the inconvenience to myself. In spite of the fact that you have attempted to make fun of me, I will nevertheless tell you what you need to know about being an employee here.'

'Look, I truly am most awfully sorry.'

The dragon lady ignored her. 'I am Miss Rachel Chambers and I am the deputy lady almoner at the infirmary. That means I assess a patient's ability to pay for treatment and I also organise convalescent care when the patient leaves hospital. This role keeps me fully occupied, but in the interests of serving my country and doing my bit, I am now in overall charge of this shared canteen facility. My responsibilities include the supply of equipment and fuel and ensuring that the Ministry of Food's guidance on nutrition is followed. I am also responsible for all matters appertaining to the staff, including pay, holidays and changes to the workforce. I do not personally write the staffing rotas, but I do expect those who write them to keep me informed of any problems, however small.'

Miss Chambers glanced away for a moment. She had a perfect profile, with a straight nose and a graceful neck. She returned her attention to Alison.

'You, Miss Lambert, are here because I permitted it. Had I declined to have you, that would have been the end of it.' Miss Chambers paused again. It wasn't a friendly pause that invited questions. It was simply a way of making Alison wait. 'I did, however, permit you to come here. I'm sure you understand that I'm wondering if I have made an error. Miss Emery wishes me to allow you opportunities to spend time with me, learning about my role as the overseer of the canteen, but now that I know you are the sort to speak in disparaging terms of a senior colleague behind

her back, I consider myself to be under no obligation to fulfil Miss Emery's request. You have made a remarkably poor
first impression, Miss Lambert. I shall be keeping an eye on
you. Step out of line once more and you'll find yourself
back on the other side of the Pennines before you can say
Jack Robinson.'

CHAPTER NINE

Joan hurried home after her shift in Lost Property, eager to get back to the dog. She had never had a pet before and she felt extra responsible for this one, because Bob had rescued it purely to please her. Their different shifts today meant that he had been able to take care of it until two o'clock or so, after which the dog would have been on its own until Joan got home. She had a huge smile on her face as she almost threw open the front door. She had stopped off at the butcher's and been allowed to have a couple of bones, much to the disgust of other shoppers, who swore they could have used those bones to add flavour to their stews and hadn't been at all impressed by Joan's tale of an abandoned dog.

But when she opened her sitting-room door, looking forward to what she hoped would be a friendly greeting, she found the room empty. The breath caught in her throat. The dog had escaped and might even now be chewing its way through Sheila's clothes. Then common sense reasserted itself. If the dog had got out, it had managed to close the sitting-room door very neatly behind itself.

She went into the kitchen, where Sheila was rinsing out her underwear in the scullery.

'Where's the dog?' Joan asked without preamble. 'Has Jimmy taken him for a walk?'

'Jimmy's not back from school yet,' said Sheila. 'He'll be roaming about with his friends. I put the dog out.'

'You did what?' Joan went cold all over.

'I put him out. That's what you do with dogs. You put 'em out for the day to wander around as they please and they come home at teatime.'

'But he doesn't know this is his home,' Joan exclaimed. 'He doesn't know to come back here.'

Sheila looked at her. 'Then you won't have to be bothered with him, will you? What have you got there?'

'Bones.'

'Oh, good. I'm making parsnip soup later. If you want to add them to the pan for flavour, we can share.'

'They're for the dog,' said Joan.

She put the bones in the meat safe. Would the dog get to enjoy them or would they end up as flavouring because the dog was never seen again? She ought to go out searching, but suppose the dog found its way back in her absence and Sheila thought it wasn't time to let it in yet? It might wander off again and, having been rebuffed, might not come back. The thought was ridiculously distressing.

The front door opened and Jimmy called, 'Mum! Come and see. I've found Fido's twin brother.'

Sheila groaned. 'Dear heaven, not another flaming dog.' She raised her eyebrows at Joan. 'See what you've started.'

Joan went into the hallway. There was Jimmy in his duffel coat, school cap askew and his socks in wrinkles round his ankles. Joan's heart leaped. With Jimmy was – no, it wasn't. Her dog – she hadn't chosen a name yet, but it wouldn't be Fido, assuming he ever came home – was on the shaggy side. This one was smooth-haired. But that face, those eyes as dark and gleaming as blackberries, and those floppy ears, all hairy and looking a fraction too long – surely this was . . .

The dog bounded to her, leaning against her leg and curving its body in delight as she bent to stroke and pat it.

'Be careful about fussing it,' warned Sheila.

82

'I know you don't want another dog in the house,' said Joan.

'What are you on about? Don't you recognise your own dog? So much for taking your life in your hands to rescue it.' Sheila rolled her eyes. 'Your Bob took him to the vet's this morning and apparently it's in good health, though underfed, and its coat was matted, so the vet shaved it.'

Crouching, Joan hugged the dog to her. No wonder he had flinched once or twice when they had touched him. The matted hair must have tugged at his skin. Poor thing.

'The vet said to be aware that it might still feel tender for a day or so,' said Sheila. 'Are you listening to that, Jimmy?'

'Will Uncle Bob help me build him a kennel?'

It was on the tip of Joan's tongue to say you couldn't expect a dog to sleep outdoors these bitter nights, but she bit back the words. Sheila obviously had clear ideas about how dogs should be treated and it wasn't for Joan to contradict her in front of Jimmy. She let the lad give the dog one of the bones in the sitting room, her heart warming at the pleasure in Jimmy's face. She thought of her own child growing up with a dog, the two of them devoted to one another, and her heart swelled with excitement.

'You've got a collar,' she said to the dog. Trust Bob to have sorted that out; there would be a lead as well. Dangling from the collar was a little disc. It was blank on both sides. 'We'll have to give you a name, won't we?'

'It's not going to answer, you know,' Sheila remarked, and returned to the kitchen.

'Fido,' said Jimmy. 'That's what Nan called him.'

'It was just the first name she thought of.'

'When you said "we" would have to choose a name, did you mean me an' all?'

'You can make suggestions, if you like,' Joan said carefully, 'but it'll be for me and Uncle Bob to decide.'

'Spike,' said Jimmy.

'Not Spike.'

'Why not?'

'He doesn't look like a Spike.'

'Shrapnel, then,' said Jimmy.

'Shrapnel?'

'Aye, because usually I find shrapnel when I'm out, but this time I found a dog.'

'You'll be wanting to call him UXB next,' said Joan. '*No*,' she added as Jimmy's blue eyes lit up in his round face. 'You haven't even taken your coat off yet and it's nearly tea-time. Go and wash your hands.'

'I never had to do that before you came.'

'You should always wash your hands before a meal, especially if you've touched shrapnel or a dog.'

'Or a dog called Shrapnel.'

'Hands, Jimmy,' said Joan.

Grinning, he dashed off. A moment later, he dashed back to close the sitting-room door. Joan had grown to love Jimmy, but, goodness, he could be exhausting company.

Sheila was due to work the night shift at the munitions. Sometimes she left Jimmy with Joan and Bob, but the lad was also a regular overnight visitor at his nan's and this was one of those nights.

'Can I take the dog with me?' he asked.

Sheila laughed. 'I can just see your nan's face.'

'No,' Joan said firmly. 'He belongs to me and Bob, so it's up to us to look after him. We need him to get used to us and his new home.'

When Jimmy and Sheila had both gone, Joan took the dog for a walk. It might have spent the afternoon roaming around, but going for walks was part of being a responsible dog owner. Bob had propped up their new dog licence on the mantelpiece. When they got back, Joan made some cheese scones. Knowing she was to have this evening to herself, she had invited Persephone round. She left the scones cooling on the wire rack and went into the sitting room, where the dog was sound asleep and twitching in front of the fire. It raised its head and blinked blearily when the doorbell rang.

'A fine guard dog you are,' said Joan, but she knew the animal must be exhausted. Who could say what kind of life it had had before being left tied to that fence? That matted coat didn't suggest a life of ease and plenty.

She went to let in her friend.

'Is it all right to leave my bike propped up out here?' asked Persephone. She wriggled her shoulders in a shivery way as she came in. 'Cycling over was supposed to warm me up, but it's proper parky tonight, as Mrs Mitchell would say.'

Mrs Mitchell, who was a distant relative of Mabel's and a good friend of Mrs Grayson's, was the housekeeper at Darley Court, where Persephone lived as the guest of the elderly owner, Miss Brown.

'Give me your coat,' said Joan. 'I'll hang it over a chair by the fire for you – though I warn you there may be competition for the warmth.'

'Between us, you mean?'

'From the dog.'

In the sitting room, Persephone went straight to the dog and settled herself on the hearthrug with it. Graceful and slender, with honey-blonde hair and violet eyes, Persephone looked every inch the lady that she was – or perhaps it would be better to say she looked every inch the Honourable that she was – but there was nothing hoity-toity about her and she clearly didn't care in the slightest about getting dog hair on her clothes. The dog lifted its head and nuzzled her hands, then settled back into a doze as Persephone stroked it and murmured soothingly while Joan told its story.

'So you've had a short back and sides, have you?' said Persephone. 'Poor old you, but your coat will grow back in no time, never fear. What are you calling him?' she asked Joan.

'Haven't decided yet. Mostly, I've been fending off Jimmy's suggestions.'

'If I might add to the unwelcome suggestions, what about Brizo? He looks just like the real Brizo, or he will when his coat comes back.'

'Does Brizo belong to your family?'

'No, he's a dog in a painting I saw at the Wallace Collection before the war. He looked just like this, the colour of a ginger biscuit, with a rough coat and long, hairy ears. The real Brizo was an otterhound, I believe. Yours isn't big enough for that, but in other respects, he looks pretty Brizo-ish, including the soulful eyes. The painting was called *Brizo, a Shepherd's Dog*. This could be Brizo, a signalman's dog.'

'Brizo. I like it,' said Joan. 'I'll suggest it to Bob.' But she already knew he would agree, because he only ever wanted her to be happy. 'I've made cheese scones. Would you like one?'

'Yes, please. I don't mind eating mine dry. I don't want to rob you of your precious marge.'

Joan grinned. 'I think I can spare you a scrape.'

She went into the kitchen, returning with a tray of tea and scones. Brizo sniffed and woke up, looking interested. Persephone fed him a bit of her scone.

Joan followed suit. 'Is it all right to give cheese scones to dogs?'

Persephone laughed. 'I can tell you're new to this dog-owning lark. In wartime, dogs and cats take whatever they can get.'

'I tried to get some tinned dog food on the way home from work, but there was none to be had,' Joan mourned.

'It's pretty scarce these days. You must give him all your scraps – not that anyone has much in the way of scraps these days. You must think of the dog as a pig bin on legs. My mother feeds her dogs on fish offal, shredded wheat and horsemeat. She has a recipe for home-made dog biscuits. I know it involves Oxo. I'll write and ask for it.'

'That would be wonderful – such a help. Thanks.'

'My pleasure. What does Sheila make of having a dog under her roof?'

'She doesn't seem to mind. I don't like to ask outright, actually, in case she says she isn't happy about it.'

'Tricky,' agreed Persephone.

'As a matter of fact, it's possible we might not be here that much longer. We're hoping to find somewhere else to live now we've got the baby on the way.'

'How exciting,' said Persephone. 'I hope you do find somewhere, but it won't be easy. Lots of families are crying out for homes.'

'I know, and I feel guilty about hoping for more than I've already got. This is a comfortable billet and there's really nothing wrong with it. It's just that . . .'

'You'd rather not live in Sheila and Jimmy's pockets when the baby comes. It's understandable and there's no reason to feel guilty. Naturally, you want the best of everything for your child.' Persephone nudged her. 'You've already provided him or her with a dog, which is what every child longs for, so you're off to a good start. Now you just need to make room for a pony.'

Joan laughed. Persephone was such good company. Fancy her, Joan Hubble, being friends with an Honourable. It would have been unimaginable before the war. Their paths would never have crossed. Were it not for the war,

Joan would have spent the whole of her working life in Ingleby's sewing room, making clothes for their better-off customers, middle-class women who wanted a smart evening dress or a new costume for Sunday best. A memory popped in her mind: Letitia's voice, clear as a bell—

'Penny for them,' offered Persephone. 'You were miles away.'

'I was thinking how the war brought us together, you and me and the others. I was thinking of Letitia too. I remember her saying – please don't take this the wrong way, but I remember her saying she was enjoying the war, because of the opportunities it had given her. She was very clever, you know. In the munitions, when the engineers designed the shells, her job was to double-check their maths.'

'That's something to be proud of,' said Persephone.

Sadness washed through Joan. What a waste of a life. 'What I'm trying to say is that as damnable as the war is, it's brought some good into our lives. I love working for the railways and feeling that I'm doing my bit, and I love my friends. I'd never have met Bob if I hadn't had to learn first aid for the war effort. Yet the same war that gave me Bob took Letitia from me.'

'Nothing's straightforward, is it? As you say, it's damnable. All we can do is make the best of what we've got, here, now. Seize the good things and rejoice in them.'

'Like America joining the war.'

'Actually, I was thinking in terms of your being in the family way, but, yes, the Yanks as well.'

'And Brizo,' said Joan.

'Glimmers of light in the darkness,' said Persephone, 'and the more of them, the better.'

CHAPTER TEN

Armed with a scraper and a bundle of oily cloths, Margaret set to work on the wheels. It was a filthy job, but hugely important. First, she had to scrape out all the grime and grease from every crevice in each wheel. After that, the wheel had to be thoroughly cleaned with the oily cloths. Once they were dry, the wheeltapper had to test every wheel for cracks. Mabel's grandfather had been a wheeltapper, apparently, which just went to show how fortunes could change for a family, because Mabel's father, the wheeltapper's son, had set up his own factory and was now very well-to-do and Mabel had been sent to a private school. From wheeltapper to private boarding school in two generations. Mind you, it needn't take that long for a family to change substantially. In her own family, it had happened in the blink of an eye, though it hadn't been financial change in their case, but her own disgrace.

Alice, the girl whose mother had received the telegram last Friday, was back at work now. Previously she had been a bonny lass with roses in her cheeks, but now her skin was sallow and she looked fragile. Nevertheless, she worked harder than ever, though whether this was for solace or from a fiery determination to win the war single-handedly, Margaret couldn't tell. It was Alice's brother who had copped it. Margaret remembered only too well that feeling of the family no longer being complete, the feeling that nothing would be quite right ever again.

89

'At least your mum didn't live to know about this.' Dad's words, harsh and unforgiving. 'That's my one and only consolation.'

Had he meant it? Or had the words been uttered out of a desire to punish her for the terrible wrong she had done to her family?

Margaret stopped work for a moment to roll her shoulders. Cleaning the wheels and the undercarriages of the engines and coaches was the dirtiest jobs of all for an engine cleaner. The girls all fastened their boiler suits to the neck and wore mob caps on top of their turbans, but it didn't matter what precautions you took. You still ended up taking loads of grime home with you. At the end of those days, Margaret always turned her regulation five inches of bathwater black and emerged feeling as if she needed another bath to get clean from that one, and Mrs Cooper had soon learned to put a cloth over Margaret's pillow on those nights.

Some of them were meeting in the buffet later – Joan, Persephone, Cordelia and herself. The arrangement had been put in their notebook under the buffet counter last week, immediately after their post-Christmas meeting . . . before Margaret had seen Joel. Since then she had felt as if she were being pulled in a dozen different directions all at the same time. She longed for the support and guidance of her friends, but how could she ever tell anyone the whole story? She couldn't.

Predictably, in the buffet, the first topic of conversation was Alison.

'I'm sure Mrs Cooper will hear from her in the next day or so,' said Cordelia.

'When we get her address,' said Persephone, 'we can all bombard her with letters.'

Margaret bit the inside of her cheek. Would she have to write to Alison? Saying what? *You're better off where you are, out of Joel's way . . .* ? That was what she ought to say – ought to, but couldn't. Writing it down, committing it to paper, would be even worse than speaking of it, because writing was evidence. Proof. And if it should fall into other hands . . .

Yet how could she write an ordinary, chatty letter?

The conversation had moved on while she was thinking. Now the others were talking about Joel. Persephone and Joan were telling Cordelia what good company he was and how much they had liked him.

Cordelia turned to Margaret. 'Did Mrs Cooper and Mrs Grayson approve of him?'

Margaret nodded, trying to smile, though she felt more like dissolving into tears. Her muscles relaxed in gratitude, which made her realise they had been clenched tight, when Persephone took up the conversation.

'Poor Alison.' Persephone laughed as she said it. 'First she took Joel home to introduce him to her family, then she had to introduce him at Wilton Close. It must have felt like having three mothers.'

Joan and Cordelia laughed too. They were happy for Alison. Everyone was. Yet again, Margaret asked herself what she was to do. Tell Alison to be careful? Warn her off? But that would be impossible without revealing her shameful secret, and she couldn't do that – but that meant she might be placing Alison in a vulnerable position.

What sort of friend did that make her?

'Well, that's a turn-up for the books.' Bob blew out a breath. 'I know we were hoping for more space, but – this.'

'I know,' said Joan. 'Do you think we should go and look?'

The surprise had been delivered by Persephone earlier on when the four friends who had met up in the buffet were saying their goodbyes. Persephone had asked for a quick word with Joan – and that word had been the offer of a home at Darley Court.

'I hope you don't think I was gossiping about your business, but I told Miss Brown about your wish to move on from Sheila's and she suggested you come to Darley Court. You know both her and Mrs Mitchell and you know you'd be welcome. Talk it over with Bob and see what you think.'

As Joan had travelled home on the bus, she had turned the offer over and over in her mind. Life seemed full of new things: the baby, the dog and possibly a new home – at Darley Court, of all places. The sheer unexpectedness of it made her want to laugh.

She had arrived home to an ecstatic reception from Brizo. Bob had gladly agreed to the name when he got in from work last night and he had promised to see to Brizo's name disc this morning.

'Just his name for now,' he'd said. 'He'll have to wait to have his address engraved on the other side.'

Would *Darley Court* appear on the reverse of Brizo's name disc?

Bob came home around half past ten to a supper of scrambled egg and fried bread. Then Joan took him through to the sitting room and shut the door. She had been dying to tell him while he ate, but what if Jimmy had crept downstairs for a drink of water, or if Sheila had arrived home from the pictures and had overheard something? They didn't know yet about Joan and Bob's hopes, and if Joan and Bob failed to find another billet, they never would know. Joan had felt uncomfortable yesterday asking Persephone not to mention it to Dot, but Persephone had shrugged it off with, 'It's for you to tell the others if and when you're ready to.' She was a good sort.

'Darley Court, eh!' Having recovered from the surprise, Bob patted Brizo, who was sitting pressed up against his legs, and fondled the dog's ears. 'What d'you think of that, boy? You might be going from being tied to a fence to living on a posh old estate.'

'Shall I tell Persephone we'd like to go and see?' asked Joan, smiling.

'It'd be foolish not to, not to mention rather ungracious. It's a kind offer. What do your shifts look like? The sooner we can go, the better.' Bob kissed her hair. 'Have a word with Persephone tomorrow.'

The visit to Darley Court was arranged for Thursday morning. It was another bitterly cold day with heavy skies. Joan and Bob cycled to Chorlton, veering off the main road when they were alongside Southern Cemetery and heading in the direction of the Mersey. They cycled beside the old brick walls that surrounded the estate until they came to the gatehouse. Beyond the gardens, which had been given over to crops, the big house was visible, its most notable feature other than its size being a huge covered porch that stuck out at the front. In days gone by, carriages would have halted beneath it to protect the grand ladies and gentlemen from the weather as they alighted.

Instead of a doorbell, there was an old-fashioned bell pull at the side of the heavy front door. Before he rang it, Bob made a face and Joan chuckled. The door swung open and there was Mrs Mitchell, a tweedy, middle-aged woman, who was as keen a cook as Mrs Grayson.

'How nice to see you both. Miss Brown is expecting you. Leave your bikes there and come in.'

She gave Bob a minute to remove his bicycle clips. Joan gazed around the entrance hall, which boasted more floor space than she and Bob had in their two rooms in Sheila's house put together. There was wood panelling everywhere, but it was covered in hardboard.

'For protection,' Mrs Mitchell said, seeing Joan looking.

'From bombs?'

'Or fire. Or, frankly, at the start of the war, it was also in case the house was commandeered to be a hospital or a school. Miss Brown's in her sitting room. This way.'

Miss Brown, an elderly but robust lady, was in a room that was smaller than Joan would have expected. Even less expected was that a bookcase and a sideboard had apparently been shunted aside to make room for a drop-leaf dining table, but then Mabel had always said what a practical sort she was.

'Come in,' Miss Brown greeted them. 'How kind of you to call.' She made it sound as if their presence was a delightful and unlooked-for treat. 'Persephone tells me you're looking for a new home. You'll be welcome here. The downstairs rooms are all spoken for, because all the local Civil Defence groups hold meetings and training sessions here, but I'm sure we can squeeze you in upstairs.' She looked at them over the rims of her spectacles. Any moment now she would take off her glasses and start waving them about, which seemed to be their main purpose as far as Miss Brown was concerned. 'But there is a rather nice sitting room downstairs that you could have as well. I do think it would be rather strange if you had nowhere of your own on the ground floor. Come and see.'

They followed her into a pleasant room with pale green walls and a white marble chimney piece.

'This used to be my predecessor's sitting room,' said Miss Brown. 'The last Lady Darley, before the family died out. Let's find Mrs Mitchell and she can show you the rooms we can offer you upstairs. Persephone says you've got a dog. You should have brought it with you. Houses like this were meant to be full of dogs.'

'Excuse me,' said Bob. 'Do you mean we'd be living in the house with you?'

'Of course.'

'Only I imagined us in the gatehouse or somewhere of the sort.'

'I put my land girls in the gatekeeper's lodge. They'll be there for the duration,' said Miss Brown, 'and all the estate cottages are occupied. You would be here in the house. Forgive my saying so, but you don't look entirely thrilled by the prospect. Why don't I give you a few minutes to talk it over? Come and find me in my sitting room when you're ready.'

As the door closed behind Miss Brown, Bob caught hold of Joan's hand.

'I'm sorry,' he said. 'I didn't mean to let you down.'

'You haven't,' Joan assured him. 'You could never do that. What's bothering you?'

Bob waved his free hand, encompassing not just the room but the whole of Darley Court and its surroundings. 'I didn't imagine we'd be living in the house. I thought they'd put us up somewhere else. Somewhere . . .'

'Less grand?' Joan suggested as understanding began to dawn.

'Imagine it,' said Bob. 'A signalman living in a posh place like this? It's not natural. A cottage on the estate, yes – but this?'

Joan moved close to him. 'I understand.'

'Do you?' Bob looked down into her face. His eyes were troubled. 'I don't. It feels like I'm putting my class consciousness above what's best for you.'

'No, you aren't. You're being honest and I respect that. The truth is, I don't really want to live here either.'

'Do you mean that?'

Joan sighed. 'I quite like the thought of moving in for a while, just so that after the war I'd be able to say I once lived in Darley Court. But as lovely as Persephone is, and as dear as Miss Brown and Mrs Mitchell are, I don't think I truly want to move in here for the duration, because . . .' And in that moment she understood the reason. 'Because if we came here, no matter how welcome we were, it would feel temporary. Maybe it's because of the baby, but I don't want to feel like that. I want an ordinary place, something down to earth that feels lasting and permanent.'

'Are you sure?' asked Bob.

'Positive,' said Joan. 'Let's go and explain to Miss Brown.'

Joan and Bob cycled home from Darley Court to be met by the next-door neighbour, who came bustling out of her front door, wiping her hands on a tea towel.

'Thanks goodness you're back. That dratted dog has done nowt but bark, bark, bark since you left. It was the same yesterday when he was in the house on his own. Can't you do something about it?'

'I'm sorry,' said Bob. 'Leave it with me.'

They stowed their bikes in the shed and went into the house, where the first thing they heard was a volley of barks from the sitting room. They looked at one another.

'I think he's recovered from being exhausted,' said Joan as they hurried to the sitting room, shedding their outdoor things in there instead of taking them upstairs. 'We can't leave him on his own if he's going to bark the house down. Sheila won't be pleased if the neighbours complain.'

Joan shared the problem the next day with Dot, who popped in during the afternoon with some baby clothes she had picked up at a jumble sale in aid of the Red Cross.

Joan sifted through the pile of garments, her fingertips lingering on them. 'Oh, Dot, they're gorgeous. Everything's so tiny.'

That made Dot laugh. 'Aye, but children grow quick, as you'll find out. One day you're rocking a newborn in your arms and next news you've got a monster like Jimmy on your hands. Him and our Jenny will be thirteen this summer. Can you believe it?'

'I can believe it of Jenny. She's such a sensible girl.'

'But not of Jimmy? He'll still be a kid when he's twenty-one. Hark at me. I sound as if I'm wishing their lives away and I'm the last person to do that. They'd stay as children for ever if it was up to me.' Dot nodded at Brizo. 'Now then, what's yon dog called? I swear Jimmy said his name were Brasso.'

'Not Brasso – Brizo. Persephone came up with it.'

'I thought it were odd, you naming your dog after brass cleaner. Mind you, with that colour of coat, Brasso would have been better than Vim or Swarfega,' said Dot. 'Jimmy said there's been a spot of bother with her next door.'

'I'm afraid so.' Joan sighed. 'Brizo spent the first day or two flaked out in front of the fire. We think he was worn out from the cold, if nothing else. But he's perked up now and he doesn't like being left on his own.'

'If he's been abandoned once, happen he thinks you might not come back. It's understandable.'

'It so happens that since the complaint, there's been one of us at home most of the time, but that won't last. Besides, we can't organise our lives around keeping Brizo company. We're worried Sheila might take against him.'

'It'll be different once you've given up work,' Dot pointed out, 'though that's no help right this minute. I know – why not take him to work with you?'

'You don't take dogs to work.'

'Why not? It's only until you leave. There's no harm in asking, chick. You don't get anywhere in this life if you don't ask. As long as he doesn't chew the umbrellas in Lost Property, where's the harm? And if the folk in Lost Property won't have him, happen he could spend a bit of time in the porters' room or by the fire in the buffet.'

'I'll ask,' said Joan, but she felt doubtful.

Dot got to her feet. 'I'd best get off home.'

Joan went with her to the front door to see her off.

'Nay, love, don't stand here with the door open,' said Dot. 'Get back in the warm. What's that racket?'

Jimmy was racing up the road, shouting, 'Sardines! Tinned tomatoes! Sardines! Tinned tomatoes!' at the top of his voice. Other boys gave up their game of football and joined in, adding to the unwelcome din. Jimmy raced home and Dot captured him in her arms.

'Jimmy! What's all this yelling? If this is a new game, you need to tone it down.'

Jimmy beamed up at her, chest heaving. 'Sardines, Nan! Tinned tomatoes!'

'I heard it the first time – when you were up the top end of the road. Why are you yelling it from the rooftops?'

'You said to. You said when I went to the shops and saw what they'd got in, I mustn't tell just Mum, I must make sure everybody knows. You did, Nan.'

'I never meant you to . . . Oh, what's the point? Listen, lad. It's not polite to belt down the road, yelling your head off. Yes, I know I told you to tell the neighbours, but I meant you to knock on their doors and tell them politely.'

'That's what a gentleman would do,' Joan added, having heard Jenny reprimand Jimmy with this.

'Oh.' Jimmy looked surprised. 'Righty-ho then. Anyroad, Nan, they've got tinned tomatoes and sardines.'

'Aye, so I heard.' Dot rolled her eyes, but Joan could see she was smothering a smile.

'Should I go back and knock on all the doors?' Jimmy offered.

'I think you've probably spread the message far and wide this time,' said Dot. 'But remember it for next time, eh?'

'Oh, a welcoming committee.' A new voice entered the conversation – Persephone. She wheeled her bicycle onto Sheila's front path, leaning it against the low wall between Sheila's and next door. 'Hello, Jimmy. Have you been up to larks again?'

'No, miss. I was on deadly serious war work.'

'Good for you,' said Persephone. To Joan, she said, 'I've brought you a note from Miss Brown.'

'I'll leave you to it,' said Dot. 'I'll see you in the buffet next week, girls. Give Nan a kiss, Jimmy.'

'Come in.' Joan led Persephone into the sitting room. What would the note say? Had she and Bob given offence by refusing Miss Brown's generous offer?

Persephone handed over a folded piece of paper before unfastening the buckled belt of her wool coat with its over-sized collar and draping the garment over the back of a chair, balancing her matching hat with its curled brim and her gauntlet gloves on top. Underneath, she wore a thick sweater in a wonderful sea-green colour, with the collar of an ivory silk blouse over the round neck. With the sweater, she was wearing crisp slacks. Gran was dead against girls wearing trousers. To her, wearing slacks meant you were slack in other ways too, but more and more women were wearing them these days. They were so practical and, in this weather, warm too.

'Read it now,' said Persephone. 'Don't mind me.'

Joan unfolded the note. In accordance with wartime regulations, Miss Brown had reused a piece of paper. On one side was what looked like a hand-drawn map showing crop rotations and on the other, in spiky-looking handwriting, was Miss Brown's message.

Joan breathed a sigh of relief. 'She says she quite understands why we don't wish to live in Darley Court, but that the offer will remain open and she will keep us in mind, should any of the cottages become available. Isn't that kind of her? And you're kind, too, to bring it.'

'Pleasure.' Persephone had already dropped onto her knees to fuss Brizo. 'How's my new chum?'

Joan explained the problem of the barking.

'You can't blame him,' said Persephone, echoing Dot. 'He had a rough time before you took him in.'

'Unfortunately, I don't think that will cut any ice with the neighbours. Dot suggested I take him to Victoria.'

She expected Persephone to pooh-pooh the idea, but instead Persephone smiled at her and there was a sparkle in her violet eyes.

'Dot is absolutely right. And I know all the whys and wherefores that will make it possible.'

CHAPTER ELEVEN

It was now Friday and Alison still felt shocked when she thought of the ruthless dressing-down she had received from Miss Chambers on Monday. She had never wanted to come to Leeds, but now she found herself in the position of working her socks off to ensure she stayed there. Although she longed with all her heart to return to Manchester for good, the thought of being sent home in disgrace made her muscles tighten in humiliation. She was too ashamed to tell anyone what Miss Chambers had said to her. Had there really been any need for the deputy lady almoner to come down on her quite so hard? Just for referring to her as the dragon lady? But Alison knew Miss Chambers had been in the right, especially after that unguarded remark about Alison having expected the dragon lady to be older. She had kicked herself for that afterwards. It wasn't all that long since she herself had been on the receiving end of patronising treatment from men who thought women had no place on the railways.

After their meeting, she had returned to the kitchen and asked if she could work two extra hours to make up her lost time instead of having her pay docked. Miss Chambers was in charge of signing off all the rotas and time sheets and Alison hated the thought of the dragon lady coming to hers in the pile and twisting her lips into a knowing sneer at the sight of those two missed hours.

Mrs Bertram had in due course handed Alison over – complete with an explanation about why two more hours of work was necessary – to Miss Fanshawe, who was the cook in charge of the next shift.

'Keep your eye on this one,' said Mrs Bertram, making Alison feel two inches tall. 'She's spent her life behind a desk and doesn't know the first thing about kitchens or canteens.'

After her first shift, Alison had been given a series of night shifts at the railway station.

'Don't fret,' said Betty. 'You were down to do them in any case. You aren't being banished.'

'It's hard work at the station,' Eddie told her, 'especially the night shift. They move troop trains at night, see? They move 'em during the day as well, of course, but they do it a lot at night and that means it can be non-stop for the station staff. The station canteen has been open twenty-four hours a day since the war started.'

Eddie was correct. It was jolly hard work, but there was a strong sense of all hands to the pump and that carried everyone through. The staff generally got around half an hour's notice of the arrival of a troop train and there might be four, five or six hundred men crammed aboard, every single one of them in need of a hot drink and something to eat. The sandwiches, sausage rolls, pork pies, baked vegetable rolls and rock cakes that the staff had got ready would all vanish, and when all those boys had departed, the staff immediately had to start preparing for the next lot.

'Go and collect all the crockery you can find,' Alison was told on her first shift. 'We can't afford for any of it to be overlooked or go missing.'

Alison had scoured the station for cups and plates, returning them by the tray-load to the canteen. They were all over the place – on window ledges and luggage trolleys, on benches in the waiting rooms, underneath the benches as well.

Back in the canteen, the urns were being topped up in preparation. In the back, the washing-up was under way.

'That's everything, as far as I can tell,' Alison had said.

'As far as you can tell?' One of the washer-uppers turned a scornful glance on her. 'You haven't tried very hard then, have you? What about all the jam jars?'

'Jam jars?' Alison repeated.

'Aye. We use them as cups – or haven't you been paying attention? There's a crockery shortage, you know.'

Alison did know. Who didn't? She retraced her steps and found plenty of jam jars. How could she have missed them before? It must be because she was tired. Not that that was any excuse. She vowed to pull her socks up and not make any more mistakes. She wasn't used to this, to being the one who made mistakes and let the side down.

'Sorry to have missed them before,' she said cheerfully as she returned with jam jars stacked on a tray. 'Stupid of me. It won't happen again.'

She had soon got used to the way of things on the night shift and her week had picked up considerably when letters started to arrive from home. Yes, they brought on a wave or two of homesickness, but mainly she had concentrated on how good it felt to have such dear friends keeping in touch with her, as well as Mum and Lydia. She had written back to Mum, asking her to share the letter with Lydia. She also wrote to Mrs Cooper, knowing the letter would be read out in Wilton Close, and she wrote to Dot with the request, *Please share this in the buffet.* Best of all, she had heard from Joel, and was it daft of her to sleep with his letter under her pillow?

He was going to come over to Leeds on Saturday to see her and she couldn't wait to be reunited with him. They had had so little time together and she had wasted most of it by holding back her true feelings.

He was going to stay in Leeds overnight and travel back on Sunday. Alison had asked Mrs Freeman to recommend a bed and breakfast where he could stay and her landlady had predictably taken the opportunity to remind her of the rule that no lodger was permitted to entertain a visitor of the opposite sex.

'I'll knock on your door before I retire for the night,' Mrs Freeman promised.

'Feel free,' Alison had retorted. 'You won't find Dr Maitland in there with me.'

'Actually, I'll be making sure you're here in your own bed and not at the B & B in his.'

Alison was supposed to be at work at the station on Saturday night, but as she had expected, the girls sometimes swapped shifts around if they had a special occasion, and seeing Joel was certainly that as far as she was concerned. Had she been here long enough to ask for a favour, though, especially after her shaky start? What would Miss Chambers think if she saw the change that had been made on Alison's time sheet? Then Alison had decided she didn't care what Miss Chambers thought on this particular matter. By swapping shifts with Betty, who had kindly made the offer, Alison would be able to spend more time with Joel and that mattered a great deal more to her than any wigging Miss Chambers could dish out.

Now it was Friday night and she was on her way to the station. A troop train was already there when she arrived, the canteen so thick with tobacco smoke that she could barely see across the room. She spent most of her shift making sandwiches, standing at a long counter in a line of women all mucking in with the same task. By now, she was as quick as any of them and joined in with their chatter. Her spirits bubbled up in excitement every so often as she thought of seeing Joel later on and she laughed good-naturedly at the teasing she received from the others, especially once they knew that he was a new boyfriend. It all added to her happiness. She had got through her first week in Leeds – well, nearly – and she had survived intact with only a few emotional bruises.

The next train drew in, covered in wet streaks – not rain but snow.

'It's coming down hard,' said the soldiers as they queued for their tea and sandwiches.

At last, Alison's shift ended. She pulled on her outdoor things, including the mittens Mrs Grayson had made on top of her gloves for extra warmth, and left the station, ready to crunch her way home through a coating of freshly fallen snow, only to have the breath whipped from her lungs by a strong wind carrying a chill sharp enough to make her gasp. The view before her made her think for one startled moment that fog had descended, but, no, the air was thick with falling snow.

'Turn around, all of you!' shouted their supervisor. 'Our shift doesn't end until we know for certain everyone from the next shift has arrived.'

Alison's heart sank straight into her shoes. *Joel.* But she had no choice. She returned with all the rest and continued working. Most of the workers for the next shift were already there. The others arrived gradually, looking soggy and telling tales of the sudden blizzard that had caught everyone unawares. An hour and a half after her proper finishing time, Alison was given permission to leave. Wrapping herself up once more, she set off to trudge through snow already several inches deep. Her feet were frozen by the time she arrived at Mrs Freeman's and she feared her shoes would never be the same again. She cadged some newspaper from her landlady to stuff inside them while they dried. Mrs Freeman also let her leave her coat in the kitchen, hanging over the back of a chair beside the fire.

Alison prepared hot-water bottles, grateful as never before to have a pair of them, and went to bed to get some sleep. Disappointing as it was that Joel couldn't get here before mid-afternoon, at least it gave her time to grab enough shut-eye that she wouldn't be bog-eyed and weary. Setting her alarm clock, she snuggled down in bed, drawing up her knees and rubbing her feet together to try to coax the life back into them, all the while picturing the charcoal-grey jacket and skirt and cherry-red jumper she planned to wear. For Christmas, Lydia had made her a lovely satin slip with satin ribbon shoulder straps and she was going to wear that underneath, though now she wondered if she would be warm enough. On the other hand, once Joel arrived, she would be too happy and excited to notice the cold.

She awoke before the alarm, senses alert with happiness. The hot-water bottles were still warm, thanks to their knitted covers, courtesy of Mrs Grayson, but the air in the bedroom was cold. Alison slid from the bed, reaching for her dressing gown and pushing her feet into her fluffy mules. She popped her clothes into bed with the hot-water bottles. While they warmed through, she reached across the table in the dormer window to draw aside the blackout curtains and peep through the bedroom curtains. It was still snowing.

She dressed quickly, admiring the sleek lines of her jacket's padded shoulders and topstitched panels that were cleverly shaped to show off her waist and make her look trim. Oh, for a full-length mirror! She picked up her hairbrush. Her hair came a little past her shoulders when it was properly curled and styled. Her natural parting was over to one side, but she preferred a centre parting and, like so many girls, she'd had her hair cut into the pageboy style that was so easy to put into curls and brush away from the face. She wore her fringe curled and flicked back too.

Alison knew she wasn't a beauty like Persephone – well, no one was a beauty like Persephone! She didn't have Mabel's striking good looks and she would never have Cordelia's classic elegance, but she knew she was nice-looking in a fresh-faced, unpretentious kind of way.

It was too early to head to the station but too cold to remain here. She decided to go to the station and nurse a hot drink while she waited for Joel's train. She retrieved her coat from the kitchen and pushed her feet into her shoes, which were still vaguely damp, though the newspaper had kept their shape.

Opening the front door, Alison stopped dead. The snow was at least a foot deep and it was still coming down.

'Wellingtons,' came Mrs Freeman's voice behind her. 'And shut that door. You're letting the snow blow in.'

'I haven't brought wellies with me.' Alison turned to her landlady.

'I'm not going out again today. You can borrow mine. Your feet are smaller, so you'll have to wear a pair or two of socks, but they won't come amiss in this weather.'

Wellies! They wouldn't exactly create the romantic picture she wished to present as Joel descended from the train and hastened along the platform to see her for the first time since last weekend. But it wouldn't be very romantic to catch a chill either, or to ruin her shoes beyond the point of salvation. With her shoes in a cloth bag, Alison set off.

It took longer than usual to get to the station and she slipped a few times, though managed to keep her footing. The concourse was busier than normal, but it was a different sort of busy. There was a sense of unease, as if the air was packed with invisible questions. Alison glimpsed worried faces, frowns, repeated glances at the clock.

'Where are you hoping to get to, miss?' asked a ticket inspector.

'I'm not. I'm meeting my boyfriend.'

'Where's he travelling from?'

'Manchester Victoria. His train is due at ten past three.'

'Sorry, miss,' said the inspector. 'You'll have a bit of a wait. There's heavy snow everywhere and it's never easy to cross the Pennines when it's like this.'

Anxiety uncurled in Alison's stomach. 'But he will get here, won't he?' Oh, she couldn't bear it if he didn't!

'Eventually. Lives here, does he?'

'No, he's just visiting. He's to go back tomorrow afternoon.'

'If you'll accept a word of advice,' said the inspector, and Alison nodded, 'tell him to turn straight round and go home again. If previous experience is anything to go by, this weather is here to stay.'

CHAPTER TWELVE

If it hadn't been for the fact that she felt so cold, Margaret was sure she would have ached all over. Cleaning locos was a doddle compared to this. Teams of railwaymen and -women were out at all hours, digging through snow three or four feet deep to get to the frozen points – and there were an awful lot of points to get to. Everything was frozen. Even the grease in the locos' axle boxes had solidified. When she wasn't part of a clearing gang, Margaret was on coal duty. Coal could no longer be tipped out of wagons, but had to be chopped out using pickaxes. It was back-breaking work and you had to be careful, because every now and again a small piece would fly straight at you. There were tales of a girl in Wigan who had received a sharp bit right in her eye, damaging her vision.

At home, they had an unexpected visitor – Tony, Colette's husband. Colette's widower, to be precise, poor chap. He had walked all the way from Seymour Grove – well, not so much walked as trudged.

'It must have taken him ages,' Mrs Grayson whispered when Margaret helped her to make a pot of tea, 'but he won't be drawn on how long.'

He had lost his looks in the short time since Colette's tragic death. His narrow face was now gaunt and there was a layer of desperation in his hazel eyes.

'I've come to make sure you're all right,' he said.

'That's very good of you,' said Mrs Cooper, 'but you really shouldn't have.'

'Colette would want me to. She thought well of you. I can give you some advice about the water.'

'Of course,' said Mabel. 'You work for the water board, don't you?'

'Pipes are bursting all over the show,' said Tony. 'The best thing you can do to prevent it happening here is to run all the taps and flush the lavatory regularly. That means during the night as well as in the daytime.'

'I remember having to do that a couple of years ago,' said Mrs Cooper, 'before my Lizzie joined the railways. That was another bad winter.'

'We'll have a rota and we can all muck in,' said Mabel. 'We can set the alarm to go off during the night.'

'You girls needn't do it at night,' said Mrs Grayson. 'You need your sleep, with all the heavy work you're doing in the daytime. Mrs Cooper and I will do the taps at night.'

'No, you won't,' Mabel said firmly. 'We'll all do it.'

When Tony had left, they all commented on his changed appearance. Then sadness descended. They were still getting used to knowing they would never see Colette again.

'At least he looked as if he was wearing several layers,' said Margaret. 'That is, if his body has gone as thin as his face, then he must have been.'

Everyone was bundled up in extra layers. Even Mrs Cooper, who was a little sparrow of a woman, looked well rounded these days.

'I'm wearing a vest, both my petticoats, a blouse, two jumpers and a big cardigan over the top,' she told them. 'The cardy didn't use to be this big, but I forced it on over everything else. I wish I could say I feel snug, but I don't.'

They soon took to living in the kitchen, where together the stove and the fireplace made it the warmest room in the house.

'If there was room for our beds here, I'd move them in,' said Mabel, and she wasn't entirely joking.

The cold was agonising. There was frost on the insides of the windows and the towels froze on the rail in the bathroom. They shoved rugs and doormats into the gaps under the doors in an attempt to seal them.

Margaret tried to persuade Mrs Cooper to stay inside.

'Mabel and I will do the shopping. I don't like to think of you having to go out in this.'

'Bless you, aren't you kind? But I can manage. Folk have dug tracks through the drifts now, so I can get to the shops.'

'As long as the tracks take you where you want to go,' said Mabel.

'Not that the shops have much in stock – even less than usual, I mean,' said Mrs Cooper. 'Normally, they don't have all that much as there isn't much to go round these days, but now there's even less because deliveries can't get through.'

Travelling to and from work took far longer. One day, Margaret's bus got lodged in a snowdrift and the passengers helped to dig it free. That same week, as she was nearing the end of her journey home, the bus driver attempted to negotiate the turn into Chorlton terminus, only for the bus to keep on turning. Fear poured through Margaret. Would the vehicle topple over? She and her fellow passengers hung on to the backs of the seats in front of them. The bus made a full circle and ended up facing the wrong way.

'I don't mean to sound unsympathetic,' remarked Mrs Cooper, 'but I'm fed up of hearing folk talking about their chilblains. It seems to have turned into a competition. You should have heard these women in the grocer's this afternoon. "Mine itch." "Well, mine are sore." "That's nothing.

Mine are itchy *and* sore." Really, there are some things that are best kept to yourself.'

There were power cuts and they eked out their precious stock of candles. They had to be careful with the coal too and they took to cuddling hot-water bottles whenever they sat down for any length of time. Mrs Grayson sent Margaret and Mabel to work with flasks of soup as well as the usual sandwiches or barm cakes.

'And it still doesn't look like letting up any time soon,' said Mrs Cooper.

The first thing Joan learned was not to look up into the trees, because it was distressing to see the poor birds frozen solid on the branches. She couldn't help wondering what would have happened if Brizo's previous owner had kept him a few more days and abandoned him immediately before the snowstorm. Would he have frozen to death, tied to that fence?

'There's nothing to be gained by dwelling on what-ifs,' Bob pointed out gently. 'Brizo is safe with us and that's what counts.'

Brizo had a job now, for which Joan felt she would be eternally grateful to Persephone, who had heard of a couple of station dogs who wore little collecting boxes on their backs, attached to a strap that fastened around the animal's middle. The dog-loving public couldn't resist the appeal of a fundraising dog and by and large were only too happy to pop a couple of coins through the slot in the box.

'I know of one dog that raises money for the railway company's orphanage,' Persephone had explained, 'and another that collects for the Red Cross. Of course, you'd need permission from the powers that be at Victoria Station, but I expect Miss Emery could help with that.'

Miss Emery was pleased to do so. 'But there seems little point in bringing Brizo in until after the snow has gone,' she suggested.

But Joan didn't want to leave him at home. 'If he starts coming with me now, he'll get used to it while there aren't many people about.'

Throughout those difficult days of extraordinarily heavy snow, when travelling was virtually at a standstill, the few people there were in Victoria couldn't help but smile at the sight of Brizo. To start with, he sat in Lost Property, on the passengers' side of the counter, where Joan could keep an eye on him and introduce him to anyone who asked about him, but Dot and Persephone had other ideas.

'I'll walk him up and down the concourse during my lunch break,' said Persephone. 'We might not have trains running, but people are coming here to eat in the buffet and the restaurant.'

'Aye, and the station porters are keeping the fires going in the waiting rooms,' Dot added. 'I think folk are popping in just to thaw out.'

'I'm sure Brizo and I can raise a bit of money,' said Persephone.

'Make sure you smile at all the men,' Dot advised with a chuckle. 'A beautiful girl and a bonny dog – the fellas will be queuing up to make a contribution.'

'I've had a word with the kitchen staff,' Persephone told Joan, 'and they'll save scraps for you to take home.'

That was Persephone all over. She wasn't pushy or bossy, but my goodness, she knew how to get things done. It was all achieved with good manners and smiles.

'Brizo thanks you,' said Joan, 'and so do I.'

'I suggest you hide the scraps inside your gas-mask box,' said Dot, 'or you'll have every dog in Manchester following you home.'

'Not to mention Brizo attempting to scrabble through your pockets and your handbag while you're on the bus,' Persephone added.

They were joking, but it was worth taking the idea seriously. Joan couldn't risk being asked to leave the bus because Brizo wasn't behaving himself. So far, he had been as good as gold on public transport. If he was in the company of at least one of his people, that was all he asked of life. Mrs Grayson had knitted him a brown and gold double-thickness coat to keep him warm while he was on his travels. Several regular passengers admired it and Joan had ended up taking orders, which Mrs Grayson said she would be happy to fulfil.

It wasn't long before Joan was moved out of Lost Property. There wasn't enough work to keep the staff busy. Joan wasn't sorry to leave the office. It was so cold in there that she was sure the baby must be shivering inside her. She and her colleagues had appropriated every piece of sacking and cardboard they could lay their hands on and stuffed them into the cracks in the floorboards to try to keep the bitter draughts at bay.

She had been instructed to move to First Aid, usually a small place, but it had moved into a larger room now, while the filthy weather lasted. Previously, the first-aid post had mainly been used for blackout injuries, but now there was an abundance of strains and sprains and even the occasional fracture because of the snow and ice. To begin with, Joan had panicked lest she had forgotten her training through the lack of needing it now that the air raids had largely tailed off, but then common sense reasserted itself and she felt her confidence returning.

She was allowed to take Brizo with her into the first-aid post and he proved popular. She was careful to keep him out of the way when necessary, but there were times when his presence soothed a distressed patient. He was happy to be fussed over or just to sit by quietly. Most patients, or the person accompanying them, asked about his collecting box and lots of them dropped in a small donation.

Joan took Brizo with her to check that Gran was all right and found her hopping mad, which initially caused Joan's spirits to dip as memories came storming back of Gran's brusqueness and the way she had ruled her little household with a rod of iron. Yet at the same time, Gran's attitude was oddly reassuring, because if Gran was vexed, that meant she was all right.

'It's the billeting officer's fault,' Gran declared. Then she spotted Brizo and her strong features settled into lines of surprise and suspicion. 'Is that dog following you? Tell it to go home. You can't have strange dogs latching on to you.'

'Too late,' Joan said lightly. 'He's already latched on. We've adopted him. Are you going to let us in? Both of us,' she added, in case Gran was thinking of shutting Brizo out.

Gran stood aside for them to enter the house. 'You've got a baby on the way. You can't be doing with a dog as well.'

'Yes, I can. His name is Brizo and he's here to stay. What's the billeting officer's fault?'

'This!'

Gran threw open the door to the dining room, releasing a smoky smell. Joan went in, stopping dead at the sight of a sizeable heap of snow under the back window. Two of the boys who lived over the road were shovelling the snow out through the window again. Brizo darted past.

'What happened?' asked Joan, then had to hurry round the table and seize Brizo by his collar as he started digging in the snow. 'Let's go in the kitchen and put the kettle on. Come on, Brizo.'

While the kettle boiled, Gran explained. 'I've kept the dining room shut up since the snow started, so I thought I'd better get the fire going today to warm the room and air it. Then someone came to the door and it was the local billeting officer.'

'What did he want?' Joan already knew the answer, but she asked anyway.

'He wants me to take in a lodger.'

'Which means you have to,' said Joan. You weren't allowed to say no to the billeting officer.

'I let him look round the house and when he opened the dining-room door, the chimney was smoking. There must be a blockage. So he opened the back window to let the smoke out and carried on looking round the house. I took it for granted that he would have shut the window, but obviously not. The next time I looked, I had a snowdrift in the room.'

'Any damage?'

'Nothing that won't dry out.'

Joan grinned. 'At least you've got help to get rid of it.'

She took the two lads hot drinks, then she and Gran settled in the parlour. Brizo lay at Joan's feet.

'What does young Mrs Green think of having a dog in her house?' Gran asked.

'She doesn't mind, and Jimmy loves it, of course.'

'Children generally do love dogs,' said Gran. 'We had dogs when I was a child.'

'I didn't know that.'

'There's a lot about me you don't know.'

A fraught silence descended, jam-packed with the lies Gran had told in the past.

Someone knocked on the parlour door and one of the lads popped his head round. 'All done, Mrs Foster. We've put our mugs back in the kitchen.'

Gran stood up. 'Thank you for your help. Let me give you something for your trouble.'

'Mum said we weren't to let you pay us, but . . .'

'I am not going to deceive your mother, if that's what you're hinting at.'

The boy sighed. 'Thought not.'

While Gran saw the lads out, Joan went into the dining room to make sure the window was shut. As she turned to leave the room, her gaze landed on the photograph of Daddy, which until last year had always been displayed in the parlour. How handsome he had been. Letitia had inherited his looks in a softened, feminine version. In no way was it good or right or acceptable that Letitia was dead, but at least she had been spared knowing the truth. Joan's hand itched to lay the photo face down. She curled her fingers round, making her nails dig in to her palms, and left the room.

Bob had been gone for two days and nights. He had taken his sleeping bag with him in case he wasn't able to get home, but now, as the time approached eleven o'clock at night, he was back and Joan flew along the hallway to draw him inside and shut the weather out. She helped him out of his wet overcoat and when his own fingers were too cold to manage, she peeled his gloves off for him.

'Come and get warm – or come and thaw out, more like. I made a pan of soup just in case. It won't take two minutes to heat up, and you can have a pasty as well.'

Bob grinned. 'You just happen to have a pasty to hand?'

'If you hadn't come home, I'd have eaten it myself tomorrow and then made something else, just in case.'

Soon, Bob was eating off a tray beside the fire in the sitting room. Jimmy was spark out on the sofa, wrapped in a blanket. Before Bob had disappeared with his sleeping bag, he had brought mattresses downstairs so they could all share the sitting room and keep the fire burning low all night. Sheila slept on Jimmy's single mattress on the floor in front of the sofa, and space had been made for Joan and Bob's double mattress by pushing furniture about, something Jimmy had been more than happy to help with. He thought sleeping on the sofa was a great adventure, especially as Brizo was allowed to curl up at his feet, though each morning, boy and dog were side by side, all cuddled up.

After Bob had eaten, he had a strip-wash and prepared for bed. They were all wearing jumpers and trousers over their nightwear. In the firelight, Sheila smoked a final cigarette.

'You've never been stranded in your signal box all this while,' she said.

'No. I'd be a giant icicle by now if I had been. Anyway, many signal levers aren't working now because they're frozen in position, and even if they did work, we still couldn't use them, as the weight of the snow and ice on the signal wires has brought down lots of the poles. It's not just the signal poles, either. It's telegraph poles too, and you know how sturdy they are.'

'I heard they're having a terrific struggle in the marshalling yard,' said Joan. 'The only way they can separate the couplings is to hammer them apart.'

'The RAF have had to drop food parcels to villages that are cut off,' said Bob, 'as well as to trains that are stuck for any length of time. I heard of one train that was caught in a snowdrift from the morning of one day until the afternoon two days later.'

'Those poor people,' said Sheila.

'It must have been an ordeal,' said Bob, 'but they all survived and that's the main thing. Even the snowploughs are getting stranded.'

'I heard of a goods train that ran into the back of a mail train,' said Joan. 'In such appalling weather conditions, it was impossible to telephone for help, plus of course all the points were frozen, and it was twelve hours before the line was cleared. But the good news is that nobody was hurt, just shaken up.'

'I don't want to upset you,' said Bob, 'but I heard of that too, and I'm sorry to say there were a couple of serious injuries, but that's hush-hush because of the censor.'

'Censorship is wrong.' Sheila blew a stream of smoke straight upwards. 'It treats the public as if we're children, but we're entitled to know.'

'Censorship is there for public morale,' Bob reminded her. 'We can't afford for folk to get downhearted.'

'Morale is important,' said Joan, 'but so is the truth.'

It was impossible not to think of all the lies Gran had told. Perhaps Bob could read her mind, because his arm tightened about her. It wasn't possible to say anything more just then, but the next morning, after Sheila and Jimmy had disappeared upstairs to get dressed, Joan and Bob had a quick word.

'I'm sorry if you feel Sheila and I ganged up on you last night,' said Joan.

'Not at all. I agree it can be frustrating to know we aren't always being told the whole truth, but this is wartime. Anyway, it wasn't wartime censorship you had in mind, really, was it?'

'Not if I'm honest, no. Censorship means lies, and I grew up being fed hateful lies about my mother, just so that Gran could build up a favourable picture of Daddy – an image he didn't deserve in the slightest, as it turned out.'

'I understand how much it matters,' Bob assured her.

'It feels . . .' Joan struggled for the right word, ' . . . unresolved. If only Gran had apologised, I might have been able to draw a line of sorts under it, but she said that her lies about Estelle were less damaging than the truth about

119

Daddy would have been.' She blew out a long breath. 'But that isn't the point.'

'What is the point?' Bob's voice was soft.

'I can hardly believe I'm about to admit this, but I can see why Gran hid the truth about Daddy from Letitia and me. I can see that by doing that, she protected us – though I know she did it as much for his sake as for ours, because she wanted us to worship his memory. But that doesn't mean I'm getting round to her way of thinking,' she added quickly, her voice rising. She took a moment to calm herself. 'Gran didn't need to tell lies about Estelle, she really didn't. She did that because she hated Estelle and couldn't forgive her for being unfaithful to Daddy. But shall I tell you what really worries me?'

For an answer, Bob folded her into his strong arms. She snuggled close, feeling safe, knowing she could say anything to this wonderful man she loved so much.

'Our children are going to have the most devoted possible Hubble grandparents who will love them to bits, but when they ask questions about their Foster grandparents, which they're bound to, we'll have to lie to them. I dread the possibility that one day our children might feel about us, about me, the way I now feel about Gran.'

CHAPTER THIRTEEN

The snow lasted until the end of the month, after which came the thaw, which brought another set of problems on a grand scale. February was a long and tiring month, with swollen rivers, overflowing drains, sodden coal and mountains of slush. Illness, too. Exhausted, many succumbed to influenza. Alison hoped fervently that she wouldn't. Imagine falling ill while away from home. But as the days went by, the chill in the air became less piercing and the trees shed their heavy burden of white. After the profound snow-silence that had blanketed the country, the sound of birdsong was silvery and pure.

In her bedroom, Alison found it safe to put water in her ewer once more without the fear of solid ice cracking the china; and from the cupboard under the stairs, Mrs Freeman brought out a bowl of daffodil bulbs that she had kept in the dark all winter, the stems now growing well, the flowers preparing to bloom.

So we'll have springtime indoors, Alison wrote to Mum, *even if it hasn't arrived outside yet – though it's on its way.*

In the park, snowdrops peeped through beneath trees that were bright with new growth, and the park-keeper assured Alison that it wouldn't be long before the primroses appeared.

'Nature manages better than we do,' he said. 'When my wife comes home from the shops, she says that the only conversation in the queues these days is about cracked roof tiles and burst pipes.'

Isn't it exciting to see the landmarks reappearing? wrote Persephone. *I walked across Chorlton Green the other day and the lychgate at the old churchyard, which has been a massive blob of white for weeks, has gone back to being a lychgate.*

That made Alison yearn for home, but she was determined to make the best of things. She didn't want others to resent her for not wanting to be here. She had become friendly with Betty and Eddie and the three of them chatted about all sorts of things. As the days gradually lengthened, they enjoyed some walks together through the thaw, brushing past dripping hedges, their footsteps unavoidably splashing in puddles that had lasted for ages.

'It won't be long before you can see your boyfriend again, Alison,' said Betty. 'Have you missed him?'

Alison laughed, making light of it, though when she said 'Just a bit', she knew Betty and Eddie would understand her real meaning. 'I can't wait.'

'We'd all like to have a handsome doctor in tow,' said Eddie.

'Joel's an unusual name,' Betty remarked.

'It's uncommon,' said Alison, 'but it isn't new. It comes from the Bible.'

Eddie grinned. 'I bet you didn't know that before you met your Joel.'

'No, I didn't,' Alison admitted cheerfully.

Eddie grabbed her arm and squeezed it, leaning close to tease. 'Oh, she wants to know every little thing about him, doesn't she?'

'It's a good thing we work in the kitchens,' said Betty. 'If we were in an office, she'd write his name on her ruler.'

'Don't give her ideas,' said Eddie. 'I bet you anything she starts carving his name into the veg after this.'

Alison laughed along with them, loving being teased about Joel. She was very fond of Eddie and Betty and knew how lucky she was to have met girls who had taken to her straight away. Even so, they would never replace her friends at home in Manchester. She, Cordelia, Dot and the rest had gone through so much together, most recently the terrible shock of losing Colette before Christmas. Earlier last year, for the first few months after Paul dumped her, Alison had gone through a dark time during which she had kept her friends at a distance. It was only towards the end of the year that she had emerged from her heartbreak and realised how misguided she had been to separate herself like that and how much she truly valued and needed the others.

And now here she was without them.

She missed Joel with an urgency that made her skin tingle and the blood run warmly through her veins. But he wasn't the only one she missed. She missed her family and the Wilton Close ladies, and she missed the friends who had never given up on her.

As February went on and things returned to normal, Margaret wondered whether it was happening more quickly than it would have done in peacetime. The country couldn't afford to lag behind in any way while it was at war. Moreover, now that winter was finally behind them, being attacked became a real possibility once more.

Nevertheless, everyone was grateful to see the back of the bad weather and everybody had an anecdote or two to share. Was Margaret alone in facing the coming spring with a feeling of growing dread? She had managed to avoid thinking about Alison and Joel all this time, only too glad to postpone it because it was such a difficult subject, but she had to face it now. She must decide what to do.

If she was any sort of friend, she would warn Alison – but then Alison would ask 'How do you know?' and what was she supposed to say to that? She couldn't, absolutely couldn't tell the truth. There were some things that you simply never spoke of again.

But what if she failed to warn Alison and then the same thing happened to Alison as had happened to her two years ago? How would she feel then? She would hate and despise herself; it would be an additional shame.

She wanted to be a good friend, but . . . but she had to be true to herself and that meant keeping her secret.

The dilemma was exactly the same as it had been when she had seen Joel in Mrs Cooper's front room at the beginning of the year. She was no closer to knowing the right thing to do. Turning it over and over in her mind was of no use. She just kept banging into the same brick walls.

Joan.

Joan knew what had happened two years ago – well, not the beginning of it, but she knew the end result. Being friends with both Margaret and Alison, she would see it from both points of view. Would she be able to bring some clarity to the matter? She would certainly bring sensitivity and kindness. Joan had been good to Margaret, drawing her into the group of friends and even inviting her to be one of her bridesmaids. She had flatly refused to be put off by Margaret's past, which, after the way Dad had turned his back on her, had meant the world to Margaret.

Dad.

Margaret closed her eyes for a moment as the old memory arose and horror and shame washed through her, knotting her belly and thickening her throat.

Being carried across the rubble that had once been the front of their house, securely strapped to a stretcher . . . . She ran her hands up and down her arms, touching the places where the straps had held her . . . here on her upper arms and here on her forearms. Dad had been told by an

ARP warden what had happened to her, and she, with her arms pinned to her sides, hadn't even been able to cover her face while Dad, shocked and furious, had berated her at the top of his voice, in the process informing the world and his wife what she had done.

She had fallen for a baby, that was what she'd done. She had got pregnant – and Dr Joel Maitland was the father.

Oh, she had loved him. Now Margaret couldn't imagine what she had ever seen in Joel Maitland, but at the time she had adored him. He was good-looking and amusing and he was a wonderful dancer. That was how they had met. She had been at a dance with friends. It was shortly before Christmas, during the Phoney War, a little more than two years ago.

She could still remember what she had worn: a dark blue velvet-rayon dress printed with white diamonds. Hems were longer in those days and the skirt had swirled attractively below her knees. It was Anna's dress, really, but before she was evacuated she had given it to Margaret, along with a pink shirtwaister.

'My two nicest pre-pregnancy dresses. I'll enjoy thinking of you wearing them.'

Margaret had missed Anna dreadfully when she went away, but she consoled herself with the thought that it was a temporary separation, unlike missing Mum, who was gone for good. With William away in the army, that only left herself and Dad at home, rattling around in the tall house opposite Alexandra Park. Anna and her husband hadn't lived with them, but her absence from Margaret's everyday life made the family home feel emptier.

The Phoney War, or the Bore War, as some called it, had still been going on when Margaret and her friends went to that particular dance before Christmas. The band played

'Deep Purple', 'Wish Me Luck (As You Wave Me Goodbye)' and the poignant 'I'll Be Seeing You'. Some girls only wanted to dance with boys in uniform, but Margaret couldn't tear her eyes away from a tall, good-looking civilian with blue eyes that crinkled warmly when he smiled. He smiled a lot and appeared very good-natured.

When he approached and politely asked her to dance, she was thrilled. His name was Joel Maitland and he was a doctor – a paediatrician, no less. Not so long ago, that wouldn't have impressed her particularly, but with Anna in the family way, it struck a chord.

'But once the war gets going, we'll need all the surgeons we can get,' he said as they waltzed, 'so I'm going on an intensive training course in surgery.'

'But children will still need doctors.'

'They will, and it's the work I'll return to after the war, but for now,' he said, softening the words with a smile, 'my duty lies in the operating theatre.'

Margaret felt a chill of apprehension, in spite of – or perhaps because of – the attraction that heightened her senses and made her feel fluttery inside.

When the waltz ended, Joel bought drinks and they sat out the next dance, chatting. Then they had a quickstep before he returned her to the group she had come with, but not before he had asked if he could see her again. Margaret had spent the rest of the evening dreaming of Joel sweeping her into his arms for the last waltz, but instead the band had played 'There'll Always Be an England', followed by 'We'll Meet Again', and everyone had crowded towards the stage, singing their hearts out. Margaret and her companions flung their arms around each other's shoulders as they swayed in time to the music. Margaret caught Joel's eye across the gathering and sang, feeling proud and patriotic and unutterably happy.

That winter was a bad one and what with heavy snow and plunging temperatures, no one had done much in the way of socialising. Besides, Joel had worked extra shifts. For her own part, Margaret had all but frozen to death doing her fire-watching duty on Ingleby's roof.

Then came the spring and at last she was able to see more of Joel. They went dancing and he took her to the pictures. She had never known happiness like it. When Joel told her he would be going to Leeds for intensive training in surgical work, it was all she could do to congratulate him when what she really wanted was to demand, 'Why can't you do your training here?' She had a mad urge to hang on to him and never let him go. She longed for him to say, 'I wish I was staying here for the training,' but he was pleased to have the arrangements sorted out. All he was waiting for was the dates. This was his bit for the war effort and he was eager to get on with it.

When they were together, which couldn't be often enough for Margaret, she felt safe and complete. Her heart beat faster when he walked into the room and the tiniest of accidental touches made her tingle all over. She wished she could see more of him, but as a bachelor, Joel made a point of taking on extra night and weekend shifts so that his married colleagues could spend more time with their families while the Phoney War lasted. Margaret admired him for his generosity, but she secretly cursed it too, because it meant he saw less of her.

And then – and then came the night of the party. One of Joel's colleagues had a sister who worked for the Ministry of Food and she had been sent to Manchester to work in the Town Hall. She and another Ministry of Food girl had been billeted on a couple in Fallowfield. The couple had gone away for a few days and had given permission for the girls to have their friends round.

Margaret told Dad she was going dancing. He was a real old fuddy-duddy and he might not approve of a party, though there was no reason to suppose it would be anything other than tickety-boo. The house was a semi that had been built in the thirties. There was lively conversation, cigarettes and drinks, and Margaret felt very ritzy and up to the minute, all the more so because she was one of the girls with a boyfriend. A fellow called Angus sat on the arm of his young lady's chair, with his arm draped loosely around her shoulders. It was rather thrilling to see a couple behaving like that in public. Margaret had never had a boyfriend before and her social life had always involved going dancing or to the pictures with other girls. This evening felt like a rite of passage. There was a gramophone and someone had brought the latest recordings. One of the chaps suggested pushing back the furniture for dancing. It was huge fun and very sophisticated.

The other girls were drinking gin and orange. Margaret had never tried it before. The most she'd ever had was a weak port and lemon, which was all Dad would permit. When she tasted the gin, she found she didn't really care for it, but feared looking silly if she said so. A young man called Richard had appointed himself the barman and he was nothing if not keen to do his job properly. He kept topping up everyone's drinks, which was very hospitable, but Margaret found it at first difficult and then downright impossible to keep track of how many she'd had. Saying 'Not for me, thanks' didn't work, because he poured more in anyway. Margaret let someone light another cigarette for her and she took another drink.

At some point, Angus and his girl changed places. Now he was in the armchair and she was on his lap, and the two of them weren't sitting up straight either. They were snuggled up close and they were – well, smooching was the only word. But instead of shocking her, the spectacle made Margaret experience a burst of desire. She wished that Joel—

'Lord, I'm a bit squiffy,' announced one of the Ministry of Food girls – Helen. She laughed as if it was a great joke.

Margaret didn't like that. Mum wouldn't have approved. It took her a moment to realise that no one was looking at Helen in disapproval. If anything, they seemed amused.

'Oh well,' said Richard the barman. 'Too late to do anything about it now,' and he topped up her glass.

Did that mean it was all right to get tiddly in public? Perhaps it was allowed among friends. But it went against everything Margaret had been taught. Before she could think about it properly, Helen swooped on Joel, pulling him to his feet for a dance, and a burning sensation flared inside Margaret's chest as jealousy took possession of her.

She surged to her feet. At least, that was what she intended, but somehow she managed to stumble. Richard caught hold of her and steadied her with one hand while putting down the bottle of gin with the other.

'Oops-a-daisy,' he said and swung her into the dance.

She tried her best to match his steps, desperate not to make a fool of herself, but dancing didn't altogether suit her just then because her thoughts couldn't quite keep up. Then Richard twirled her to a standstill. Inwardly, she was still spinning.

'Excuse me.' Richard tapped Helen on her silk-clad shoulder. 'I hereby declare this to be an excuse-me dance and I've chosen you, you lucky lady.'

'You're supposed to excuse the man, not the lady, you twit,' said Helen, but she moved willingly into his arms and Richard delivered Margaret into Joel's . . .

CHAPTER FOURTEEN

It was the beginning of March and Joan's last week at work. She was meeting up with her friends that evening before they all went home. It was busy in the buffet, which was as good a sign as any that things were back to normal, and her heart lifted as she threaded her way across the crowded room, one hand in front of her holding her tea, the other behind her holding Brizo's lead. With barely enough room on the table for their cups and saucers, her friends were all squeezed in next to one another, but they cheerfully shunted round to make a space for her.

'Here, share with me,' offered Persephone, sliding to the edge of her chair, 'and Brizo can go under the table. He'll be out of everyone's way and he won't get trodden on when other people come and go.'

'In you go, boy,' said Mabel. 'Sorry about all the feet.'

'What were you talking about?' Joan asked, looking around the group.

'Japan,' said Cordelia. 'It makes a change from endlessly discussing Germany, though not a good change, I'm afraid.'

Joan shuddered inwardly. Time and again, she was grateful that her husband was in a reserved occupation that meant he wouldn't be called up. Now that Japan was in the war, there was yet more to worry about. In the middle of February, Singapore had fallen and thousands upon thousands of troops were now prisoners of war. And at the end of the month, the Allies had failed in their attempt to prevent the Japanese from attacking Java.

'But it's not all bad news,' said Dot. 'We've got a deputy prime minister now, the first time we've ever had one of those. He's a good man, is Mr Attlee. I like it that Mr Churchill has given the job to a Labour man instead of another Tory.'

'How are you feeling, Joan?' Cordelia asked.

'Fine, thanks. I'm doing well.'

'You're six months along now, aren't you, chick?' said Dot. 'It's time you stayed at home and put your feet up. Make the most of it. When the second one comes along, you won't get any rest.'

'The second?' Joan laughed. 'Steady on. Let's bring this one into the world first.'

'How do you feel about leaving work?' asked Margaret.

'It's nothing like as busy in First Aid now, so it feels like the right time, but I'll miss all of you.'

'You don't get rid of us that easily,' Persephone declared. 'We'll all be coming to see you, and you'll be calling round at Mrs Cooper's, won't you?'

'You'll soon be wrapped up in preparing for Baby,' said Cordelia.

'Have you chosen any names?' asked Mabel.

'You shouldn't ask,' Dot said at once. 'Just before the war, when my niece Cora was expecting, she wanted Lily Rose for a girl, but her sister made a joke out of it, because that's the name of one of the kids in that children's story that came out a few years back, *The Family From One End Street*. So Cora gave up on Lily Rose, which was a real shame, because she had a lovely little girl.'

'What name did she choose in the end?' asked Margaret.

'Cecilia – Cissie.'

'That's pretty,' said Joan.

'It is,' agreed Dot, 'but it wasn't Cora's first choice. My advice to you, love,' she added, looking at Joan, 'is not to talk about names until you've chosen for definite.'

'I don't think we ever will choose, since you mention it,' said Joan. 'There are names we quite like, but not enough to say "*That* one." The only one that is definite is Letitia as a middle name for a girl.'

'That's perfect,' said Mabel.

'Yes, it is,' agreed the others, and Dot pressed Joan's hand.

'And I can share two names that have been crossed off,' said Joan, and told them about Hebe and Sybil.

'What's wrong with them?' Margaret asked.

'Give her a minute,' smiled Mabel, 'and the penny will drop.'

Margaret frowned as everyone looked at her, then her expression cleared and she said, 'Ah, I see,' and they all laughed.

'What are everyone's plans for the weekend?' asked Cordelia. 'I'm working on Saturday and then going to a bridge evening.'

'We're having Sunday dinner with Bob's family,' said Joan, 'and then popping round to Wilton Close on the way home, so I might see you then.' She looked at Mabel and Margaret.

'Sorry,' said Mabel. 'I'm seeing Harry.'

'I'll be there,' said Margaret.

'And Alison is away in Leeds,' said Joan. 'This is her first real weekend away from home. What I mean is, she couldn't have come any earlier because of the snow and the thaw. Is Joel going to Leeds to see her, does anyone know?'

'Yes,' said Mabel. 'Mrs Cooper had a letter from her yesterday.'

'What about Brizo's job here after you leave, Joan?' asked Persephone. 'He's quite a feature of the station these days.'

'I could collect him from you and bring him with me,' said Dot, 'and Persephone could look after him during the day. Once you've left, Joan, she'll be the only one of us working all day on the station.'

'That sounds like it could work.' Joan made a point of smiling, but actually she felt rather iffy about it. Everyone else would carry on working – even her dog! She was going to miss her job and the comradeship.

'There's Miss Emery,' said Dot. 'I think she's heading for us.'

As elegant as ever in a red felt hat and a smart grey mackintosh with a tie belt, Miss Emery made her way across the crowded buffet, smiling at the friends to show she was indeed coming to speak to them.

'Good evening, ladies,' she greeted them. 'I thought I might find you here.' She addressed Joan. 'Could you pop across to Hunts Bank tomorrow and see me, Mrs Hubble? Don't look alarmed. I have some good news for you – well, I hope you'll think it's good.'

'Can't you tell me now?' Joan asked. 'I'm happy for you to talk in front of the others, now that I know I'm not going to be hauled over the coals.'

'I don't see why not,' said Miss Emery. 'Is that your dog I can see under the table?'

'Yes,' said Joan. 'Mrs Jessop knows he's here. I have permission to bring him in.'

'It's because of him that I'm here.' Miss Emery smiled. She never gave a broad, eye-crinkling smile, or at least she never did when she was at work. 'I'm here to ask you if you would like to appear in a short feature in the LMS staff magazine, Mrs Hubble, to talk about your fundraising dog.'

'Oh, Joan,' said Margaret. 'How exciting.'

'You are going to say yes, aren't you?' Mabel encouraged her.

'Drat,' said Persephone with a laugh. 'I wish I'd thought of it. I could have written an amusing little piece for *Vera's Voice*.'

Everyone was looking at Joan.

'I'd love to,' she said.

'Good,' said Miss Emery. 'I'll arrange everything and let you know. They'll want to take a photograph of you and . . .'

'Brizo,' said Dot.

' . . . you and Brizo. You shan't mind that, shall you?'

'You can talk about how you rescued him after he was abandoned,' said Persephone. 'It'll make a lovely article. It's a shame it's an in-house magazine and will only be seen by the staff.'

'That's quite enough publicity for Brizo and me,' said Joan.

'It might encourage other station staff to do something similar with their own dogs,' said Cordelia.

'Wouldn't that be something?' said Mabel. 'You see what you've started, Joan?'

'It was Persephone who started it,' said Joan. 'It was her idea.'

'Actually, it wasn't my idea at all,' Persephone corrected her. 'I pinched the idea from another station.'

'It doesn't matter who started it,' Dot declared. 'It's a nice way to celebrate our Joan and the special work done by Brizo. You can cut it out of the magazine and keep it for ever, Joan.'

'You can show it to your grandchildren one day,' Mabel teased.

Joan put her hands over her ears. 'Stop it! I've already told you: let's get baby number one out of the way first.'

It was exciting to think of appearing in the staff magazine, though Joan was well aware it was Brizo who would be the star of the article. She couldn't wait to get home and tell Bob.

He was proud, just as she'd known he would be.

'We'll have to give him an extra brushing on the morning of the interview to get him ready for his photograph.' Bob laughed. 'You can have an extra brushing too.'

'They won't want me in the picture,' said Joan. 'It's Brizo they're interested in.'

'When will the interview take place? They'll have to get a move on. You're leaving on Friday.'

'I could always go back, if necessary. Just because I won't be an employee any more doesn't mean I can never set foot in Victoria Station again.'

Did other girls feel this way when they left? Surely she was meant to be dying to leave so she could be at home all the time, preparing for her baby – and she was looking forward to doing that, she really was, but she loved being a railway girl and hated to think of giving it up.

This week, she and Bob were both on early daytime shifts, so they had late afternoons and all the evenings together. They went to see some accommodation that had been advertised, but at the first house they didn't even get over the threshold because the landlady refused on the doorstep to take a dog. The other property shared a party wall with a bombed-out house that was more rubble than house.

'That party wall may well stay intact for years,' said Bob, 'but it would be daft of us to take that flat.'

On their way home, the air was bright with the scent of privet and there were daffodils and primulas in the gardens, tucked away in corners so as not to encroach on the space needed for home-grown vegetables. Bob let Brizo off the lead to go off and have a good sniff around, but he didn't stray far from them. In fact, he spent a significant portion of his time off the lead, circling the two of them as they walked along. They had noticed this behaviour before and found it endearing.

'He's keeping us together,' said Joan.

'You can tell the man who interviews you about this,' said Bob.

Joan had a date for the interview now. It was to be on Friday, her last day at work.

'When you finish work,' said Bob, 'you'll have time to follow up more advertisements for accommodation.'

'I think it's time to tell Sheila we're thinking of leaving,' said Joan. 'It's only fair. I'd feel rotten if the first she knew of it was when we give notice.'

'*If* we give notice – if we find somewhere.'

When they arrived home, Dot was there to collect Jimmy, who was to sleep at her house. Sheila had already gone to work.

'Been anywhere nice?' Dot asked.

Joan felt a flicker of embarrassment, but it wouldn't be right to inform Dot before Sheila.

Bob said easily, 'Just for a walk.' He described Brizo's way of circling round them.

'He knows another trick an' all,' piped up Jimmy.

'Oh aye?' said Dot. 'What's that, then?'

'This,' said Jimmy. 'Brizo-zo-zo-zo-zo.'

The dog lifted his tawny head and howled.

'Stop it, Jimmy,' said Dot. 'Did you teach him that? I'm so sorry,' she added to Joan and Bob.

'I never taught him,' Jimmy said indignantly. 'I just happened to say "Brizo-zo—" I mean, I just said it and he howled, so I did it again to make sure. Now he does it every time. You could tell them that in your interview, Auntie Joan.'

'Fetch your stuff, our Jimmy.' Dot shook her head. 'I'll get him out of your hair.'

'We don't mind,' said Bob. 'We're fond of him.'

'He thinks the world of the pair of you,' said Dot, 'especially you, Bob. It's good of you to pay him as much attention as you do.'

After Dot and Jimmy had gone, Joan and Bob looked at one another.

'She's right,' said Joan. 'He adores you. He's going to miss you dreadfully if we move.'

'I know and I feel bad about that, but we can't stay just for Jimmy's sake. Remember, we're leaving, or hoping to, for Junior.'

Joan raised her eyebrows. 'Junior? Is that the best you can do?'

Bob grinned. 'It's the safest.'

'The other day, Dot mentioned a baby whose mum wanted to call her Lily Rose.'

'That's pretty,' said Bob.

'That's what I thought. I'm not suggesting it, mind, but it made me think of flower names. I like Violet, but might it sound old-fashioned nowadays? We don't want to saddle a little girl with a great-auntish sort of name.'

'What about Charlotte?' suggested Bob. 'We could call her Lottie.'

'Lottie is a bit close to Letitia. I wondered about Martin for a boy.'

'Martin Hubble. I like that.'

'Leslie and Philip are nice too,' said Joan.

Bob gave her a hug. 'We need a name that's better than just nice. This is our first-born child we're talking about.'

Joan laughed. 'Perhaps we should ask Persephone. She came up with the perfect name for Brizo. There are lots of names I like, but none that I love . . . not since I had to give up Hebe and Sybil, anyway.'

'A son wouldn't thank us for calling him Hebe.'

137

'You daft ha'p'orth.'

Now it was Bob's turn to raise his eyebrows at her. 'A daft ha'p'orth, am I? You won't want me to kiss you, then. No sensible girl wants kisses from a daft ha'p'orth.'

'I'll make an exception,' said Joan, lifting her face obligingly. 'Just this once.'

CHAPTER FIFTEEN

It was the first Friday night in March and Alison was on the night shift, hard at work in the kitchens alongside Betty and Eddie.

'This must be like déjà vu for you, Alison,' said Betty. 'You were on the night shift the last time Joel was due here for the weekend, weren't you?'

'Yes,' said Alison, 'but I was working at the station then, not here.'

'Let's hope he doesn't bring a snowstorm with him this time,' said Eddie.

'Just a love-storm,' chuckled Betty.

The other two laughed. Alison blushed, but she was pleased as well. Goodness, but she was looking forward to Joel's arrival. It was all she had thought about for days. She hadn't seen him since that all too brief visit in January, which had been cut short by the snow. What with that and the prolonged thaw, not to mention their clashing shift patterns, it hadn't been possible for them to see one another since. But now, at long last, Joel was coming to Leeds. Like last time – or rather, like last time should have been – he was coming on Saturday afternoon and staying until Sunday afternoon. Alison couldn't wait.

The three girls were on sandwich duty, making up the night trays for staff working overnight in this building and in the hospital, as well as in Civil Defence roles.

'I do enjoy this job,' Betty remarked. 'I find it restful.'

'Restful?' said Alison. 'Working like a maniac to produce hundreds of sandwiches?'

Betty's knife stopped for a moment, then resumed spreading the fish paste. 'The job's the same as it always was, but it feels different these days – or these nights, I should say.'

'Do you mean because you're in a new building and a different kitchen?' Alison suggested, though she couldn't see why this would make that sort of difference.

'No, it's nothing to do with that,' said Betty. 'When we started, we were doing night trays for the rescue services, weren't we, Eddie? Now that the air raids have stopped, touch wood,' she added, tapping her head, 'our job hasn't changed, but it feels calmer.'

'When the raids were on,' Eddie continued, 'the WVS ladies came in during the day and we helped them make sandwiches for their mobile canteens to hand out to repair squads and demolition boys – '

' – and the bomb-disposal lads and the firemen – '

' – and the chaps sorting out the gas and water supplies,' said Eddie, 'and don't forget the gravediggers.'

'Gravediggers!' Alison couldn't help repeating it, then wished she had held her tongue. Why be surprised? It made sense. The air raids had devastated entire communities.

As she worked, Alison kept an eye on the clock, her heartbeats coming a little faster each time she pictured seeing Joel again. Early in the battle against the snow, one of the women in the station canteen had said, 'If nowt else, love, you'll find out if your feelings for one another are real, with you not having known one another very long, I mean. You're bound not to see one another for some time if this winter is anything like the other bad ones we've had recently. Absence might make the heart grow fonder – or your feelings might just fizzle out altogether.'

Well, that certainly hadn't happened. Having feelings for Joel was the most exciting thing to have happened to Alison in a long while. Her long-standing relationship with Paul had been steady and predictable, which had been satisfying at the time, but now Alison relished the exhilaration of starting afresh.

At the end of her shift, she walked home as quickly as possible without actually breaking into a run. A smile tugged at the corners of her mouth. So what if she ran? She was happy and she didn't care who saw it. That was another reason why embarking on this new relationship was a good thing. When she had been in a couple with Paul, there had been a shameful amount of pretence. Desperate to get engaged, she had constantly looked for the next likely opportunity when Paul might pop the question – and she had just as constantly had to pretend not to be disappointed when it didn't happen. But with Joel, once she had finally accepted that seeing him and developing a new relationship was truly what she wanted, there was none of that. Yes, she wanted to get married one day, of course, but right now what she wanted was the joy and fun of getting to know her lovely new boyfriend without the pressure and worry that she associated with an engagement ring. Getting a ring on her finger had once been all-important to her, but not any more.

She went to bed, though she didn't sleep much. Nevertheless, she sprang out of bed as if she'd had a full eight hours. She had brought with her a navy dress with white polka dots and a white collar and white cuffs at the short puff sleeves. She almost hadn't packed it, because it wasn't a winter dress and she had hoped that she would be back in Manchester well before the spring, but now she was glad Mabel had persuaded her to bring it with her.

At least she wouldn't have to wear wellingtons this time. She titivated her hair and put on her felt hat. Some girls had stopped wearing hats these days, but how could you look your best bareheaded? She wanted to look her best for Joel – and for herself too, because she always took pride in her appearance.

At the station, she purchased a platform ticket and walked through the ticket barrier to wait for Joel's train. A woman porter with a flatbed trolley came onto the platform and found a space, apparently at random, but Alison was well aware that this would be exactly where the guard's van with all the parcels would stop. Presently, puffs of white cloud came into sight as the train approached. It coasted alongside the platform and a hissing sound came from the top of the engine as it headed towards the buffers. As the brakes shrieked, some of the doors banged open and passengers started spilling out even before the train came to a halt.

Alison watched everyone alight, her gaze darting about in search of the one person she longed to see. Then – there he was. The rest of the world receded into a distant background hum as her gaze locked onto him. He carried a valise in one hand and a large suitcase in the other. Typical Joel, helping a fellow passenger, an older gentleman with a walking stick. Joel handed the suitcase to a porter with a sack trolley before exchanging a few words with the gentleman, then they parted company and Joel looked around, eagerness in his expression – eagerness to see her.

Their eyes met and Alison felt a burst of emotion that almost made her want to cry. They hurried towards one another. Joel deposited the valise at his feet and they went into each other's arms, just like in a film. Joel kissed her, not a long, passionate kiss, but a gentle, brief one that was filled with promise. As he held her close to him, Alison released a deep sigh, not just of happiness, but also of relief. Here, in Joel's arms, was where she wanted to be.

When they broke apart, they both started to speak at once, stopping at the same moment, too, and laughing. There was so much to say and yet no need to say anything.

'Practicalities first,' said Joel. Let's go to the B & B, so I can dump my valise. Is it the same place as last time?'

'Yes,' said Alison. 'Afterwards, I thought we'd go for a walk and have a meal later. We can go to the pictures this evening, if you like.'

'No, I want to be with you properly, not gazing at a screen. I want to hear about everything.'

Alison laughed. 'You make it sound as if we haven't exchanged any letters.'

'You can repeat every word you wrote, if you like. I just want to hear your voice.' Joel groaned. 'Sorry, that sounded rather trite, didn't it, not to say downright cheesy. But it's true. I've been looking forward to seeing you so very much.'

They dropped off Joel's luggage before setting off to amble around the centre of the city, talking about anything and everything.

'How are you getting on in your digs now?' asked Joel.

'So-so. Actually, more than so-so, really,' Alison admitted. 'I slept under the dining table during the snow, because my room was like an ice cave. The water in the ewer didn't just have a layer of ice on the top, it was frozen solid all the way to the bottom.'

'Do you ever think of finding somewhere else and leaving?'

'If I'm honest, it has crossed my mind more than once, but looking for a better billet would be like settling in properly, as if I'm intending to stay – and this is definitely a temporary arrangement. I can't wait to get home. When I next get a couple of days off together, I'll go home and see everyone. I do appreciate your coming just for twenty-four hours.'

'A great pleasure, I assure you.'

'I feel a bit mean, actually. My friends are putting on a special do for Joan tomorrow and they wanted me to be there, but it isn't until the afternoon, so as soon as Joan arrived, I'd have had to set off to catch the train back here.'

'Nothing to feel mean about,' said Joel. 'It would have been different if the do had been tomorrow morning.'

Alison had booked an early table for them in case they went to the pictures afterwards.

'Now we can relax and take our time,' said Joel. 'What would you like?'

Alison had the rabbit stew followed by sultana pudding, and Joel chose the vegetable pie with cheesy oatmeal topping followed by marmalade pudding.

'It must be nice to be waited on instead of doing all the work,' he remarked.

'It is. I feel very spoiled and I can't help thinking about everything that's going on behind the scenes. I'll never take eating out for granted again.'

'Your letters made it sound as if you've done your share of the behind-the-scenes work.'

'Basically, all I've done is four jobs – peeling, prepping, serving and washing up. I can do them all in my sleep at this point.'

'I realise you have to do your share of the work,' said Joel, 'but what about being shown the ropes for how the canteen is managed? I thought that's why you were sent here.'

'It was, but also to help out, because the Park Square canteen is a new one.' Alison hesitated. She hadn't mentioned this before. 'As for learning the ropes, I'm afraid I fell foul of the lady in charge on day one.'

'You didn't mention that in your letters.'

'It wasn't my finest moment. I'm rather ashamed of it, to tell the truth. It's the first time I've ever behaved in such an unprofessional way. If I'd seen a girl behave like that when I worked in an office, I'd have known precisely what to think of her.'

'I can't imagine you letting yourself down,' said Joel.

She shrugged. 'Let's just say I opened my mouth and put my foot straight in it.'

Joel laughed. 'Moving swiftly on . . .' He changed the subject.

After their meal, they went dancing. Outside, the blackout was in force, but inside, the lights twinkled below the high ceiling. The band was accomplished and the bandleader was an engaging MC. Joel and Alison had several dances one after another, then Joel bought drinks and they sat out for a while.

Over Joel's shoulder, Alison saw – oh no. She groaned inwardly while making sure she kept the smile on her face. Coming in their direction was Miss Chambers, the dragon lady herself. She wore a long damson-coloured dress shot through with silver threads that winked as they caught the light. Around her slender shoulders, she wore a pale grey wrap that was so fragile-looking it might have been made of cobwebs. Her hair was swept back and her dark eyes were striking in her lovely face.

Alison nodded politely and Miss Chambers returned the casual greeting. She glanced automatically to see whom Alison was with, but then, instead of walking past as Alison had expected her to, Miss Chambers looked a second time at Joel, and then she stopped.

'Why, Joel, *darling*. How perfectly wonderful to see you.'

Laughing in surprise, Joel rose politely to his feet. Alison gazed up at the pair of them and saw how good they looked, standing next to one another. She saw, too, the way Miss Chambers' rapt gaze was fixed on Joel.

'Aren't you supposed to be in Manchester?' Miss Chambers asked him. 'What brings you back to Leeds? Not that I'm not pleased to see you,' she added with an engaging laugh that made her face light up and added to her beauty.

'I'm visiting my girlfriend,' said Joel. 'This is Alison Lambert. Alison, this is Rachel Chambers, a friend.'

'A friend? Is that all?' Miss Chambers pouted. No girl had any business looking that good when she pouted. Then she laughed. 'There's no need for introductions, Joel, darling. Miss Lambert and I are old friends. She works for me in the canteen.' With that, Miss Chambers sat down and joined them. 'Just for a minute.' She looked at Alison. 'You don't mind, do you? Only I haven't seen Joel in ages.' As he sat down, she said to him, 'How is everything in Manchester?'

'Fine, thanks, especially now that the snow's gone and I can get across the Pennines to see Alison.'

Miss Chambers' gaze flicked to Alison and then back to rest on Joel's face. 'How nice for the two of you to be reunited.'

'Yes, it is,' said Joel. 'How are things at work?'

'As busy as ever. Busier, in fact. I have two jobs these days. No rest for the wicked, so I must be very wicked indeed. I'm the deputy lady almoner at the infirmary and I'm also in charge of overseeing the Park Square canteen and kitchen where Miss Lambert is employed.'

Miss Chambers glanced over her shoulder and waved at some people at another table. As she stood up, Joel rose too.

'I must go. My friends are waiting for me. It's lovely to see you again, Joel. If you're going to be a regular visitor, maybe we'll bump into one another again.' Miss Chambers glanced at Alison. 'Good evening, Miss Lambert.' She placed a hand on Joel's arm and kissed his cheek. 'Goodbye, darling, until next time.'

Alison's mouth started to fall open and she snapped it shut. The only thing that made her feel better – and even that didn't make her feel entirely better – was that Joel's rather sheepish look suggested he felt that Miss Chambers – Rachel – had overstepped the mark.

'As you've probably gathered,' he said, 'Rachel is an old girlfriend.'

'She didn't behave much like an old one. "Joel, *dar*ling," indeed!' How waspish she sounded – how jealous. Alison pulled herself together. This was Rachel's fault, not Joel's. 'Did you go out with her for a long time?'

'No, not really. We met when I was here doing my surgical intensive training.'

'So . . . two years ago?' The tension drained out of her as the threat receded. Threat? 'She did rather gush over you, didn't she?'

'Well, it wasn't how I imagined this evening,' said Joel. 'Forget Rachel. It was just one of those things. Would you like another dance? Would you do me the honour?'

'With pleasure.'

Alison gave him her hand and he led her onto the floor, taking her into his arms for the quickstep. Although they'd had hardly any opportunity to dance as partners, their steps fitted perfectly and he was a better dancer than Paul.

'Here, you're meant to let me lead,' said Joel with a laugh.

'Sorry.' Had she been trying to steer him away from where Rachel Chambers and her cronies were seated? How silly. How needless. 'I just want to dance right in the middle under the chandelier.'

'Your wish is my command.'

Joel expertly whirled her into the throng of dancers, well out of sight of anybody sitting in a particular section of the seating area. Good. Even so . . .

There wasn't going to be a ladies' excuse-me dance, was there?

CHAPTER SIXTEEN

On Sunday, Bob suggested taking a taxi to Stretford.

'Can we afford it?' Joan asked.

'Can I afford to take proper care of my beautiful wife? Most certainly, always and for ever.'

It might have seemed like an extravagance, but it made sense too, because it saved them from getting two buses.

'You put your feet up, Joan, while we see to the dinner,' said Mum, adding, when Joan protested, 'Make the most of it, love. You'll have plenty to do when the baby comes.'

They were all there, apart from Glad, who was working.

'More elbow room for the rest of us,' said Bob.

After dinner, they chatted and played a few hands of whist, then it was time for Joan and Bob to go to Wilton Close.

'Let's walk there,' said Joan. 'We've never thought anything before of the distance, and it's a lovely bright day.'

'You're six months along, though,' Bob pointed out. 'Are you all right walking?'

'Of course I am, fusspot. It won't be long before I'm as big as a tram, so I want to make the most of this while I can.'

At Wilton Close, Mrs Cooper let them in – and was she trying not to laugh as she opened the front-room door for them? Yes, she was – because the room was full of their friends.

As well as Mrs Grayson, Cordelia and Dot were there, as were Mabel, Margaret and Persephone, and Cordelia's daughter, Emily. Seated on the sofa were Miss Brown and

Mrs Mitchell from Darley Court. Joan exclaimed in delight as her friends got up to draw her into the room and hug her. Tony was there, too, Colette's husband, looking a bit awkward, but Bob made a point of going straight up to him and shaking his hand. The party was completed by a middle-aged couple whom Joan thought she recognised, though for the life of her she couldn't think where from. Mrs Cooper introduced them as her sister and brother-in-law, Mr and Mrs Bryant, and Joan remembered. Lizzie's funeral. Of course.

All the chairs in the house had been brought into the front room and there were jokes about musical chairs as everyone found somewhere to sit after all the greetings had been exchanged.

'I didn't know you were all going to be here,' said Joan.

'That was the whole idea,' said Mabel.

'Before you girls sit down again,' said Mrs Cooper, 'let's bring it forward, shall we, so Joan and Bob can open it?'

Margaret and Persephone pushed their dining chairs aside as best they could to make space for 'it' to come through. It was a large, indistinct shape, loosely covered in sheets of newspaper that had been stuck together.

'It's for you, Bob and Joan, from all your railway friends, including Alison, even though she can't be here. It's also from Mrs Grayson and me – and Miss Brown and Mrs Mitchell.'

Overwhelmed with delight, Joan raised her hands to cover her mouth. Bob gave her a gentle push.

'Go on,' he said. 'Open it.'

Stepping forward, Joan lifted off the paper as carefully as possible. No one casually tore paper off these days. Bob took the paper from her and Joan gasped at the sight of a wooden rocking chair. On its seat was a buttoned cushion in faded red velvet, with a matching cushion against its ladder-back. Over one arm was draped a piece of colourful patchwork and on the seat cushion was a large brown paper bag whose crumpled appearance showed it had been much used.

'The rocking chair belonged to Mrs Masters,' said Mrs Cooper, 'and now it's yours.'

'Oh, I couldn't . . .' Joan began.

'Yes, you can, and you will,' Cordelia said in her calm voice. 'I used to sit in it when I was nursing Emily. Now it's your turn to make use of it.'

'Are you sure?' Joan whispered.

'It's a great pleasure to pass it on to you.' Cordelia smiled at her. Her smile always looked cool and restrained compared to other people's, but that didn't mean she was a cold person.

'The velvet cushions came from Darley Court,' said Persephone.

'You're most welcome to them, my dear,' said Miss Brown.

'Look at the patchwork,' Margaret urged, and Joan picked it up. It was a quilt for a baby's cot. 'We all helped make it.'

Joan ran her fingertips over the pretty patchwork design, holding out the quilt for Bob to admire. How lucky they were to have such good friends to care about them and wish them well in such a practical and helpful way.

'Don't forget to look in the bag,' said Dot.

The brown paper bag contained a selection of knitted baby clothes – matinee jackets, bootees and bonnets in a range of colours.

'You'll have the best-dressed baby in Withington,' said Mabel. 'We all made at least one thing, including Alison. She can't be here because of her shifts, but she sends her love.'

'Here,' said Mrs Cooper. 'You haven't tried the chair yet. Sit down.'

As Joan sat in it, feeling its gentle rock, her eyes filled and she felt almost light-headed. In that moment, she couldn't speak because the tears were too close.

'Thank you,' said Bob. 'Thank you all. This is – well, it's overwhelming. You're so kind. You gave us the perfect wedding reception – and now this.'

Joan reached for his hand and he squeezed hers. 'Yes.' She sniffed away the tears. 'You're the most wonderful friends we could possibly have. Thank you.'

She got up and went to where Cordelia was sitting. Bending, Joan hugged her, murmuring her thanks. After that, there were hugs and kisses all round, amid laughter.

'This is like getting married again,' said Bob. 'I kissed an awful lot of ladies that day too.'

Tony Naylor looked embarrassed. 'I'm sorry to intrude. I didn't know something special was happening this afternoon. I came to do the garden.'

'You're not intruding,' Mrs Grayson told him. 'We couldn't have you working outside while we're all in here celebrating.'

'Poor fellow,' Mabel murmured to Joan. 'We didn't expect to see him again after losing Colette, but he says that keeping on with Mrs Cooper's garden gives him something to do.'

Joan's heart reached out to the young widower. They all missed Colette deeply, but it was so much worse for Tony. No wonder he needed to keep himself occupied.

Mrs Bryant pressed Joan's hand. 'Many congratulations, love. Me and my husband dropped by without warning and ended up sharing your special celebration, so I hope you don't mind.'

'Of course not,' said Joan.

'The more the merrier,' said Bob.

Mrs Bryant looked misty-eyed. 'Well, it's a pleasure to be here. Me and our Jessie,' she glanced at her sister, 'we both wed lads who didn't have brothers and sisters. Me and Ernie were never blessed, unfortunately, so there were only Lizzie . . . Me and my big mouth.'

'Don't feel bad for mentioning Lizzie,' said Dot, slipping an arm around Mrs Cooper and giving her a squeeze. 'We always like to hear her name, don't we, chuck?'

'Aye,' said Mrs Cooper. She was still smiling, but the smile had vanished from her eyes.

Miss Brown attracted Joan and Bob's attention. 'The land girls will deliver the rocking chair for you in the horse and cart, so don't worry about getting it home.'

'Thank you,' said Joan. Leaving Bob talking to Miss Brown and Mrs Mitchell, she chatted with Mrs Cooper.

'Did you know I've taken on a woman to help me with Magic Mop?' asked Mrs Cooper.

'I'm pleased to hear it,' Joan said sincerely. 'Needing another cleaner is a sign of how pleased your clients are.'

'The lady is called Mrs Wadden and she's the mother of one of the girls Mabel works with.'

'Is someone taking my name in vain?' asked Mabel.

'I thought you were supposed to be out with Harry today,' said Joan.

'I just said that to throw you off the scent,' said Mabel. 'Are you going to put the kettle on, Mrs G? I'll come and give you a hand – and then I want to hear about your interview for the staff magazine, Joan.'

'We all want to hear about that,' said Dot.

'Not one word until I get back,' Mabel ordered Joan, 'or there'll be no tea and buns for you. Come on, Emily. You can help in the kitchen.'

Tony took the opportunity to slip outside and was soon to be seen, jacket off and sleeves rolled up, digging over the soil, a cigarette dangling from his lips.

'I'll go and lend a hand,' said Bob, seeing Joan watching Tony through the window.

'Me an' all.' Mr Bryant stood up. 'Then you ladies can relax and have a proper talk.'

Mabel, Emily and Mrs Grayson returned with trays and soon everyone had a cup of tea in the pretty china that belonged to Mrs Morgan, whose husband owned the house. The Morgans had decamped to North Wales for the duration.

'Brizo, here, boy.' Persephone patted her thigh and the dog went to sit beside her. She fondled his hairy ears. 'Tell us all about your interview, Joan. What questions were you asked?'

'I just talked about Brizo, really,' said Joan. 'He's the one the article is going to be about, not me. I explained how we got him and talked about his little ways.'

'You didn't tell them about the you-know-what?' asked Dot.

Joan grinned. 'I certainly did – and Brizo kindly demonstrated.'

'What's the you-know-what?' asked Margaret.

'Brizo-zo-zo-zo-zo,' chanted Joan, and Brizo lifted his head and howled, making them all laugh. 'When we go out for a walk and let him off the lead, he likes to run around us in circles to make sure we keep together, so I said that as well. But mainly the interview was about his charity work on the station.'

'When will it be published?' asked Persephone.

'Next month,' said Joan, 'or possibly not until the month after.'

'Did they take photographs?' asked Mrs Cooper.

'There were a few pictures of Brizo, including one of him wearing his collecting box on his back. They won't use all the photos. They just need several to choose from. And there was one of me and him together.'

'Did you have to pose?' asked Mabel.

'I didn't want to show off my bump, so we got Brizo to sit down and then I crouched behind, with one arm around him.'

'That sounds like a nice picture,' said Dot. 'You'll have to get in touch with the magazine and ask if you can have a copy.'

'Were you in uniform?' asked Cordelia, and when Joan nodded, she added, 'That would make a lovely souvenir of your time on the railways.'

Mrs Grayson lifted the lid off the earthenware teapot. 'Shall I put the kettle on again? I'm sure we can squeeze some more flavour out of these leaves.'

'I'll do it.' Margaret got up. She smiled an invitation at Joan, so Joan got up too.

'I hope you aren't intending to do any work, chuck,' said Mrs Cooper. 'You're the guest of honour.'

'And you're lovely to make such a fuss of me, but mainly I'm your ex-lodger and I know my way around the kitchen.'

When Joan accompanied Margaret from the room, she was surprised when Margaret pushed the kitchen door closed behind them.

'Is something wrong?' Joan asked. She was very fond of Margaret.

'I was wondering if we could have a talk – not now, but soon. It's important.'

'Of course.'

'It's nothing for you to worry about,' Margaret said quickly. 'I just need to talk something over to help me sort out my thoughts.'

The door opened and Mabel appeared with an empty plate. 'Any more buns? Sorry, am I interrupting?'

'Not at all,' said Joan as Margaret turned away to pick up the kettle from the stove and take it into the scullery.

What did Margaret want to discuss with her? She'd seen worry in her friend's eyes. But when Margaret returned with the full kettle, she smiled at her and gave her hand a secret squeeze, so whatever it was, it seemed Margaret wanted to reassure her that she mustn't fret over it. Good. That left Joan free to concentrate on what a wonderful afternoon this was, filled with warmth and love. How lucky she was to have such thoughtful, caring friends.

When Joan and Bob were getting ready to leave, Mrs Cooper lent them a pillowcase to put the baby clothes and the little patchwork quilt in. There were lots of goodbye hugs, then they set off, turning at the gate to wave at the smiling friends who had spilled out of the front door to see them on their way.

After exclaiming over what an enjoyable afternoon it had been and how kind everybody was, the two of them fell silent.

'Are you thinking what I'm thinking?' Joan asked.

'I expect so.' Bob smiled at her. He had such a kind smile. 'It's the right thing to do.'

So they went to Torbay Road, where Gran was pleased to see them. Not that she made a fuss, she never did, though it was even more obvious than usual after the loving generosity in Wilton Close.

In the parlour, they told Gran about the rocking chair, then Joan took out the contents of the pillowcase to show off.

'You have kind friends,' said Gran. 'Capable, too. This is good craftsmanship.'

Joan fingered a matinee coat. 'I can't get over how tiny everything is.'

'I've done some knitting for the baby too,' said Gran, 'but I've concentrated on bigger clothes that he can grow into.'

'He?' joked Bob. 'Have you been reading your tea leaves, Mrs Foster?'

'He or she,' said Gran.

'Thank you for doing the knitting,' said Joan. 'May we see what you've made?'

Gran got to her feet and went to the sideboard, taking out a small pile of garments.

'Here,' she said.

'They're lovely,' said Joan, looking through them. 'Oh, look, Bob, this one's got a little hood. Thank you, Gran.'

'You've been busy,' said Bob.

'Some of the neighbours are knitting for the baby as well,' said Gran. 'They remember you when you were a baby.'

'Everyone is so kind,' said Joan.

'Everybody wants to help when there's a baby on the way,' said Gran.

'All the more so in wartime, I imagine,' said Bob.

'Have you heard back from the billeting officer?' asked Joan. 'It was a while ago that he came round – during the snow.'

'I have a Miss Wentworth moving in on Tuesday,' said Gran. 'It's a temporary billet, just for a few weeks. I asked for someone temporary.'

'While you get used to it.' Joan nodded understandingly. She and Bob left shortly afterwards, adding Gran's baby clothes to their gifts.

'It won't be easy for Gran to have a stranger in the house,' said Joan. 'She's a very private person.' A new thought struck her. 'Or is it that circumstances have forced her to be private?'

Bob laughed. 'If you're asking if I can imagine your gran in her younger days joining in with a good old knees-up and a sing-song, the answer's no.'

But Joan couldn't help wondering. Before the family tragedy happened, what sort of person had Gran been?

CHAPTER SEVENTEEN

It was noisy in the canteen. The sounds bounced off the walls, adding to the volume of the chatter and making the footsteps on the polished floorboards seem sharp. Even the tiniest clink of cutlery against a plate had an extra *ting*. The aroma in the air that day was savoury and oniony, with a hint of cheese as you passed the pudding section of the long serving-counter. The soup of the day was potato and the main courses were either corned-beef rissoles and vegetables or a vegetable casserole. For pud, the choice was raisin pudding or a cheese muffin.

Alison was on serving duty. She wore a white overall and a white cap beneath which she had put her hair into a snood, which was apparently one of the rules Miss Chambers had brought in when she was put in charge of the canteen. Some of the women wore hairnets – and that was the rule, really: hairnets for women serving food – but Alison wouldn't be caught dead in one of those. She wore a snood made from quite a chunky wool, just so that there could be no doubt that it was a snood and not a heavy-duty hairnet.

Apart from the surprising effort involved in standing still for hours on end, Alison quite liked serving. It was far more enjoyable than being on washing-up duty. Most folk who came into the canteen were polite, friendly even, though a few had a high opinion of themselves and barely glanced at the staff serving their meals. Even their thank-yous were automatic. At first, Alison had felt like pointing out that she was a grammar-school girl, with a School

Certificate to her name, and that she had trained in office work and had now been selected to learn about a variety of roles on the railway because she had been singled out as having potential . . . but by this time, it had long ceased to rile her. If some folk were snooty, so what? It said more about them than it did about her, if they looked down their noses at people in 'lowly' jobs.

Alison served the carrot-and-swede mash that went with the rissoles, which were being served, on her left, by middle-aged Mrs Laider. On Alison's right, giggly Miss Richards was in charge of winter greens. Alison gave every customer a smile, but not too big a smile. She had found out that some men couldn't tell the difference between being pleasant because it was part of your job and being pleasant because you were in the market for a boyfriend. She had been asked out several times when she'd started working in the canteen. There was one gap-toothed chap who had been persistent and she had grown to dread spotting him in the queue, wishing she could hide under the counter until he passed by.

In the end, Mrs Laider had told him bluntly, 'Knock it off, lad. She's spoken for.'

The young man had blushed deep red and had barely waited for his meal to be dished up.

Alison felt embarrassed too, but at the same time it was a relief. 'Thanks. He was becoming a bit of a pest.'

'Why didn't you just tell him you had a boyfriend?' asked Mrs Laider.

'Because that shouldn't matter,' said Alison. 'Because if I'm not interested, that should be enough.'

Mrs Laider was unimpressed. 'Huh. You don't know much about men, do you?'

Alison had felt needled by that comment, but the problem had been solved, which was the main thing. After that, she'd reined in her smile.

Now, as she dished up the carrot and swede onto plate after plate, she glanced along the queue towards the doors to see if there was likely to be any let-up soon – and there in the doorway was Miss Rachel Chambers, talking to a pair of suited men and a woman with cherries on her hat. Rachel – she wasn't Miss Chambers in Alison's mind any more, not after Saturday night – was evidently showing those people around. One elegant hand performed a graceful movement, indicating the dining room in all its glory.

Rachel wore the same jacket she'd worn the first time Alison had seen her, but this time with a matching skirt and a pink blouse with small white spots and a frothy jabot. She wore pearly-pink earrings and the brooch on her lapel had a discreet sparkle. It was impossible not to admire her appearance, which was both professional and feminine. Alison had always been good with accessories and finishing touches, but Rachel Chambers was an expert.

Well, she would take her little entourage off somewhere else in a minute, and good riddance. But no. The elegant hand that had invited her guests to look over the dining room was now ushering them towards the queue. Alison groaned inwardly. Oh, that was just what she needed – her in her overall, dishing up carrot and swede for the beautiful Rachel Chambers, Joel's former girlfriend. Please let her opt for the vegetable stew and walk past the other veg on offer, but no, Rachel had to choose the corned-beef rissoles. Mrs Laider took the next plate off the heated pile and used a wide fish slice to place two rissoles on it, handing the plate to Alison, who took it, using a mitt to protect her fingers.

'We meet again.' Rachel appeared in front of her.

'Carrot-and-swede mash?' Alison offered.

'Yes, please.'

Alison served a helping and passed the plate along to Miss Richards. This was emphatically not the way she wanted Joel's old girlfriend to see her – but why not? It wasn't as though Rachel was unaware of Alison's job here, and providing tasty, nutritious meals for hundreds of people a day was important. And it didn't matter in the slightest that Rachel and her visitors sat at a table adjacent to the counter; neither did it matter that they were directly in Alison's line of sight.

'What are you scowling at?' asked Mrs Laider.

'I'm not scowling.' Alison smoothed her features and dished up carrot and swede to the next person.

When Rachel's group finished their meal, they loaded their trays with used crockery and carried them over to the wheeled shelving units for the staff to clear away. Rachel escorted the others to the doors and there was a small pantomime of her pointing to something or somewhere outside the room and waving them through the doors before she turned back. Oh, crikey, what now? Well, it couldn't be anything to do with Alison.

But it was. With a beguiling smile and a murmured, 'Excuse me. I promise I'll be just one moment,' Rachel inserted herself into the queue in front of Alison and Mrs Laider. 'That was a delicious meal. Thank you.' She addressed Mrs Laider as if she personally had cooked it. Then she looked at Alison. 'Miss Lambert, if you could come to see me in the private room at – four o'clock, shall we say?' Then, to the two people she was standing between, she said, 'Thank you,' and slipped away.

Well! What was that about?

'Have you done something wrong?' asked Miss Richards.

'Not that I know of,' said Alison, pretending not to notice the glances coming her way from people in the queue. They would all be aware of who Rachel Chambers was. Alison lifted her chin. She didn't want anyone speculating about her being in hot water.

At the end of her shift, she shed her overall and white cap and took off her snood, shaking out her hair before she gave it a brush. She wasn't going to be in trouble for wearing a snood instead of a hairnet, was she? No. Such a thing wouldn't be nearly important enough for an interview in the private room.

It would be a good idea to arrive first. The private room was a sort of no-man's-land, so by getting there first, she could choose where to sit. It was a small way of asserting herself. Rachel had kept her in a humble job ever since she'd come to Leeds, something that Alison might or might not have deserved, and she wanted to show it hadn't broken her spirit. Or maybe Rachel had left her in the kitchens and never given her another thought.

At a quarter to four, Alison went to the private room and slipped inside, only to stop dead as two faces turned towards her in surprise. Rachel was already there with a middle-aged woman, who looked distressed.

'Oh – I'm sorry,' said Alison. 'I didn't realise.'

'If you wouldn't mind . . .' said Rachel.

Alison retreated, kicking herself for her mistake. It hadn't occurred to her that the room might be in use. It was the sort of mistake an office junior might make, not a girl in her twenties who considered herself to be experienced in the workplace. She retreated along the corridor and waited.

Shortly before four o'clock, the door opened and Rachel showed the woman out. She looked more composed now, as she thanked Rachel and went on her way.

'You may come in now,' Rachel said to Alison, and disappeared back inside, leaving Alison to follow.

'I apologise for walking in like that.' Determined to get in the first word, Alison spoke the moment she crossed the threshold. 'It was thoughtless of me. I don't normally do things like that.'

'We'll say no more about it. Have a seat.' Sitting in one of the armchairs, Rachel put on her spectacles and reached for some papers on the table. She glanced through them, then removed her glasses and put the papers down. 'I'm pleased with your performance, Miss Lambert. You have pulled your weight, so I've decided to give you the opportunity to spend some time on the other side of the fence, so to speak, seeing how things are run.'

'Thank you, Miss Chambers.'

'You can start by observing me in my role as deputy lady almoner. It isn't strictly what you were sent here for, but I'm sure you'll find it interesting. Do you know what the almoner's office does?'

'In general terms, yes.'

'I'll be happy to show you in detail. I intend to involve you in the pie scheme as well.'

Alison smiled, starting to relax. 'Now that I do know about.'

It was a national scheme through which nutritious pies were provided at reasonable prices in agricultural areas, so that farmworkers, land girls and others could be sure of a decent meal.

'I'll arrange for you to go out on one of the pie runs for a week or two.' Rachel smiled. 'You ought to see the scenery when it's not under six feet of snow.'

Alison drew in a deep breath, savouring the moment. This was more like it! This was the sort of thing she had expected when she was sent here. Information, variety, responsibility.

'You shall spend tomorrow and Wednesday in the canteen, so they aren't left up a gum tree,' said Rachel. 'Then you'll be in the almoner's office at the infirmary with me on Thursday, Friday and Saturday.'

'Oh.' Alison couldn't hide her disappointment. 'I was meant to have this weekend off. I had intended to go home.'

'I see,' said Rachel. 'It's up to you, of course. You could come to the almoner's office next week instead – no, not next week. That isn't convenient and neither is the week after.' She spread her hands. In anyone else, it might be a gesture of helplessness. Coming from Rachel, it was an intriguing mixture of charm and challenge. 'There we are. Either you put off your weekend away or you postpone coming to the lady almoner's. Which is it to be?'

Joan walked home from the shops feeling pleased with herself because she had got two nice pieces of cod; she would make a fish pie tomorrow. The moment she opened the front door, the kitchen door opened and Sheila appeared, beckoning her. Puzzled, Joan went into the kitchen. As she took off her coat and hat, she couldn't help glancing around. It was second nature now. For all Sheila's good points, she wasn't the tidiest person. She and Joan each had a different cupboard-top for preparing their meals and Sheila's was routinely invisible beneath a mishmash of knives, pans and jars that hadn't been put away. Joan tried hard to feel that it was none of her business what Sheila's work surface looked like, but sometimes her fingers itched to clear away for her.

Not that it would make any odds if she did. Sheila seemed to spread untidiness wherever she went. She often left her coat hanging on the back of a kitchen chair or kicked off her shoes at the foot of the stairs. But she kept the kitchen table clear of mess, and that was something. Joan knew her well enough to guess how it must have looked before she and Bob lived here, with the milk bottle in the middle, and a wet spoon dumped in the sugar bowl, and probably a make-up bag and yesterday's newspaper, not to mention Jimmy's latest piece of shrapnel. These days, the milk was in a jug that was put away on the marble slab after use and the table was always tidy, with the cruet set Joan and Bob had been given as a wedding present in the middle, next to the ashtray. Joan would have dearly loved to move the ashtray elsewhere, but everybody had ashtrays all over their houses and removing one from the kitchen would be tantamount to saying the kettle shouldn't live on the stove.

'You've got a visitor,' said Sheila, turning her head away to blow smoke not quite over her shoulder.

'You've let someone into my room?'

'She said she's your grandmother – and she didn't look like the sort of person you say no to.'

That was Gran, all right. But why had she come? She had never visited Sheila's house before.

'How long has she been here?' Joan asked.

'Half an hour.'

'Thanks for the warning.'

Joan ran upstairs to put away her outdoor things and change into her slippers. If she and Bob had a place of their own, maybe they wouldn't need to stuff their coats into the hanging cupboard.

Downstairs, she entered the sitting room to find Gran sitting bolt upright in an armchair, still in her coat and hat.

'Gran – this is a surprise.' Joan bent to kiss her cheek. 'You haven't taken your coat off.'

'I'm not one to do that until I'm invited to.'

'You should at least have got the fire going.' Joan threw on a couple of lumps of coal and set to work with the poker, stirring up the fire she had banked down that morning. 'Take your coat off while I pop the kettle on.'

'I don't want to take up your time. I expect you want to get Bob's tea ready.'

166

'He won't be home for ages yet. This is a special occasion, your first visit. We're having savoury vegetable fritters. I could add more potato and then it would stretch to enough for three.'

'There's no need, though it's a kind gesture to an unexpected visitor.'

Joan hurried to make a pot of tea. When she carried the tray through, Gran was still in her coat, though she had unfastened it.

'The room will soon warm up,' Joan promised.

'I shan't stay. I have a proposition to put to you.'

'That sounds important.'

'I know we haven't seen eye to eye for some time,' said Gran.

About to say, 'That's putting it mildly,' Joan pressed her lips together to stop the words popping out.

'But I hope you won't dismiss my idea out of hand.' Gran stopped, and was that a flicker of uncertainty that fluttered across her strong features? 'I don't know how settled you are here, but – but my house is bigger, and if you and Bob would like to move in, in order to have more space for the baby, then I think that would be appropriate. The dining room could become my bedroom and you could have the whole of upstairs. We'd share the kitchen and bathroom.'

Joan felt almost breathless with surprise. 'I had no idea what you were going to come out with, but I never expected that.'

'It's the reason I'm having a temporary lodger,' said Gran. 'I took the liberty of telling the billeting officer my granddaughter and her family might be moving in with me.'

Joan shook her head in disbelief. 'That was . . . quite a liberty. Why didn't you say this when we called round?'

'Had I known you were coming, I might have. As it was, I felt unprepared. Besides, this is better discussed between ourselves. No disrespect to Bob.'

'I don't know what to say.'

'Don't say anything – not yet,' said Gran. 'This isn't about you and me or anything that has happened in the past. It's about providing for the baby. I know all about doing that in difficult circumstances. If you feel you can't return to the house, I would understand that, but if you and Bob want to talk it over, the offer's there.' She rose, straightening her hat and coat, even though they didn't need it. 'Don't get up. I'll see myself out.'

As Gran quietly left the room, shock sent Joan's heartbeat racing – shock, indignation and a rush of anger. How dare Gran . . . ? How *dare* she? After everything she had done, all the pretence, all the *lies*. She had spent years maligning Joan and Letitia's mother, years making out their father was some sort of saint, when the truth was – the truth was . . .

Gran had brought them up believing that Estelle, their mother, had run away with her lover, leaving poor darling Daddy to die of a broken heart. This was the secret they had never been allowed to tell anyone: that their mother had abandoned her family to run off with her fancy man. But the real secret was far worse. The truth, which Joan had uncovered last summer, was that Daddy had committed a terrible crime. Yes, Estelle had had a lover, and maybe she'd been going to run away with him, but Daddy had found out and – and he had strangled Estelle to death, a crime for which he had paid the ultimate price. Would Estelle have disappeared with her man friend if she'd had the chance? No one knew what she had intended, because no one knew the man's identity and he had never come forward, no doubt thanking his lucky stars that he'd been spared involvement in the scandal. Maybe he'd been married, too, and had gone slinking back to his unsuspecting wife.

And Gran had brought up Letitia and Joan to believe it was all Estelle's fault – that she really had run away, leaving Daddy so desolate with unhappiness that he had lost the will to live. As if that wasn't bad enough, she hadn't expressed so much as an iota of shame or remorse when Joan had found out the truth and confronted her. As far as Gran was concerned, it was better for the girls to think their mother had abandoned them than to know that their father was a murderer. Nothing Joan could say had swayed her from this position.

And now Gran thought Joan might actually return to her childhood home and live with her. As if!

But even as the indignation pounded through her, the old ache started up inside her chest and she wrapped her arms around her stomach, anxious to protect her precious baby. All this time, her happiness with Bob had kept her safely cocooned, but now her heart thumped in a slow, heavy beat as the memories crowded around her – the memories, and the new knowledge she had gained last year. Return to Torbay Road? She shut her eyes and didn't want to open them again.

Lying cuddled up in bed, Joan and Bob talked long into the night about Gran's astounding offer.

'I don't know where to start,' said Joan. 'There are so many thoughts bashing about in my head.'

'That's hardly surprising,' said Bob in his usual kindly way. He had always understood and Joan found comfort in that now.

'I never imagined being asked to go back,' she said.

'It's the baby,' said Bob. 'Babies change a lot of things. They can bring people together.'

'I'm not sure I want to be brought together with Gran. Sorry. That was a horrid thing to say. I feel all churned up.

Things have never been easy with Gran, but these past months, since we got married, we seem to have reached a state of . . .'

'Armed neutrality?' Bob suggested.

Joan couldn't help smiling. 'We're not as bad as that.' She tried to quantify it. 'We're civil to one another, and sometimes we visit Letitia together.'

'That's important.'

'Yes, it is. Letitia was always the one who held us together as a family – and she's still doing it.'

'Maybe the baby will do it in future,' said Bob.

'I hadn't thought of it that way,' said Joan. 'Maybe it will.' She moved restlessly. 'But though our baby is all about the future, I can't forget the past. I'll never forget what Gran did, the lies she told. I can't believe I didn't throw her invitation straight back in her face.'

'You were too surprised,' said Bob. 'From the way you described it, it sounds like Mrs Foster left pretty quickly afterwards.'

'Probably so I couldn't say no on the spot.'

'Very likely. Is that what you want to do? Say no?'

'I feel we ought to as a matter of principle,' said Joan.

'Then that's what we'll do.'

Oh, how lucky she was to be married to this man. Joan snuggled closer, resting her head on Bob's chest. 'You'll back me up whatever I want, won't you?'

'Of course I will. We'll say "No, thanks" to Mrs Foster and carry on looking.'

Joan propped herself up on her elbow, looking at Bob. 'But that's the trouble, isn't it? We haven't found anywhere else – and now Gran has come along with the offer of the whole of the upstairs of her house. It's what we've dreamed of – and that makes me feel unprincipled, because in spite of everything, I do feel tempted, even after the way Gran brought up Letitia and me to believe all those lies about our mother. What sort of person does that make me?'

'You're a mother-to-be and you want the best for your baby,' said Bob. 'Life in wartime is all about compromises and making the best of what you've got.'

'But we aren't making the best of it, are we?' said Joan. 'Or we'd be happy to stay here at Sheila's.'

'With the baby coming, we need a place that feels like our own. There's nothing wrong with that,' Bob reassured her. 'And I'm not specifically talking about your gran's house when I say it would be good to live in Chorlton. That's where you're from, so you know it inside out. You'd be happy there, and you'd be close to our friends in Wilton Close. They'd be delighted to have us near and they'd give you a lot of support. I have to say, I like the thought of that. And we'd be closer to my folks, too, if we moved to Chorlton.'

'But do we want all that so much that we're prepared to live with Gran in order to get it?' Joan lay down again, shifting a little so that her face was nestled under Bob's chin. 'Shall I tell you what worries me most about living there?'

'That Mrs Foster would rule the roost?'

'No. I've grown up a lot since I found out the truth about my parents and I'll never let Gran get the upper hand again.'

'So what would be the worst thing?' Bob asked.

'If Gran thought that us living there meant that I had accepted what she did. I couldn't bear it if she thought that. I'll *never* accept it.'

Alison found working in the lady almoner's office deeply interesting. She had opted – of course – to postpone her weekend away, aware of how bad it would have looked had she chosen it over this opportunity at work. She knew how disappointed Mum and Dad must be, but they would understand, as would Joel and her friends. The war effort came first. Compared to the sacrifices so many women and girls were making, with husbands and sweethearts overseas for months on end, if not years, her missing one weekend at home was nothing.

The lady almoner's role was to enquire into a patient's financial position to determine whether they should be asked to contribute to their treatment. Many patients who could afford to do so paid into special schemes that would make a payment if hospital care was required.

'My dad subscribes to the Hospital Saturday Fund,' said Alison.

'I wish more people did,' said Rachel, 'or to be more accurate, I wish more people could afford to. In the almoner's office, we also visit patients at home after they've been discharged, to see how they're getting on, and we provide advice about things like hygiene and nutrition and alert the local doctors and district nurses to situations we think they ought to be aware of.'

As well as learning about the work of the almoner's office, Alison picked up a juicy piece of gossip about Rachel, though she had no way of knowing how accurate it was.

During a quiet tea break, Miss Finch, one of the clerks, asked how she was finding things in the lady almoner's office.

'It's fascinating,' said Alison, 'and so busy. I'm surprised Miss Chambers has the time to oversee the Park Square canteen and kitchens as well.'

'She might not if she was an ordinary human being like the rest of us,' said Miss Finch.

Alison wasn't sure how to respond to that. 'She obviously works hard.'

'Oh, she does that all right.' Miss Finch's tone didn't suggest a compliment. She sat forward. 'Would you care to hear how she got the extra job?'

Alison knew she should say, 'No, thanks.' She knew she should draw back, but the temptation of hearing about Joel's former girlfriend proved too much. She nodded.

'The lady almoner put her forward for it,' said Miss Finch. 'It's most unusual to have a deputy lady almoner. We only have one because this is a big hospital and we're so busy. The deputy's post was created at the beginning of the war. The idea was that the deputy would support the lady almoner, but it hasn't necessarily worked out quite that way. Miss Chambers is highly efficient. The first thing she did when she arrived was to update some of our clerical systems. It caused quite a stir, but to give her her due, everything runs far more smoothly now.'

'That's a good thing,' commented Alison.

'Yes, but she rattled a few cages, you might say, especially the lady almoner's. When the war ends, we won't need a deputy lady almoner any more.' Miss Finch stopped speaking and looked squarely at Alison.

A tingling sensation pattered across Alison's skin. 'You don't mean to say that Miss Chambers has her eye on the lady almoner's position?'

Miss Finch shrugged. 'So people say. That's why the lady almoner got her shunted over to Park Square, to keep her occupied elsewhere, only it hasn't had the desired effect, because Miss Efficiency is now holding down both jobs successfully. She's going to come out of this looking highly capable, if you ask me. And when the war is over . . .'

'Goodness,' murmured Alison.

'I rather think,' said Miss Finch, 'that what Miss Chambers wants, Miss Chambers gets.'

173

It came as no surprise to hear that Rachel was efficient and if she had indeed improved the office's clerical methods, that was something to be admired. It showed that hers had been a good appointment . . . or did it show that the lady almoner herself was set in her ways? Was the lady almoner right to fear for her future?

Or, of course, the whole story could be pure gossip of the worst sort, Alison realised. She really ought to give Rachel the benefit of the doubt.

Ought to.

At midday on Saturday, Rachel suggested she and Alison go together for a bite to eat.

'Not in Park Square,' she said. 'I'll show you a little place I go to sometimes.'

Rachel's 'little place' was tucked away down a side street. Above a pretty bow window, the words *Tabitha's Tea Shop* were painted in fancy lettering.

'It used to be rather charming before the war,' said Rachel, 'but now, with shortages and rationing, it's become a glorified café, but they do their best, and a very good best it is too.'

Soon they were seated and the waitress had taken their order. Alison looked round at the cotton tablecloths and basic white crockery.

'You have to imagine it with lace-edged linen and the prettiest china,' said Rachel. 'They had to put it all into storage.'

'It's clean and pleasant,' said Alison. 'I'm sorry.' She pulled a face. 'That sounds like damning with faint praise.'

'Not at all,' Rachel replied. 'Clean and pleasant is all you need at the moment. I wanted to bring you here as a little treat to make up for doing you out of going to Manchester for the weekend.'

'You didn't,' said Alison. 'It was just the way things worked out.'

Rachel nodded approvingly. 'Good for you, taking it on the chin. I knew you'd be a good sport about it, Alison – may I call you Alison? And I'm Rachel, though not at work, of course. But when it's just the two of us, like now, in a social setting, I think first names should be the order of the day, don't you? After all, we've got our darling Joel in common, haven't we?'

CHAPTER EIGHTEEN

Joan had invited Margaret round on Saturday afternoon to talk about whatever was on her mind and stay for tea afterwards, by which time Bob and Jimmy would be home from an inter-schools football competition that Bob had been roped into helping with.

'Will you still come and play with me after you move?' Jimmy had asked.

'It depends on where we move to,' said Bob, 'but I promise you haven't seen the last of me.'

Although he was being brave about it, Jimmy was upset that they wanted to leave, which made Joan feel guilty, but she had to put her own child before Sheila's. Sheila didn't seem too bothered one way or the other about their going, but Joan had always found her a difficult person to read. Although there was no suggestion of ill-feeling in the house, the two of them hadn't become friends. Joan found Sheila affable and had got used to her flippancy. They rubbed along together well enough and Sheila had certainly made full use of Joan and Bob's willingness to mind Jimmy, but no real closeness had grown out of it, which Joan knew was Sheila's choice rather than her own. Maybe having her mother-in-law's friend under her roof had made Sheila want to keep her distance.

Dot had popped round to say, 'Our Jimmy told me you're looking for somewhere else to live, chick. It's understandable, with a baby on the way, but we'll all miss you.'

'We might not find anywhere,' Joan had pointed out.

'Well, I hope you do, if it's what you want. There are plenty of folk shacking up together these days and it must be a strain. If you find somewhere that feels right, grab it with both hands.'

Now Joan prepared as much of the tea as she could in advance of Margaret's arrival. She baked potatoes in their jackets and fried some chopped vegetables. Then she scooped out the flesh from the potatoes and mixed it with the veg before stuffing it all back into the jackets, ready to be heated through before being served. For afters, she had made carrot scones. She put everything on the shelf in the larder, under fly nets.

Just in time too. Brizo's excited barking alerted her and she went to open the door. Margaret was leaning her bicycle against the garden wall. She removed her headscarf and shook out her hair. She had pretty hair that held its shape well. From the wicker basket on the front of her bike, she removed the russet jumper with the cream stripe that her sister had knitted her for Christmas. Joan took her jacket from her as she came inside and Margaret draped the jumper around her slender shoulders. The tough physical work of engine cleaning had honed her, adding a confidence to the way she moved.

Margaret crouched to fuss Brizo, then rose and surprised Joan by kissing her cheek.

'Thanks for letting me come.'

'You don't need an invitation. We're friends. Come and sit down. I'll put the kettle on if you like, or I've got a bottle of lime cordial.'

'I don't remember the last time I had that.'

'Make yourself comfy and I'll bring it in.'

She fetched two glasses of cordial and returned to the sitting room, where Brizo appeared to be under the impression that Margaret had come round specially to admire him eating a bone.

'You've put the rocking chair by the window,' Margaret observed. 'I expected it to be beside the fire.'

'I thought it'd be nice to watch the children playing outside while I'm knitting.'

'I can't imagine not going to work every day,' said Margaret.

'I know what you mean. I started work the day after I finished school, when I was fourteen. Letitia started at the same time. She was a year older, but she went to grammar school, so she stayed on until she was fifteen and did her School Certificate.'

'Clever girl,' Margaret remarked.

'She was – and funny and kind. She was the best sister ever.'

Margaret smiled. 'I've got one of those too, a best sister ever. What's it like being a full-time housewife? I bet you don't miss having to drag yourself out of bed at some unearthly hour of the morning to go on the early shift.'

'But I have a husband who has to get up for the early shift, so I still have to get up. Bob would be happy for me to have a lie-in, but I wouldn't dream of not making his breakfast.'

'It's what marriage is about. Looking after one another. My mum said that.'

'She was right.' Joan took a refreshing sip. 'I don't want to rush you, but you said you wanted to discuss something and it sounded important. We don't want the boys coming home in the middle of it.'

Margaret folded her arms and then unfolded them. She looked away and then back again. 'I hardly know where to start.'

The change in her from composure to anxiety concerned Joan. It just showed – no matter how someone appeared on the surface, you didn't know what was going on underneath. She was about to offer reassurance, but Margaret spoke first.

'I feel bad about telling you.'

'Why? It's what friends are for. It's like what your mum said about married couples taking care of one another. Friends do that too.'

'What I mean is, you're in the family way, so you shouldn't be upset.'

'Don't be daft. I've never felt healthier. And the only thing that's likely to upset me is you choosing not to confide in me. I know exactly what my gran would say in this situation. She'd say, "Don't prevaricate, Margaret." So stop making excuses and talk to me.'

Margaret looked at her hands for a few moments, then released a long breath and met Joan's gaze. After a false start or two, she said, 'It's to do with . . . with what happened that time in our cellar when you were on first-aid duty.'

Joan hoped she hid her surprise. She hadn't had any idea what to expect, but what she felt was more than surprise. It was shock. Before the war, she and Margaret had both worked at Ingleby's, though in different departments. During the Phoney War, they'd become fire-watching colleagues. Then Joan had left Ingleby's to join the railways and hadn't seen Margaret again until . . .

Until one night in the early summer of 1940, when, in her capacity as a first-aider, Joan had climbed down into the cellar of a badly damaged house to tend to a girl known to be trapped down there. That girl had been Margaret and she'd had an ankle injury, though that was the least of her problems, because that night she suffered a miscarriage. Margaret, an unmarried girl, had had a miscarriage. Although Joan knew she had to be professional and detached, she had felt deeply shocked. She hadn't known Margaret was that sort of girl. Afterwards, as if things hadn't been bad enough for poor Margaret, her father, having been given the news by an ARP man, had berated her loudly and at great length as she was carried away on a stretcher.

The next time Joan had seen Margaret had been last spring in the engine sheds at Manchester Victoria. At first, Margaret had pretended not to see her, but Joan had persisted and Margaret had confided the rest of her story, describing how she and her father had been billeted on a neighbour, who hadn't been pleased to have a harlot under her roof. Nor had Margaret's father forgiven her for her fall from grace, and finally Margaret had left the Alexandra Park area where she had grown up and had moved into a grotty bedsit, from which Mrs Cooper and Mrs Grayson had rescued her towards the end of last year.

Now Margaret blushed deeply. As her gaze fell away from Joan's, Joan left her armchair and moved across to take her friend's hand.

'Here,' said Joan, 'let's sit together on the sofa, shall we? Then you can tell me what's worrying you.'

What on earth could it be? What could possibly relate back to . . . that?

'It's Joel,' said Margaret.

'*Joel*? Alison's Joel?'

'Before he was Alison's Joel, he was my Joel. Well, I thought he was. He left me high and dry. He – he got me pregnant and left me high and dry.'

'Joel?' Joan repeated. 'Joel did?'

'Please don't say it in that tone of voice, as if you don't believe me.'

'Of course I believe you,' said Joan. 'Of course I do. It's just . . .'

'I know. He's good-looking and educated and clever and funny and everybody likes him. If villains would all wear top hats and long black cloaks and go around twirling their moustaches, life would be much simpler.'

Joan said softly, 'He was the father of your baby?'

Margaret nodded. At first she seemed too full of emotion to speak, then she tightened her free hand into a fist and huffed out a breath. 'I thought the world of him, I honestly did, or I'd never have . . . Mind you, the gin probably had something to do with it.'

Joan sucked in a sharp breath. 'He got you drunk?'

'No – no. In fairness, I did a pretty good job of that myself. We were at a party and people were getting sozzled. I'd never drunk like that before, but everyone else seemed to be knocking it back – all the girls were drinking freely, I mean – and as stupid as it sounds now, at the time it felt sophisticated. Anyway, one thing led to another, as the saying goes, and – and I woke up in the dead of night, lying on the bed where everyone had left their coats, and . . . Joel was beside me.'

'Oh, sweetheart,' Joan whispered.

'My head thumped and my mouth felt like I'd eaten a doormat, but I was stone-cold sober. I was utterly appalled to realise what I'd done. I flung on my clothes and crept out. When I got home, I sneaked inside with tears pouring down my face. My dad was out fire-watching, so I could have marched in quite safely, but I quaked with fear, as if he was going to burst out of his bedroom and haul me over the coals for being a stop-out. I stayed awake the rest of the night, feeling ashamed, but later on I started to tell myself that it takes two and that if I loved Joel, which I did, then it wasn't such a bad thing to have done . . . though, if he wanted to do it again, he'd have to wait until we were married.'

'What happened?' asked Joan.

'Nothing. Absolutely nothing. We had a prior arrangement to meet outside the cinema a couple of days later and he – he stood me up. I waited outside and he didn't come, so I kidded myself that we were meant to meet up inside, but he wasn't there either, so I went back out again. I waited and waited . . . I was there so long that another bloke tried to pick me up.'

'You poor love,' Joan whispered.

'It turned out Joel had gone. Cleared off. He'd got what he wanted and that was that. He didn't even have the guts to tell me it was over.'

Joan rubbed Margaret's arm. This went against everything she knew about Joel – but what did she know, really? The truth was she hardly knew him at all. He had all the qualities Margaret had attributed to him – looks, education, brains, a sense of humour, to which Joan would have added kindness and consideration – but the fact was, she had taken him at face value.

'Then I found out I was in the family way.' Margaret closed her eyes. A tear squeezed out of one corner. She sniffed and opened her eyes, their hazel colour seeming paler, as if washed clear by memories and distress. 'I had no choice but to go to the hospital and ask for him, but – but he'd gone to Leeds.'

Leeds! 'He really did run away, then.'

'He didn't go there just to escape from me, if I'm honest. He was due to be sent there anyway, but he went off without even saying goodbye. So that's how it happened, you see. That's how I ended up having a miscarriage in the cellar, without a ring on my finger.'

'Margaret, I'm so sorry that all this happened to you.'

'So am I,' said Margaret. 'It's cast a long shadow over my life. Dad and I are estranged now and I feel weighed down by this terrible secret that I've never confided in my sister, and we used to be so close. I even lost my job because of it, because I was so scared that one of our old neighbours might come shopping in Ingleby's and they'd see me there and complain that a respectable shop of such long standing shouldn't be employing the likes of me.'

'It's too horrid for words,' said Joan, 'but I'm grateful you came to work on the railways, because it brought us together.'

'You're a good friend.' Margaret gave her a watery smile. 'I was ready for you to turn your back on me for being no better than I should be, but you didn't. You took me into your circle of friends and introduced me to Mrs Cooper and Mrs Grayson. I owe you a lot.' She shook her head. 'Look at me, repaying you by dumping this problem on you.'

'You aren't dumping it on me. You've turned to me for help and I'm glad you have. You must have been twisting yourself inside out with worry.'

'I just don't know what to do.'

'You have to tell Alison. She needs to know what sort of man Joel is.'

'D'you think I don't know that?' exclaimed Margaret, with fire in her eyes. 'But I can't tell her about Joel without telling her about me, and it isn't the sort of thing you spread around. I'm only able to talk to you today because you already know about – about my miscarriage.'

That silenced Joan. Margaret was right. For an unmarried girl to find herself in the family way wasn't something she would ever live down if it became common knowledge. Look at the lengths Margaret had gone to in order to keep her secret.

'I feel I'll be a really bad friend if I don't tell Alison,' said Margaret, 'but every time I get to the point of deciding to tell her, I then think "But what about me?" After everything that's happened, after everything I've lost, it feels as though if I don't look after me, no one else is going to. I know how selfish that must sound.'

'It isn't selfish,' said Joan. 'I'm sorry. It never occurred to me how alone you must feel. I realised that was how you felt when we met up again last summer, but I imagined that with you now lodging with Mrs Cooper and being one of the group—'

'That all was right with the world? Sorry – that sounded cynical and ungrateful. My life is immeasurably better now. And you're right. I don't feel alone in a day-to-day sense. I love living in Wilton Close and I love my friends. You've all enriched my life and helped me to feel so much better. I really believed I'd put the past behind me. If Alison hadn't met Joel – but she did. I'd taken all the bad things and tucked them away in the back of my mind, where I thought I needn't look at them ever again, but now they've all come tumbling out all over the place. And it's worse this time. Before, I just had to – "just"! Hark at me, making it sound so simple. All I had to do was keep my secret. I found a new job and a new home – well, a new place to live, anyway. That awful bedsit was never a home. I told myself I'd made a fresh start and nobody would ever know about my past. Then I met up with you again and things started looking up.'

'Until now,' said Joan.

'Until now. This time, it isn't just about me. It's about Alison too – my friend. I want to do right by her – but I also feel strongly that I'm entitled to my privacy. I worked hard to put the bad things behind me and I don't want cats jumping out of bags now. Yet how can I not warn Alison? Just think what she's already been through. She was distraught when Paul left her – and on top of that, she had to cope with her sister's surprise wedding. Things were so hard for her for a long time. Seeing her recover has meant a lot to all of us. Imagine if I now tell her the truth about Joel. What would it do to her?'

184

Joan cast about inside her mind for something helpful to say. 'When I lived in Wilton Close, I grew close to Mabel. I assume you're closer to her now than you used to be, because of sharing a room.'

'Are you going to suggest I confide in her?'

'No, I'm building up to asking if you feel closer to Alison.'

Margaret laughed, a brittle sound. 'Close enough that when she was unsure about going out with Joel, I encouraged her, I actually encouraged her. I didn't know who he was at that point, of course, but if I hadn't done that . . .'

'You did it because you're a loving friend who wanted her to be happy. And you're still concerned about her now.'

'Yes, I am. I know I ought to warn her, but at the same time I can't bear to tell her my secret. I've never even told my sister and I'm closer to her than to anyone, especially since we lost Mum. Part of me feels angry with Alison for possibly being entitled to be told something I've never shared with Anna. And if I do tell her – *if* I tell her – as soon as I do, I lose control, because she'll act on what I say.'

'She won't tell the others,' Joan said at once.

'She might tell her sister. She might need someone to talk to and she'd see no harm in telling Lydia, because Lydia isn't one of us. She'd tell *her* sister something that I've withheld from *my* sister and I hate the thought of that.' Margaret dashed aside a tear. 'Even if Alison doesn't talk to anybody else, there's still one person she'd be certain to speak to: Joel. If I make this accusation against him, she's bound to ask him about it. Bound to!'

'It's not as though he could defend himself for getting what he wanted and then abandoning you.'

'No, but he could tell Alison a thing or two about me. He could say I got drunk. He didn't set out to get me drunk. It happened because I hadn't had gin before and I had too many. That doesn't put me in a good light, does it?

185

And – and when we . . . what I mean is, I was perfectly willing. That's another thing against me, because good girls aren't supposed . . . well, they just aren't supposed to. Joel could say all that about me and it'd be true.'

Joan pressed her lips together and thought hard. This was more complicated than she'd supposed. She wanted to do the right thing by Margaret, but she also wanted to do the right thing by Alison. Was it possible to do both? It felt as if it wasn't. Then an idea occurred to her and she brightened.

'I have a suggestion. Please think about it before you say no.'

'That sounds ominous,' said Margaret.

'I don't know what to suggest to help you through this. I think you and I will just talk our way round and round in circles, but . . .'

'Go on,' said Margaret.

'I can think of someone who might be able to help.'

'Who?'

'Dot. Wait – hear me out. You know how sensible and down to earth she is, and how kind. She has a way of seeing through to the other side of things. When I started on the railways, I had trouble with a creepy man I used to work for. I told Dot and Cordelia and they sorted it out for me. I don't know what they did, but he never bothered me again.'

'Hang on,' said Margaret. 'You said Dot. Now it's Dot and Cordelia.'

'I'm not suggesting confiding in both of them. Just Dot.'

'If I don't want to tell Alison, what makes you think I'll tell Dot?'

Joan had a moment of insight. 'Because she won't judge you and you're frightened that Alison will. You are frightened of that, aren't you? I guarantee that Dot won't, because firstly, she's got the biggest heart of anyone I've ever met, and secondly, she was in the club when she got married. She told me that herself – and I'm not breaking any confidences in telling you, because there were others there when she said it. She said it because she wanted to make sure I didn't end up in the same situation. She said I didn't have a mother of my own to warn me, so she'd taken it upon herself to say it.' Joan smiled. 'She once said we're all her daughters for the duration. Well, it seems to me that another of her wartime daughters needs a spot of guidance now. What d'you think? Could you face telling Dot?'

Margaret more than half hoped that Dot wouldn't be at home. She'd thought hard about Joan's suggestion of confiding in Dot. She'd wanted to refuse because she didn't want her secret to go any further, but at the same time she understood that Joan was right. So here they were now, on their way to Dot's house.

Heathside Lane, where Dot lived, had smaller dwellings than the road where Joan lodged with Sheila. The Heathside Lane houses were older, the road narrower. Dot occasionally mentioned having grown up in a poky little cottage with her numerous brothers and sisters, so coming here when she got married must have felt like a big step up in the world. Knowing Dot, she must be proud as punch to think of her son and his family now living somewhere larger.

Dot answered the door to them, her face breaking into a warm smile.

'This is unexpected. Come in.'

'Are you alone?' asked Joan.

'That's an odd question. As it happens, Reg is digging for victory in the back garden, but aside from that, it's just me. Park yourselves in the kitchen and I'll put the kettle on.'

'Actually, Dot,' said Joan, 'we can't stay very long. We have to be home when Bob and Jimmy get back.'

'Oh aye, the football competition.'

Margaret couldn't leave all the talking to Joan. It wouldn't be fair. 'We've come here for advice – well, I have. Joan's come with me to hold my hand.'

'Right, then,' said Dot. 'We'll go in the parlour. Reg might come barging into the kitchen. Sit yourselves down. What's this about, chick?' she asked Margaret.

Margaret suddenly felt ridiculously close to tears as all the worry of recent weeks rose up and washed over her, leaving her feeling weak and trembly. Might Dot truly be able to help her?

'Do you want me to explain to Dot?' Joan asked gently.

'No.' Margaret pulled herself together. 'It's my story and I should be the one to tell it.'

'Go on, then, love,' said Dot. 'I'm all ears.'

Margaret drew in a slow breath and released it before embarking upon her tale. She didn't dwell on the details. She seemed to have thought of little else ever since the evening back in January when she had seen Joel in Mrs Cooper's front room and now she just wanted to get it over with.

When she had finished, Dot said, 'Oh, my love.' She smiled sadly. 'Well, that answers one question.'

'What?' asked Margaret.

'I've sometimes wondered why a pretty girl like you doesn't have a boyfriend. It seemed a shame, because you're a lovely lass, but now . . . I don't suppose you've felt like getting involved again, have you? Sorry if I'm speaking out of turn.'

'It's all right,' said Margaret. 'You're correct, as it happens. I spent a long time looking the other way when other girls were eyeing up the men. To be honest, after I made friends with all of you and moved into Mrs Cooper's, I was starting to feel that my life was getting back on track and maybe there might be someone out there for me. When Alison confided in Mabel and me about Joel before Christmas, I even felt just the tiniest bit envious.'

Dot covered Margaret's hand with her own. 'Eh, you poor lass. What a lot you've had to go through.'

'What should she do now?' asked Joan. 'She needs to keep her secret, but she's also concerned about Alison.'

Dot gave them both a wry smile. 'And you think I'm the oracle who's going to come up with the perfect answer? I'll tell you right now. I don't think there is a perfect answer.'

Disappointment clenched in Margaret's stomach. She swallowed hard, realising how deeply she had been relying on Dot to come up with the advice she needed.

'I don't know how useful this will be, chick,' Dot said to her, 'but it's what springs to mind. Forget about Alison for the time being.'

'What?' Margaret and Joan said together.

'It seems to me,' said Dot, 'that the person you ought to speak to is Joel.'

CHAPTER NINETEEN

Waking before her alarm clock rang, Alison took a moment to stretch her limbs and squeeze her toes. So what if she was getting up at five for a six o'clock start at work? She felt uplifted. Now that she'd had a break from canteen and kitchen work, she felt better about things in general. Although she had applied herself to the peeling, prepping, serving, clearing away and washing-up with a good grace, the work had never really suited her, and though she had enjoyed the company of the other girls, especially Betty and Eddie, Mrs Laider had been something of a disappointment. Alison had hoped for another Dot, warm-hearted and commonsensical, or another Mrs Cooper, compassionate and practical. Mrs Laider's common sense was nothing if not practical, but she lacked the warmth of the other two women; nor did she have Dot's quick sense of humour.

Last week's experience in the almoner's office in the infirmary, while unrelated to railway work, had been most enjoyable. There had been something reassuring and comfortable about returning to an office environment, and learning about the patients and their personal circumstances had been deeply interesting and informative. Rachel had offered to let Alison accompany her on a future occasion when she visited patients at home to ascertain each family's ability to provide proper aftercare.

'Or not, as the case may be,' Rachel had said.

This week, Alison was due to work on the pie scheme. While this would involve plenty of peeling and prepping, that would be more than made up for by the promise of travelling around to deliver the pies to people scattered throughout the countryside.

She put on the tailored trousers Mum referred to as her trews because of the small tartan pattern in dark blue, and a lightweight jumper over her blouse. After the bitter winter temperatures, the spring was overcast and chilly but becoming discernibly milder. Alison smiled to herself. Good weather for driving around the countryside.

Of course, there was a lot more than that to the job. It called for an early start to get all the pies and pasties made.

She was assigned to a girl called Barbara, who had dark hair and a clear-skinned, outdoorsy look.

'First job – get those rabbits skinned and gutted.' Barbara grinned. 'Sorry, couldn't resist. It's all right. I wouldn't dump that job on you on your first day, not unless you're a butcher's daughter. You can help chop the veg – of which we have masses, as you can see. This is Angela. You can work with her.'

As they worked, Alison asked about the pie scheme.

'The WVS are marvellous at it,' said Angela. 'We couldn't manage without them. They do heaps of baking and distributing all over the country. In some villages, they have their own stall at the weekly market. Finished those carrots, have you? The rabbits are done now, so you can help put them in water.'

Alison nodded. It was something Mum did at home, leaving the rabbit in salted water for an hour to ensure it was clean.

'We're doing three different pies today,' Barbara told her. 'Over there, ingredients for rabbit pie, with plenty of seasoning and some bacon. In the middle, root vegetables – they'll go into pasties. And over there, beans, oatmeal and corned beef.'

The pies and pasties were assembled and put into the ovens in batches. Soon the air was filled with the aroma of baking, making Alison's mouth water.

'It's essential to make the pies as nutritious as poss,' said Barbara, 'and as tasty as we can too, of course. But nutrition is the most important thing. Have you heard of the Oslo Meal they give to children at school? Basically, it's as much veg as you can get your hands on, mixed with salad dressing and dried milk powder, and accompanied by wholemeal bread, an apple and, if possible, a couple of ounces of cheese. Apparently, the kids who are fed it daily do really well. They grow taller and I don't know if it's true, but it's said they learn better too. So we sometimes do an Oslo pasty that we serve with a hunk of wholemeal bread and sometimes an apple, though we can't manage the cheese, not in those quantities.'

'Before I came here,' said Alison, 'I'd never appreciated what goes into planning meals and trying to keep everyone healthy by providing good nutrition.'

'As they keep telling us,' Barbara replied, 'food is a munition of war.'

'War is a terrible thing,' said Angela, 'but having the country engaged in the war effort has had one good outcome, at least. Children from backgrounds of poverty and deprivation are receiving better food than they've ever had in their lives.'

Later in the morning, Barbara, Angela and Alison loaded up a battered old van and set off to drive through Leeds and out into the hills.

'We've got just enough petrol to do our round trip,' said Barbara.

Angela laughed. 'Do you remember that time when the lane we were in was blocked by a fallen tree and we had to turn round and find another route?'

'The detour took way longer than we thought,' said Barbara, 'and we spent the homeward journey willing the motor not to pack up on us.'

'We drove that final couple of miles on fumes,' said Angela.

They visited farmland and a couple of villages. Angela and Barbara seemed to know everyone they met and there was a lot of banter as they sold their wares, counting the money and keeping a record of everything.

'Record-keeping is part of the job,' said Barbara. 'It's important.'

'One WVS woman – a woman as opposed to a lady, if you get my drift – told me that she'd learned more about maths from running her local pie scheme than she ever learned when she was at school.'

As they drove around, they swapped personal information. Barbara was like Lydia. Her chap was in the army and he had dashed home for a quick wedding and then gone back again more or less straight away. Angela didn't have a boyfriend, but she wrote to a dozen servicemen.

'Just as a friend, you understand,' she said. 'Letters mean such a lot to them.'

In return, Alison talked about Joel. There was no need to mention Paul. Much as she looked forward to going home to Manchester, one of the good things about being here was that nobody knew about the disastrous end of her long-term relationship. To people here, she wasn't Alison who'd had her heart broken by Paul. She was Alison, who had a lovely new boyfriend called Joel, who was a doctor.

'Have you and your Joel got any plans to see one another soon?' Barbara asked.

Alison turned her face up to the skies as happiness bubbled up inside her. 'We're seeing each other this weekend.

He's setting off early on Saturday and I'm going to meet him off the mid-morning train.'

'Lovely,' said Barbara.

'How long is he here for?' asked Angela.

'He'll go home again on Sunday afternoon,' said Alison, 'so we'll have practically the whole weekend together.'

'How gorgeous for you.' Barbara gave a sentimental sigh. Was she thinking of her husband far away?

'I've booked him into the same B & B as before.'

That made Angela laugh. 'Some couples have a special tune or a special table in their favourite restaurant. You two have a special B & B.'

As Alison's second day drew to a close, Rachel sought her out.

'I was out and about, so I thought I'd see how you're getting along.' Although she smiled at Alison, she raised her eyebrows interrogatively at Barbara.

'She'll do,' said Barbara with a smile. She glanced at Alison with a nod that showed that although the words sounded almost offhand, she was pleased with Alison's performance as one of her crew.

'Good,' said Rachel. 'You'll have her back next week, then?' Goodness, was that the dragon lady making a joke?

'More than happy to,' said Barbara.

'I'd be glad to spend another week doing the pies,' said Alison.

'I've already put her on the rota for every day next week,' said Barbara. 'She's just Monday to Friday this week.'

'She's spending the weekend with her boyfriend,' put in Angela.

'Really?' Rachel remarked politely. 'Is he coming here, Miss Lambert, or are you going there?'

'He's coming to Leeds.'

'Well, I hope you both have a good time.'

The rest of the working week flew by. Alison enjoyed the work, especially going out in the van to sell the pies and pasties she had helped to make. She was on pastry duty on Thursday and acquitted herself well, for which she sent silent thanks to Mum for teaching her – thanks that she duly added to a letter home. On Friday, she was filled with high spirits and didn't care who knew it.

At the end of the day, when they worked alongside the other teams, cleaning and stacking the trays. Barbara disappeared into the office, as she always did, to coordinate all the paperwork, of which there was masses.

She emerged from the office, looking serious. She took Alison to one side.

'Look, I hate to do this to you, but I have to ask you to come to work tomorrow. I'm sorry. I know it's your special weekend with your chap, but it can't be helped. I've had a message from Miss Chambers. She wants to poach one of the girls – Valerie – who was due to be in tomorrow. A girl in the almoner's office heard today her husband has been shipped home with bad burns, so she's going down south to see him, and Valerie used to work there, so it makes sense for her to provide cover, but it leaves me one down on tomorrow's pie runs. You're my only extra person at the moment, because I've got two people off sick. Would you mind awfully?'

Alison went very still. Although Barbara was asking politely, she knew it wasn't a request. It was an order, more or less. Barbara was her boss at present and when your boss asked for extra work in wartime, you didn't say no.

She hoisted a smile into place. 'Of course I'll stand in. I'm sorry to hear about the man with burns.'

'Good show,' said Barbara.

Drat and drat again. Alison concentrated on feeling fierce because otherwise she might get tearful and that would never do. But however disappointing this was for her, it was nothing compared to what the injured soldier and his wife were going through.

As she gathered her belongings together, getting ready to leave for the day, Rachel Chambers came hurrying in. If anyone else hurried, they might look flustered or possibly a little rumpled, but neither of those applied to the elegant Miss Chambers, who managed to hurry and look immaculately turned out at the same time. She carried a clipboard in the crook of her arm and she produced her spectacles with such a graceful movement that it wasn't possible to say where she got them out from. She pushed them onto her face, but not all the way. When they were half on, she held them there so she could consult the top page on her clipboard, then she removed them. It was the sort of thing you might expect Hedy Lamarr to do on the silver screen.

Rachel spoke briefly to Barbara, then, looking round, saw Alison and went over to her.

'I gather you've stepped in to help tomorrow. Thank you.'

'She deserves an extra-big thank you,' said Angela, 'because she's giving up a day with her young man to do it. He's due in at the station tomorrow morning.'

Barbara came over to join in. 'Can you get a message to him?' she asked Alison.

'Short of sending a telegram, all I can do is telephone the hospital and leave him a message.'

'And then there's the worry of the message not being passed on,' Angela said sympathetically, 'though I imagine they must be good at that sort of thing in hospitals.'

'Not to worry,' Rachel said to Alison with a smile. 'I'll meet him off the train for you and look after him until your shift finishes.' To the others, she added, 'Joel and I are old friends.'

Alison stiffened. Rachel – meeting Joel from the train? How had that come about? Could it be – surely not, but could it be that Rachel had used the bad news about the injured soldier as a means of removing Valerie from tomorrow's rota, knowing that Alison would be asked to step in? Surely not. It was too convoluted. But all the same . . .

What was it Miss Finch in the almoner's office had said? 'What Miss Chambers wants, Miss Chambers gets.'

CHAPTER TWENTY

A week had gone by since Dot had suggested that Margaret speak to Joel. All week, Margaret had gone into a tizz every time she pictured it – but only an internal tizz. No one observing her would have had any idea of the way the nerves were rolling around inside her belly while thoughts clattered about in her head – not so much actual thoughts as little streaks of panic. Talk to Joel? Talk to Joel! She couldn't, simply couldn't, but even as she told herself that, she knew that Dot had hit upon the answer, the only answer. One of the reasons Margaret was so reluctant to speak to Alison was because she knew Alison would then demand an explanation from Joel, and who knew what he might say? But if Margaret tackled Joel, that might contain the situation. Might. She could warn him off ill-treating Alison and with luck and a prevailing wind, he would be too ashamed to breathe a word to her.

Oh, how simple it sounded, put like that, but what if Joel didn't respond the way Margaret intended? It was all very well her writing a script in her head, but she couldn't actually be certain how Joel would react.

At some point during the week, her thoughts had switched around and she'd begun to focus on her father. To avoid thinking about Joel? Possibly. Probably, if she was honest. She would go and see Dad. With her former circumstances and her shame playing on her mind almost non-stop, she felt a strong need to make her peace with him, a yearning for his approval. Dad knew about her job on the railways, because her sense of duty had impelled her to write and tell him when she had gone to work for LMS. The memory of writing that letter brought forth a bitter laugh. An unwanted tart of a daughter she might be, but at least she'd had the good manners to inform her father of her change in circumstances. If Dad couldn't approve of her in the usual way, maybe he could respect her for her war work. Maybe that could be a new start for them. Or was she kidding herself?

In a letter to Anna, she had mentioned that Dad hadn't responded to her Christmas card and Anna's reply had been unequivocal.

Don't give up. Wait a while and try again – to please me, if for no other reason. Mum always said Dad could be a stubborn old basket, so if you want a reconciliation, it'll be up to you. Please don't stop trying.

Thank heaven for engine cleaning. The hard physical graft provided a welcome routine that was oddly soothing, the work's purpose an important counterpoint to the turmoil of her thoughts. Comfort also came from putting in a request for some holiday so that she could go and visit Anna.

She didn't mention Dad in the buffet, but she was happy to tell the others about her intended holiday with her sister.

'How lovely,' said Persephone. 'Where is she living at the moment?'

'In the Severn Valley, not far from Bridgnorth. She was evacuated to Bridgnorth originally, but she moved after it was bombed.'

'You don't think of a little place like that getting bombed,' Cordelia commented.

'They think it was Jerry getting rid of some final bombs after a raid on Coventry,' said Margaret. 'It's only happened that one time, but the billeting officer gave Anna the chance to move a short distance away. She didn't do it for herself. She did it for the sake of the children.'

'When shall you go?' asked Cordelia.

'Don't know yet. I've said I can be flexible. With Easter not far away, I'm sure they'll want to let staff with families have first dibs on time off, so I said I don't mind.'

'That was kind of you, love,' said Dot, 'but don't forget you're entitled to time off the same as anybody else.'

Now it was Saturday afternoon and soon she would be on her way to Dad's digs. She put on the pink shirtwaister Anna had given her, teaming it with a plum-coloured cardigan from the clothes exchange. The pink and the plum ought to have been an awful clash, but actually they toned in together, much to Margaret's delight, as purple was her favourite colour.

As she went downstairs, the doorbell rang and she let in Emily Masters, Cordelia's daughter – a pretty, dark-haired girl, with blue eyes in a heart-shaped face with a dainty chin.

'I've come to take Mrs Grayson to the hairdresser's,' said Emily. 'Is she ready?'

'Come on in,' said Margaret.

She hadn't known Mrs Grayson back in the days when an overwhelming fear of leaving the house had kept her confined indoors. These days, the lodgers and other friends accompanied her on excursions to the shops or to church, short journeys that she had come to know well and which now held no fear for her as long as she had a trusted friend by her side.

Mrs Grayson and Emily set off; Mabel was out for the day with Harry. That left Margaret in the house with Mrs Cooper.

'You look nice, dear,' said Mrs Cooper.

'It makes a change from wearing a boiler suit,' said Margaret. Perhaps that wasn't the most gracious way to receive a compliment, so she added, 'Thank you. It's actually my sister's cast-off.'

'And isn't that the cardy you got from the clothes exchange? They go well together.'

'You must enjoy volunteering there and helping ladies find something different for their wardrobes.'

'It's such a good idea, isn't it? I'm glad it's been set up. I enjoy sorting through the donations and I'm learning how many points to give to the donors for them to use. But it does have its moments. There's a strict rule that you can get something from the exchange just once a month and there was a bit of an altercation the other day, because a woman tried to come before the month was up. A WVS lady dealt with it, fortunately.'

Margaret smiled. 'I can't imagine you giving anyone what for.'

'I can be very firm when I have to be,' said Mrs Cooper.

'How is Mrs Wadden getting on?' Margaret asked.

'Fine, chuck, thanks for asking. It's a big help to me having someone to call on. She's a very good cleaner.'

'She'd have to be to be good enough for Magic Mop,' said Margaret.

'Are you going somewhere special?' asked Mrs Cooper.

Margaret gave it one moment's thought – just one – and then she told the truth, or at least as much of it as could be told without losing the good opinion of this dear lady whom she had grown to love.

'I'm going to see my dad.'

'I thought you were . . .'

'Estranged, yes.'

'Are you hoping to mend some fences?' asked Mrs Cooper.

'I'm not sure if they can be mended as such, but maybe we can build some new ones.'

Mrs Cooper gave her a hug. 'My dear lass, I do hope so. Family is so important, even more so in wartime when life feels so fragile.'

Not for the first time, Margaret wished she had known Lizzie. She returned her landlady's warm hug. Mrs Cooper was a thin little woman, but she had a heart the size of Albert Square.

Mrs Cooper gave her a little push. 'Off you go, chuck.'

It was a bright afternoon, warm in the sun, but chilly out of it. Margaret took the bus to Alexandra Park. She felt self-conscious as she walked along the road where she used to live. At least when she'd come here with her Christmas card, it had been dark. What if the neighbours saw her? People had long memories for scandal and Dad's rejection would ensure that they never forgot. Walking past what remained of her old house gave her an odd feeling. Now it was a pile of rubble with a couple of walls stubbornly standing, but before that, she had grown up in it.

Dad's billet was further along the road. What would happen, what would be said when Mrs McEvoy answered the door? Margaret felt increasingly quivery inside and it was all she could do to keep her arms down when what she wanted was to fold them across herself, as if that barrier would keep her safe. Then she saw Dad digging for victory in the front garden. He was in his shirtsleeves and braces, with his tweed jacket hanging on the handle of the garden fork stuck in the soil. His hair, what was left of it, was grey, his eyes brown. Margaret remembered running to him as a little girl, his mouth stretching into the widest of smiles at the sight of her.

'Hello, Dad.'

He looked up and saw her. The brown eyes that should have been warm dulled and the mouth that should have been generous thinned.

'Margaret.' He gave her a nod – no, not so much a nod as a jerk of the chin.

'How are you?' she asked.

'What brings you here?' Dad glanced at the house.

Margaret glanced too. The net curtains didn't twitch. 'I wanted to see you. I hoped we might talk.'

Dad rolled down his sleeves. He fastened his top button and straightened his tie before putting on his jacket, removing his rolled-up cap from the pocket and jamming it on his head.

'Let's go over the road and sit in the park,' he said. 'There are still a few benches here and there among the vegetable plots.'

And that said it all, didn't it? He wouldn't or couldn't take her inside the house where he lived. Margaret's throat bobbed with distress and humiliation, but she swallowed hard. Now wasn't the time to be upset.

They crossed the road. Times were when Dad would have taken her arm or even held her hand and never mind that she was grown up, but those days were gone. They walked along a path between plots where middle-aged and elderly men were weeding seedbeds and digging well-rotted manure into the soil. Dad headed for a bench in the shade.

Sitting, he fished his cigarettes from his pocket and offered her one.

She shook her head. 'I don't any more.'

She hadn't smoked since the night she'd slept with Joel. Hadn't smoked, hadn't touched gin. She didn't want to be sophisticated ever again.

'What do you want to talk about?' asked Dad. 'Not about . . . that, I hope.'

'I came to see how you're getting on.'

'Fine. Printing works by day, Home Guard in the evenings and some nights. It keeps me busy. But I expect you already know about all that from Anna.'

'That's not the point. I wanted to hear it from you.' Margaret smiled at him, but he looked uncomfortable, and she felt it as a cut all the way to her heart. 'I enjoy working on the railways.' She waited.

'Good.'

Not 'I'm pleased to hear it.' Not 'Tell me about it.' Just 'Good.' Margaret told him about it anyway, but it was a strain trying to hold a conversation with someone who clearly didn't wish to participate.

It was time to dive in. What did she have to lose?

'Dad, can't we please be friends again? I miss you. I want us to be on good terms.'

Dad looked at her. 'To be friends? That's what you said? Friends?'

'Yes,' she said.

'That's what you think fathers and daughters should be, is it? Friends?' Dad waved his cigarette in front of her and the smell of tobacco went up her nose. 'You're not meant to be my friend, Margaret. You're meant to be my daughter. You're meant to follow my rules and remember the way I brought you up. You're meant to live by my standards. Daughters behave like decent girls and their fathers take care of them. That's what's meant to happen. That's what I thought I had. Only I didn't, did I? My little Margaret, my precious one, the baby of the family, ended up with a bun in the oven. That's what happened to my girl.'

Margaret flinched. Dad inhaled deeply and blew out a stream of smoke, lifting his chin to do so.

'I don't know where I am with you any more,' said Dad. 'You aren't the girl I thought you were. You aren't the girl I

brought up. And you come here wanting us to be friends –
friends, I ask you. That's adding insult to injury, that is.'

Margaret felt like slumping against the back of the bench,
but she forced herself to remain upright. Tears appeared,
but she brushed them aside.

'Don't turn on the waterworks,' said Dad.

'I wasn't.'

'It won't work with me,' he said, as if she hadn't spoken.
Throwing his cigarette onto the path, he ground it beneath
the sole of his shoe.

Margaret stood up. At least she could hang on to the
remnants of her dignity by standing before he did, before
he could rise and walk off, abandoning her.

'I'm sorry to have . . .' she began.

He tilted his head to one side as he looked up at her.
'Sorry you came? Sorry you wasted your time? Not to mention my time.'

'I'm sorry . . . just sorry. I'd hoped you might be ready to
forgive me.' Even now, there was the tiniest glimmer of
hope. Would he take her hand, call her his precious girl?
'But I think I knew, really, when you didn't ask me into the
house.'

Was this it? Was this the moment? In Margaret's heart,
this was the moment when Dad was overcome by love for
her, when he said, 'I can't ask you in there – so I shan't stay
there. I'll find myself another billet, one where my daughter
will be welcome.' That was what she longed for.

'I can't have you in there,' said Dad. 'Mrs McEvoy
wouldn't stand for it – and who could blame her?'

CHAPTER TWENTY-ONE

Joan opened the oven a crack to peer inside at the tray of small biscuits. She wasn't sure why she bothered, because it wasn't as though she knew what they were meant to look like. Actually, they didn't look all that different to when she had put them in. The doorbell rang and she went to answer it.

Dot was on the step. 'Afternoon, chick. First day of spring today, isn't it, March the twenty-first? How are you? You look blooming.'

'Thanks. I'm fine. Come in. You don't need to ring the bell, you know. You should pull the key through the letter box.'

Dot shook her head. 'Not now you're a full-time house-wife. You don't want folk barging in. I don't want to take liberties.'

'You'd never do that. Come through to the kitchen. I'm about to take something out of the oven.'

Dot sniffed. 'It doesn't smell like a cake.'

'It isn't cake.'

Putting on the oven mitts, she removed the tray.

Dot peered at the biscuits. 'I don't mean any offence, love, but they're not the most appetising things I've ever seen. Is it one of them wartime recipes? You'd think the Ministry of Food could come up with summat better than this.'

Joan laughed. 'They're dog biscuits. The recipe came from Persephone's mother. Do you think this is how they're meant to look?'

'I've no idea. What's in them?'

'Wholemeal flour, Oxo, fragments of fat saved from the meat, and bits of bacon rind.'

'Well, the dog won't care what they look like. Where is he? Shouldn't he be trying to get at them before they cool down?'

'He's not here. Bob has taken him for a long walk.'

'In case the smell of dog biscuits baking proved too much for him?' asked Dot.

'Something like that.'

'You should have called him Lucky, because he's jolly lucky to be looked after so devotedly by you and Bob.'

Joan transferred the biscuits onto a wire rack. 'Thanks for taking him to Victoria with you all week, so he can carry on raising money.'

'Don't thank me. All I did was deliver him in the mornings and fetch him home in the evenings. Persephone is the one who sorted out who would be responsible for him at different times every day. A great organiser, is our Persephone.'

'Now that I've settled into a routine of housework and shopping, plus the knitting circle and other things,' Joan said as she put the kettle on, 'I'll bring Brizo to the station myself once or twice a week. I don't want to lose touch.' She stopped speaking as a thought occurred to her. 'Perhaps I'd better ask Miss Emery if that's allowed.'

'Why wouldn't it be?'

'I'm not an employee any more. It's one thing for Brizo to be supervised by someone in uniform, but I'd be in my own clothes. Passengers wouldn't realise Brizo is a railway dog.'

Dot chuckled. 'You don't want folk thinking you've found a clever way of raising money for your holiday.' She pretended to look over her shoulder. 'I shouldn't say that out loud in case our Jimmy gets ideas.'

'You're safe. He's out with his pals. He promised to look in the shops on his way home to see if any new stock came in today.'

'He's a good lad at heart,' said Dot. 'He's just what you might call overenthusiastic.'

Joan warmed the pot and made the tea.

'Would you like a biscuit?' she asked.

'As long as you don't give me one of Brizo's by mistake.'

'They're ginger biscuits. Mrs Grayson gave me her recipe.'

'Talking of recipes,' said Dot, 'I've got one for a herb salve that's good for nappy rash. It might come in handy.'

'What's in it?'

'Elderflowers and other herbs. Lard. I know lard might not sound like something you'd like to rub on skin, but it does the job.'

'These wartime recipes are so clever,' said Joan. 'They use all sorts of ingredients you'd never expect.'

Dot gave her a wry smile. 'It's my mam's old balm, actually, but I've seen similar recipes recently. It just goes to show. It's all very well having fancy new products, but the old ways are the best, not least because they don't vanish off the shelves in wartime. Mam used her balm for everything – insect bites, chapped lips, you name it.'

As they went into the sitting room, Dot's gaze went straight to the rocking chair.

'It looks good in the window,' she said.

'I love it,' Joan enthused. 'Everyone was so kind that day.'

'We all think the world of you – Bob an' all.'

'Sit down,' said Joan, offering the plate of biscuits.

'You don't mind if I dunk it, do you?' asked Dot. 'Any luck yet finding a new home?'

'Not yet. The trouble is, what we've got here is pretty good, so it'll take a lot to improve on it. Miss Brown offered to have us at Darley Court.'

'She never.' Dot laughed. 'Are you telling me our Sheila's house is better than Darley Court?'

'Bob didn't want to live there, not in the house itself,' said Joan. 'It would have been different if there'd been a cottage available.'

'Too posh for a humble signalman? I don't blame him. Mind you, it would have been summat to tell your grandchildren about one day.'

'Grandchildren! Give us a chance. We haven't had baby number one yet.' Joan cradled her bump lovingly. 'Dot, can I talk to you about something?'

'Course you can, chick, anything.'

'You're an easy person to talk to.'

'I take that as a compliment. Was it your idea for Margaret to come and talk to me last weekend?'

Joan nodded.

'Thought so,' said Dot.

'Have you seen her this week?' Joan asked. 'Did you have a chance to ask if she . . . ?'

'I didn't ask, but she told me she's going to see her dad first before she thinks about seeing Joel. Poor lass. She's got a lot on her mind.' Dot looked directly at Joan. 'And what's on your mind?'

'Gran has offered us a home with her – not right away; she has a lodger at the moment, but that's a temporary arrangement. If we move in, Gran says she'll have the downstairs back room as her bedroom, so we can have upstairs to ourselves, though the kitchen and bathroom will be shared, obviously.'

'That's a generous offer,' Dot commented.

'It is. She seems keen to be a great-grandmother. The thing is, having the whole floor of a house to ourselves is our idea of the perfect home.'

Dot arched her eyebrows. 'But?'

Joan sighed. 'Exactly. But.'

'I know things have been difficult between you and Mrs Foster ever since she threw you out.'

Joan winced at the memory. 'Things were never easy under Gran's roof. It was Letitia who made it all right. She was Gran's favourite and she could get round Gran if she needed to.'

'And when she died, you lost the person who'd held your family together.'

Joan's heart filled with gratitude. 'I knew you'd understand.'

'You don't have to be Einstein to understand that, love,' said Dot. 'But there's more to it than that, isn't there? And it's nowt to do with your Letitia.'

A rush of panic sent Joan's pulse jumping in her wrists, but she kept her voice steady as she said, 'I don't want to go into detail. That might sound hypocritical of me after the way I encouraged Margaret to bare her soul to you.'

'It's not hypocritical. Everyone has things they want to keep private. I'll tell you what I think – and I'm not pushing for confidences. I'm just telling you my ideas, which, incidentally, I haven't shared with anybody else, so don't go thinking I've been talking about you behind your back. I wonder if summat happened when you went down south last year to find out what you could about your family. Before that, you were the child in your relationship with Mrs Foster. You were deferential to her. But after you came home, I got the impression that you'd changed towards her. Instead of her being the adult and you being the child, you were an adult facing up to another adult. But that's only my impression.'

Joan hoped her surprise didn't show. To hear it put into words, and such accurate words, was startling. But what she felt more than anything was trust and confidence in her dear friend.

'Gran brought up Letitia and me on a diet of lies and I want her to be sorry, but she isn't.'

'That must hurt,' said Dot.

'It's frustrating, to put it mildly.'

'And now you're worried that if you move into her house, she'll think you've forgiven her.'

'That's exactly it,' said Joan. 'Trust you to see straight to the heart of the matter. The house is precisely what we want in terms of space and privacy. That's what we haven't really got here in Sheila's house – privacy. I don't mean any disrespect to Sheila and Jimmy when I say that.'

'Don't fret, love. I understand.'

'And Gran's house is in Chorlton, where I grew up, and it's near to Wilton Close, and we'd be considerably nearer to Bob's family.'

'And if the house belonged to anybody but your gran, you'd move in like a shot.'

'We would,' agreed Joan, 'but I don't want her to think she's been forgiven.'

'Does she want your forgiveness?' Dot asked bluntly.

'Well – no. I don't know, but I don't suppose so. When you're in the right, you don't require other people's forgiveness, do you? I imagine that's how she sees it. What I mean is, I wouldn't want her to think I'd accepted what she did. As well as that, I don't want to compromise myself. It would feel hypocritical to resent what she did and then move in anyway. There's that word again – hypocrisy. But then I think of how Gran brought us up, and never mind the lies she told, I owe her a lot. Besides, she's not getting any younger and I do feel a certain responsibility towards her. I don't necessarily want to feel it, but I do.'

'That's because you've got a good heart. It's also because –
dare I say it? It's because your gran brought you up to have
certain values.'

'She wasn't all bad. I know that.'

'But she lied to you and you felt hurt and betrayed when
you found out. There are no easy answers, chick. Sorry if
you thought I might come up with a solution.'

'Why should you, when Bob and I can't? All we do is go
round in circles – I say "we", but I really mean me. It has
been good to talk it over with you though, Dot. Thank you
for coming round in my circle with me.'

'It's not easy being a parent,' said Dot. 'It's the most wonderful thing in the world, but it isn't easy. That's what
started this off, you being in the family way and wanting
the best possible start in life for your baby. And part of that
is your sense of honour.'

Joan almost laughed. 'My what?'

'You heard. You said yourself, from a purely practical
point of view, you've got the chance of the perfect home,
but your sense of honour is involved an' all and that's to
your credit. You want to bring your baby up in a home
where there are no dark misgivings lurking in the corners.'

'You understand,' Joan breathed.

'Aye, I do. We'd all like our lives to be straightforward
and we'd all like to do the right thing – well, most of us
would, anyroad. But life has a habit of being more complicated than that and yours sounds more complicated than
most. A word of advice?'

'Please,' said Joan.

'You've got a breathing space at the moment, while your
gran's lodger is still there. If thinking about you and your
gran is sending you round in circles, then you need to try
thinking about it in a different way. Think about your baby,
and remember that life doesn't run in straight lines. Hark at

me. I sound like one of them crystal-ball readers at the fair. I can see it now: Discerning Dorothea Divines Your Darkest Dilemmas.'

'Is Dot short for Dorothea?'

'Nay, lass, I'm plain old Dorothy. I'm saving Dorothea for if I ever go on the stage.'

'Bob's mum and her two sisters were all named after music-hall stars. Bernice, Florrie and Marie.'

'*Hold your hand out, naughty boy,*' sang Dot. 'That was Florrie Forde. With a voice like mine, I'd best stick to the crystal ball.'

Joan got up. 'I'll put those dog biscuits in a tin before Bob brings Brizo home.'

She returned to the kitchen. The biscuits had cooled. She popped them into a tin and put it on the shelf. When she went back to the sitting room, Dot was at the window, looking along the road.

'I'm just watching our Jimmy,' said Dot. 'There must be summat good in the shops, because he's knocking on every door as he comes down the road.'

'He's telling all the neighbours, just like you said he should.'

'Some of the women have come outside and they're talking to one another,' Dot said approvingly, 'so it must be summat worth having. I just hope they don't all fling their coats on and rush down there to buy it up before Jimmy gets here and tells us what it is. Anyroad, I must make tracks. I promised to help our Jenny cut out a skirt pattern. She wants me to help her draw the shape of an inset pocket, because that'll use less fabric than a patch pocket would.'

'There are so many restrictions now on what new items of clothing we are allowed to have,' said Joan. 'You wouldn't think that reducing the number of buttons would help win the war, would you?'

'It's all to do with cutting back on everything we can in order to preserve what we've got,' said Dot. 'Eh, times are hard, and they'll get harder before they get better. We've a long way to go yet – and a long time to go. Three cheers for the Yanks, that's what I say, or the time would be even longer. Sorry, chick, I don't mean to leave you on a note of gloom.'

'We all feel the same, Dot.'

She helped Dot on with her coat and opened the front door in time for Jimmy to come trotting home, a big smile on his freckled face, his blue eyes shining.

'Hello, Nan. Hello, Auntie Joan.'

'Well, our Jimmy, is there anything good in the shops? Oh,' said Dot, as a group of housewives, most of them in pinnies and curlers, appeared behind Jimmy.

Joan thought they must be about to praise the lad for his generosity in telling them about the latest deliveries, but then she saw the sour expressions on some faces and the screwed-up brows on others. Several of the women had their arms folded. Joan exchanged surprised glances with Dot.

'What's all this, then?' asked Dot.

Jimmy, apparently oblivious to the following he had gathered, burst out, 'Tinned pears! Safety pins! Sanitary towels!'

Joan's ears filled with the sound of the collective intake of breath of a dozen women. One of the gasps was her own.

'Jimmy,' breathed Dot, 'you never went from house to house, saying . . .'

'I did, Nan – just like you told me to,' said Jimmy and there was a vexed rumble behind him. 'It's a good mixture today, isn't it? Tinned pears! Safety pins! Sanitary towels! What are sanitary towels, Auntie Joan?'

*

Alison had fumed silently all day, finding no pleasure whatsoever in the job she had enjoyed so much all week. *What Miss Chambers wants, Miss Chambers gets.* She had well and truly got Joel today – and all under the guise of doing Alison a good turn by meeting her boyfriend off the train when she'd been unavoidably detained. Or was Alison putting two and two together and coming up with an answer considerably more than four? Was meeting Joel nothing more than Rachel's way of helping out in an unfortunate situation? Was it all perfectly innocent?

But Alison was haunted by memories of a girl in a green dress, tapping her on the shoulder during a ladies' excuse-me dance and then whirling away in Paul's arms. That had been the beginning of the end for Alison and Paul.

But that was Paul, she told herself. This was Joel. He was a different person altogether and he thought the world of her.

Paul had thought the world of her once.

Alison felt an unpleasant fluttering sensation in her chest as her thoughts ricocheted all over the place. She felt anxious and conflicted. Did Rachel intend to win Joel back? Alison knew what it was to be pursued by someone who found you attractive, because that was how Joel had finally got her to take him seriously. What if he should now start to notice Rachel? Rachel was clever, poised, beautiful. What man wouldn't be tempted?

During the long drive back to Leeds after making the day's deliveries, Alison made an effort to chat to the others she had been teamed up with, but her heart wasn't in it. They probably thought she was being moody because of having to give up her day off. She couldn't wait to get back to base and get the trays washed and the inside of the van cleaned.

At last she hurried back to Mrs Freeman's to spruce herself up before setting off to meet Joel and Rachel outside Tabitha's Tea Shop. Just as she was about to leave her room, she turned back, remembering the gift from Persephone. *Emergency present to be opened when you need cheering up.* That was what the label had said and now seemed like just the right moment. She opened her top drawer and felt about at the back, drawing out the little packet wrapped in brown paper. It felt squidgy; she had forgotten that. Removing the paper, she discovered that the reason for the squidginess was that Persephone had wrapped whatever was inside in scrunched-up newspaper. Alison smiled. It felt like a game of pass the parcel. Pulling off the newspaper, she unwrapped – a lipstick. That was a generous present because make-up was increasingly hard to come by and it was typical of Persephone that she had made it even more special by writing the accompanying label.

Alison applied the lipstick, pressing her lips together, and admired the effect in the mirror. Her spirits lifted and she set off with a lighter heart.

But as she turned the final corner, hoping to see Joel and Rachel outside Tabitha's, her heart sank. They weren't there – but she was five minutes early, so she oughtn't to mind. She made her way along the road, taking her time – killing time, more like. She stopped outside the tobacconist's next door to the tea shop and looked up and down the road. They were bound to appear around one corner or the other any moment now.

They didn't. Alison waited, trying to leave long gaps in between the times she checked her watch. Where were they? She'd been waiting for this moment all day. It was too bad. She walked back to the corner, then back to the tobacconist's, and they still didn't appear. She might as well walk to the other corner and back. As she passed Tabitha's Tea Shop, she glanced through the window and there, between the strips of anti-blast tape, she could see Rachel and Joel sitting together at a table. Alison's heart thumped. She was annoyed with them for being inside when the arrangement was to meet up outside, but she was annoyed with herself too. What had made her wait outside the tobacconist's? If she had walked on just a few more paces . . .

Never mind that now. She pushed open the door and the little brass bell tinkled above her head. Joel had his back to her. Rachel was leaning towards him, laughing at something he said. Then she saw Alison and waved. Joel turned round, hooking his arm over the back of his chair, and in spite of her vexation, Alison's pulse raced at the sight of his smile. Perhaps she ought to cross the room and join them – well, there was no perhaps about it. But her emotions welled up and she found herself waving to them and pointing through the window before she left to wait on the pavement.

A minute later, Rachel joined her, coming straight towards her as if about to embrace a friend. Alison couldn't help it; she took a step backwards.

'Where have you been?' Rachel exclaimed. 'We've been waiting and waiting. We were starting to worry.'

'I've been waiting out here – like we agreed.'

Joel emerged from the tea shop, slipping his wallet into the inside pocket of his jacket. He was smiling. Alison had thought of it as his special smile, just for her, but now she wasn't so sure.

Rachel slid her arm through his. 'Joel, you won't believe this. Alison has been waiting out here for us, the poor lamb.'

Joel frowned. 'You said we were to wait for her inside.'

'That was what we'd agreed,' said Rachel.

'You said outside,' said Alison. Did she sound ratty?

'No, inside.' Rachel smiled. 'That makes much more sense.' She held out a hand towards Alison, as if offering her to Joel. 'I'll leave you with your lovely girlfriend, Joel darling.' She unhooked her other arm from his, but left her fingertips on his arm and looked up into his face. 'Thank you for your company.'

'I should be the one thanking you for stepping in when Alison had to work.'

Was he about to kiss Rachel goodbye? She was close enough, and was that upturned face an invitation? But now Joel looked at Alison, the warmth in his expression sending a tingling sensation coursing through her veins. How could she ever have held this man at arm's length? Forgetting Rachel, Alison went to him, easing close to him as he lifted his arm and placed it around her shoulders. Rachel stepped back from them, her smile not faltering.

'Enjoy your evening together,' she said.

'Thanks,' said Joel. 'We shall.'

Rachel went on her way. Alison started to draw Joel in the opposite direction.

He laughed. 'This is the wrong way if you want to go to the pictures. I used to live here, don't forget.'

'Let's forget the flicks. I'd rather just be together and talk.' As they walked along, Alison squeezed Joel's arm, suddenly overcome with the joy of being together.

Joel stopped walking and turned her to face him. He looked searchingly into her face and her heart did a little flip. He took her hands in his, fingers intertwining. The brim of his hat cast a light shadow over the upper half of his face, but there could be no room for doubt as to what was in his eyes.

'This is what I wanted to see when I got off the train,' he murmured. 'My girl's face. You're all I thought of all the way here.'

'Really?' A smile pulled at her lips.

'Really. Shall I tell you what else I was thinking?'

'Go on.'

'It's more a case of having to show you,' said Joel, and he kissed her.

CHAPTER TWENTY-TWO

Margaret stood in the bay window, looking out at the garden, where Tony Naylor was planting potatoes. She turned from the window and looked at Mrs Cooper and Mrs Grayson, who were busy knitting for the railway orphanage on this fine Saturday afternoon at the end of March.

'I always feel guilty when I see Tony out there, working in the garden,' said Margaret.

'I imagine it's a comfort to him,' said Mrs Cooper.

'It probably makes him remember coming here with Colette every weekend,' said Margaret. 'That must be bittersweet, but I imagine there is solace in it.'

'At least it gets him out of his house.' Mrs Grayson turned her knitting and started the next row. 'That's better for him than sitting at home stewing over things.'

Margaret nodded, though she tactfully didn't say anything. Mabel had told her – not in a gossipy way, but just so that she didn't put her foot in it – about the tragic death years ago of Mrs Grayson's only child, which, combined with the less than compassionate treatment she'd received from her husband and his parents, had ultimately led to the agoraphobia that had dominated her life for so long. Only now, all these years later, was she gradually returning to a more normal life, thanks to the patient support of her friends. It was no wonder she was in favour of Tony continuing to visit Wilton Close once a week.

'What do you mean about feeling guilty?' asked Mrs Cooper.

'I feel as if I ought to be out there helping him,' said Margaret. 'I don't want anyone to think I'm lazy.'

'Goodness,' said Mrs Cooper. 'With the job you do, no one could ever accuse you of that, chuck.'

'Besides,' added Mrs Grayson, 'you and Mabel do your share in the garden. We all do.'

Margaret glanced through the window again. At least while she and Mabel were out there, they had a laugh while they worked. Tony looked . . . intent. Margaret couldn't come up with any other word to describe it. Poor chap. If throwing himself into things was meant to alleviate his grief and ease his heartache, it didn't altogether look as if it was working, though making the effort to lend a hand in someone else's garden had got to be better for him than staying at home and staring at his own four walls.

Cordelia and Emily appeared at the gate and Emily opened it to let her mother in first. Smiling, Margaret waved to them, then turned to the others.

'Here's Mrs Masters. Emily's with her.' She went to answer the door.

'Hello, Margaret.' Cordelia looked very swish in a light-weight blue-and-green herringbone coat with a silk scarf in the same colours, which looked flattering against her fair skin and ash-blonde hair.

'Come in,' said Margaret. 'Let me hang up your things for you. Go right in.'

Beneath her swing coat, Emily wore a cream blouse and grey wool skirt. That was the problem with girls' clothes, Margaret thought. You had to dress as a girl, complete with ankle socks, until you left school and then you went straight into women's clothes. There ought to be a carefree, pretty style specially for the unmarried under-twenty-ones.

In the front room, Mrs Cooper stood up to greet her visitors.

'I'm here to do the monthly check,' said Cordelia.

'And I'm here to take your minds off it,' Emily added.

'Bless you, chuck,' said Mrs Cooper. 'I don't mind the check in the slightest. Mr Morgan would never have installed me as housekeeper without knowing your mum would be keeping an eye on me.'

'Well, I don't like it,' said Emily. 'The Morgans accepted you on Mummy's recommendation and that ought to be sufficient. As if you need to be watched over! You're completely trustworthy.'

'Emily,' murmured Cordelia, 'it's not your place to speak like that about your elders, even if there is a compliment involved.'

Mrs Cooper's thin face lit up. 'Thank you for saying so, Emily.' To Cordelia, she said, 'Inspection first and tea afterwards, as usual, Mrs Masters?'

'I think so. Thank you.'

'I'll put the kettle on,' Margaret offered.

'I'll help,' said Emily.

In the kitchen, Margaret lifted the kettle and gave it a shake to see if there was enough water in it before lighting the gas.

'Are you still working in your dad's law firm?' she asked Emily.

Emily pulled a face. 'Yes. 'Fraid so.'

'Don't you like it?'

'I loved it to start with. It was new and different and I felt very grown-up, but being the office junior isn't particularly interesting. I do endless filing and I take letters to the pillar box and I'm learning to type. Oh yes, and I make the tea,' she added as Margaret warmed the pot.

'It's a good job, though,' Margaret pointed out. 'It'll set you up for the future. There will always be a need for clerks – assuming that you still work after the war. I suppose girls of your class mainly stay at home until they get married.'

Emily applied herself to laying the tray. 'This office job is Daddy's way of keeping me safe until after the war – to stop me doing proper war work. As for when the war ends, maybe he thinks being the office junior will have bored me into wanting to stay at home.'

'You can understand his point of view.' Margaret spoke mildly enough, but inside she felt a sharp pang. She had been Dad's precious girl once.

'I'm sixteen now,' said Emily. 'That means it's another five years before I'm allowed to make decisions for myself and even then it'll be a struggle, with a father like mine. Don't misunderstand me. I love him to bits, but I think growing up happens a lot more quickly in wartime.'

They finished preparing the tea. Margaret got out a mug for Tony, then took the lid off the biscuit tin and removed some of the cheese straws that Mrs Grayson had made from some dry cheese. When the tray was ready, Emily picked it up and Margaret opened the door for her just as Cordelia came downstairs. Leaving the others in the front room, Margaret nipped outside with Tony's mug. She invited him indoors, but wasn't sorry when he declined. Was that mean of her? She hoped not, but they would be more comfortable without him.

As she returned to the front room, Cordelia was saying, 'Everything is as clean and tidy as always, Mrs Cooper.'

Margaret couldn't help picturing her previous digs. Yes, she appreciated the cleanliness and good order that held sway in Wilton Close in a way she had never truly appreciated in her family home, where Mum had kept everything spick and span. But more important than Mrs Cooper's housewifely skills was the sense of warmth that her gentle but capable personality gave to the house and which made it into a home. Margaret had felt happy here right from her very first visit when she had come to see Joan try on her wedding dress. Being invited to move in had been the best thing that had happened to her in a long time and she knew she would never forget it.

'Have you got your holiday dates yet for visiting your sister?' Cordelia asked her.

Margaret felt a little burst of happiness inside at the thought of it. 'I've been offered the choice of two different weeks in April, going on the Wednesday and coming home the following Monday.'

'That's good news,' said Mrs Cooper. 'Which dates?'

'Wednesday the first or Wednesday the eighth.'

'The first?' Cordelia exclaimed. 'That's next week. You haven't got long to decide.'

'I know,' said Margaret. 'That one was a last-minute option because of someone else changing their plans. If I choose it, that will give me the Easter weekend, but I feel as if I should leave that free in case somebody with family commitments wants to have a last-minute Easter break.'

'You have family, too, Margaret,' said Mrs Grayson, 'and you haven't seen your sister for a long time – and you've never met her little ones.'

'If I go on the eighth, that week is closer to my birthday. I'd have to come home the day before it, but Anna and I could still celebrate.'

'And we'll have a celebration here on the day itself.' A familiar light appeared in Mrs Grayson's eyes: she was planning a cake.

'Yes, do choose the second week,' said Mrs Cooper, sitting forward and looking at her, 'because then you'll be here for the Easter weekend.' She beamed round at all of them. 'I had a letter from Alison this morning. She'll be here over Easter. She's having a couple of nights with her parents first, then she'll come here.'

Margaret went cold right to the core of her being. Alison – here. Thank goodness she had been warned before she'd made firm arrangements about Shropshire.

She stood up. 'I'll just nip out and see if Tony's finished with his mug.'

She couldn't possibly be here when Alison visited, she just couldn't. She would write to Anna this very day and tell her to expect her on the first. April Fool's Day. How appropriate.

It was the last day of March, Margaret's final day at work before heading off for the Severn Valley to stay with Anna and meet her nephew and niece. It was staggering to think of it. Tommy and Anne-Marie were two years old and had never met their auntie Margaret. Guilt tightened in the back of her throat. It was her own fault they hadn't met. After the emotional devastation of her unwanted pregnancy and her miscarriage, she had been preoccupied with hiding herself away. She had never confided in Anna about what she had gone through. She had been too ashamed and Dad had made her feel even worse about herself.

But now she felt better equipped to face the future, even if Dad had made it clear that he didn't want to know. She pushed the thought of her father to the back of her mind. She was going to concentrate on Anna and the children for now. A warm feeling spread through her. She would be with them tomorrow.

She was due to spend today cleaning the motionwork, which was what they called everything underneath, in between the wheels. Margaret and the rest of her gang made their way towards their allocated locomotive. Mr Ramsden, their foreman, carried a large red board on which was written NOT TO BE MOVED, which he placed on the lamp at the rear of the engine. When Margaret had first been taught to clean the motionwork, she'd been told that the secret was to clean every single bit, the inaccessible as well as the accessible, but 'especially the inaccessible, because those are the bits the inspector checks first, and if they haven't been done properly, you'll end up having to do the whole lot all over again.'

Last week, Alice had offered to swap shifts with Margaret so that today she could finish work mid-afternoon instead of late in the evening.

'Ta very much.' Margaret had beamed at the other girl. From now on, instead of thinking of her as the girl whose brother had copped it on the day Margaret found out that the Joel Alison was going out with was Dr Joel Maitland, she would always think of her as the girl who had helped her be reunited with Anna.

With her colleagues' good wishes for a happy Easter ringing in her ears, Margaret hurried home to get ready. Mrs Grayson helped her wash her hair and produced a pair of cardigans she had knitted for the twins.

'That's so sweet of you,' said Margaret.

'I've made them a bit on the big side, so they can grow into them.'

'Anna will be thrilled. I know she'll write and thank you.'

Mabel was out at work, but she had already offered Margaret the pick of her clothes. Margaret had looked at Mabel's array of garments, all of the best quality, hanging up in her side of the wardrobe they shared. Margaret's side contained relatively few things.

'It's kind of you,' she'd told Mabel, 'and I appreciate it, but I'll stick with my own. I want Anna to see the real me.'

The real me, the real Margaret. No one had seen the real Margaret for a long time, but she was coming out of her shell now and had made a vow to herself to tell Anna what had happened to her. She couldn't bear to think of Anna reacting in the same way as Dad, but neither could she bear to keep her secret any longer. She wanted and needed her sister to know.

While Margaret was packing the suitcase, Mrs Cooper appeared with her ration book.

'Don't forget this.'

'Thanks.'

'And don't forget to bring it back with you as well – eh, I'm sorry, chuck. That sounds as if I'm wishing your holiday away and I'm not. I hope you have a wonderful time.'

Pure excitement made Margaret hug her landlady. 'Now that it's all arranged, I can't believe how long it's taken me to get round to it.'

'It'll be very special, seeing your sister again after so long and seeing her little ones for the first time. It's just a shame you won't see Alison. I know she'll be sorry to miss you.'

Margaret folded a blouse and laid it on top of the other things in the suitcase. 'Yes, it's a shame. It's just the way things worked out. Someone else desperately wanted the other dates, as it turned out, so what could I do? Besides, I'll see Anna a whole week sooner.' She ran her hands over her packing, smoothing what was already smooth. Was she overexplaining? She looked at Mrs Cooper and smiled. 'I'll see Alison next time.'

'Next time she comes,' said Mrs Cooper, 'I hope it'll be for good. She's been away a long time. That's how it feels, anyroad. It's the end of March now and she went to Leeds before the middle of January.'

Margaret didn't want to think about any of that, not about Alison, not about Joel, especially not about Joel. But she would have to when she came home from the Severn

Valley. That was the deadline she had set herself. See Anna. Meet the twins. Then come home and face up to what had to be done.

With a huge effort, she shoved it to the back of her mind. All that mattered now, right now, was being reunited with her sister. Everything else was for the future.

CHAPTER TWENTY-THREE

Margaret's journey was long and frustrating, with unexplained hold-ups, and would have been easier to bear if the train hadn't been overcrowded, but this was the normal state of travel for passengers in wartime. IS YOUR JOURNEY REALLY NECESSARY? asked the posters in case you were in any doubt as to the relative importance of troop trains and trains conveying munitions and food.

On the last leg of her journey, helpful locals ensured that Margaret got off at the right place. She just had time to register that Hampton Loade was a small country station that would undoubtedly have been chocolate-box pretty with tubs of flowers before the war, when there was a flutter of activity further along the platform and in the next moment she and Anna were running into one another's arms. They clung together, burying their faces in each other's necks. Anna smelled of soda crystals and baking and sunshine.

At last, laughing and crying, Anna pushed Margaret away. 'Let me look at you. My little sister, as beautiful as ever.'

'I was never beautiful.'

'You are to me,' said Anna. 'Your face is thinner,' she added.

Margaret shrugged. 'We're all thinner than we used to be. You look well. You've got roses in your cheeks.'

Anna laughed. 'Fresh air and country living. It's either that or because I'm puffed out from running around after two little tearaways.'

'Where are they?' Margaret looked down the platform, eager to see her niece and nephew.

'Mrs Andrews is looking after them. I warn you, your arrival is more hotly anticipated than Father Christmas's and the Second Coming combined.'

Margaret felt a flicker of joy. There was no one in the world she wanted to be with more than Anna, and to have Anna's children looking forward to her visit filled her with happiness.

Holding hands, the two of them walked back along the platform to where Margaret had dumped her luggage. A lad of eight or nine was standing there, clutching the end of a length of rope that was attached to the front of a wheeled cart, which was obviously home-made.

'Is this the one, missis?' he asked Anna.

'This is Hughie,' Anna told Margaret. 'You're an evacuee, same as me, aren't you, Hughie?'

'Shouldn't you be at school?' Margaret asked in a pretend-stern voice.

'Nah, miss. Us vaccies go in the morning and the locals go in the afternoon. It's the only way they can fit us all in. It's great. We get a holiday every afternoon.'

'But this isn't a holiday,' Anna said, deadpan. 'This is work.' To Margaret she said, 'Hughie is going to take your suitcase to Mrs Andrews' cottage for us.'

'That's kind of you, Hughie,' said Margaret.

'No, it isn't, miss. It's a job. Mrs Dixon said she'll give me a – a small consid'ration.'

'Did she really?' Margaret exchanged amused glances with her sister. 'Well, if you get my suitcase to wherever it's going without it falling off the cart, I might give you a small consid'ration too.'

'Cor, thanks, miss.'

Grasping its handle, Hughie heaved the case onto his cart and set off. Anna and Margaret watched the cart wobbling on its way, then turned to one another again. Anna's fair hair was longer than Margaret remembered, or maybe Anna had less time for curlers these days. Her blue eyes were the same as their brother William's. She looked slender in a green dress printed with a pattern of daisies and a fawn cardy.

It was late afternoon and the day was cooling as they walked to Margaret's temporary billet. Hughie soon pulled well ahead of them, spurred on, no doubt, by the promise of not one but two consid'rations. Instead of being rumpled and tired from her long journey, Margaret couldn't have felt brighter. She linked up with Anna.

'It's good of Mrs Andrews' friend to put me up,' she said. 'I've brought her a slab of cake and a jar of carrot marma-lade from Mrs Grayson.'

'I'm glad to think of you living with those two ladies.' Anna squeezed her arm. 'Especially after that previous place you lived in. You should have told me what it was like – while you were still there, I mean, instead of waiting until you found somewhere better.'

'I didn't want you to worry,' said Margaret. 'Anyway, I've got a wizard billet now and that's what counts.'

Her digs for the next few days were with Mrs Fennell, an elderly woman who looked as if no one had told her the nineteenth century had drawn to a close more than forty years ago. She wore a white cotton cap over her snowy hair and a full-length apron over a long black skirt. Her home was a dinky old cottage with a stable-type door. The first time Margaret saw it, the top half was open, with a damp rag rug draped over the lower half to dry. The building was a two-up two-down with a boxed-in staircase that emerged into the rear of the two small bedrooms.

On the wall of Margaret's bedroom were shelves holding various items of medical paraphernalia – an eyebath, a throat spray, an inhaler made of earthenware and some smelling bottles, not to mention an earthenware bedpan.

'I gather Mrs Fennell used to tend to the locals' medical needs in days gone by,' said Anna as, after each giving a delighted Hughie the princely consid'ration of thruppence, they headed for Mrs Andrews' house.

Margaret laughed. 'I'm staying with the village wise woman.'

'Here we are,' said Anna as they turned a corner.

Margaret was about to ask which house she lived in when, towards the far end of the row, a wooden gate creaked open and two small children came hurtling along the dusty path. Tommy wore a knitted jumper and knitted shorts and Anne-Marie was in a cotton dress, the smocking at the chest making the rest of the dress flare outwards above her chubby knees. Anne-Marie's feet got in a tangle and she fell over, immediately releasing a prolonged wail. When Anna scooted around Tommy to get to her daughter, Tommy lost his nerve. Finding himself approaching this unknown auntie without his mummy there to protect him, he stopped dead. Dropping into a crouch, Margaret smiled and started to offer encouraging words, but this only had the effect of making the little boy burst into noisy tears.

Swinging her daughter up onto her hip, Anna smiled ruefully at Margaret. 'Welcome to the madhouse.'

Margaret sat on Anna's bed, close to the cot, watching the children as they slept. 'I'm sorry I didn't come to see you before now.'

'It couldn't be helped. You're here now and that's all that matters.' Anna gazed at her slumbering children. 'But it's a shame you haven't been able to watch them grow. Their dad has never seen them at all.'

Margaret stroked her sister's arm. 'It's hard for everyone.'

'I know.' Anna sighed. 'They can't stay in that cot much longer or it'll stunt their growth.'

'Where will they sleep then?'

'They'll have to have my bed, though I'll need to put the mattress on the floor so they can't fall out.'

Margaret glanced around the bedroom. How had Anna managed to cram her life into such a small space? Not only that but she was ruthlessly tidy about it – well, she had to be, didn't she? It was the only way. The room contained a bed, a chest of drawers and a chair. A washstand in the corner was home to an earthenware basin and a jug of water on the top, with a towel hanging from a hook on the side. With the mattress on the floor, there wouldn't be much floor space left, if any.

'Where will you sleep then?' Margaret asked.

'I'll curl up with the children.'

'Sounds cosy.'

'When they're a bit bigger, the mattress can go back on the bed and they can top and tail – and don't ask where I'll sleep. I'll worry about that nearer the time.'

'Maybe the billeting officer could find you somewhere bigger,' Margaret suggested.

'Maybe, but it's not everyone who would welcome a stranger with young twins into their home. You do hear stories of billets that don't work out for one reason or another. I like Mrs Andrews. She's been very accommodating, but she's not a spring chicken and she finds the children tiring – though, as she says, that's a different thing to finding them tiresome. I try to keep out of her hair as much as I can. When I was billeted in Bridgnorth when I was first here, I got friendly with another mother-to-be whose landlady made her stay out all day from after breakfast until teatime.'

'How horrid.'

Anna nodded. 'It was. I'm sure Mrs Andrews would never stoop so low, but I want to be careful not to outstay my welcome.'

'Does that put a strain on you?' Margaret asked, feeling concerned.

'No more strain than I suppose Mrs Andrews feels at having been lumbered with a family to look after. Don't worry about me. I'm fine and so are the twins.'

'Is that why you got your little cleaning job?' Margaret asked. 'To show willing?'

'Yes – though even that relies on Mrs Andrews' goodwill, because I can't leave the children unattended. Not that she is called on to do anything as a rule, because they're fast asleep.'

'Don't the ladies you clean for mind having their cleaning done in the evening?'

Anna grinned. 'It's not altogether convenient for them, but it's a lot more convenient than having no cleaner at all.'

They fell silent for a spell, gazing at the children. Anne-Marie was curled up in a ball, huffing quietly. Tommy slept flat on his back, arms flung out.

'I love watching them sleep,' said Anna.

'I like their names,' said Margaret. 'Anne-Marie is pretty.'

Anna smiled. 'The child or the name?'

'Both. She's gorgeous. They both are. I like the name Anne-Marie because, at the same time as having her own name, she is almost named after you and Mum.'

'She was very nearly Mary-Ann. I wanted Mary, for Mum's sake.'

'Why didn't you call her that?'

'Think about it. Mary-Ann Dixon. MAD. So I chose Anne-Marie instead.'

Margaret laughed. 'A wise decision. Besides, there are lots of Mary-Anns, but Anne-Marie is a bit unusual. And you called Tommy after Mum as well.'

'It broke my heart when she died.' Anna spoke almost in a whisper. 'She was far too young to go. And then, even though having the twins made me happier than anything else ever has in the whole of my life, my heart broke all over again, because Mum will never see them and they'll grow up not knowing her. Naming them after her wasn't something I had any choice over. It was something I had to do.'

'I miss her too.' Margaret squeezed Anna's hand. The old grief came back, slowing her heartbeat.

Anna pulled her hand free and smeared away a tear. 'Enough of that. This is meant to be a happy time. You're here for a holiday and that pleases me more than I can say.'

'Me too.'

It was indeed a happy time. The weather, though not overly warm, was fine and dry and after the long, harsh winter, the countryside was filled with fresh growth. The pace of life seemed gentler than Margaret was used to, though when she said so, Anna burst out laughing.

'Gentler? Is that what you call racing around after these two? But it is a different way of life. Forget keeping rabbits in hutches like townies do. Here, the cat goes hunting at night and often as not, Mrs Andrews finds a rabbit on the doorstep when she comes down in the morning.'

They went for walks together. Anna had managed to get her hands on a pushchair, which she had to steer with one hand while carrying the other child on her hip.

'That's your job while you're here,' she told Margaret. 'You can do the carrying.'

Margaret was only too happy to oblige. Holding a child in her arms caused a distant yearning inside her. What of her own baby? What if . . . ? But she would never have been able to keep it. If she was honest, she wouldn't even have considered trying. The shame and the stigma would have been unbearable. Nevertheless, when she picked up Anne-Marie and the child placed one hand on her chest and sat up straight, looking all around while her chubby legs dangled, it made something inside Margaret ache and wonder.

On Saturday, she and Anna helped at an Easter picnic for the children from several miles around. Masses of old wool was produced for the children to make pom-poms, to which they stuck paper eyes and little bits of twig for legs, the women and the older girls helping the youngest children. Someone took a photograph of all the children proudly holding up the finished articles and Margaret thought what a shame it was that the resulting black-and-white picture would give no indication of the multicoloured array of Easter chicks.

Afterwards there were sack races and three-legged races, the picnic ending with everybody standing for the national anthem, which Brown Owl played on the recorder.

'These two are more than ready for a nap,' said Anna as they made their way home, 'so we can have a bit of time to ourselves.'

Presently, Tommy and Anne-Marie were flaked out in their cot. Mrs Andrews promised to listen out for them and sent the sisters for a walk. Although it was sunny, the afternoon was cooling, so they put on jumpers and set off for the river, stopping to watch the cable ferry cross to the other side before they wandered on and chose a spot beneath the trees, where the new greenery lent a bright sweetness to the air. Sitting, they stretched out their legs in front of them, leaning back on their hands.

'I was sorry to hear that Dad didn't want to make it up with you,' said Anna. 'Give him time.'

'I will,' said Margaret.

But how much time? And anyway, Anna had no idea of the real reason for their dramatic falling-out. Margaret had simply told her in a letter that she hadn't got along with Mrs McEvoy and so had moved out, which had made Dad flip his lid because he didn't want her going off on her own. It had seemed rather a feeble reason, but Anna had never questioned it.

Now, though, was the perfect time to share the truth, just as Margaret had promised herself she would. She sat upright, drawing her knees close to her chest and wrapping her arms around them. After a moment she changed her mind. She didn't want to huddle and look small and ashamed – even if she was ashamed. The most important thing now was the love and trust between her and her sister. She wouldn't shrink and seem to ask for sympathy. Swinging round, she leaned on one hand, facing Anna.

'Didn't you think it strange that Dad fell out with me for finding my own billet?' she asked. 'The thing is . . . there was more to it than that.'

Anna tilted her head to one side. 'Do you want to tell me about it?'

Margaret's heart thudded, but she refused to duck out of it now. Slowly, her voice hitching here and there, she started to tell her tale, jerking her hand away when Anna reached out to her.

'Don't,' she said. 'Let me finish. This is hard for me to say.'

'You don't have to say anything,' Anna told her gently. 'I already know what happened.'

Margaret stiffened in shock. 'You what?'

'Dad told me.'

Margaret felt it as a smack in the face. Dad! 'So not only did he blab to all and sundry the night of the air raid, he also blabbed to you.' She went cold right to the centre of her being. 'He hasn't told William as well, has he?'

'No. I know for a fact he hasn't. And before you ask, I haven't either. I wouldn't dream of it.'

Margaret shook her head. 'I can't believe Dad told you.'

'He was very upset.'

'*He* was upset? What about me?' Margaret stared at her sister. 'You've known all this time. Why did you never say anything?'

'Because you never did. I wanted to respect your privacy.'

Her privacy? What a joke. Dad had made sure she had none of that left. 'You ought to have told me you knew.'

'No, that wouldn't have been right. It would have put you under more pressure. I thought it better to wait for you to tell me, if you wanted to. I thought that would be of more help to you. If I'd come wading into the situation, it would have piled more shame on top of you and I didn't want to do that.'

'So you just waited for me to tell you.'

'Yes.'

'What if I never had?'

'That would have been your choice, your decision.'

Margaret stared at her hands as if they contained the answers to all of life's questions. 'I can't take it in. You've known all along and you never let on.'

'I don't know the whole story, though, do I? I only know what Dad told me – that you'd suffered a miscarriage. Why don't you tell me the rest? Please. I want to understand. I want to know what my little sister went through.'

As Margaret told Anna about Joel, she felt a pang of guilt that Anna wasn't the first person with whom she had shared her story. On the other hand, having already told Joan and Dot made it easier to tell Anna, because the words were already there.

'Why didn't you tell me when you first knew you had a baby on the way?' Anna asked gently.

'How?' Margaret suppressed a shudder as the old fear washed through her. 'I couldn't tell anybody. I was too frightened to make any proper decisions. And then . . .'

'And then you miscarried, but instead of being able to keep the secret and put it behind you, Dad blew his stack in front of the world and his wife.'

Margaret shut her eyes against the memory of a humiliation so great that she had ultimately been unable to remain in the place where she'd grown up.

'I'm so sorry you had to go through all that,' said Anna. 'Thank you for telling me. Thank you for trusting me.' She moved close, put her arm around Margaret's shoulders and kissed her hair. 'There is nothing you could do that would make me turn away from you. You know that, don't you? You're my sister and I love you, and nothing could ever change that.'

'Dad's my father, but things have certainly changed for him.'

Margaret felt a soft breath against her temple as Anna released a sigh.

'I've worried about you ever since Dad wrote to me about it, especially when things were so bad that you moved out of Mrs McEvoy's.'

'But you understand why I had to go, don't you?'

'Of course I do. I think you've shown great bravery.'

That surprised a laugh out of Margaret. 'Brave? Me? You're kidding.'

'I mean it. You've been through so much, but you did your best to make a new start. You went to work on the railways and made new friends. I was thrilled when you were asked to be a bridesmaid.'

'The wedding dress that Joan wore . . .'

Anna tilted her head. 'What about it?'

'It was mine. I bought it. I was so desperately in love with Joel, and I saw this wedding dress. It was the most beautiful gown I'd ever seen and it was on sale. I could never have afforded it at full price, so I . . . I bought it. I knew it was a crazy thing to do, but I couldn't help it. When I got it home, I wrapped it up carefully and hid it in a cupboard in the cellar.' Margaret half laughed, scorning herself. 'Which meant, of course, that it was one of the very few things to survive the bomb blast. So you see what a complete twit I was.'

'Don't do yourself down. You were in love and we all do mad things then. You're a good girl at heart and that's what counts. You made one mistake and got caught out, but look at you now, eh? Working for the war effort and living in a nice house with Mrs Cooper and Mrs Grayson fussing over you. That's – that's what Mum would have wanted for you after everything you've been through.'

'Mum? Really? I thought – Dad said—'

'Nonsense,' Anna said firmly. 'If Mum had still been with us, she'd never have let Dad carry on the way he has. She'd have stood by you. You'd have told her, wouldn't you, when you knew you were expecting?'

'I suppose so.'

'I know so,' said Anna. 'You couldn't tell Dad and I wasn't there, but you'd have told Mum. Even if you'd been too scared, she'd have realised something was wrong and she'd have got you to open up. You know she would. She'd have been upset, of course, but she'd never have turned her back on you, not for one moment. She'd never have let you feel grubby or small. She loved you so much and she'd have loved you even more, because you needed her more at that time.'

'Really?' Margaret whispered. Hearing Anna's words, she knew they were true, but she wanted to hear them again. She wanted to be told that Mum would have stood up for her, no matter what.

Oh, Mum. She had never missed her more than in this moment.

CHAPTER TWENTY-FOUR

Alison hummed to herself as she got ready to go out on Saturday evening. It felt so good to be home. She had two homes now, Mum and Dad's and here with Mrs Cooper. She had come over to Manchester on Thursday and spent a couple of nights at Mum's and today she had travelled to Wilton Close, where she was to stay until Monday. In Leeds, she had filled her suitcase with her winter clothes and had unpacked them earlier while Mrs Cooper sat on her bed, watching.

'I hope coming back to this room isn't a disappointment,' Mrs Cooper had said. When Alison had looked at her in surprise, she explained, 'I mean, because it's small. From what you said in your letters, your bedroom in Leeds is rather bigger.'

'And rather colder,' said Alison, 'not to mention being on the wrong side of the Pennines. I can't tell you how glad I am to be back. I just wish I didn't have to go away again.'

'But when you go back to Leeds, it won't be for such a long time, will it?'

'No, it won't,' Alison had replied. She didn't know whether it was true, but she wanted it to be – needed it to be. She wanted to come home and feel settled and get on with having a proper relationship with Joel . . . without Rachel Chambers being anywhere in the vicinity.

This evening she and Joel were going out in a foursome with Mabel and Harry. Alison wanted to look her best for a night of dancing at the Ritz, with its famous revolving stage.

While she was staying at Mum's, Lydia had given her an evening dress, her best one, a rayon dress with a long blue skirt and a silvery-blue beaded bodice with a sweetheart neckline.

'I can't take it,' Alison had protested.

'Yes, you can. It's not as though I need going-out clothes any more now that I'm married with my husband away in the army. I'd rather you had it than anyone else. And think of all those things you gave me for my home – your entire bottom drawer.'

Alison had laughed. 'Oh yes, I let you have household linen and fish knives and goodness knows what else, even a doormat, as I recall – and you give me a lovely evening dress. That's my idea of a good swap!'

Now, Alison slipped into her new dress, enjoying the feel of it as it whispered against her skin. She twisted gracefully to and fro, making the skirt swish. Leaving her room, she went along the landing, knocked on Mabel's door and popped her head in.

'Do you mind if I gaze at myself in your mirror?'

'Gaze away.' Mabel glanced round from her seat at the dressing table, where she was doing her hair. 'Gorgeous dress. Is that the one Lydia gave you? It suits you. I've got something that might . . .' Her voice trailed away as she got up and rifled through a drawer. 'Here, try this.'

Alison's breath caught in pure pleasure. It was a snood of silvery thread.

'Let me put it on for you,' Mabel offered. 'Take a pew.'

Alison sat at the dressing table. Moments later, she looked at herself, turning her chin to the side to get a better glimpse of the snood that looked as if it had been made specially for this dress.

'You'll knock Joel's socks off.' Mabel stood behind Alison, smiling at her reflection over her shoulder. 'I bet he can't wait to see you again.'

'I can't wait to see him either. It hasn't been easy being apart from one another.'

'I know,' Mabel said sympathetically. 'I'm the same with Harry.'

'At least I'll end up back home again when my stint in Leeds is finished, but you'll always be at a distance from Harry.'

'It makes the times we're together all the more special,' said Mabel. She sounded bright and positive, but it couldn't be easy for her to be apart from Harry nearly all the time. But that was Mabel for you. She took things on the chin and now that Alison thought of it, she was good at keeping her troubles to herself. Just look at how she had kept the truth about her friend Althea's death secret for such a long time.

Alison reached and caught Mabel's hand and they looked at one another.

'I'm trying to think of something helpful to say,' Alison admitted, 'something to show I understand about you and Harry not seeing much of one another, something to show I care.'

Mabel gave her a hug, a careful one that didn't muss up her appearance. 'Bless you, I know you care, but thanks for saying so. Harry and I are old hands at being apart. I'm not saying it's something you get used to, exactly, but it's the way things are for us. At least we do get to see each other every so often, which is a lot more than most couples can say these days. It can't have been easy for you these past few weeks, not having Joel close by, just when you were starting to get to know one another.'

'No, it hasn't,' Alison agreed. 'I wish I didn't have to go back to Leeds.'

'We all want you to come home for good.' Mabel tilted her head. 'There's more to this than just wanting to come home, isn't there?'

Alison could feel the truth welling up inside her. 'You have no idea.'

Mabel looked serious. 'Then you'd better tell me.'

She sat on her bed and Alison swivelled around on the dressing-table stool to face her.

'It wasn't all that long ago that you were in here, with Margaret and me encouraging you to make a go of things with Joel,' said Mabel. 'You haven't changed your mind about him, have you?'

'Lord, no! If anything, being separated from him has made me want to have the chance to be with him all the more.'

'Don't tell me he's going off the boil.'

Alison laughed, but it wasn't a real laugh. 'You do get straight to the point, don't you?'

'Tell me to take my nose out of your business if you want to, but it sounds to me as if you want to talk. Come on, sweetheart. You've been over there in Leeds all on your own for however many weeks it's been, but you're home now, with the people who know you and care about you. Let me help. Even if I can't help, let me at least listen.'

Alison's insides seemed to vibrate as she released a long, slow breath. She was annoyed and worried about Rachel, but until this moment she hadn't realised – hadn't let herself realise – how deeply upset she really was.

'Actually,' she admitted, 'I'm feeling quite rattled. It's to do with Rachel – Miss Chambers, the deputy lady almoner.'

'Rachel? First names? I didn't realise you were friends.'

'We aren't, not really. That is, I'm not sure. She behaves as if we are, but . . . She's an old girlfriend of Joel's.'

Mabel's eyes widened and she let out a low whistle. 'Well, that's a bit of a turn-up. Is it a problem? I thought you got on with her. She got you that stint in the lady almoner's office, didn't she? And she put you on the pie scheme. You enjoyed both of those – unless you were lying through your teeth in your letters.'

'Of course I wasn't. They were a big improvement on doing the donkey work in the canteen. But Rachel didn't start giving me interesting things to do until after she knew I was going out with Joel.'

'Coincidence, surely.'

'Possibly.'

'What else would it be?'

'I never said anything about it in my letters, but right back on my first day, I got on Rachel's wrong side. Never mind the ins and outs of it, but I spoke out of turn and she wasn't pleased. She never said in so many words that she was going to keep me on peeling and prepping duty as a punishment, but she didn't give me the chance to see the management side of things, which was what she was supposed to do.'

'But she came good in the end and gave you those opportunities, didn't she? Maybe she decided you'd served your punishment and it was time to let you do the things you'd been sent to Leeds to do.'

'Maybe,' Alison was forced to concede, 'but that wasn't until after she knew about Joel and me.'

'Why would she start being nice to you because of Joel?'

'I think she wants him back.'

'Crikey.'

'Exactly. I can't prove it and sometimes I think I'm seeing things that aren't there, but – but I can sense it. The last time Joel came over to Leeds, I had to work an extra shift, so I missed meeting him off the train and couldn't see him until later. In the meantime, guess who stepped in and looked after him.'

'Did Rachel give you the extra shift?'

'No. Someone else did. And I ought to say that the reason behind the extra shift was real. It was to do with someone's husband who had been badly injured. It's just that . . . it sounds ridiculous to say it, but – well, things worked out very conveniently for Rachel.'

'Assuming she wants Joel back, that is. Did she say or do anything untoward while she was with him?'

'No, I'm sure she didn't, but they obviously still get along and she's very charming.'

'What does Joel have to say on the subject?'

'I haven't asked.'

'Sorry to state the blindingly obvious, but maybe you should.'

Alison looked squarely at her friend. 'It's not that simple. I don't want to make a complete clot of myself if Rachel is just being a friend to Joel. I don't want to seem jealous or clingy. I've always rather looked down on clingy girls. Mind you, that was when I was with Paul and I thought we were the perfect couple, more fool me.'

Mabel said gently, 'This isn't about Paul. It's about you and Joel.'

Alison swallowed as a lump appeared in her throat, clogging it. 'But it is about Paul. Don't you see? He and I were a couple for such a long time – several years – and Joel knows about it and he doesn't mind.'

'Of course he doesn't,' said Mabel. 'Why would he?'

'He and Rachel met when he was in Leeds doing intensive surgical training. That was early in the war. I don't know exactly how long they were seeing one another, but it can't have been all that long, because Joel came back to Manchester immediately after his training finished and she stayed in Leeds.'

'So it was a short-lived thing,' said Mabel. 'Nothing like you and Paul.'

'Can you understand my point of view?' Alison asked. 'If Joel doesn't mind about Paul, who I was with for years and thought I was going to marry and spend the rest of my life with, I can hardly make a song and dance over Rachel, can I?'

'Mmm.' Mabel frowned down at her hands. 'I can see that.' Then she looked at Alison and her face broke into a smile. 'Here's the plan.'

'Plan?'

'You don't turn to me for support and get fobbed off with a "There, there, dear, never mind." Here's what we're going to do. I'll ask Mrs Cooper to cut along to the phone box and telephone Persephone and ask her to nip round sharpish with a sackful of swag – jewellery, scent, evening gloves, maybe a chiffon wrap – anything that could help you look even more gorgeous than you do already. Then we'll go out and have a wonderful evening and Joel will fall for you all over again.'

Alison laughed, not exactly forgetting about Rachel, but swept up by delight.

'Are you seeing him again tomorrow?' asked Mabel.

'I'm going to meet his sister. We're going there for tea.'

'Lovely. Tomorrow morning, go to the early service at church, then spend the rest of the morning writing a report for Miss Emery about everything you've done in Leeds and what you've learned from it. While you're being entertained to tea and cake by Joel's sister, I'll go to Darley Court and Persephone and I will type up your report for you – and before you ask, yes, Miss Brown has a typewriter. Then, when you leave here on Monday to return to Leeds, go early to Victoria, so you can nip across to Hunts Bank to see Miss Emery. Give her the report and ask her how much longer you have to stay in Leeds. That's not an unreasonable question. If she's not in her office, leave the report with

Mrs Jessop and I'll deliver it to Miss Emery at the first opportunity and ask on your behalf about a leaving date. Even if she's too discreet to tell me, it will spur her on to write to you.' Mabel's smile held more than a hint of wickedness. 'The report's the important thing here, you see. It gives the impression of things drawing to a close.'

'And once I have a finishing date . . .' Alison pictured it.

'Exactly,' said Mabel. 'You'll breeze through your remaining time because the end will be in sight. If Miss Rachel Chambers crosses your path, take a deep breath and smile. That's all there is to it. Then you can come home and never think about her ever again.'

CHAPTER TWENTY-FIVE

When Alison went upstairs to get ready to go to Joel's sister's for tea, Mabel followed.

'What are you going to wear?' Mabel asked.

Alison opened her hanging cupboard. She had known Paul's relations inside out, especially his mum, whom she had been very close to – indeed, whom she had fully expected to live with after her marriage. She had always wanted to look nice when she saw Paul's family, but today's outing felt different.

'Meeting a chap's family for the first time isn't something I've done for several years,' she told Mabel.

'Butterflies?'

'Not exactly. It's not as though I'm shy. But it matters. I want to make a good impression.'

'Speaking as the person responsible for making you look like a star of the silver screen last night,' said Mabel, 'I suggest you don't go overboard on the dressing up. Wear something fairly simple. Smart, of course, appropriate to the occasion, but simple. Joel saw you at your most devastatingly swish last night and, believe me, he was the proudest man in the ballroom. Now show him you're natural and unaffected too. Wear something pretty. Demure. That's the word: demure.'

Alison couldn't help laughing. 'Never mind being a lengthman. You should have a job organising people's love lives.'

'Perhaps I will, after the war. Mabel's Matrimonial Bureau. How does that sound? Let's see what you've got.'

Alison drew out her pale yellow dress. It had a boat neck, slight puffs on the short sleeves and a gathered skirt.

'Perfect,' Mabel declared. 'Stylish but not fussy. You wore it as your bridesmaid's dress, didn't you?'

'Fancy you remembering.'

Mabel helped her to dress and did her hair for her, using her own tortoiseshell combs to scoop it tidily away from her face.

'Now come and look at yourself in the big mirror,' Mabel invited, leading the way along the landing to the room she shared with Margaret. 'There. Happy?'

'Cardigan or jacket?' asked Alison.

'Cardy,' Mabel decreed. 'You'll do Joel proud.'

A while later, when Joel arrived, he caught Alison's hands in his and stood back to look at her.

'Will I do?' she asked.

'More than,' he told her.

She took him into the front room to spend a few minutes with the others.

'Where does your sister live?' Mrs Cooper asked.

'Victoria Park,' said Joel.

'Very nice,' said Mrs Cooper.

Alison hadn't heard of Victoria Park, but the impressed looks on Mrs Cooper's and Mrs Grayson's faces told her something.

'Have you got the packs of cards in your bag?' asked Mrs Grayson.

'Safely tucked away,' said Alison. To Joel she explained, 'They're for your sister's boys.'

'That's kind of you,' said Joel. 'Venetia will appreciate it.'

Soon it was time to go. Mabel kissed Alison's cheek and whispered, 'Remember, the future of my matrimonial bureau rests on you.'

Joel had ordered a taxi and they held hands in the back as they travelled, Joel only letting go to lean forward and say to the driver, 'It's over here on the left after the pillar box.'

The motor pulled over and Joel helped Alison out. While he paid, she looked at the house on the other side of the wall. It was double-fronted with a flight of stone steps leading to a front door in between a pair of bay windows. No wonder Mrs Cooper and Mrs Grayson had been impressed.

'Let's go in,' said Joel, smiling at her.

They entered the garden. A path made a square, with four narrow paths leading into the middle, creating four smaller squares. These must have been filled in with lawn before the war but now they contained vegetable beds, in the centre of which was a fountain, with spray spurting upwards and turning to diamond droplets in the spring sunshine.

As they walked up the path to the house, Alison saw a figure in the bay window on the right. Her first impression was one of slenderness and fair hair. She expected the woman to move away, having been caught peering, but she didn't.

'My sister, Venetia,' said Joel. He waved to her and she waved back.

The door was opened by a maid who was in her sixties or thereabouts, wearing a black skirt and blouse.

'Good afternoon, Grace,' said Joel. 'Happy Easter. This is Miss Lambert.'

'Afternoon, miss.'

They handed over their coats and hats and Joel opened the door to the front room, where a carpet in muted reds and blues covered most of the floor, and the furniture included a grand piano – not just a piano, but a grand. Alison had only ever seen those in concert halls. Crikey, there was some money here.

Venetia came forward, taking Joel's hands and offering her smooth cheek for a kiss. She wore her fair hair caught up at the top of her head at the back, from where it tumbled in a mass of tiny curls. They fell to shoulder level, which meant that, uncurled, her hair must be pretty long. Like Joel, she had blue eyes. Her smile was pretty and everything about her was graceful and attractive. If she was anything like her brother, then she must be older than she appeared. When Alison had first seen Joel, she had thought him in his late twenties or early thirties and now she knew him to be at the top end of that range.

Joel performed the introductions. 'Venetia, this is Alison Lambert, my girlfriend. Alison, this is my sister, Venetia Clifton. And this,' he added as a yellow Labrador climbed off the sofa and ambled across, rear end shaking from side to side with the energy of the tail-wagging, 'is Honey.'

Alison shook hands with Venetia. Venetia's handshake was firm and cool.

'Hello, old girl.' Joel was fussing the dog, so Alison did too. 'There. Is that enough for now? Honey's job,' he told Alison as Honey returned to the sofa, 'is to make sure the furniture doesn't fly away.' To Venetia he said, 'I thought Honey's place was that old chintz monstrosity in the corner.'

'She's been promoted,' Venetia replied. 'I'm so sorry, Alison – may I call you Alison? Imagine the dog sitting down first.'

'That's the Maitland family's manners for you,' said Joel.

'Come and sit here,' said Venetia, waving Alison to a wingback armchair upholstered in beige and caramel with just a hint of pink. Venetia took her place on the sofa with the dog. 'We sit here and miss Larry and the boys together. Larry's my husband. He's in the navy.'

'How long is it since you've seen your children?' Alison asked.

'I'm lucky, really. I've been to see them twice each year. Many parents only manage once, and some not at all.'

'Poor Venetia rattles around in this place all on her own,' said Joel, 'apart from dear old Grace.'

'Don't listen to him,' said his sister. 'The house is full of civil servants and I run a WVS jam factory in my kitchen.'

'My mum's in the WVS,' said Alison.

'Good for her,' said Venetia. 'I work in the Citizens Advice Bureau most days and with the WVS in the evenings. Joel says you work for LMS. What do you do?'

'I started out as a wages clerk. Since then I've done various things.'

'Alison is being trained up,' said Joel. 'No pun intended.'

'They must think well of you, then,' said Venetia. 'What are you up to currently? Or aren't you allowed to say? Keep mum, and all that.'

Alison smiled. 'As a matter of fact, I'm delivering pies outside Leeds.'

'Leeds? I assumed you were a Manchester girl.'

Alison felt a bit taken aback. It wasn't the response she'd expected. 'I am, but I've been working in Leeds since January.'

Venetia glanced at Joel, then returned her attention to Alison. 'I see. I didn't realise. When Joel went over there for those weekends, I thought—' Did Joel catch Venetia's eye, or was that Alison's imagination? 'Never mind. It doesn't matter. Pies, you said?'

Alison explained about the pie scheme. 'The WVS are very involved in it.'

Venetia gave Joel a mock-stern look. 'And don't say they have their fingers in many pies.'

Joel grinned. 'Wouldn't dream of it.'

Alison felt it was time for her to ask a question instead of leaving the work to her hostess. 'Are you allowed to say what your husband does in the navy?'

Venetia lifted her chin. 'He's a doctor.'

'It runs in the family,' said Alison. 'Joel says your father's a doctor too.'

Venetia laughed. 'Is that what he told you? Father is a consultant and eminent in his field. What does your father do?'

'He's a builder.'

'He must be exceptionally busy at the moment, and for the most tragic of reasons.'

'He says he's never been busier. He works in Heavy Rescue as well, because of his specialist knowledge.' Alison leaned down and picked up her handbag, removing the packs of cards. 'I brought you these for your sons. I hope they'll like them.'

'How perfectly sweet of you,' cried Venetia. 'I know one is supposed to say, "Oh, you shouldn't have," but I never say that where my sons are concerned, with everything being in such short supply. Thank you a thousand times. They'll be so pleased.'

'I was with Joel when he got them the paintboxes for you to give them for Christmas,' said Alison. 'Did he tell you about that?'

'Don't tell me he did a smash-and-grab on the toy shop.'

'He tackled a war profiteer.' Alison told the tale, proud all over again of the way Joel had handled what could have become a very sticky situation. 'He was a hero,' she finished.

'Steady on,' said Joel.

'Everyone in the queue thought so,' Alison replied staunchly.

'You see,' Joel said to Venetia, 'you don't appreciate me as you should.'

'Well, I'm glad you were with him on that occasion, Alison,' said Venetia.

'So that she could sing my praises afterwards, you mean?' asked Joel.

'So that she knew about the boys and was kind enough to bring them these presents.'

'They aren't new packs, I'm afraid,' said Alison, 'but all the cards are there. I've checked.'

'The boys will be thrilled.'

'It was my mum's idea to bring them something,' Alison admitted. 'Mrs Grayson, who does the cooking for us, usually sends a jar of one of her jams or one of her cakes when one of us is invited to someone's house, but Mum thought something for the children would be more imaginative.'

'She was correct,' said Venetia. 'And she has her own cook. That makes her very fortunate these days. I wish I'd been able to keep mine, but she stays at home now to look after her grandchildren while her daughters work in the munitions.'

Alison felt a flutter of alarm. 'No, you misunderstand. Mrs Grayson isn't my mum's cook. In fact, she's nobody's cook in that sense. It's not her paid job. It's just something she has a talent for and she cooks for everybody at my digs.'

'Did your mother lose her cook to the war effort?' Venetia asked.

How on earth had the conversation taken this turn? 'She's never had one. We're just an ordinary family.'

Joel said mildly, 'Not everyone learned to walk with a pile of books on their head, Vee.'

'Very funny, I don't think,' his sister retorted before saying to Alison, 'Joel likes to bring me down to earth if he thinks I'm being posh. Father sent my sister and me to finishing school, you see. Hence the dig about books on heads.'

'Venetia's idea of cooking is – or used to be, before the war – choosing the menu, arranging the flowers and working out the most tactful and socially and professionally advantageous seating plan.'

'Mock all you like,' Venetia replied spiritedly, 'but dinner parties are important if a man wants to get on in life. It's a wife's duty to support her husband in his career. Don't you agree, Alison?'

'I'd never thought of it that way,' said Alison. 'I've always thought of marriage in terms of taking care of one another, not helping your husband to rise in the world.'

Venetia picked up a dainty brass bell from the table beside her. She gave it a little shake. 'After all that talk of fancy dinner parties, we'll be having wartime meat paste with radishes from the garden, and sultana scones.'

'Sultanas, eh?' said Joel. 'We're honoured.'

'You jolly well ought to be,' said Venetia. 'I practically had to sleep with the grocer to get them.'

Grace brought in the tea on a wheeled wooden trolley and they chatted as they ate. Alison asked about Venetia's children.

'What are they called?'

'Son number one is Lawrence after his father and son number two is Jonty, short for Jonathan, which was the name of . . .' Venetia glanced at Joel.

'The name of our brother who died,' Joel said quietly. 'Alison knows about him.'

'I was very sorry to hear it,' said Alison.

'I wanted to name my son after him, but didn't want the child to be known as Jonathan,' said Venetia. 'It wouldn't have felt right.'

'I can understand that,' said Alison.

They talked about what it had been like coping with the fuel rationing in recent weeks and about the German aerial attacks on Malta and the Maltese people's heroic struggle.

When it was time to leave, Venetia asked Joel, 'Shall you telephone for a taxi?'

'It's such a lovely day,' said Alison. 'Let's walk to the bus stop.'

'You'll wait ages for a bus on a Sunday,' said Venetia.

'Then I'll spend longer with Alison,' said Joel.

Venetia rolled her eyes and punched his arm. She kissed him goodbye. When she shook hands with Alison, she leaned forward slightly and for a moment Alison thought Venetia might be about to kiss her too, but she didn't.

Venetia stood at the top of the front steps as they left and they turned at the gate to wave. As they walked down the road, Alison said a few complimentary things about Venetia and her home and then, hoping it didn't sound as if the previous remarks were just a smokescreen, she asked the question she'd been dying to ask most of the afternoon.

'When I said I worked in Leeds, Venetia started to say something about your recent visits there.' She kept her voice light, her tone casual. 'Did she think you'd gone to see Rachel?'

'Apparently so.' Joel appeared unperturbed by the question. 'Venetia was very fond of Rachel.'

All Alison's senses perked up. She had only ever thought of Rachel as the temporary girlfriend across the Pennines. It had never occurred to her that Rachel might have had a foothold in Manchester . . . in Joel's family.

'How did they meet?' she asked. 'Through you, obviously. I'm really asking where.'

'Venetia came over to Leeds for a visit.'

Good. That was all right. There was no threat in that.

'And Rachel also came over to Manchester with me,' Joel added.

Alison's skin prickled. She willed Joel to extend the sentence. Once? Twice? A dozen times? She gave a little laugh. 'Did she get invited to tea as well?'

'Venetia asks all my girlfriends to tea,' said Joel. 'Sorry, that makes it sound as if they roll up at her door by the busload.'

'You said Venetia was very fond of Rachel.'

'I did,' said Joel, 'and she was.' Stopping, he turned Alison to face him, gently lifting her chin with the knuckles of one hand. 'And I – ' kiss ' – am very fond – ' kiss ' – of you.'

As they had each night of her stay, Margaret and Anna sat chatting quietly as they watched the children sleeping. All through her time here, Margaret had harboured a strong desire to talk to Anna, really talk to her, to have deep, important conversations, but that was impossible when you had a pair of lively toddlers permanently in tow. That had made the quiet times they had managed to have together all the more special. Not that Margaret hadn't loved every moment of being with her niece and nephew. She had. They were adorable and she had taken them off Anna's hands for a spell each day, not just to give her sister a break but also because she wanted to start to build a special relationship with them. It definitely wouldn't be two whole years before she saw them again. She had promised herself that – and had promised Anna too.

A pang cut through her at the thought that her visit would end tomorrow.

Anna reached to rearrange the blanket Anne-Marie had kicked off, saying to Margaret, 'I'll miss you when you leave. It's been wonderful having you here.'

'I've loved it too, for all sorts of reasons. Not just being with you and the children, but because you've made me feel better about myself, with what you said about Mum and how she would have stood by me.'

'Of course she would have,' said Anna. 'Don't ever doubt it. She'd have brought Dad round too.' She smiled sadly. 'But don't tell him I said so.'

Margaret didn't look at Anna as she asked, 'Do you think he'll ever forgive me?'

'I don't know. I've tried telling him that Mum wouldn't want the family to be split apart, but it doesn't do any good. It doesn't help that he still lives where it happened and where everybody knows, but as he made clear to me, why should he be required to leave the place he's lived in all his life because of your transgression? So he stays put and feels all the time that he's being talked about behind his back.'

'Which he probably is, if Mrs McEvoy has anything to do with it,' Margaret said drily. 'You should have heard the row she had with the billeting officer the day I left hospital and he took me round there to live with Dad. Anyway, let's not rehash all that. It's my last night here. Let's end my visit on a cheerful note.'

'Good show,' said Anna. 'Tell me more about your friends and the ladies you live with.'

Margaret was happy to oblige. Anna listened and nodded along, asking a question or making a comment here and there.

'I haven't forgotten I must write and thank Mrs Grayson for the children's cardigans.'

'I could take the letter with me, if you like,' Margaret offered.

'No, I'll post it. It might look a bit casual if you take it, and I wouldn't want to give that impression. I want her to understand how much I appreciate her kindness.'

'She's a kind person,' Margaret agreed. 'So is Mrs Cooper.'

'You're lucky to have them.'

'Believe me, I know it.'

'I like to think of you being properly looked after. It's what Mum would have wanted and it makes me feel better about you.'

'When you write to me from now on,' said Margaret, 'I'll be able to picture the people and the place.'

'I wish I knew what your friends look like.'

Margaret had a thought. 'I've got a photograph I can send you. It's not of everyone, but I'd like you to have it. When Alison was sent to Leeds at the beginning of the year, Joan got her wedding photographer to make copies of the picture of her and the bridesmaids. She gave one to each of us, which was jolly generous of her as well as being a lovely surprise. We all knew she was getting one for Alison, but we had no idea she was doing it for all of us. I'll send you mine.'

'I can't take your precious photo from you,' said Anna.

'You're not taking it. I'm giving it – gladly. I want you to have it. I know how much I'll enjoy imagining you and the twins being here now that I've seen it for myself. I'd like you to be able to picture my friends.'

'Thank you,' said Anna. 'Don't forget to write the names and the date on the back. Is . . .' She reached for Margaret's hand. 'Is your friend who was killed in the picture?'

Tears thickened the inside of Margaret's throat. She nodded. 'Colette. Yes. She was matron of honour. She died before Christmas, and now we've just had Easter.'

'I know,' Anna said softly. 'Are you sure you want me to have the photograph?'

'Positive. It's not just for you. It's for the children as well, so they don't forget what their auntie Margaret looks like.'

Anna swiped at a tear. 'Sorry. It's the thought of you going home.'

'Right now, I don't want to leave, but I know that when I get home, I'll be happy to be there. I'm lucky to have two places where I want to be.' Should she admit it? Yes. She could say anything to Anna. 'For a long time, I had nowhere I wanted to be, just places I had to be. I felt completely alone.' For a moment, all the old anguish coursed through her and she felt trapped, but then she emerged on the other side of the wave of emotion. She smiled. 'But I'm not alone any more. I have my friends and my job and a lovely home. And I have you.'

'You've always had me,' said Anna.

'I know that now. I should have turned to you sooner, but I was too ashamed.'

'I don't mean to trivialise your feelings, but I hope I've helped you feel less ashamed.'

'You have,' Margaret assured her. 'It was what you said about Mum. All this time, I've seen everything through Dad's eyes. You've made me realise there's another way of looking at it.'

'Mum's way,' said Anna. 'She would have stood by you, come what may. Never let anyone tell you different. I'm glad it's made you feel better about yourself.'

'It has and it's helped me make a decision that I'd like to share with you. I've thought hard about it and I'm going to change my name – my surname.'

Anna frowned. 'Dad won't like that.'

'He can't have it both ways. He can barely look me in the eye because he's so ashamed of me. He ought to be pleased I'm not going to be a Darrell any more.'

'Well, he won't be. He just won't. The only reason for a girl to change her name is through marriage. That's how he'll see it.'

'What about you?' Margaret asked. 'How do you see it?'

'It's come as a surprise. I just want to be sure you aren't doing it for the wrong reasons.'

'To get back at Dad, you mean? No, it's not that. It's nothing to do with Dad. It's to do with Mum.' A feeling of contentment expanded inside her chest. 'I'm going to be Margaret Thomas, in honour of Mum.'

'Goodness,' breathed Anna.

'Why "goodness"? You've got Mary as your middle name and you've named both your children after her, and William is William Thomas. Why shouldn't I be named after her as well?'

Was Anna going to object? But Anna moved to wrap her arms around her and held her close.

'I think it's perfect,' Anna whispered.

CHAPTER TWENTY-SIX

As the bus approached Joan's stop, she started to get up, but the conductor, an older man who looked like he had come out of retirement to take a younger man's place for the duration, leaned down to speak to her.

'Nay, lass, you stop where you are until the bus halts. Don't fret. I'll make sure you get off safely.'

Joan smiled and nodded. Folk were so kind. She was seven months along now and the more obvious her condition had become over time, the more consideration she had received. She never had to queue for anything, but was waved to the front every time. Even before she had looked pregnant, as soon as anyone realised she possessed a green ration book, she was immediately given preferential treatment. There was no law or regulation that said mothers-to-be should be favoured. It was just something that everyone did and now she was this far along, Joan was glad of it.

The bus pulled in at the stop and the passengers who had already stood up to wait in the aisle filed off.

'Your turn now, love,' said the conductor. He stood on the platform at the rear of the bus, refusing to let the queue move forward until Joan had alighted.

She made her way to Victoria Station, her spirit reaching out instinctively to the sharp-sweet aroma of smoke and steam and the sounds that lifted up into the overarching canopy and echoed back down again. She loved Bob with all her heart and was excited about the baby, but it wasn't wrong, was it, to love this place and all it represented?

In the buffet, Mrs Jessop wanted to hear how she was getting on.

'Do the others know you're coming?' she asked.

'No, but I know they're meeting today. Mrs Green told me.'

'The buffet isn't too busy,' said Mrs Jessop. 'You'll be able to push a couple of tables together.'

'I'll do it now.'

'You most certainly will not.'

Mrs Jessop and her young assistant came out from behind the counter and placed one table next to another.

'You sit down,' Mrs Jessop told Joan. 'Dolly will bring your tea across.'

'There's really no need,' Joan protested.

Mrs Jessop lifted an eyebrow in a knowing way. 'Make the most of it, love. You'll be rushed off your feet once the baby's here.'

Joan laughed and thanked her, but as Mrs Jessop threaded her way back to the counter, Joan released a soft sigh. Pushing two tables together was a treat rather than a necessity these days, without Colette and Alison. At least Alison would be coming back.

It wasn't long before her friends started to arrive, waving to her as they joined the short queue. Each time one of them sat down, Joan had to answer the same questions all over again.

'I'm fine, thanks. Starting to be uncomfortable, but nothing to write home about. Sorry if this is indelicate, but the baby likes using my bladder as a trampoline. Aside from that, I've never felt better.'

'Any luck finding a new home yet?' asked Mabel.

'Still looking.'

'If you don't find somewhere soon,' said Cordelia, 'you'll have to wait until after you've had the baby.'

'Look, here comes Brizo,' said Mabel.

Persephone had appeared in the doorway with Brizo on his lead. The dog spotted Joan and bounced about excitedly, but when Persephone spoke quietly to him, he calmed down. She brought him across and after joyfully greeting Joan, he sat beside her, pressing as close to her as he could.

'He behaves much better for you than he does for Bob and me,' Joan told Persephone.

'I grew up with dogs, so I've got the knack. The collection box is safely locked away and today's money has been totted up.' Persephone scratched Brizo's ear. 'You're a good boy, aren't you? People love giving you money.'

Persephone went to join the queue. Soon all the friends were together.

'What brings you here, chick?' Dot asked Joan. 'Not that we aren't delighted to see you.'

'First of all,' said Joan, 'I want to hear all about Margaret's trip to see her sister.'

Everyone turned to Margaret, eager to hear everything. Margaret described Anna's billet, the folk she had met and the Easter picnic.

'You've clearly had a good time,' said Cordelia. 'I'm pleased for you.'

'We all are,' said Dot.

'It was a wrench to come back,' Margaret admitted.

'It's a shame you had to be away while Alison was here,' said Mabel.

Margaret turned to Joan. 'You said, "First of all" about my trip. That suggests there's a second of all.'

'Yes, there is.' Delving in her bag, and having to push Brizo's nose out of the way, Joan produced her copy of the latest issue of the LMS magazine and held it up.

'Is your interview in it?' Persephone asked.

'Oh, let's see!' said Margaret.

Opening it at the correct page, Joan passed it to Mabel beside her. Mabel immediately held it up for the others to admire the photograph of Joan with Brizo.

'That's a bonny picture,' said Dot.

Mabel placed the magazine on the table between her and Margaret. Together, they scanned the article.

Margaret read a bit out loud. 'Listen to this: *Mrs Hubble, a smartly uniformed brunette, used to sew made-to-measure ladies' clothes for a prestigious shop in Manchester. Like so many of the fair sex, she gave up her womanly task to become a porter-ette, thus releasing a man to do his patriotic duty.*'

'Crikey,' said Mabel. 'You're the brunette porterette.'

'And you gave up your "womanly task",' Margaret added. 'How patronising.'

'That's the way women war workers are portrayed in the press,' said Persephone. 'Unfortunate, but there it is.'

'Luckily,' said Joan, 'most of the article is about Brizo.' She bent down to fuss him.

Dot, who was seated on Brizo's other side, laughed. 'Normally he gives me the loving treatment, but now I know it's only because he knows I'm going to take him home to you.'

Joan felt a warm glow of pure happiness. How good it was to be with her friends again, and especially to be with them here in the station buffet, which had always been their special place. Moreover, it was the place the others had chosen for her wedding reception after the church-hall kitchen had been flooded. What might have been a disaster had been transformed into the most wonderful wedding reception ever, as far as Joan was concerned.

When the meeting broke up, Joan was passed from friend to friend as they all hugged her, including Dot, even though they were going to travel home together.

'I'm glad you came to see us this evening,' Dot said as she and Joan sat together on the bus with Brizo squashed between them on the floor.

'So am I,' said Joan. 'I miss you all and I wanted to share Brizo's big moment with you.'

Brizo lifted his tawny head and Dot patted him. 'Yes, we're talking about you, boy.'

'I thought I'd take it round to show Gran,' said Joan.

'Good idea,' Dot said immediately. 'It's a generous thing to do, a way of including her in your life without any strings.'

'Thank you,' said Joan. 'I know it's the right thing to do, but I needed to hear you say it, just to make sure.'

'Eh, you daft ha'p'orth, of course it's right. Listen to me, Joan Hubble. I know you're struggling with the question of where to live, but I know you'll find the right answer in the end, because you've got a good heart and so has your Bob.'

'Oh, Dot, you are kind.'

'No, I'm not. I speak as I find, that's all.'

Yes, she did, Joan realised. Dot always said what she meant, but her manner of doing so, however forthright, was also compassionate. Yes, she could be blunt, but she was sensitive too. What a contrast to Gran, who also spoke her mind and was proud to do so, but Gran's manner was brusque and judgemental and left nobody in any doubt that Beryl Foster knew best.

But this magazine article would provide them with a safe topic of conversation. A dull, heavy feeling crept into Joan's chest. How sad to need safe topics.

She went to see Gran on Saturday, calling in beforehand at Wilton Close, where Mrs Grayson was copying out a recipe.

'I'm going to send it to Margaret's sister,' she told Joan. 'I had such a chatty letter from her, thanking me for a little something I sent her children and telling me all about their life in the country, so I thought I'd write back with a recipe she might like to try.'

'She'll love that,' said Margaret. 'I've told her all about your cooking and baking.'

'Will her landlady let her use the kitchen?' Joan asked.

'Definitely,' said Margaret. 'It isn't one of those households where the lodger is made to live separately and has to obey all sorts of rules and pay extra for the use of the cruet. Anna, Mrs Andrews and the children live as a family, the same way we do here. That's the way Mrs Andrews likes it.'

'It must be a big support to Anna,' said Mrs Cooper.

'It is,' said Margaret. She turned to Joan. 'Have you brought the magazine to show Mrs Cooper and Mrs Grayson?'

'I have, unless they've already seen it.'

'Mabel brought a copy home,' said Mrs Cooper, 'but I'm very happy to look at it again.'

'There's no need,' said Joan.

'Yes, there is,' was the immediate reply. 'It's about you and your clever dog, so we want you to talk us through it – don't we, Mrs Grayson?'

'Yes, please,' said Mrs Grayson, 'and you can tell us the things you told the interviewer that ended up not being included in the article.'

Touched by their generosity, Joan was more than happy to oblige. Afterwards, Margaret touched her arm and, with the tiniest tilt of her head in the direction of the door, invited her for a private word.

'Come and see the blouse I'm making,' said Margaret. 'You can tell me where I've gone wrong.'

They went into the dining room, where Mrs Morgan's treadle sewing machine stood in the corner.

'I've got something to tell you,' said Margaret. 'I want to tell you first because of how you've helped me. Don't look

269

so worried. It's a good thing.' She drew in a breath. 'I'm going to change my name – my surname, not my first name.'

'Why? And what to?'

'Margaret Thomas. Thomas was my mum's maiden name. Anna and I talked a lot about what happened to me and she made me see it differently. I realise now that it would have been different if Mum had been alive. She would have stood up for me. Dad has made me feel nothing but shame and humiliation. Mum would have been hurt and upset, and I suppose she'd have been angry too – but she would have ended up giving me a big hug and she would have faced the situation with me.'

Joan's heart swelled with emotion. It was an honour to be told before the others.

'Do you remember telling me ages ago that I shouldn't go on punishing myself?' Margaret asked. 'You said I had a new life now and that I deserved a second chance. Well, I'm finally ready to do that. I feel stronger than I have done since I can't remember when. I want to create a new beginning for myself and changing my name is part of that.'

'What reason will you give the others?'

'I'll say it's in honour of my mother and a way of keeping her memory alive.'

'What does your dad say?'

'He doesn't know yet,' Margaret admitted. 'Anna offered to tell him for me, but it's something I have to do myself.'

As Joan walked the short distance to Torbay Road, she thought about Margaret's decision. It was good to know that at last Margaret had found new strength, but oh, how she must be missing her mum now. Joan made herself concentrate on her friend's situation. When other people talked about their mothers, it was all too easy for her to slide off into thinking about Estelle.

Gran opened the door to her and they went into the parlour, where sunshine poured through the windows, adding a rich glow to the heavy old furniture. How different it was now to the days when she and Letitia had lived here.

'You may sit in my chair if you like,' said Gran. 'It's firmer than the other one and may be more comfortable for you.'

Had anyone other than Gran ever sat in that chair? Then Joan noticed a matchbox on one of the arms – and a few buttons on the other arm.

'What are they for?' she asked.

'Nothing.' Gran scooped them up and pushed them into the sideboard drawer.

Joan sat in her usual seat, leaving Gran's chair for her.

'I brought this to show you.' Joan produced the magazine article. 'It's about Brizo.'

'That dog?'

'Not *that* dog. *My* dog. I've told you how he raises money. Here's a picture of him with his collecting box on his back. And there I am, the brunette porterette.'

'The what?'

Joan grinned. Getting up, she moved the pouffe so she could sit beside Gran while they looked through the article together.

'Though whether I'll be able to get up afterwards is another matter,' she joked.

'I thought you'd made a mistake when you took in that animal,' said Gran, 'but credit where it's due, I think you've made a good job of it.'

'The fundraising was Persephone's idea.'

The parlour door opened and an auburn-haired girl looked in.

'I'm off now – oh,' she said in a plummy voice. 'Pardon the interruption.'

'This is my granddaughter, Mrs Hubble,' said Gran. 'This is Miss Wentworth, my lodger.'

'How do?' said Miss Wentworth. 'I shan't be needing an evening meal, Mrs Foster. Sorry for the short notice.'

When she had departed, Joan closed the magazine and returned to the armchair.

'Miss Wentworth has given notice,' said Gran, 'which means the time is approaching when you and Bob need to give me an answer about moving in. The billeting officer won't hang about while you make your minds up.'

It wasn't the most gracious of invitations, but then Joan noticed the way Gran had clasped the fingers of her left hand inside those of her right. Was she anxious about the situation?

'When does Miss Wentworth move out?' Joan asked.

'For heaven's sake!' Gran exclaimed. 'Such prevarication. I wish you'd just say it.'

'Say what?'

'That you have no intention of living here. Well, you don't – do you?'

CHAPTER TWENTY-SEVEN

'I'll make a trench cake for your birthday,' Mrs Grayson told Margaret. 'I know it might not seem very festive, but they're long-lasting, which makes them perfect for posting to our boys overseas. We can send some to your sister so she can share it with the people you met in Shropshire.'

'She'd love that,' said Margaret, 'and so would I. Thank you.' She laughed. 'Shropshire isn't exactly overseas.'

'We'll send a piece to your brother – three or four pieces, so he has something to share around.'

'Steady on, Mrs G,' said Mabel, 'or there won't be any for us to have at home.'

'Thank you for arranging my birthday tea,' Margaret said to Mrs Cooper. 'If you wanted to invite your sister and her husband, I wouldn't mind at all.'

'Bless you, chuck. Ernie wouldn't be able to come because he'll be at work and Olive has to be there when he comes in for his tea, but thank you for thinking of them.'

'We could change it to the Saturday if that would help,' Margaret suggested. A thought struck her and she almost added, 'Then we'd have to invite Tony Naylor as well,' but she changed it just in time to, 'Then we could invite Tony Naylor. He's so good about helping in the garden – though … well, he's never seemed like one of us, if you know what I mean. I've seen far more of him than I have of Harry or Bob, but I feel I know them much better.' She could have added that she liked them better too.

'I had hoped,' said Mrs Cooper, 'that by now he would have stopped coming round – by which I mean,' she added quickly, 'that I hoped it for his own sake. I hoped he would start to move on. Anyroad,' and her voice brightened, 'we're not moving your party to Saturday. Your birthday is on Tuesday, so that's when we'll have it.'

On Tuesday, Margaret got up early for her shift. She was never interested in eating this early in the morning, no matter how ready she was for meals at other times of day, but Mrs Cooper wouldn't let her leave the house with nothing inside her.

'This came for you yesterday,' said Mrs Cooper.

She handed Margaret an envelope with a card from Anna. Beneath the printed greeting, Anna had written *Sending lots of love and all good wishes to my wonderful sister.* Underneath that, she had put her name and some kisses and at the bottom she'd written in brackets: *(from one wonderful sister to another!)*. Opposite were some green dashes with *(Tommy)* written next to them, and purple scribbles with *(Anne-Marie)*. It might be a flimsy wartime card, but it was the best one Margaret had ever received.

She went to work with a light heart. How different this birthday was going to be from last year's.

When she came home later, Mrs Cooper ushered her straight upstairs.

'Go and get ready and don't come down until we call you.'

She gave herself a thorough strip-wash. There really ought to be a more generous soap ration for engine cleaners. Mabel came upstairs to do her hair for her and Margaret sat at the dressing table in her dressing gown. Presently, there was a tap at the door and Joan came in with a dress draped over her arm. She held it up. It was the lilac dress that Joan had originally made for Letitia. Margaret had worn it when she was Joan's bridesmaid.

'It's your birthday present from me,' said Joan.

Margaret's lips parted in a small gasp of delight. 'Are you sure?'

'Positive. You looked lovely in it when you were my bridesmaid and I'd like to give it to you.'

'Put it on,' said Mabel.

Margaret did so and Mabel gave her a gentle push to make her stand in front of the mirror. Not that Margaret needed any persuading. She loved this dress. The elbow-length sleeves and round, collarless neckline suited her, and the matching belt was the perfect finishing touch.

'I'll give you my present as well,' said Mabel, producing a bottle of hand lotion. 'Here, smooth some on.'

Margaret was grateful to her friends for their kindness. Being made a fuss of created a little spark of excitement too. This was going to be a wonderful party.

A tap on the door heralded the arrival of Mrs Cooper. She was about to speak, then she stopped and looked at Margaret in admiration. 'You look a picture, chuck. Are you ready? It's time to come down.'

They all went downstairs together. Dot, Cordelia and Emily were in the front room and they all wished Margaret a happy birthday as she entered.

'Unfortunately, there's no Persephone,' said Cordelia. 'She was given an extra shift.'

'But there is a present here from her,' Dot added.

The table that normally stood beside Mrs Grayson's chair was in the centre of the room. It was covered by a cloth that looked lumpy and bumpy because of whatever was underneath it.

'No one has any wrapping paper,' said Mrs Grayson, 'so you have to put your hand under the cloth and bring something out.'

Laughing, Margaret knelt down and slipped her hand underneath. Something smooth. A jar. She drew it out, expecting jam.

'It's bath salts, home-made by Emily,' said Cordelia, 'with best wishes from both of us.'

Margaret twisted off the lid and sniffed. 'Lavender. It smells gorgeous. Thank you.'

'What's next?' asked Dot.

Margaret lifted the edge of the cloth to put her hand under again.

'This is like those parties where you're blindfolded,' said Mabel, 'and you have to put your hand in jelly and they tell you it's entrails.'

'Goodness me,' said Mrs Cooper. 'What sort of parties do you go to?'

'This was Halloween at school,' said Mabel. 'One of the things was gobstoppers in soil and they were meant to be eyeballs.'

Margaret drew out –

'Knicker elastic,' said Dot. 'You couldn't get that for love nor money by the end of the last war, so consider yourself blessed.'

Everyone laughed.

'I'll hide it away,' said Margaret, 'so no one can get their hands on it.'

Mrs Grayson had knitted her a cardy in a pretty stitch.

'It looks almost like lace,' said Margaret.

'It's called hyacinth stitch,' Mrs Grayson told her. 'Some people find it fiddly to do, but the effect is lovely. The buttons are from Alison. She found them on a market stall in Leeds.'

From Persephone, there was a length of parachute silk and from Mrs Cooper, a home-made shopping bag made of sturdy striped fabric.

'One of the ladies I clean for had an old deckchair she wanted to get rid of,' said Mrs Cooper. 'She let me have the canvas.'

'And you made this,' said Mabel. 'Clever old you.'

'Thank you – all of you,' said Margaret.

She and Mrs Grayson went to fetch the tea and everyone chatted over sandwiches and small pieces of lemon tart. Wanting to make the most of her special tea, Margaret made sure that she spoke to each guest.

'I hope it was all right for me to come,' said Emily. 'I didn't want to barge in, but Mummy said it would be fine.'

'Of course it is,' Margaret was quick to reassure her. 'You're one of us and you must never feel we put up with you for your mother's sake. How's the job going? Any improvement?'

'No such luck.'

'At least, being the boss's daughter, you were able to take time off to come here.'

'You're kidding. I had to write a memo to request time off, the same as everybody else in the office. It's one of Daddy's rules that I'm treated the same as everyone else.'

'It's better than being resented by your colleagues,' said Margaret, then wondered if that sounded holier-than-thou.

The trench cake was brought in. There were no birthday candles, but Mabel lit a match and held it up for Margaret to blow out, which she did to great applause.

'Make a wish,' Joan called.

'Close your eyes,' said Dot.

Margaret did so. It wasn't so much a wish as a feeling. Being with Anna and talking about Mum had caused a new strength to begin to stir inside her, a new belief in herself. She wanted that feeling to continue. She wanted it to grow.

Slices were passed round and everyone congratulated Mrs Grayson on the cake's quality, then Margaret told her friends about her forthcoming change of name.

'I don't want to say anything against my dad, but he and I don't get along any more, which is very sad, but there it is. I want to do this in honour of my mum. Anna and I talked about it a lot when I was in Shropshire and it feels like the right thing to do.'

'How do you go about it?' Mrs Grayson asked.

'You'll need a new identity card,' said Mrs Cooper.

'Are you even allowed to change your name in wartime?' Mabel asked, then answered her own question. 'Yes, of course you are or Joan wouldn't now be Mrs Hubble.'

'You have to do it by deed poll,' said Cordelia. 'I'll ask my husband for the details.'

'Nay, don't bother him with it,' said Dot.

'It wouldn't be a bother,' said Cordelia. 'It's a simple question for him to answer.'

'All the same,' said Dot.

'I'm sure Daddy won't mind,' said Emily. 'He thinks highly of all of you after the way you rescued Mummy when she was buried alive.'

'Buried alive?' Cordelia murmured. 'Don't be dramatic, darling.'

'Well, you were,' said Emily with a trace of stubbornness, 'and I'll be grateful to your friends for ever and so will Daddy.'

'There's one thing wrong with that sentence, chick,' said Dot. 'You said "your friends" and you should have said "our friends".'

Emily blushed and Margaret saw Cordelia mouth 'Thank you' to Dot.

Soon after that, the tea party ended. Saying her good-byes and thank-yous, Margaret felt unexpectedly tearful. Her friends had gone to so much trouble for her. When the visitors had left, she wasn't allowed to wash up or put furniture back, so she went upstairs to where her final present was waiting. Anna had given it to her shortly before she had left to catch the train home.

It was inside a small, much-crinkled, cone-shaped white bag, the sort you got from the sweet shop. It was folded over and when Margaret unfolded it, she found that Anna had written: *Dad gave both rings to me, as the oldest, but I think you should have this one.*

Margaret's heart thudded as she opened the bag. Inside was Mum's engagement ring, a narrow gold band, worn thin because it had originally belonged to Dad's mother, with five little diamonds set in a row. It was a simple ring, but unutterably precious because of the memories it evoked. Margaret felt a swelling sensation inside her chest as she tried it on and then stood gazing at the engagement ring of the late Mary Darrell, the former Mary Thomas, which now belonged to her daughter, the future Margaret Thomas.

CHAPTER TWENTY-EIGHT

Although the April nights could be chilly, the days were milder and seasonal showers encouraged new growth. Alison's heart rejoiced at the sight of blossom. Wherever you looked – in kitchen gardens, allotments, even in window boxes – folk were busy sowing carrots, leeks, peas, cabbages, swedes and more. Alison and the other lodgers mucked in to help Mrs Freeman protect her precious seedlings, using newly darned netting and cold frames.

In the evenings when she was on her way to a night shift, Alison looked up at the skies. Better weather and clear nights made her think of one thing: air raids.

Just as she now did every morning, even before she padded down to the floor below for her stint in the bathroom, Alison took the envelope out of her top drawer and crossed off another number. She was counting down to the day she would finally leave Leeds for good. It had been a clever idea of Mabel's to get her to write that report and ask for her finishing date. Miss Emery hadn't provided one on the spot, but had promised to write.

Three days after Alison returned to Leeds, Rachel had sent for her, asking her to report to the private room. A subtle reminder of their first meeting, when Alison had made a colossal ass of herself?

Rachel had looked as immaculately turned out as ever in a pretty linen dress. She wore a corsage of silk flowers on the front of one shoulder and Alison noticed the matching silk flowers on one side of Rachel's hat. She could hardly help noticing since Rachel had placed her hat on the seat next to her with the decoration on show.

'You've been working hard, Miss Lambert,' Rachel said, 'and doing well, by all accounts. Congratulations. I'm pleased with your performance.'

Did she talk to all her staff in that way? Or just Alison? In fairness, it was probably the former. She couldn't have risen to her current position without the ability to assert herself and keep others in their place.

'Thank you,' Alison said. The devil in her was tempted to bob a curtsey and she had to swallow a smile.

'Do sit down,' said Rachel. 'I've given some thought to your position here and what remains that you can usefully do. I have been in contact with Miss Emery and she agrees with me that you shall remain here until the middle of May.'

That had happened on the Thursday. On the Saturday, Alison had received a letter from Miss Emery, giving her final day in Leeds as Saturday, 16 May. Miss Emery's decision – or Rachel's? It wasn't something Alison could ask, and it didn't matter anyway. All that mattered was that the end was in sight.

She had immediately counted how many days she had left to go. Including today, there were thirty-six days to her finishing day. On the back of an old envelope, she had gleefully written 36, 35, 34 . . . all the way down to 1, immediately crossing off day 36. Since then, she had started off each day by crossing off the next number. Her final day was still a long way off, but today was the start of a new week and this coming Friday the start of a new month, and after that she would feel like she would soon be going home.

She had spent part of April in the Parks Department, which used crop rotation to supply the Park Square, station and WVS canteens.

'I thought that would be interesting for you,' Rachel had said.

'It is,' Alison answered. 'Thank you.'

She didn't enjoy being beholden to Rachel, but there was no avoiding it.

Joel had come to Leeds for a couple of days last week and Alison hadn't told anyone he was coming, because she didn't want word getting back to Rachel. It had been easy enough to keep quiet about it, as she had been dividing her time between the Parks Department, where she had been passed around from pillar to post and consequently hadn't really got to know anybody, and the lady almoner's office, where she had gone out visiting patients at home with the lady almoner herself.

'I thought you'd appreciate the opportunity,' said Rachel.

'I do. Thank you.'

She and Joel had spent a lovely couple of days together. They had a day walking in the countryside, and one evening they went to the theatre, but best of all, they talked about anything and everything and Alison had felt them drawing ever closer.

When Joel went back to Manchester and Alison had returned to work, there was no need to keep quiet about his visit any longer and she had talked about it freely.

This week was her last one in the Parks Department and she would have her final couple of outings with the lady almoner. She went to work with a light heart. It was another busy and interesting week. She might feel threatened by Rachel for personal reasons, but professionally speaking, she owed her a lot.

Letters from home had helped the time pass by. Her friends' letters hadn't tailed off. Between them, they still made sure she received a letter almost every day. She got letters from Mum and Lydia as well. Rather to her surprise, she had found that Margaret wasn't much of a correspondent. There was something reserved, stilted even, about her style that made her letters less of a pleasure to read. Maybe that was because she was anxious about changing her name; she had told Alison she would have to appear before the magistrate early in May – but Alison had noted Margaret's reserve way before that.

May Day came round and Alison was in the Parks Department for the whole day. In the morning, she was taken to visit various greengrocers who supported the department's crop-rotation scheme by supplying foods that the department couldn't, and she spent the afternoon in the office, helping with clerical work.

She did some typing, then there was filing to do.

'I didn't realise Joel had been over here.'

Rachel appeared at Alison's side, not looking at her but apparently looking into the depths of the filing cabinet into which Alison was placing documents.

Alison didn't stop what she was doing. 'It was a last-minute arrangement.' She wished she could say, 'There was no reason why you should realise. It's none of your business,' but good manners – and the knowledge that Rachel could condemn her to peeling duty – prevailed.

'You and I have hardly seen one another recently,' said Rachel. 'You'll be down to your last fortnight next week. We ought to meet up in Tabitha's.'

'That'd be nice,' Alison murmured. She picked up the next bundle of documents, hoping that Rachel's suggestion was just one of those things people said to be polite without any intention of actually doing them, but no, Rachel really meant it and Alison had no option but to make the arrangement. It wasn't as though she could get out of it by lying about her work commitments to Rachel of all people.

When they met in Tabitha's Tea Shop the following Tuesday, Alison was determined to keep the conversation on the topic of work or the air raids that had devastated some of Britain's most beautiful historic cities – anything, in fact, but the personal.

But that didn't stop Rachel.

'You haven't told me about Joel's visit.'

Alison answered as briefly as she could without being rude.

'I'm so sorry to have missed him.' Was that a little pout? 'That reminds me. It's ages since I wrote to Venetia – Venetia Clifton, Joel's sister. Have you met her?'

'We went to her house for tea at Easter.' Alison's voice was remarkably steady, considering she was boggling at the idea that Rachel and Venetia had a correspondence going, but at least it didn't sound as if letters were flying to and fro on a regular basis.

'She's such a dear girl, don't you think?' asked Rachel. 'You'll be going home for good next week. I don't suppose . . .' A faint blush appeared in her cheeks. 'I don't suppose Joel is coming over here before that, is he?'

'No,' Alison said bluntly.

'Not even to assist you with your luggage when you go home?'

'No.' She couldn't keep saying 'No' or she would sound churlish. 'He's working on the Friday night and then on the Saturday, which is my last day, he's going to his sister's that afternoon.'

'Venetia or Caroline?'

'Venetia. They're cooking up plans to gather toys for children who are in hospital long-term.'

'That doesn't surprise me. Joel intends to return to paediatrics after the war, you know. He has a true calling.'

It was galling to have to sit and listen while this girl – this beautiful, poised, clever girl, which made it infinitely worse – pumped her for information about her boyfriend and then presumed to tell her about his plans. Alison was sufficiently riled to ask a question she would never otherwise have asked.

'Will you give me a straight answer to a straight question?'

Rachel raised her eyebrows. 'Heavens, how intriguing.'

'You didn't start giving me interesting work until after you found out I was Joel's girlfriend. Was that a coincidence or was Joel the reason?'

To Alison's annoyance, Rachel laughed. 'You think Joel was the reason? Goodness me, how unexpected – and how very disappointing. Are you really one of those girls who sees her own value purely in terms of the man in her life? Honestly, Alison, I had thought better of you than that.'

Margaret hadn't been worried about having to present herself before the magistrate. It wasn't as though she had been summoned to court. She was to meet the magistrate in his chambers. Then a request came from the magistrate's clerk, seeking character references. That made her appreciate how serious this was and she started experiencing the occasional flutter of nerves. Now it was Tuesday and thank goodness it was a buffet evening.

'I can't help feeling concerned about your going there alone,' Cordelia remarked.

'But all the rest of us are working,' Dot added.

'I shan't be alone,' Margaret told them. 'I'll have Joan with me for moral support.' She explained about having to provide references. 'One has to be from my – quote – "landlord", as if there's no such thing as a landlady.' She looked at Cordelia. 'And I wondered if you would write one for me, please?'

285

'With pleasure,' said Cordelia. 'I'll ask my husband to write one as well. I'm sorry to say it, but his word will carry more weight. He doesn't know you well, but he can certainly testify as to your courage and efficiency in a crisis.'

'Thank you,' said Margaret.

'Is there anything worrying you about it?' asked Persephone.

'It sounds so trivial,' said Margaret, 'but I'm bothered about my nails. It's so difficult to get them properly clean. I'll wear gloves on Friday, of course, to be smart, and that'll hide them, but suppose I have to sign something? Am I supposed to take off my gloves to do that? Or if I have to swear an oath? What will the magistrate think if I have dirty nails? Might he turn me down?'

'If he so much as frowns at your nails,' said Mabel, 'you just tell him what your war work is.'

'Aye, and then tell him to put that in his pipe and smoke it,' Dot added.

That boosted Margaret's spirits and made her laugh. Good old Dot. She had a knack for saying the right thing, whether it was a nugget of compassion or a jokey put-down.

As they all left the buffet, Dot drew Margaret aside for a moment.

'I'm not being nosy, but have you spoken to Joel yet?'

'Not yet. I want to sort out my change of name first.'

'Fair enough – as long as you're not making excuses to avoid it.'

'I'm not, I promise well, maybe I am a bit, but things have been tough for me over the past couple of years and it feels right to do this important thing for myself before I tackle anything else.'

'You're a lovely lass, Margaret, and don't forget it.'

Margaret was startled, but mainly she felt touched by Dot's words. Being approved of by Dot made her feel good about herself and she recalled Dot's kind words a few times over the next couple of days.

Thursday came round, the day before she was to see the magistrate. Cordelia caught her before she went home at the end of the day and handed her an envelope.

'Your reference,' said Cordelia. 'It's sealed because my husband said it's important that the magistrate knows he's the first person to read it, but I've written good things about you.'

'Thank you.'

'My husband also said that since the magistrate asked for two references, it would be better to supply two, not three. We discussed whether he or I should write the second reference and he said I should. His only real knowledge of you comes from the courage you showed when I was trapped underground. That was entirely commendable, of course, but the magistrate will want a fuller picture of you.'

Anxiety built upside Margaret and she rubbed the back of her neck, though she tried to smile.

'I know how important this is to you,' said Cordelia, 'so I shan't tell you not to worry, but my husband assures me the process is merely a formality.'

'Let's hope so,' said Margaret.

She headed for home. Upstairs, she scrubbed at her nails until her fingertips felt red-raw. Getting the oil and grime out from under them was always a task and a half, but this evening of all evenings, just when she most needed them to be perfect, the thin black lines where white met pink under her nails wouldn't budge. They were nothing more than the thinnest of lines, but they were horribly noticeable.

The doorbell rang and a few moments later Mrs Cooper called up the stairs.

'Margaret, can you come down, dear? Miss Persephone is here to see you.'

Margaret went down to the front room.

Persephone smiled at her. There was a twinkle in her beautiful violet eyes. She held up a small bottle. 'Ta-da!'

'Is that nail varnish?' asked Mrs Grayson. 'I thought that was almost impossible to get these days.'

'It is,' said Persephone, 'but I happened to know that my sister has been hoarding a bottle, so after we met in the buffet on Tuesday, I telephoned her and asked her to send it.'

'And she did,' said Mrs Cooper. 'How generous.'

'I told her that if she didn't,' Persephone said cheerfully, 'I'd tell Ma what really happened to the trifle all those years ago. Sit here, Margaret, and let me work my magic. It's a pretty colour, don't you think? It's called Autumn Rose.'

They settled down, Persephone bending over Margaret's hand.

'It's such a nuisance when you can't get the dirt out from under your nails,' said Persephone. 'The land girls are always complaining about it.' Lifting her face, she gave Margaret a mischievous glance. 'I'll have to post this back to Fudge double quick before they get wind of it.'

'You are a card, Miss Persephone,' said Mrs Cooper.

'Who, me?' Persephone asked innocently. 'I'm deadly serious at all times. Other hand, please.'

Margaret switched hands. 'This is very good of you – and your sister.'

'I hope you don't mind, but I took the liberty of mentioning to my father about your being sent for by the magistrate and he said it should be a formality.'

'That's what Mr Masters said too.'

'After all,' said Persephone, 'if someone intended to change their name for nefarious purposes, they're not going to do it properly through the court.'

'For what purposes?' asked Mrs Cooper.

'Nefarious.'

'That's a new one on me. I'll use it if someone tries to fob me off with a short measure.'

'Let those dry,' Persephone told Margaret, 'and then we'll do the second coat.'

'Feeling better now?' Mrs Grayson smiled at Margaret.

'Definitely,' Margaret answered.

She was too. That was what friendship could do for you.

CHAPTER TWENTY-NINE

Margaret dressed with care. Mrs Grayson had sponged and pressed her lilac dress and Cordelia had lent her a pair of discreet clip-on pearl earrings. Mabel had offered her the loan of her cream jacket and Persephone had offered a navy one.

'The cream looks better with the lilac,' Persephone had declared when Margaret had tried them on, 'but it does rather suggest you're going out to a special occasion.'

'Changing her name is a special occasion,' said Mabel.

'Very true.' Persephone smiled. 'It's a question of how you wish to appear to the magistrate. I think the navy looks more serious.'

Margaret had opted for the navy.

Now she picked up her hairbrush and tweaked one or two curls, then slipped her feet into her court shoes, which she had polished yesterday evening. Picking up her handbag, she went downstairs and put her hat on in front of the mirror in the hall.

She entered the front room to an array of approving looks.

'You look very smart, dear,' said Mrs Grayson.

'Have you got everything?' Joan asked.

Margaret opened her handbag. 'Birth certificate, references, identity card. Letter from LMS to say I work for them; letter from Ingleby's confirming the dates I worked there.'

Joan stood up. It took a bit of a heave these days for her to get out of an armchair.

'We'd best be off, then,' said Joan.

They walked to the terminus and caught the bus into town. Inside the building, Margaret announced herself at the reception desk and was asked to wait. Presently, a gentleman approached them. He was perhaps fifty and had an aroma of pipe tobacco about him. His hairline had receded right to the top of his head, leaving a broad forehead beneath which was a strong nose. Margaret frowned to herself, sure she knew him from somewhere.

'I think he lives in Chorlton,' whispered Joan.

He introduced himself as Ronald Shires, one of the magistrates' clerks.

'My job is to make sure there are no breaches of law or procedure,' he explained. 'I'll show you where to go. You do understand, don't you, that this isn't a court proceeding today? You'll be in a chamber, which is a private room.'

'Like an office?' Margaret asked.

'You'll see soon enough.'

'I've brought my friend with me. This is Mrs Hubble.'

'Good morning,' Mr Shires greeted Joan. 'I'm afraid you won't be able to go into the chamber, but you can sit outside.'

'Oh, but she's here to give me moral support,' Margaret said, dismayed.

'I'm afraid it won't altogether convey the right impression if you seem to need a boost,' said Mr Shires. 'Mr Brent-Williams won't like it.'

'Why not?' asked Joan. 'This is an important matter for Miss Darrell. It's natural to wish to have a friend close by.'

'Perhaps you had better wait outside,' said Margaret. She wanted to do this correctly. 'Don't worry. I'm a big girl.'

'This way, please, ladies,' said Mr Shires.

He took them across the foyer, their footsteps ringing on the tiled floor. There was a wide staircase with shallow treads. At the top, Mr Shires escorted them along one or two corridors lined with doors, all closed. Finally, he opened a door and before waving Margaret inside, indicated some chairs in the corridor.

'If you wouldn't mind waiting here, please, Mrs Hubble.'

'Good luck,' said Joan as Margaret went inside.

A long, polished table with three shield-back chairs behind it faced the room. The back wall of the room – the chamber – was lined with shelves of leather-bound books on either side of a door. Over to one side was a pair of desks, side by side. There was a single chair in front of the table.

Margaret eyed the three chairs behind the table. 'I thought there was going to be one magistrate.'

'No, there'll be three hearing your case today.'

Her case? So much for the reassurances of this being a mere formality.

'Mr Brent-Williams is the magistrate in charge,' Mr Shires told her. 'He'll sit in the middle, with Mr Unsworth on one side and Mrs Ames on the other. This is where you are to sit.' Mr Shires indicated the lone chair in front of the table. 'When Mr Brent-Williams enters, he'll wait for me to announce the matter formally, but don't worry. That's just his way.'

Margaret sat down. Mr Shires went to one of the desks at the side of the room, where he was joined by another clerk. Margaret smiled at the newcomer, but he didn't appear to see her. The two men spoke to one another in low voices. At first Margaret kept her handbag on her lap, but what if that made her appear nervous or, worse, like a suspicious-looking character? So she placed it on the floor beside her.

The door at the rear of the room opened and the clerks stood up, Mr Shires motioning to Margaret to do likewise. A tall, well-built man with craggy features and dark eyes walked in first. This must be Mr Brent-Williams. Mr Unsworth was older, with a Humpty-Dumpty sort of face, bald and shining with big blue eyes. Mrs Ames was a stout lady who wore the longer hemline of the previous decade. A pair of spectacles dangled from a silver chain around her podgy neck. These must be reading glasses, because when she sat down, she looked at Margaret and gave her a smile and a nod, which was more than the two men did. Margaret relaxed. She had an ally. Thank goodness for Mrs Ames, because otherwise the stern look Mr Brent-Williams gave her would have made her uneasy.

The magistrates sat down, followed by the clerks and Margaret.

'Clerk of the court, if you please,' said Mr Brent-Williams, speaking in a grand voice. 'I beg everyone's pardon. The law in its wisdom would have it that this isn't a court matter.' He bestowed a gracious nod on Mr Shires. 'Magistrates' clerk, if you please.'

Mr Shires stood up. 'The magistrates are convened on this eighth day of May to hear the matter of the proposed change of name of Miss Margaret Stephanie Darrell.'

Speaking under his breath but nevertheless audibly, Mr Unsworth said, 'Stephanie? What sort of name is that?'

'I think it's charming,' said Mrs Ames.

'It's because I was going to be Stephen if I was a boy,' said Margaret.

Mr Brent-Williams gave her a hard look. 'Miss Darrell, this isn't a coffee morning for chit-chat about recipes and knitting patterns. Protocol dictates that you speak only when invited to do so.' With a flash of irritation, he went on, 'What has her middle name got to do with this matter, anyway? It's her surname we're here to talk about. Changing one's surname for reasons other than marriage or adoption is a serious matter and doubly so in wartime. What possible reason can you have, Miss Darrell, to wish to make this change?'

'Family reasons, sir,' said Margaret.

'I see. Darrell is your stepfather's name, is it, and you wish to revert to your father's name?'

'It's in honour of my mother, sir. Thomas was her maiden name.'

'And is Darrell the surname of your father?' enquired Mr Brent-Williams.

'Yes, sir.'

'Are you illegitimate?' asked the magistrate. 'Is that why you wish to use your mother's name? Because you have no legal right to your father's?'

'Certainly not,' retorted Margaret, indignant on Mum's behalf. 'My parents were legally married.'

Mrs Ames leaned towards Mr Brent-Williams and murmured something.

'Yes, yes, if you must,' he muttered in reply.

Mrs Ames addressed Margaret. 'You must forgive Mr Brent-Williams's bluntness, my dear, but I'm sure you understand that we need to be in full possession of the facts.'

'Of course.' Thanks goodness for Mrs Ames.

'Well, then,' said Mr Brent-Williams. 'Let's start with the facts, shall we?' He looked across at Mr Shires. 'The evidence, if you please.'

Mrs Ames murmured to him once more.

'What?' said Mr Brent-Williams. 'Of course it's evidence.'

Mrs Ames gave Margaret a sympathetic smile. 'Evidence of good character, I'm sure.'

Mr Shires approached Margaret. 'Do you have the papers you were asked to bring?'

She took them from her bag and handed them over. Mr Shires laid them on the desk in front of Mr Brent-Williams. He unfolded her birth certificate, scrutinised it and then looked at Margaret through narrowed eyes, as if assessing if she really was who she claimed to be. He examined her identity card and then opened the envelopes one by one and read the contents. Only when he had finished did he permit his colleagues to see the documents.

Mr Unsworth scanned the birth certificate. 'So her parents are married.'

'It doesn't necessarily mean they were married at the time of her birth,' said Mr Brent-Williams. 'The parents of illegitimate offspring can apply for a fresh birth certificate if they marry within a year of the birth.'

Mrs Ames had put on her spectacles to read the letters. Now she removed them, holding them by one of the arms, as if she might wave them to emphasise a point. 'Miss Darrell has a full record of employment, including important war work. And these references are excellent.'

'The one from the landlady leaves something to be desired,' said Mr Brent-Williams.

'Surely not,' said Mrs Ames. 'It says—'

Mr Brent-Williams cut her short. 'I'm referring to the standard of the woman's education. Look – basic sentences. No subordinate clauses. Common or garden handwriting.'

Margaret spoke sharply. 'So far we've established that my parents were married and my landlady didn't go to grammar school. What does any of that have to do with my change of name?'

Mr Brent-Williams glared at her. Margaret braced herself for a voice of thunder, but he didn't raise his voice, though the level of sternness increased.

'Kindly don't interrupt, young lady. You want to know what all this has to do with your change of name. The answer is – everything. It all speaks to what sort of person you are. It isn't natural for a girl to want to change her name other than through marriage. Moreover, you want to do this in wartime. You are taking up my valuable time, and that of my colleagues, because we are obliged to investigate this bizarre wish of yours. You have stated that you want to . . .' he made a point of referring to his notes, ' . . . to honour your mother. Why? Is she some sort of war heroine?'

'She died some years ago, sir.'

'You must miss her,' said Mrs Ames.

'I do, madam.'

'Plenty of people miss their mothers,' said Mr Brent-Williams, 'but they don't all express their sorrow through deed polls. I'll ask you again. Why do you want to honour your mother's memory?'

Margaret lifted her chin. 'Because I loved her and I miss her.' Emotion built up inside her, forcing her to stop.

'Not good enough,' snapped Mr Brent-Williams. 'I loved my old golden retriever and I miss him bringing me my slippers when I arrive home. It doesn't mean I'm going to change my name to Rover.'

Mr Unsworth leaned towards him, speaking quietly.

'Good point, sir, good point,' said Mr Brent-Williams. He looked at Margaret. 'My esteemed colleague has suggested I may be pursuing the wrong question. The issue here isn't why *do* you want to be Thomas, so much as why *don't* you want to be Darrell? Well? Speak up, girl. Cat got your tongue, has it?'

What could she say? 'I . . . don't see eye to eye with my father.'

'So you propose to change your name out of childish spite?'

Margaret forced herself to remain calm. 'Not at all, sir. I told you. It's to honour my late mother.'

'So you keep saying.' Mr Brent-Williams drew the letters towards him and glanced through them. 'I see there is no letter here from your father. Do you have his permission to do this?'

'No, sir,' Margaret admitted.

Mr Brent-Williams cast the letters aside. 'Then you're pursuing this against his wishes?'

'He's unaware of it.'

Mr Brent-Williams's eyebrows climbed up his forehead. 'Unaware? Unaware, you say?'

'I don't require his permission.' Margaret made sure she sounded polite. 'I'm over twenty-one.'

Too late, she saw Mrs Ames shaking her head in warning. The lady magistrate stopped abruptly as Mr Brent-Williams glanced her way. Then he returned his attention to Margaret before picking up the papers from the table and ripping them in half. Margaret gasped and her skin tingled all over. Good grief, had he just torn up her birth certificate?

'That's what I think of your character references,' Mr Brent-Williams declared. 'They're not worth the paper they're written on. When an unmarried young female brazenly tells me she's over twenty-one and therefore can do as she pleases and doesn't care what anyone thinks, I know that her so-called character references are a pack of lies. No decent, rational person would supply such good testimonials for one such as you. Over twenty-one, indeed!'

'If I may, Mr Brent-Williams?' asked Mrs Ames. 'Girls today are engaged in war work. Many, if not most, are obliged to live away from home for the first time. They're bound to grow up quickly. Indeed, it would be detrimental to them if they didn't. I'm sure Miss Darrell intends no disrespect to her elders when she states she is over twenty-one.'

'On the contrary, she intends every possible disrespect to her father if she hasn't told him of her plans,' said Mr Brent-Williams. 'What do you say to that, Miss Darrell?'

'We are . . . estranged.'

'So badly that you wish to discard his name?' Mrs Ames asked kindly.

'You're all looking at this in terms of my father,' said Margaret. 'I'm looking at it in terms of my mother.'

Mr Brent-Williams huffed out an irritated breath. 'Yes, yes, and your wish to honour her memory.'

'But it's true,' said Margaret. 'I've no desire to upset my father.'

'Balderdash. This will hurt him profoundly. It would injure any right-thinking man.'

'He turned his back on me when I needed him most – and my mother would never have done that. That's why I want to use her name.'

'What happened?' Mr Brent-Williams demanded.

'Miss Darrell is entitled to her privacy,' said Mrs Ames.

Mr Brent-Williams brushed that aside. 'Not in wartime. The only people who can't be open and honest in wartime are spies and traitors.'

In the ensuing silence, Margaret felt all eyes upon her. Her heart beat hard. It seemed the others would neither speak nor move until she did, but she couldn't tell them, she couldn't.

Mr Brent-Williams broke the spell with a loud noise that sounded like 'Pshaw!'

Mr Shires left his seat. For a mad moment, Margaret thought he was coming to arrest her, but he walked past her to the door.

'Where are you going, Shires?' demanded Mr Brent-Williams.

Mr Shires turned briefly. 'Excuse me for one moment, sir,' and he left the room.

'Most irregular,' Mr Brent-Williams muttered before his attention homed in on Margaret once more. 'You needn't think I've forgotten you. You say your father turned his back on you. Your attempt to make him appear to be the one at fault won't wash with me. Answer me this, if you please. What did you do to make him turn away?'

Margaret felt her expression freeze. Her pulse picked up speed until she thought her heart would explode.

'Struck a nerve, have I?' The way Mr Brent-Williams twisted his lips made him appear insufferably smug. 'I'll repeat the question. What did you do that was so bad that your own father couldn't bear to look at you?'

Margaret swallowed.

'Well?' said Mr Brent-Williams. 'I'm waiting.'

It felt as if the whole world was waiting.

'I – I fell pregnant out of wedlock,' she whispered.

'*What?*'

Was Mr Brent-Williams so appalled that his deep voice had turned soprano? It took Margaret a moment to realise that the screech of disgust had come from Mrs Ames.

'Pregnant out of wedlock? That's shocking – disgraceful,' ranted Mrs Ames. 'There's a word for girls like you. No wonder you're in need of a new name.'

Margaret stared at her in disbelief. Mrs Ames – her ally – had turned on her and was being far more vicious than Mr Brent-Williams.

Mrs Ames jerked her head in Margaret's direction as she addressed Mr Brent-Williams. 'She's not a spy or a fifth columnist. She's a dirty little trollop who thinks that a new name will wipe out the stigma of her past.' Mrs Ames stared at Margaret, her nostrils flaring. 'Well, it won't, I tell you. Girls of your sort used to drown themselves and the world was well rid of them.'

Margaret was too stunned to think, let alone speak. She was dimly aware of the door opening. Slowly she turned her head to see who had come in to witness her humiliation.

Mr Masters. What was he doing here? Was Cordelia with him? Had they heard? Oh, crikey.

'What is this?' barked Mr Brent-Williams. 'Who are you, sir? What is the meaning of this intrusion?'

'Pardon me, sir,' said Mr Masters, 'but I am Kenneth Masters of Wardle, Grace and Masters. I am Miss Darrell's solicitor and I hope soon to represent Miss Margaret Thomas. I made arrangements with the magistrates' clerk that I would sit outside and he would call me in, should the need arise. Judging by my client's stricken expression, I deduce that the need has indeed arisen.'

'This is most irregular,' said Mr Brent-Williams.

'Possibly, sir,' agreed Mr Masters, 'but if you have reduced my client to a state of distress, it seems to me that your conduct has been irregular too. This is a meeting to discuss a change of name. There can be no excuse for causing such upset.'

'Are you aware of what this – this person has done?' asked Mr Brent-Williams. 'Are you aware of the reason behind her wish, her need, I may say, to change her name?'

Margaret held her breath.

'No,' said Mr Masters, 'and neither do I wish to know. In peacetime, no one would dream of asking such personal questions.'

'This is wartime, sir,' said Mr Brent-Williams.

'And the correct procedure is simply to ascertain that this young lady is who she says she is and is of sound character – and that's all. For you to hound her with questions – which is what I must assume took place here – means that you have acted beyond your authority, sir. This is a matter I should be most interested to pursue. You are in a position of influence and authority and I suggest you have abused that.'

'How dare you, sir?' thundered Mr Brent-Williams, but there was a note of bluster in his voice. 'One more word and I'll have you removed from my chamber.'

Mr Masters spoke calmly, without raising his voice. 'You are a magistrate of many years' standing, Mr Brent-Williams, and you have acquired a great deal of legal knowledge, but you don't know the law as well as I do or as well as Mr Shires does. I am not alone in believing you have overstepped the mark. Shires does too or he wouldn't have summoned me. Do you really wish to pursue this discussion, Mr Brent-Williams?' Mr Masters paused briefly, but it was clear he didn't expect an answer. 'I thought not. You shall, of course, write a formal letter to the effect that the magistrates hearing this matter have found no reason whatsoever why Miss Darrell should not change her name.'

Mr Brent-Williams spluttered, but was forced to agree.

'Thank you,' said Mr Masters. 'I'll send my clerk round to fetch it later on. Now, if I might have my client's personal papers, please? Thank you, Mr Shires. I see some of them have been torn up. I consider that to be distasteful and unprofessional. I hope the birth certificate and identity card have not been damaged or I shall register an official complaint. No, I see they are intact.' He gave everything to Margaret. 'Would you like to put these in your bag? Are you ready to leave?'

Margaret stood up. She felt wobbly, but only for a moment.

'One final thing, Miss Darrell,' said Mr Brent-Williams.

'There's no need to stay and listen,' Mr Masters said quietly. 'Come along.'

As she headed for the door, Margaret tried not to hear Mr Brent-Williams's parting shot, but it was inescapable.

'How do you think your late mother would feel to know that the daughter who brought shame on her father's name now intends to hide behind her mother's?'

CHAPTER THIRTY

Joan gazed at Mr Masters through new eyes. Not that she could claim to know him particularly, but she had always thought of him as starchy and rather fond of his own opinion. Truth be told, she had always felt that Cordelia deserved someone nicer . . . kinder. But not any more. Now Mr Masters had taken on a distinctly heroic aspect.

Margaret looked pale and shaky as Mr Masters guided them from the building.

'Allow me to escort you to my offices in Rosemount Place,' he said. 'It will only take a few minutes to walk there. You can sit in a private room to have a cup of tea and gather your thoughts before you go home. If you wish, since you have the necessary paperwork with you, you could fill in your deed poll.'

'I've already made arrangements with another solicitor in Chorlton,' said Margaret.

'With whom, if I might ask?'

'Mr Hughes on Barlow Moor Road.'

Mr Masters nodded his approval. 'A sound fellow. You'll be in good hands.'

'I think Margaret was in very good hands just now,' said Joan, 'thanks to you.'

'It was my wife's idea, but I was happy to comply with her wishes.'

'It was a good job you were,' Margaret said quietly. 'They'd have torn me to pieces in there otherwise.'

'I knew things were bad when Mr Shires came out to fetch me. Are you up to walking to Rosemount Place? I can get a taxi, if you prefer.'

'I'd rather go straight home, if you don't mind,' said Margaret.

'As you wish,' said Mr Masters. 'I'll pay for a taxi – no arguments. If Emily were ever to need help because she was upset, I hope someone would do the same for her.'

Margaret hesitated, then said, 'Mr Masters, I don't know how much you heard when we were leaving that room—'

'I heard nothing,' was the stout reply. 'But please be assured that had I heard every word, I would regard it as a confidential matter.'

'Thank you,' Margaret whispered.

Mr Masters flagged down a taxi and paid the driver in advance, slipping Joan a shilling with a murmur of 'The tip.' The girls climbed in and held hands all the way to Wilton Close.

'What happened?' Joan asked softly and listened in horror as Margaret described what the magistrates had put her through. 'That's appalling. Such unkindness, such lack of respect.'

'They didn't think I deserved respect,' said Margaret. 'You should have heard the lady magistrate once she heard about – ' she glanced at the back of the driver's head '– about the baby,' she whispered. 'She said I was . . .' Her voice hitched and she couldn't continue.

'Hush,' said Joan. 'It doesn't matter. I don't care what she said. She was wrong. You're one of the best people I know, and I'm proud of you. Those magistrates were brutes to put you through all that and they should know better.'

'It was vile at the time. The worst part was knowing that what the lady magistrate said about me was what most people would say. But now here I am with you and you always make me feel better about myself. You and my sister both do that for me.'

Joan squeezed her hand and they rode on in silence. Margaret seemed deep in thought and Joan didn't want to intrude.

Presently, Margaret said, 'All I'll say if anyone asks – which they will, because they care – is that it was tougher than I was expecting and the magistrates harped on about not having asked for Dad's permission.'

'All of which is true,' said Joan. 'What happens next?'

'When the change of name happens, I have to inform everyone who needs to know. I'll have to take the deed-poll document to the bank and so on, and show it to Miss Emery.' Margaret paused. 'I'll have to tell my father. Perhaps I should have got Anna to tell him. She did offer.' She laughed, but it wasn't a real laugh. 'We'll be home soon. Let's talk about something else. I don't want to arrive looking upset. What else are you doing today? Are you keeping an eye on Jimmy after school?'

'It's Sheila's day off, so she's at home. Mrs Grayson has invited me for a bite to eat and then I'll go and see Gran.'

They arrived back in Wilton Close to the aroma of baking. Mrs Grayson came out of the kitchen, wiping her hands on a tea towel.

'How was it?' she asked.

'Fine, thanks,' said Margaret, 'though it was a bit taxing.'

Mrs Cooper came downstairs, dressed in her wrap-around pinny and a turban, bringing with her a whiff of turps and vinegar, two of the ingredients for home-made furniture polish.

'Shouldn't you be out at work?' Margaret asked her.

'I got Mrs Wadden to do my jobs today. I wanted to be here when you got home.'

'So you're cleaning our house instead of someone else's.' Margaret gave her a hug. 'Thank you for being here – both of you,' she added, looking at Mrs Grayson.

Margaret looked better than she had on the way home, Joan thought. This was what she'd needed – to feel cared for.

Mrs Cooper took off her pinny while the girls set the table and Mrs Grayson dished up. They soon settled down to their potato soup. Mrs Grayson used potatoes in lots of different ways, because they were ship-savers, meaning more space on merchant ships could be used for war materials instead of food.

'And for pudding,' said Mrs Grayson, 'I've made a trifle to celebrate.'

'Trifle!' Joan exclaimed. When was the last time she'd had trifle? When was the last time anyone had?

'Mum used to make trifle every Christmas as a treat,' Margaret remembered.

'Not like this, she didn't,' said Mrs Grayson. 'Tea buns instead of sponge cake, cooked fruit instead of jelly, and thin custard over the top.'

'At least it has the custard,' smiled Mrs Cooper.

'Potato flour and flavouring,' Mrs Grayson admitted, 'but who's counting?'

Afterwards, Joan hugged Margaret before setting off to see Gran. Truth be told, she was feeling a bit jumpy with nerves. She hadn't been to Torbay Road since Gran had made it clear she didn't expect Joan and Bob to want to move in. It couldn't be pleasant for Gran to think that her granddaughter wasn't exactly leaping at the chance to live with her – but then what had she expected? Anyway, after all the agonising and the toing and froing, they had made up their minds now – and they weren't going to move in. Plenty would say they were mad to give up the chance of such a good billet, but there was so much more to it than that. Battling with the heartache and the memories would be a high price to pay.

Gran opened the door to her and the first thing Joan saw when she walked into the parlour was Daddy's photograph, back on the sideboard. Should she comment? It would be unnatural not to.

'I see you've brought Daddy's photograph back in from the dining room.'

'I might as well have it on show. It's not as though you're going to live here.'

Before Joan could say anything, Gran went to the sideboard. Was she about to pick up the picture? No, she opened one of the drawers and took something out.

'Here, this is for you – for the baby.'

Joan took it, curiosity turning into delight as she realised it was a rattle made from a matchbox with a toothbrush for a handle. She shook it. 'What makes the noise?'

'Buttons.'

'You were making this when I was here before.'

'Baby things are in short supply these days.'

'It's wonderful. I love it and the baby will too. Gran, I've got something to say—' Joan was interrupted by the sound of the doorbell. 'I'll get it.'

She went to the door and found a stranger, an older man, perhaps on the way to sixty. As he raised his trilby to her, his eyes were bright with delight.

'Good afternoon,' he said. 'Am I addressing – well, I don't need to ask, do I?'

A frown tugged at Joan's forehead.

'Who is it?' called Gran. A moment later, she appeared at Joan's side. 'What do you want? I don't buy at the door.'

A grin appeared briefly on the man's face, then his features went serious, though there was no hiding the pleasure in his eyes. 'Well, well, well. Estelle Henshaw's daughter – and Donald Henshaw's mother. I do believe that's what they call hitting the jackpot.'

They let him in. What choice did they have? He had found them – Estelle's daughter and Donald Henshaw's mother. They couldn't close the door on him in case he went up and down Torbay Road, asking questions, and they couldn't utter a word on the doorstep for fear of a neighbour passing by. Forced to step aside and permit the threat to enter the house, they stood close together, bumping shoulders. Gran's fingers tangled with Joan's. The breath in Joan's lungs had turned to ice. This couldn't be happening.

But it was.

In the hallway, he turned and looked at them, now that he was safely inside the house. Before he had come in, he had introduced himself as Geoff Baldwin, a reporter. Given how he had hunted them down, given what he no doubt intended to do to them, he ought to have been thin and weaselly with shifty eyes, his suit shiny with wear. Instead, he was well built, with broad shoulders inside a single-breasted jacket, and the squareness and set of his jawline made his pitted and pockmarked cheeks look characterful. He had removed his hat as he walked in, revealing a full head of silver hair.

'Thank you, ladies,' he said. 'Most obliging of you. This way, is it?'

And he walked straight into Gran's parlour.

Joan and Gran sagged against one another, united in terror and despair.

Joan drew herself upright. Never in her life had she felt stronger than Gran, but she did now. Was this strength? Or was it no more than the knowledge that she had to behave as if she was strong?

'Come on,' she whispered.

Holding hands – clutching hands – they went towards the parlour. Outside the door, Gran stopped. Swallowing hard, she pushed back shoulders that Joan would have sworn had never before been anything other than dead straight and rigid.

Gran walked in and Joan followed. It wouldn't have come as a surprise had Mr Baldwin already helped himself to a seat, but he hadn't. He stood by the sideboard with his back to them. When he turned round, he was holding Daddy's photograph.

Gran seemed rooted to the spot, then with a small jerk she got herself moving. She snatched the photograph from Mr Baldwin's hand and replaced it on the sideboard. Then she went to her armchair and sat down, wrapping her fingers around the fronts of the arms, scrunching the cotton arm caps that protected the upholstery from wear.

Joan sat opposite her. She perched right on the edge. A strong instinct urged her to place her arms around her bulky stomach, to hold her baby and provide protection from . . . from whatever was about to happen. Would she and Bob have to disappear and start a new life two hundred miles away, like Gran had done all those years ago? But if this reporter wrote a story for the national press, there would be nowhere they could be safe and ordinary . . . nowhere their baby could grow up without the stigma of the family scandal and Donald Henshaw's crime.

'Aren't you going to offer me a seat?' asked Mr Baldwin. 'I'm happy to stand.'

Gran's jaw worked, her eyes turning to flint. She didn't speak, just nodded, which Geoff Baldwin took as permission to lower himself onto the sofa, placing his trilby beside him.

He held up his hands, palms out. 'Look, no reporter's notebook. I'm just here to test the water, you might say.'

He looked from one to the other without moving his head. He smiled, not so much a smile as a smirk, which he quickly smothered, though there could be no doubting his complacency. He was so pleased with himself that it was a wonder all the pits and pocks in his cheeks didn't fill with fresh skin and become smooth.

'What . . .' Gran started to say, but it came out as a croak. She closed her eyes for a moment. 'What do you want?'

'I think we all know the answer to that, Mrs Henshaw – although it's Mrs Foster now, isn't it? You'll have to excuse me if I slip up and call you by your real name. I only came across the Foster name a few minutes ago. Clever, that, changing your identity, but only to be expected, I suppose.'

'How did you find us?' Joan asked.

'I didn't find "us". I found you, Mrs Hubble – or rather, you found me.'

'Don't speak in riddles,' Gran snapped.

'Right,' said Mr Baldwin. 'I can see this is a shock for you, so I'll do the talking for now and then it'll be your turn.'

'Never,' Gran declared.

'Oh, I think you'll talk – but we'll come to that presently. Your granddaughter asked how I found you. It was that interview in the railway magazine.'

'But that's an in-house publication,' Joan exclaimed.

'Let me go back to the beginning.' Mr Baldwin sounded like a friend about to spin a rattling good yarn. 'I remember when Estelle Henshaw was killed – murdered, strangled. I sat through the trial and reported on it. Afterwards, I tried to find out what had become of the children. I assumed the Hopkins family, their mother's family, would have taken them in, so I went to see them. Although Estelle Henshaw died young, her parents had pre-deceased her. The children had an aunt and a couple of great-aunts.

None of them would speak to me, but you can always find a neighbour who's happy to gossip. The Hopkinses had come to an agreement with Donald Henshaw's mother that she would take them away and make a fresh start somewhere else.'

Joan looked at Gran. She had never known this – had never thought it through sufficiently to wonder. The Hopkins family had given up her and Letitia so that Estelle's daughters could lead a life free from shame. She touched her baby bump. Nothing would ever induce her to part with her child. But Estelle's family had done it, because they had wanted to protect her and Letitia. They had wanted it to the extent that they had severed all ties and had had no contact. What strength that must have taken. What sacrifice . . . what desperation.

'I wanted to write about it, about the children being spirited away to a new life,' Geoff Baldwin said, 'but my editor refused. He said it would reflect poorly on the newspaper if we used innocent babies as a story.'

'Your editor still might not be interested,' said Gran. 'If he wouldn't let you publish the baby story, why would he let you hound us now?'

'That was the editor of the *Bucks Herald*. I haven't worked there for years. I'm freelance now. If one paper doesn't want the story, another will. Guaranteed. Anyway, my old editor wouldn't countenance the baby story, so that was the end of that – until last week. Oh my. All these years later, I finally get my story. I was stranded on a station. Several of us had missed the last train. The stationmaster put some extra coal on the fire in the waiting room and his wife gave us all cups of Bovril. As we were settling down as best we could to see the night out, the stationmaster gave us some newspapers. In amongst them was an LMS magazine, possibly his own, that had got into the pile. Anyway, there I was, flicking through it, and I turned a page and, behold, there was Estelle Henshaw looking at me from a photograph. It was a bizarre moment. Even when I knew it couldn't possibly be her, my eyes told me I was seeing her. Then my eyes adjusted and I saw it wasn't her at all.' He looked at Joan. 'It was you, Mrs Hubble. It's a funny creature, the brain. It can play tricks. Take you, for example. You have a look of your mother about you, but you aren't her double by any means. Yet in that first moment, the resemblance was sufficient for my brain to show me not you, but Estelle Henshaw as she looked years ago.'

Joan's heart thudded along, heavy and slow. How many times had she wondered if she looked like Estelle? Now she had her answer.

'So I took a trip to Manchester and hung around Victoria Station,' said Mr Baldwin. 'Your dog is very appealing, by the way. Various people seemed to be in charge of him at different times, but the looker-after-in-chief appeared to be a real corker of a girl dressed as a ticket collector. There's something fetching about a girl in uniform, I always think. I had a go at pumping her for information, but I couldn't get anything personal about you out of her, so then I tried following the dog home.'

'You did what?' Joan demanded.

'If that's an outraged way of asking if I found out where you live, the answer's yes.'

'Then why didn't you . . . ?' This man, this reporter, this vile creature knew her home address. Her skin crawled.

'Because you are *Mrs* Hubble and I didn't want to run the risk of encountering *Mr* Hubble.'

'Oh, very brave of you.' But Joan's scorn was only on the surface. Inside she was quaking.

'I went there earlier today and knocked on a couple of the neighbours' doors,' Mr Baldwin continued. 'Don't worry. I didn't blab to anyone.' He smiled. 'There'd be no point in telling them and spoiling my newspaper scoop, would there? I just said I was an old friend of Mr Hubble's family and the lady over the road told me I'd have to wait for him to come home tonight.'

'So you thought you'd catch me on my own,' said Joan.

'That was the plan, yes. I knocked on your door and another lady answered – your landlady, I assume. I told her I was a gentleman of the press who was interested in the famous money-raising dog. She said you'd be out all morning and would probably be at your grandma's this afternoon. Well,' he said with a touch of drama, 'your grandma, eh? That was far more than I could have hoped for. I told your landlady I needed to speak to you pretty well immediately, because of my time being booked up, so she said I should try Torbay Road in Chorlton, though she didn't know the number. I came here and knocked on one or two doors, asking for Mrs Henshaw, but nobody had heard of her, so then I asked after the lady with the grand-daughter who works for the railways and I was immediately directed to your door – to Mrs Foster's door.'

Joan and Gran looked at one another. There was a sour taste in Joan's mouth. The taste of defeat?

'That's how I found you,' said Mr Baldwin. 'It makes a nice little tale, doesn't it? I might even write a book about this. The thought has always been in the back of my mind. *The Henshaws: The Murder and the Mystery.* How does that sound?'

Gran breathed in sharply; her nostrils flared. 'You rogue—' she began.

'Now then,' said Mr Baldwin, as if she hadn't spoken, 'there are two ways this can happen. You can give me an interview, the two of you – not forgetting the other grand-daughter—'

'Don't you dare—' flared Gran at the same moment as Joan said flatly, 'She died doing her duty.'

'I'm sorry to hear that,' but Mr Baldwin's eyes said he was thinking how best to work it into his story. 'As I was saying, if you consent to answer my questions, I'll present your story sympathetically. I'm very good at what I do and I'll have the readers wiping away the tears, I promise you. I came here in good faith.'

'Good faith?' Joan questioned disbelievingly.

'I could have brought a photographer with me. When you answered the door, your faces when I said your names would have made a splendid picture for the front page. I could have done that to you, but I didn't because, believe it or not, I'm a decent bloke.'

'Decent?' said Gran. 'There's nothing decent about what you're doing.'

'You'd prefer the other option, would you? The one where I write my story – and by my story, I mean, of course, your story – as a sensational piece, revealing how Donald the wife murderer Henshaw's family went into hiding and took their place in a respectable and unsuspecting northern community.' Mr Baldwin glanced towards the studio portrait of Daddy. 'The murderer's photograph on display in the parlour: that'll make a nice touch.' He sat up straight, picking up his hat. 'I'll give you a few days to think it over, ladies. I'm sure you'll see sense. Don't get up. I'll see myself out.'

CHAPTER THIRTY-ONE

Margaret felt bruised all day after her encounter with Mr Brent-Williams and his cronies, especially Mrs Ames, who, after seeming kind and sympathetic, had turned on her so viciously. *Girls of your sort used to drown themselves.* Presumably, they still should, in Mrs Ames's opinion. Well, in that case, there would be an awful lot of drownings. This far into the war, the number of what were being called 'irregular pregnancies' was on the rise, and it wasn't all unmarried girls either. Many pregnancies were those of wives whose husbands had been away for too many months for them to be the fathers. What would happen when all the husbands came back? Some men might accept a cuckoo in the nest, but plenty wouldn't. The divorce rate seemed certain to increase.

Stop it! She was letting her thoughts wander. Deep down, was she still avoiding facing what must happen next? It was time to talk to Joel. She had put it off for long enough by deciding not to tackle it until after she had tried for a reconciliation with Dad, visited Anna and the twins and then set her change of name in motion. All these things were important and she had needed to do them, but she needed to speak to Joel too. Even more so with Alison coming home for good next week. Margaret had to do this for her friend's sake.

And – something she had never realised before – she had to do it for her own sake as well. She thought about it, weighing it up. Yes, it truly was for her own sake as well as Alison's. It formed part of her new beginning. Talking with

Anna about Mum had finally enabled her to accept herself and a new strength had unfurled inside her, a strength that her new surname represented.

Doubting Thomas? Wasn't that the expression? But for Margaret, the name meant setting aside her doubts about herself. Yes, she had made a terrible mistake, but she was still a worthwhile person and her mother would have carried on loving her. Anna had given her that belief in herself and she would never forget what she owed her sister. Anna and Mum: the two most important and cherished women in her life, now and always.

All this time, she had dreaded the thought of having to see Joel again, having to discuss what had happened, the way he had treated her and the shameful aftermath she had been left to face alone. Now that dread had subsided into a quiet determination. This was something she had to do. It was an essential ingredient of her new start. She wouldn't truly feel she had made her fresh beginning without it.

How was she to find Joel? She didn't know his current address. She would have to go to MRI – the Manchester Royal Infirmary. Not that she'd be able to waltz in and hunt him down. She'd have to appeal to a clerk or a nurse to help her, and that meant she'd need a good story . . . and she knew exactly what would sound convincing.

'Did that reporter chappie catch up with you?' Sheila asked when Joan arrived home.

Catch up with her? Caught her in his trap, more like. Joan forced herself to smile. 'Yes, thanks.'

She spent the rest of the afternoon hiding in the sitting room, feeling churned up and trying not to dissolve into tears. As the time approached for Dot to bring Brizo home, she couldn't face the usual chat. Opening the sash window, she looked for Jimmy in the street. Judging by the way the children were jumping on and off garden walls and wrapping themselves tightly around lamp posts with their feet clear of the pavement, it looked like a game of ticky off the ground was in progress.

When Joan called him, Jimmy looked round from his perch on a wall. She beckoned and his freckled face screwed up in anguish.

'We're in the middle of a game. I'll get got if I have to come over there.'

When she had first moved in, Joan had let Jimmy get away with a certain amount, but over time she had learned to be firm. 'Now, Jimmy, please.'

The lad leaped down, sprinted for his mum's front wall and jumped onto it, catching at the privet growing alongside it for support.

'Here, Jimmy.' Joan tapped the window sill and after a moment, with obvious reluctance, Jimmy obeyed. 'I'm going upstairs for a nap. When your nan comes with Brizo, please can you look after him for me? You can give him his tea.'

Jimmy was always delighted to do anything that involved Brizo and he loved feeding him, but his happy smile vanished as Nessa from next door but two jabbed him in the back and immediately darted away, hitching herself onto a wall.

'You're it,' she yelled.

'Not fair!' Jimmy howled. 'I were talking to Auntie Joan. Tell her, Auntie Joan.'

But Joan closed the window and retreated upstairs, where she couldn't hold back the tears any longer.

Thank heaven Bob had the weekend off. When he came home, all Joan wanted was to cling to him as she explained.

'I'm so sorry to have brought this trouble on you,' she said.

'We'll have none of that, thank you,' said Bob. 'You're my wife. We're a team and we face everything together. Whatever happens, nothing can change that.'

What a good man he was. From the moment she had told him what she had discovered about her parents, his support had never wavered.

The baby kicked, normally something Joan loved, but this time it filled her with fear of the future. Was her child going to grow up being teased and taunted for having a grandfather who had been hanged for murder? Would other parents tell their children not to play with the Hubble child? She couldn't bear to think of it. Her muscles quivered as anger swelled inside her. Damn Geoff Baldwin. How dare he play fast and loose with their lives?

Although they talked all evening, there was no relief to be gained from it.

'We ought to have something to eat,' said Bob.

'I couldn't face it.'

'You must,' Bob said gently, 'for the baby's sake. What meal had you planned for this evening? Come on, I'll help you make it.'

'It's a good job Sheila's out at work tonight,' Joan said with a watery smile, 'or she'd complain you're setting a bad example for Jimmy by helping in the kitchen.'

At last it was time for bed. Joan felt dragged down and exhausted, but she knew she wouldn't sleep.

Lying in the dark, she asked Bob, 'Do you think we might have to move away?' She added in a whisper, 'Like Gran did when we were babies.'

'That's the last thing I want. I've always lived here and so have you.'

'But if it becomes public knowledge . . .'

Bob put his arms around her and held her close. His chest rose and fell beneath her cheek as he released a deep sigh.

'If we do end up moving – *if* – then we take your gran with us. She doesn't deserve this any more than you do.'

'I never expected to find myself on the same side as her,' said Joan.

Was she now tasting the same fear that Gran and the Hopkinses had faced after Donald Henshaw had been hanged for murder? Had their chests risen and fallen extra quickly, their breathing shallow? Had the little pulse inside their wrists jumped like this?

She didn't sleep much; neither did Bob.

At some point in the dead of night, without having to ask if she was awake, Bob said, 'I don't know how much use it will be, but the only thing I can think of is to ask Persephone.'

'She doesn't know anything about what happened.' From the core of Joan's being came the fear that had been instilled in her from her earliest childhood. No one must ever know.

'No, but she knows about journalism. She writes articles that sometimes get published in that women's magazine.'

'*Vera's Voice*,' said Joan, 'and she used to write a society column for one of the posh newspapers before the war. How can she help us?'

'I don't know that she can,' said Bob, 'but she might at least be able to tell us how these things work, how a freelance writer sets about getting something published. We wouldn't tell her about your parents, but we'd have to say that this Geoff Baldwin has uncovered a family scandal from a long time ago.'

'Would we even need to say that much?'

'We need her to understand the urgency,' said Bob. 'She might know someone who knows someone who knows Baldwin. It might be a way of appealing to his better nature.'

'He hasn't got one,' Joan said glumly, then she pulled herself together. 'Sorry. You're trying to find a solution and I'm not helping.'

'You're frightened.'

'Terrified, more like,' she admitted. 'Do you think this has been on the edge of Gran's awareness all these years? The fear of it all blowing up in our faces?'

'I wouldn't be surprised,' said Bob.

'How did she stand it?'

'She had to. Not just for her own sake, but for you and Letitia as well. I know some of her thinking was pretty twisted – hence the lies she told you about your mother – but she kept you girls safe from the Geoff Baldwins of this world.'

'Yes,' whispered Joan. 'She did.'

CHAPTER THIRTY-TWO

'I know it's unorthodox,' Margaret said, smiling pleasantly but not too widely at the clerk behind the desk in the hospital. She wanted to convey a mixture of civility and controlled emotion. 'But I hope you can appreciate how important this is. When Dr Maitland was a paediatrician, he treated my young nephew and referred him to Great Ormond Street. That referral saved his life.'

The clerk was a middle-aged woman with the drawn face of someone approaching the end of a double shift. 'I'm pleased to hear it.' Her unfailing politeness gave no indication of whether Margaret's tale had swayed her.

'The family doesn't live up here any more,' Margaret persevered, 'but I'm here for a few days, so I hoped it might be possible to see Dr Maitland just for a minute or two, to tell him what a difference he made to us. It would mean such a lot to my brother and sister-in-law if I could tell them I'd spoken to him personally.' Was she coming on too strong? She backed down. 'Of course, I quite understand if it isn't possible. If I wrote a letter instead, you'd make sure Dr Maitland received it, wouldn't you?'

The clerk pursed her lips and Margaret held her breath.

'Take a seat over there,' said the clerk, 'and I'll see what I can do.'

'Thank you,' Margaret said sincerely.

She sat down and watched as the clerk spoke into the telephone. After a short conversation, the woman hung up and beckoned Margaret over.

'You're in luck as long as you don't mind waiting. Dr Maitland is going off duty in twenty minutes and he says he'll come this way. Mind you don't hold him up or I'll send you on your way myself.'

It was nearly an hour before Joel appeared. Margaret saw him before he saw her. His face was set in serious lines, but then he smiled as he held open a door for an old boy with a walking stick, and there it was, that good-humoured expression she had known so well.

She'd been scared that the sight of him might bring all the old feelings rushing back, but no such catastrophe happened. Nor did she wonder what she had ever seen in him, which would have been upsetting in a different way, because it would have made her fall from grace seem like even more of a mistake. After the first jolt of recognition, she felt . . . 'distanced' was the best word to describe it, coupled with a vague distaste for what she was about to put herself through.

She watched Joel speak to the clerk, then stood up as the clerk indicated her. Joel turned round and stared at her incredulously before hurrying over.

'Margaret! What are you doing here? I was told—'

'I made that up so you'd come.'

Joel shook his head, bewildered. He gave a laugh, but that was the shock. 'I never expected to see you again.'

'No, I don't imagine you did. It would have suited you very well not to, wouldn't it?'

'I don't know what you mean.'

'Really?' Margaret spoke frostily but inside she was trembling with anger. 'Can we go somewhere private and talk?'

'I'm tired,' said Joel. 'I've just come off a long shift. Can we—'

'I'm friends with Alison.'

Joel frowned. 'Alison? My Alison?'

Had he ever called her 'my Margaret'?

'Now, Joel,' she said. 'I've been building up to this for a long time – since January, actually, and I don't care how tired you are. I'm not waiting any longer.'

Joan waited anxiously for Bob to return from the telephone box. He had gone to ring Darley Court to find out if Persephone was there. Would talking to her really help? Joan didn't see how, although she was trying to be positive, but Bob seemed certain that any information Persephone could provide about the newspaper publishing process would make them stronger because they would have a clearer idea of what to expect.

Joan stood at the sitting-room window, one hand on the back of her precious rocking chair. What a happy day that had been when her friends had presented it to her. What would those same friends think when they read all about her family secret? She would have to tell them in advance. They had stood by her when she had two-timed Bob before they got engaged, but it was one thing to lend your support to a girl who had lost her way while in the depths of grief and quite another to associate with the daughter of a murderer. Would other people see Cordelia, Dot and the others as tainted because they were friends with her?

There was Gran to think about too. She would never be able to hold her head up again. There would be gossip and sharp glances; people might cross the road to avoid her. Gran was a proud woman and, moreover, one who was known to be critical of the faults in others. How would she endure the public scandal?

And what about the Hopkins family? It would be unbearable for them to have the past dragged up. On top of that, the sacrifice they had made in letting go of Estelle's daughters would have been for nothing.

And all because a seedy reporter wanted to make his name.

Joan's grip tightened on the back of the rocker, her knuckles turning white.

Her heart bumped as Bob appeared at the corner and came along the road, touching the brim of his cap to a couple of neighbours with shopping baskets. Brizo accompanied Joan to the front door and greeted Bob as if he'd been gone for hours.

In the sitting room, Joan asked, 'Is Persephone there? Can we go round?'

'She's coming here. I told her we needed her help and she said she'd come immediately.'

What a good friend Persephone was. Part of Joan was warmed by the knowledge, though the rest of her was filled with panic.

'But we haven't decided what to say,' she said.

Bob placed his hands on her shoulders. 'She's your friend and she cares about you. Remember that and it'll be fine.'

It didn't take long for Persephone to cycle over from Darley Court. She propped up her bike and came inside, removing a natty beret and giving her honey-blonde hair a shake. Brizo, who was always on his best behaviour with her, came running to greet her, tail wagging madly, but he didn't jump up.

'Let's go in the sitting room,' said Joan. When they were seated, she said, 'Thank you for coming.'

'Of course I came. Bob said you needed help. I'm quite a useful person – as long as you don't expect me to deliver the baby.'

'It's a bit early for that,' said Joan and then couldn't think what to say next.

Persephone looked from her to Bob. 'What's this about?'

'We're hoping you can explain how newspapers work,' said Bob. 'Specifically, how long it might take for a story to appear if it's written by a freelancer.'

'It depends,' said Persephone.

'On what?' asked Bob.

'For a start, on whether the newspapers' own journalists are reporting on the story, in which case the freelancer won't get a look-in.'

'Supposing the freelancer is the only person who knows about this story?' said Bob.

'Then it depends on how interesting or important the story is and whether it's worth buying. If it is worth buying, the freelancer might get two or more papers bidding for it.'

Joan felt ill. 'It's worth buying, all right.'

'Please don't think I'm sticking my nose in,' said Persephone, 'but if you could give a hint as to what this is about, I might have a better idea of how to help you and what you need to do. I think you know me well enough to know I'm not a gossip.'

Bob looked at Joan. She knew this was her decision, and hers alone.

She sighed. 'Years ago, there was a scandal in my family – a bad one. It – it would have been in all the papers at the time. Yesterday . . .' She had to pause to compose herself. 'A freelance journalist has tracked me down. He intends – he's going to . . .'

'He's going to bring it all up again,' said Bob.

'It's worse than that,' said Joan. 'Gran brought Letitia and me here to Manchester when we were babies in order to escape from it. This man wants to interview us, but even if we say no, it won't stop him. He isn't just going to rehash the old story. He's going to write about how Gran ran away.'

'How did he find you?' Persephone asked.

'Through the LMS article about Brizo.'

Persephone caught her breath. 'Lumme. If I hadn't pinched that idea about the fundraising dog . . .'

'Is there any advice you can give us?' Bob asked. 'Anything you can suggest?'

'I don't think anything we say or do will stop this reporter. What's his name?'

'Geoff Baldwin,' said Joan.

'What a rotter,' said Persephone. 'And the Brizo article was such a morale-booster too.'

'Yes, it was,' agreed Joan. 'What?' she asked as, to her surprise, Persephone smiled.

'That's it. That's how we'll do it. Morale is all-important these days. Certain things are kept out of the public domain so that people aren't frightened or worried by them. It's essential that people keep their spirits up. It's part of the war effort. Resurrecting an old scandal and upsetting and publicly humiliating an elderly lady who plays her part by doing war work in the community, and her granddaughter who has done such sterling work on the railways, would serve no good purpose and would in fact cause damage, because it would show such lack of respect for the ordinary people who are the backbone of this country. Not only that, but you're a heroine, Joan. As a trained first-aider, you've taken part in rescues in numerous air raids. Your only sister gave her life in the Christmas Blitz. And you're newly married and expecting your first baby. You are not someone who deserves to be ruined by an old scandal and the public would be outraged if you were.'

'Are you sure you aren't one of Mr Churchill's speech-writers?' said Bob.

'So we have to hope Geoff Baldwin will back down for reasons of public morale?' asked Joan.

'I don't imagine that would sway him in the slightest,' Persephone answered. 'He sounds rather a worm, if you ask me. He needs to be leaned on heavily and I know just the man to do it. My father. He's a bigwig in the War Office and his brother is a High Court judge and Ma's brother is a Member of Parliament.' She smiled. 'I'm what you might call well connected.'

'Do you think your father will help us?' asked Joan.

'Yes, I do, but he won't do it just on my say-so. He'll need to know exactly what this is about.'

'You mean, what happened in my family.'

'Yes. 'Fraid so. Then, if he believes that public morale will not be served by bringing it all up again, and in particular by dragging your name and Mrs Foster's name through the mud, he can do something about it. You'll have to come over to Darley Court and speak to him on the telephone. I know it'll be wretched for you, but it'll be worth it in the end.'

'Thank you,' Bob said with feeling. 'When I rang you, I never imagined you'd have the answer to our problem.'

'Don't thank me until Pa has agreed to help.'

'Even if he doesn't,' said Joan, 'I'll never forget what you've done for us today.'

'One last thing,' said Persephone. 'I think we should bring Mrs Foster along too. Whatever the scandal was, I assume she lived through it in a way you and Letitia didn't. She ought to be told what we propose to do and we need to get her on the blower to my father.'

'Yes,' said Joan. 'We need to do this together.'

CHAPTER THIRTY-THREE

Joel opened the door and Margaret went into a consulting room. It was on the ground floor and the windows were frosted. The desk had one chair behind it and two in front. Over to one side was a narrow examination bed with a curtain on a ceiling track. In the opposite corner was a cupboard.

Margaret sat down. Joel started to walk behind the desk.

'There's no call for you to sit there,' Margaret pointed out. 'I'm not a patient.'

Joel smiled – a smile, it turned out, she remembered so clearly. 'Force of habit.' He came round the desk again and sat in the other chair, turning it so that it faced her and in the same movement pulling it a little further away. 'It's good to see you.'

'Is it?'

'I've sometimes wondered about you. The way we parted—'

'We didn't part,' said Margaret. 'You ran for it.'

'Hang on a minute,' Joel began.

'You got what you were after and off you went. I'd served my purpose. Don't deny it.'

'If you're suggesting that all I wanted was to get you into bed, and having achieved that I didn't want to see you again, then I most certainly do deny it,' said Joel. 'It wasn't like that.'

'Wasn't it?' Margaret asked scornfully. 'It looked that way from where I was standing.'

Joel moved his chair closer. He could have taken her hands, except that she had no intention of surrendering them and anyway, he didn't attempt to.

'I'm so sorry if you thought that,' said Joel, 'but I swear that wasn't how it was. I was enormously fond of you, you know.'

Fond. She had adored him and what he had felt was fondness. In a mad moment, she had even bought a wedding dress. That was how much she had loved him. A wedding dress! What an unutterable idiot she had been. But it hadn't felt idiotic at the time.

'That night we spent together – you've every right to feel sore about it,' said Joel, 'but I honestly didn't set out to seduce you. We both hit the bottle that night, as I recall.'

'You mean I asked for it.'

'I mean, the circumstances were such that it just happened. For what it's worth, I know you're not that sort of girl. When I woke up the next morning, you'd already gone.'

'And you felt no need to see me again. It's all very well saying you didn't plan it and it just happened, but you made no attempt to see me again.'

This time, Joel did catch hold of her hands. 'I was due to go to Leeds. You knew that. The next morning, I got my orders – and believe me, they were orders – to go that same day.'

Margaret was startled. She hadn't expected that. 'But we'd arranged to meet outside the cinema a day or two later. I waited for you . . . but you'd already gone away. When I say I waited, I don't just mean on that occasion. I kept on waiting and hoping.' She felt stunned. 'And you'd gone away.'

'A couple of army chaps turned up on my doorstep and gave me half an hour to pack my things and that was that. Believe me, you don't argue when the army appears at your front door.'

'It sounds rather hush-hush.'

'Not the way you mean. It was because – have you heard of Archibald McIndoe? His is a famous name in the medical world. He's engaged in pioneering work in the field of reconstructive surgery. Along with some other surgeons, I was spirited off to meet him and some of the lads he'd worked on.'

'Is that what you do now? Reconstructive surgery?'

'Not at that level. I do whatever operations come my way, both routine and as the result of air raids. But because of the air raids that were expected to start at any time, there was a need for doctors to be familiar with severe injuries and burns such as we hadn't seen before. So I spent a week with him and from there I went straight to Leeds.' He hesitated before adding, 'I'll be honest, Margaret. It was something of a relief. I knew I'd behaved badly, not the way a gentleman should, the night before the army-wallahs came to my door, and I was all too well aware that you deserved better.'

Margaret had a sensation of inner collapse as humiliation poured through her. And she had loved him so much. She removed her hands from his, not yanking them away lest he sense her feelings, but firmly, decisively.

All she said was, 'So it was a relief to get away.'

'Frankly, yes. I'm sorry, but there it is. It didn't sit well with me, though. I felt bad about it. I wrote to you, but you never replied, so I assumed you wanted no further contact.'

'You wrote? No, you didn't.'

'I did. I spent ages trying to find the right words.'

'Do you expect me to believe that?'

'Margaret, I swear to you from the bottom of my heart that I wrote to you after I arrived in Leeds.'

Margaret's heartbeat had slowed to a steady thump. 'I never received it.'

'Perhaps it got lost in the post. There's far more mail these days than there used to be before the war.' His voice dropped to a lower pitch and he said almost tenderly, 'I promise you, I did write.'

Margaret pressed her lips together as emotion welled up. What was there to say?

'And later on, when I was given a few days off, I came back to Manchester and tried to see you.'

'You can't have tried very hard.'

'I did try – and I had a reason for trying. I'd met another girl.'

Margaret's breath hitched in her throat and she went cold all over. 'You met someone else that quickly?'

'Well, it wasn't immediately,' Joel said defensively. 'It wasn't the first thing that happened when I reached Leeds. And remember, I thought you didn't want to see me again. But I still wanted to end things with you properly. It felt like the right thing to do. I'd never been to your house, but I knew you lived opposite Alexandra Park. I went there and asked after the Darrell family and found you'd been bombed out. I saw what remained of your house. I'm sorry that happened to you. A neighbour directed me along the road to where you'd been billeted, but when I knocked and asked for you, the woman who answered the door told me bluntly she wouldn't give house room to the likes of you. She made it sound as if she'd slung you out.'

'It didn't happen like that,' said Margaret. 'She made me so uncomfortable that I was forced to leave.' She shrugged. 'It amounts to the same thing.'

'She called you— well, never mind.'

'I can imagine,' Margaret said drily. Actually, she didn't need to imagine. Mrs McEvoy had called her a harlot and a scarlet woman to her face.

'I asked for your new address, but she didn't have it. Then I tried Ingleby's, but you didn't work there any longer. They told me you'd left to do war work, so that was the end of that.'

'Ah,' said Margaret.

'Ah what?'

'Nothing.'

But it was something. Alison had told her how Joel had tracked her down because he was so eager to see her again. He had made enquiries and ended up asking Miss Emery to pass on a message for him. That was how determined he'd been to meet up again with Alison, but there had clearly been no such need to see her, Margaret, again. No one at Ingleby's would have told him she was based at Victoria Station, but he could have asked for a letter to be sent on. Only he hadn't.

Lucky Alison.

'I hope you can understand,' Joel said quietly.

Oh aye, she understood all right. 'And now I want you to understand what happened to me.'

'I realise it must have been deeply upsetting for you.'

Margaret cut him short. 'I was pregnant.'

Joel's eyes widened. 'What?'

'You heard.'

'Do you mean to say . . . ? Is there a child?'

'No. I lost it. It happened the night we were bombed out. That's how Mrs McEvoy knew I was a harlot. All the neighbours knew, because my father berated me at top volume all the way to the ambulance.'

How strange to reduce it to so few words. Ever since it had happened, she had thought about it over and over, dwelling on every detail as she relived it, and she had described it fully for Anna. Yet now, speaking to Joel, she felt no wish or need to harp on about it and that was a step forward of sorts, a step away from the past.

Joel was shocked and concerned, but Margaret brushed aside his response. She had wanted him to know and he knew. That was it, as far as she was concerned. How . . . unexpected. After all this time, all the anguish, she had no need for a protracted discussion with him.

Speaking now in a businesslike manner, she said, 'I need you to know all this, because I'm Alison's friend and I care about her. To start with, I wanted to have a real go at you and tell you not to do to her what you did to me. All this time, I believed you'd taken advantage of me. I can see now it didn't happen like that, and when I've had the chance to take it in, maybe I'll feel better about it.'

'I hope you do,' Joel said softly. 'You paid a heavy price.'

'The girl always does. Isn't that what they say? I don't want Alison to pay any kind of price. I accept that you didn't set out to have your way with me, but all the same you hurt me badly. I don't want that for Alison. I'm going to watch the way you treat her.'

'Then what you'll see is your friend being cherished.'

Margaret lifted her chin. 'What are we going to tell her? We can't pretend never to have met before. The strain . . . the deceit . . . I don't want that.'

'Neither do I. Alison deserves better – and so do you. You've had a wretched time.'

Margaret drew back slightly. She didn't want sympathy. She needed to be strong. 'We can say we went out a few times before you went to Leeds to do your training and we didn't stay in touch after that.' Went out a few times! Her heart creaked.

Joel thought for a moment, then nodded. 'That should do.'

Margaret had a sinking feeling inside. 'I hate the thought of hiding behind half-truths.'

'I don't care for it either,' Joel said seriously, 'but it really is the best solution for all of us. Alison will know of our previous friendship. You'll keep your privacy and your reputation. And it spares Alison's feelings.'

'As well as letting you off the hook,' Margaret replied with a sudden note of sharpness. She pressed her fingers to her mouth for a moment. 'Sorry. That was mean. I've spent such a long time thinking that you abandoned me on purpose that it's difficult to see you through new eyes.'

'Do you doubt I've told you the truth?'

She pulled in a deep breath before slowly releasing it. 'No. After everything I went through, and everything I believed, it's . . . bewildering to have to look at it in a different way.'

'I know,' Joel said softly. 'You have deep-rooted feelings of distress and betrayal and they can't just be switched off.'

'You always were an understanding person. It was one of the things I treasured about you, but I really don't want to be on the receiving end of that understanding just now.' Margaret straightened her shoulders. It was no time to be weak. She had to concentrate on Alison. 'So it's agreed, then? We'll say we knew one another before you went to Leeds.'

Joel nodded. 'For what it's worth, I feel guilty about it too. We'll be telling the truth, but not the whole truth.'

'We can't tell the whole truth.'

'No, we can't. Do you think you can manage what we've agreed?'

'I have to. I don't want to deceive Alison and I can see you don't either, but there's nothing to be gained for any of us by telling the whole truth. It would hurt Alison dreadfully.' Margaret shook her head. 'It's funny. All along, I've desperately wanted to keep my secret and preserve my reputation. Now that I'm going to achieve it, I should feel relieved and grateful and reassured. But what I actually feel is . . . disquieted.'

*

Persephone settled Joan, Bob and Gran in what Joan thought must be a small room by Darley Court standards. It was undoubtedly a posh room, with velvet curtains and pelmet of deep red and a vast marble chimney piece. Even so, the white marble together with the blue hearth tiles, the curtains' cream lining and fringing and the colourful beaded cushions scattered on the chairs and the sofa all made the room feel pleasant and bright.

'If you wait here,' said Persephone, 'I'll put the call through to my father. I'll give him the public-morale speech and ask him to step in on your behalf. If he agrees, you'll need to speak to him yourselves.'

She left the room and the three of them sat in silence. Presently, Bob got up and stood, hands in pockets, staring out of the windows. Joan looked at Gran and her heart turned over. Gran – strong, difficult, judgemental Gran – looked old and thin. Diminished.

It felt like ages before Persephone returned, but she couldn't have been all that long because the clock on the chimney piece had chimed the quarter as she had shown them into the room and it had yet to sound the half-hour.

'Pa's on the line, waiting to speak to you,' said Persephone. 'May I offer a word of advice? Please don't be reserved or discreet or embarrassed when you talk to him. He's made it clear he isn't going to do this purely as a favour to me. He'll only do it if it's worthwhile and important and not unless.'

'We understand,' Gran said grimly.

Persephone took Joan and Gran to Miss Brown's office, where the black telephone sat on a large mahogany desk inlaid with dark green leather.

'Please address my father as General Trehearn-Hobbs,' said Persephone. 'He prefers to use his military title rather than the hereditary one for the duration. I'll leave you to it.'

The door clicked shut behind her.

Joan moved towards the desk, but Gran stopped her.

'This is for me to do, not you,' Gran said. 'I've been in the place of a parent to you ever since you were a baby and it's my job to protect you. Everything has gone wrong between us in the past year, but that makes no difference to my duty.'

She went to sit behind the desk and picked up the telephone, holding it to her ear for a moment before speaking.

'Good afternoon, General Trehearn-Hobbs. I am Mrs Beryl Foster. Thank you for consenting to hear me out. Your daughter says I mustn't hold anything back and so . . .' Gran drew in a breath. 'Does the name Donald Henshaw mean anything to you, sir? He was a murderer and – and he was my son.'

Joan heard the General speaking, but without being able to make out his words.

'My son strangled his wife in a fit of jealous rage. It was in all the newspapers day after day. The so-called gentlemen of the press were anything but gentlemanly. They hounded us – by "us", I mean myself and the Hopkinses. They were the family of my late daughter-in-law.'

It was the first time Joan had ever heard Gran refer to Estelle as her daughter-in-law. All Joan's life, Estelle had been 'your mother'.

'They even went through our dustbins,' said Gran, 'in case we'd been foolish enough to dispose of anything more interesting than the ashes from the fire. We couldn't set foot outside our front doors without being followed by a gang of men waving notebooks and cameras. We couldn't leave by our back doors either, because they hung around in the back lanes just in case. They were there all day, every day, and all night too. In the end, the landlord gave me notice. Reporters knocked on every door in Aylesbury Vale, asking questions about the family, about Donald and his marriage, and trying to find out the name of Estelle's lover.' Gran's eyes were bright beneath a sheen of tears, but her jaw hardened. 'My son was found guilty and he was hanged.' Her voice caught and she had to pause. 'My son was hanged for murder. I think of it every day of my life – and I ask myself where I went wrong.'

She stopped and listened. After a while, she nodded.

'I reached an agreement with Estelle's family that I would move away and take the little ones with me. I came here to Manchester and reverted to my maiden name of Foster, giving that name to the girls as well . . . Yes, General, that's correct – the older one, Letitia.' Gran looked at Joan. 'Persephone has told her father what happened to your sister . . . No, sir, I was speaking to my younger granddaughter, Joan, Mrs Robert Hubble. She is expecting a happy event and you can imagine the shock and distress this worry is causing.'

Again she paused to listen to the General.

'This reporter, this Geoff Baldwin, has tracked us down and intends to make a story out of our escape from the shame and scandal of the Henshaw murder. He wants us to consent to be interviewed, but will write his piece regardless. He cares nothing for us. We are merely a means to an end. We do not deserve this, sir. My granddaughter doesn't deserve it; neither does her husband or their baby. My granddaughter is a good girl and she has done her duty in wartime. Until recently, she worked on the railways and went out at night on first-aid duty. She has taken part in many rescues, as did her sister, who paid the ultimate price for her bravery. Both of them were determined to do their bit for their country. Is this a family that deserves to be turned into newspaper fodder? Does Letitia's memory deserve to be sullied? Does Joan deserve to have her life turned upside down and tarnished for ever? She didn't even know about her parents until last year. She has coped with that knowledge with dignity, grace and strength and I am proud of her.'

Joan's skin tingled all over. She'd had no idea that Gran saw her that way.

'Persephone told me I should tell you everything and I believe I have, sir,' Gran said. 'I may have the misfortune to be the mother of a murderer, but I am also the grandmother of the two best granddaughters in the world and I urge you to think of them now.'

CHAPTER THIRTY-FOUR

It was a good thing Margaret had to go back to work on Monday, because it meant the others would be safe from her. Not that she had actually lost her rag, but she'd been scared she might. After seeing Joel, she had come away feeling calm, even rather pleased with herself for having handled the encounter so well, but by Saturday evening she had begun to feel agitated, a sensation that had built up throughout Sunday into full-blown fury. She didn't know why she was angry. She didn't know at whom she was angry. Not at herself – and not at Joel, because he had turned out not to be a heartless bounder after all. She was just – angry.

And maybe she did know why. Maybe it was the whole situation, everything she had gone through, the anguish, the shame, the desperate determination to pull herself out of the moral gutter. It felt as if she'd lost a slice of her life through having had that unwanted pregnancy and miscarriage.

On Monday, she worked harder than she had ever worked in her life, throwing all her energy into venting her turbulent feelings. She mustn't let her old situation drag her down. It had changed her life, but now her life was about to change again and this time in the best possible way, because this week she had her appointment with Mr Hughes to complete her deed poll. She wasn't going to let old sorrows blight her fresh start. She was going to ask Mrs Cooper and Joan to be her witnesses, but not until after she had told Dad what was happening.

On Monday evening, she was back to her normal self, or as near as dammit. It was a buffet evening and she was glad of it. She knew she would benefit from being with her friends. Today it was just the four of them – Cordelia, Dot, Mabel and herself.

Cordelia handed her a sealed envelope. 'With my husband's compliments.' She smiled.

Margaret knew what it was and she put it straight in her bag, telling the others, 'It's the letter from the magistrate, confirming there's nothing iffy about my name change.'

'That's good, chick,' said Dot. 'Everything went well with the magistrates, then, I take it? Not that there was reason why it shouldn't.'

'It was a bit grim, actually,' said Margaret. 'Honouring your mother's memory isn't a good enough reason to give up your father's name, apparently.'

'You mean legally?' Dot asked.

'No, I mean if you're a stuffy old magistrate.'

Dot nodded. 'So when you say it was "a bit grim", what you mean is they put you through the mill.'

'Something like that,' said Margaret. 'It was rather horrid, but Mr Masters came riding to the rescue and sorted it out for me, which was ever so good of him. Now I just need to tell my father what I'm doing and then the difficult parts will be out of the way.'

It sounded straightforward, put like that, but she knew it wouldn't be. All the same, she refused to put it off. She wanted to get it over with before her appointment with Mr Hughes, so that she could attend it with a clear conscience, supported by her dear witnesses and feeling calm and hopeful. She wanted it to be a dignified occasion, not overlaid by worries.

'I'm going to see Dad straight after work tomorrow,' she told the others now, 'before he goes off to do his Home Guard stint.'

She felt wobbly inside, but she had already faced up to dragons in the magistrates' chamber. Telling Dad wasn't going to be easy or pleasant, but neither was it going to be worse than what she'd already gone through . . . was it?

Travelling on the bus from work to her old home opposite Alexandra Park gave Margaret an odd sense of déjà vu. It was a journey she had undertaken for most of her working life. In the months after Mum died, she had made the daily journey with a vague sense of sickness in her stomach at the thought of going home to a house without Mum.

Today she descended from the wooden platform at the rear of the bus and took the same old walk – the same and not the same. Nothing was the same these days, nothing and nowhere. Craters in roads meant that vehicles often had to take detours and it had become normal to see a row of buildings with a heap of rubble partway along where a house or shop used to be. There hadn't been an air raid over Manchester since January, but evidence of the Luftwaffe's attacks was everywhere you looked.

She walked along the pavement beside the park. After she had made friends with the others last year and had heard the story of their dear Lizzie, she had made a point of going to see the crater that was all that was left of the site where the park-keeper's house had been. She had stood staring at it, trying to visualise this popular girl whom she had never met but whose fate had been strangely linked with her own. The bomb that had destroyed the house and killed Lizzie had been dropped while Margaret was in her family's cellar, enduring a miscarriage. And now Margaret was friends with the very group that Lizzie had been part of. Did Joan ever make that link? She had been in the cellar with Margaret, taking care of her. If she hadn't done her duty as a first-aider—

'Margaret, what are you doing here?'

Startled, she looked across the road at the line of houses before realising the voice, Dad's voice, had come from inside the park. She turned and there he was, examining the vegetables, dressed in his Home Guard uniform.

'Come in here with me,' he said. Not 'Wait there. I'll come to you,' oh no, not that. They wouldn't exactly be hidden among the vegetable plots, but they would be much less conspicuous. Well, that suited Margaret, because what she had to say was private.

She joined him. He hadn't hugged or kissed her since before her miscarriage. Other people divided their lives into before the war and since the war started, but for Margaret, the point of division was her short-lived pregnancy.

'You look smart, Dad,' she said. 'I haven't seen you in khaki before.'

'Our uniforms were issued after – after you'd moved on.'

Dad looked surprisingly dapper. Margaret wanted to say that Mum would have been proud, but Dad wouldn't thank her for it. He would gladly have heard it from Anna, but not from her.

'What d'you want?' Dad asked. 'I haven't got long. I just came to check the potatoes before I go on duty.'

Margaret felt uncomfortable. Suddenly it seemed that this would have been a lot easier if Anna had paved the way.

'I've got something important to tell you, Dad. I'm going to change my name – my surname. I'm not going to be Margaret Darrell any more.'

Dad frowned. 'What are you talking about? You can't do that. Don't be daft.'

'It isn't daft. It's my choice. I had to appear in front of the magistrates last week—'

'In front of the magistrates! By all that's holy . . .'

'Not that kind of appearing. I haven't done anything wrong. They asked questions about why I wanted to do it. They needed to know I'm not a spy.'

'Good God, Margaret. Haven't you done enough damage to this family? Now you want to cast aside the family name.'

'If I've caused so much damage,' Margaret retorted, 'you should be relieved.'

'Don't be ridiculous. It isn't natural to give up your name. What are you changing it to, anyway?'

'Thomas. I'm going to be Margaret Thomas – after Mum.'

Dad's face slackened in shock, then hardened. Margaret felt a frisson of fear as Mr Brent-Williams's parting words returned in full force.

How do you think your late mother would feel to know that the daughter who brought shame on her father's name now intends to hide behind her mother's?

Oh, please. This mattered so much. Was Dad about to ruin it?

Dad started to speak, then stopped. He wasn't looking at her any more. He was looking over her shoulder towards the houses. The colour leached from his face, to be replaced by a look of sick dread.

Slowly Margaret turned around – and there was the telegram boy at Mrs McEvoy's house. Mrs McEvoy looked across the road at them, for once not sneering or curling her lip at the sight of Margaret. The telegram boy turned round as well and seemed to be about to leave the front door and cross the road, but Mrs McEvoy took the telegram from him and sent him on his way. He picked up the battered old

343

boneshaker he had dumped on the pavement, flung his leg over the crossbar and cycled away.

Margaret followed Dad out of the park and over the road. She ached to hold his hand, for both their sakes, but she couldn't bear the thought of being rebuffed. Worse, she couldn't bear the thought of *not* being rebuffed because Dad was too shocked by what the telegram was going to say.

Oh, good heavens, not William, not her lovely brother.

CHAPTER THIRTY-FIVE

On Thursday evening, Dot brought Brizo home to Joan as usual. He greeted Joan with enthusiasm but without being too bouncy. It was as if he understood she needed to be treated with care.

Dot patted him. 'He's such a happy fellow.'

'He's so loving and trusting – even though his previous owners abandoned him,' said Joan. 'How could anyone be so cruel?'

'We'll never know the story behind it.'

'Perhaps they went somewhere very important,' said Jimmy, joining in, 'only they went too close to a UXB at the wrong moment and were wiped out.'

'That's enough of that, thank you,' said Dot. 'Take Brizo out to play for a while. I want to speak to Auntie Joan.'

'In private,' Jimmy said wisely.

'Don't wander off,' Joan warned. 'Brizo will want his tea even if you don't.'

She watched them go, then looked at Dot enquiringly.

'Let's have a seat,' said Dot.

'That sounds ominous.'

'No, it sounds like you're nigh on eight and a half months gone and you need to take the weight off your feet.'

'I'll be glad to, actually,' Joan admitted.

'How are you feeling?' asked Dot.

'A bit twingey, to be honest.'

They sat down, Dot on the sofa and Joan in the rocking chair, which was her favourite seat now.

'It's bad news, to start with, I'm afraid,' said Dot. 'Margaret's brother has been posted as missing.'

Joan's insides gave a lurch of shock. 'Oh no. I'm sorry to hear that.'

'She told us in the buffet today. She was with her dad when he found out, but the two of them aren't close, as you know. It's a shame her sister is so far away.'

'Poor Margaret,' said Joan. 'It's one of those moments when you badly want to do something to help, but there really isn't anything anyone can do.'

'I know, chick. All we can do is be kind and thoughtful and hope for the best. Margaret was meant to change her name tomorrow, but she's cancelled the appointment. She said it wouldn't feel right.'

'She hasn't cancelled it altogether, has she?' Joan asked.

'No. She's just put it off for now. Poor lass,' said Dot. 'Anyroad, I've got summat else to tell you an' all. Persephone asked me if you could pop round to your gran's tomorrow morning – Bob an' all, if poss.'

'Bob won't be able to.'

'Never mind. She said she'll see you there after eleven.'

It must be something to do with Geoff Baldwin. Joan didn't know whether to twist her wedding ring in anxiety or sag with relief.

Dot added, 'She said to tell you not to worry.'

'Thanks, Dot,' said Joan.

'You know me,' laughed Dot. 'I deliver parcels all day, and dogs and messages on the way home. It's all part of the service.'

Dot wasn't a nosy person and she didn't pry into the meaning of Persephone's message. She left soon afterwards to go home and do the tea. Like hundreds of thousands of women all over the kingdom, she fitted her household and family responsibilities in between working flat out for the war effort.

When Bob got home, Joan relayed Persephone's request.

'It's a shame you'll be at work,' she said.

'If it's nothing to worry about, it must mean General Trehearn-Hobbs has arranged for Geoff Baldwin to be sat upon and squashed flat. A jolly good thing, too.'

It definitely sounded like the news they were desperately hoping for, but Joan wasn't going to take anything for granted. She wouldn't be able to relax until she had heard it from Persephone's own lips.

Joan set off for Chorlton in plenty of time and walked up Torbay Road shortly after ten. Each house in the long line of red-brick buildings had a front garden with a brick wall, a bay window in the downstairs front and black-tiled roofs with chimney stacks. Mrs O'Leary from up the road stopped for a chat. She was dressed in her old black coat with a headscarf tied under her chin and she carried her shopping basket over her arm. Joan answered all the usual questions about how she was feeling and, no, they hadn't settled on names yet.

'Though we'd better get a move on,' she added, 'or the baby will arrive without a name.'

'Don't you fret about that,' said Mrs O'Leary. 'Just you wait until you see him or her. The right name might pop into your head.'

Joan laughed. 'After all the names we've considered, that might be the baby's only chance.'

She went to Gran's. Gran opened the door before she could ring.

'I seem to have spent half the morning staring out of the window,' said Gran. 'I can't settle to anything.'

'I know what you mean,' said Joan. 'That's why I'm early.'

'When I got in from the WVS last night, there was a note on the doormat from Persephone. I hardly slept.'

'Likewise, though in fairness, I'm not sleeping much these days. You'll be a great-grandmother soon.'

They didn't say much while they waited. Gran had never been one for chatting for its own sake, though Letitia used to be able to draw her out. Joan felt a pang of sorrow. Letitia had missed so much this past year and a half. Now she was going to miss the chance to be an auntie.

The only subject they really talked about was Margaret's brother.

Gran said in her formal way, 'I'm sorry to hear that.'

Joan remembered Gran's reaction to Margaret's miscarriage. *'A flighty piece, a common little tart, who couldn't keep her knickers up.'* That had been Gran's assessment of the girl Joan had tended in the cellar when she had told her about it. Gran had no idea that Joan's friend Margaret had been the unfortunate girl and Joan would never tell her.

'She's here,' Gran said from the place she had gravitated towards beside the window. She left the parlour to let Persephone in.

In her heart, Joan wanted nothing more than to fly to the front door to greet her friend and draw her inside, but her girth and general discomfort scotched that. It was quicker for everyone if she stayed put while Gran did the honours.

'I can't stay long because I'm on my way to work,' said Persephone when she and Gran sat down. 'But I wanted to let you know the good news. Mr Geoffrey Baldwin will not be writing about your family now or at any other time.'

Relief and gratitude coursed through Joan. Gran, who always sat bolt upright, put her hand to her chest and slumped backwards.

Persephone immediately went to her, kneeling by her side. 'Mrs Foster, are you quite well? Shall I put the kettle on?'

Gran lifted her head. Her strong features had taken on a softer cast that Joan had never seen before. She sat up straight.

'I'm fine, thank you. I just felt overcome for a moment.'

'I don't blame you,' said Persephone. 'Not that I'm au fait with any of the details, mark you. Pa hasn't breathed a word. All I know is that he pulled a few strings.'

'We can never thank you enough,' said Joan.

'If you give me your father's address,' said Gran, 'I'll write to him, of course.'

Persephone smiled. 'There's no need for a letter. You can thank him in person. His work is bringing him up this way for a few days and he's going to pop across to Manchester so he can meet you. He hopes you'll be kind enough to dine with him. Bob's invited too, of course.'

'Truly, there's no need,' Gran began.

'Oh, please say yes,' said Persephone. 'Forgive me for being blunt, but dining with him will underline the fact that you are acquainted with a person of rank and influence.'

Joan and Gran looked at one another.

'In that case,' said Gran, 'thank you.'

'Champion,' said Persephone. 'He'll be so pleased. He asked me to apologise for not being able to take you to a restaurant in town, but he's only going to be here on a flying visit, you see, so I'll make a reservation in the first-class restaurant at Victoria Station for tomorrow evening.'

'Is he stopping off in Manchester just to see us?' asked Joan.

'Yes.' Persephone gave them her sweetest smile. 'Please don't try to wriggle out of it. If you change your minds, he won't come at all and then I shan't see him – and you wouldn't do that to me, would you?'

*

Excitement bubbled up inside Alison as she walked along the platform to board the train on Friday afternoon. She couldn't wait to get home to Manchester. Most of all, she couldn't wait to surprise Joel tomorrow when she appeared a whole twenty-four hours before he was expecting her. Saturday was officially her last day of working in Leeds and Joel thought she was coming home on Sunday, but because she'd been able to swap her shifts around, she was returning to Manchester now, on Friday, instead.

Pushing her suitcase ahead of her through the door, she climbed aboard and entered a compartment with three passengers already in it, including a young soldier, who stood up and hefted her suitcase into the webbed luggage rack above the seat. She smiled a thank you and her high spirits must have turned it into a bit of a dazzler, because the soldier's eyes widened with interest and he started a conversation.

'Going far?'

Alison set the ground rules immediately. 'Home, to my family – and my boyfriend.'

The soldier looked deflated.

Alison settled back to enjoy the journey. She had loved going home for Easter, but knowing she would have to return to Leeds had cast something of a cloud. There was no such cloud this time. This time, she could be unreservedly happy.

The journey was long, partly because the train was double-length, pulled by two locomotives. Having all the additional carriages meant stopping twice at each station, the front half stopping alongside the platform first before the train pulled forward so the passengers in the rear half could alight if they needed to and more passengers could crowd on from the packed platform.

Arriving at Victoria Station was itself a sort of homecoming. The young soldier got Alison's suitcase down for her, but instead of joining the crowd of people inching their way towards the doors, Alison waited a few minutes to let the crush thin out before she got off. She stepped down onto the platform, breathing in the scents of smoke, steam and oil and stepping out of the way of a porter with a flatbed trolley loaded with luggage and parcels.

A soppy grin formed on Alison's face when she saw the ticket collector at the barrier. Persephone squealed at the sight of her and, throwing decorum to the winds, gave her a hug.

'Do all the passengers get a welcome like that?' asked a chap in air-force blue from behind Alison. He made a show of holding out his arms and puckering his lips and the girls laughed.

'You should get home,' Persephone told Alison. 'You must be tired. I'll pop round over the weekend to see you.'

'Not Saturday afternoon,' said Alison. She couldn't add more because of holding up the queue of passengers wanting to leave the platform.

She walked onto the concourse. It was full of people, some reading newspapers while they waited, others running for trains or making for the taxi rank, some queuing to buy platform tickets from the machine so they could wave someone off or meet someone as they alighted from the train. All around her, she sensed the varying emotions – excitement, resignation, anxiety, even heartbreak at a dreaded parting. Alison felt for those people, she really did, but nothing could dampen her own happiness.

Oh, it felt so good to be back.

*

Margaret was in turmoil. Alison was back – two days early. Panic streaked through her. She had arranged with Joel that the two of them would tell Alison about having previously gone out together.

'We'll tell her gently, briefly and privately,' Joel had said. 'Then I'll take her out, so we can be alone.'

Margaret hadn't said, 'So that you can spend the evening making it up to her and making her feel cherished and important,' but she had thought it – and she had also known it was the right thing to happen.

But now, here was Alison back at home, and it was only Friday. She wasn't meant to arrive until Sunday. Margaret ran the tip of her tongue over lips that had gone dry. What was she supposed to do?

Well, she would have to tell Alison, wouldn't she? There was no choice. It would be too cowardly for words to duck out of it. Besides, the first thing Alison had said, once she had greeted everyone, was that she was going to surprise Joel tomorrow afternoon at his sister's house, which meant that there was absolutely no chance of Margaret and Joel being able to see Alison together before that.

Margaret tried to ignore the fluttery feeling in her chest. Best get it over with.

The door to Alison's little bedroom was open. She was humming 'In the Quartermaster's Stores' as she unpacked.

'Can I come in?' Margaret closed the door behind her. 'I've got something to tell you and it's not easy to say. I'm afraid it might upset you.'

'What is it?' Alison stood still. 'You're scaring me.'

'It's to do with Joel – no, don't worry. He's fine. It's that ... he and I used to know one another. We used to go out together.'

'You what?'

'It was before he went to Leeds. It didn't last long. He's a lovely chap, but he never liked me the way he likes you.'

Alison stared at her in shock and disbelief. Margaret's skin prickled.

'I don't know what to say,' said Alison. 'Why have you waited all this time to tell me – and why has Joel never said anything?'

'Please don't hold him to blame,' Margaret answered swiftly. 'He had no idea we're friends – not until last weekend. On that evening in January when you brought him here to meet everyone, do you remember how I had to work late?'

'You missed out on coming to the pictures with us.'

'I did come home late that evening – but not as late as I let everybody believe afterwards. I – I arrived when you and Joel were in the front room. I started to walk in, then I saw Joel and I couldn't believe my eyes. No one had noticed me, so I turned tail and ran for it. I was so embarrassed, not to mention shocked. It wasn't long afterwards that you were sent away to Leeds and I . . . I never got around to telling you before you went.'

'I see,' Alison said in a brittle voice.

Margaret waited. There was a weight in her chest that she knew wouldn't dissolve unless this situation was resolved with kindness and goodwill. Alison fiddled with her wristwatch.

'You wrote to me regularly. You could have told me that way.'

'Oh, Alison, it's not the sort of thing you can put in a letter.'

Alison's response was a jerk of her chin that seemed to signify agreement. At least, Margaret hoped it did.

'I went to see Joel last Saturday,' Margaret went on quietly, 'and told him about our friendship. He was surprised, to put it mildly. We knew we had to tell you. We intended to tell you together because we wanted you to see that – that it was over and done with a long time ago and you truly have nothing to be concerned about.'

Alison blew out a breath. 'I don't know what to say.' She reached for Margaret's hands. 'But it's all right. It feels odd and unsettling at the moment, but it'll be all right. I just need to get used to it. Would you mind . . . ? I'd rather be on my own for a bit.'

'Of course. And . . . thanks.'

'For what?'

'For taking it on the chin.'

Margaret went to her own room. Shutting the door, she leaned against it, her palms flat against the wood. Then she lifted one hand to swipe away a tear.

CHAPTER THIRTY-SIX

On Saturday afternoon, Alison got ready to go round to Venetia's to surprise Joel. He had specifically arranged to spend that afternoon with his sister, working on their plans to provide toys for children facing prolonged stays in hospital, because Alison would still be in Leeds – or so he thought. Alison smiled to herself. Joel would feel as if all his birthdays had come at once when she walked in.

The last time she had been to Venetia's, she had worn something simple, but this time she wanted to make more impact, and not just to knock Joel's socks off either. She remembered what Venetia had said about dinner parties and a wife supporting her husband's career. She wanted Venetia to take her seriously.

Mabel was happy to lend Alison her velvet-rayon dress. It was in two shades of green, and the buttons down the bodice, the collar, cuffs and belt all matched.

Margaret kept out of the way while Mabel was helping Alison to get ready, but that was understandable after the revelation about Joel yesterday. Besides, she must be frightfully upset about her brother. That was the sort of worry that had never touched Alison's life. She had no brothers; Paul had been in a reserved occupation and now Joel was too. The concern Alison felt for Lydia's husband was more for Lydia herself than for Alec, fond of him though she was. Alison promised herself that after she'd been reunited with Joel, she would spend some time with Margaret. Perhaps Margaret would want to talk or maybe she would just like some quiet company. Alison wanted to support her and be a good friend.

She set off for Victoria Park, walking along Beech Road to the terminus. When she got there, a young blonde woman, a few years older than herself, had just alighted from a bus, carrying a small carpet bag. She stood and looked around, smiling at Alison as she drew level.

'Excuse me. Do you know Wilton Close?'

'Yes.' Alison gave directions. 'You can walk it in five minutes.'

The young woman thanked her and went on her way. Alison crossed the terminus to stand at her stop.

It took about twenty minutes to get to Victoria Park. When she walked up the steps to Venetia's front door and rang the bell, Grace answered.

'Good afternoon,' Alison said. 'I've come to see Mrs Clifton.'

'Come in, miss. Madam is in the drawing room.'

'Thank you. I'll see myself in.'

That would be better than being announced. More of a surprise for Joel.

She went to the door. Ought she to knock? She compromised by tapping softly at the same moment as opening it.

'May I come in?'

The first person she saw was Venetia, sitting in the armchair in the wide bay window, looking elegant in rose-coloured *crêpe de Chine*. Her eyes widened in surprise, but it was nothing compared to how Joel must be feeling. Alison turned towards the sofa with a smile just for him – and the happy expression froze on her face.

Not Joel.

Rachel.

*

Margaret wasn't sure how to feel at the thought of Alison taking Joel by surprise at his sister's house. It would have been so much easier if she and Joel had had the chance to tell Alison together about their former relationship. Margaret would have felt more in control that way. But the main thing was that Alison had been told and Margaret just had to give it time to fade from the forefront of her mind.

Soon after Alison had gone out, the doorbell rang. Margaret was on her way downstairs as Mrs Cooper answered it. At the foot of the stairs, Margaret automatically glanced over Mrs Cooper's shoulder – and exclaimed in surprise.

'Anna! What are you doing here?'

'Anna?' said Mrs Cooper. 'Your sister?'

'Yes. Anna, this is Mrs Cooper, my landlady.' Margaret shook her head. 'I can't believe you're here.'

Mrs Cooper did what she always did when someone came to her door. She made Anna welcome.

'Anna – may I call you Anna? Come in, dear. Have you travelled up from Shropshire today? You must be tired.' Mrs Cooper craned her neck to look past Anna. 'Have you brought the children with you?'

'No,' said Anna. 'My landlady is taking care of them.'

'Why have you come?' Margaret asked.

'I've got some sorting out to do,' said Anna.

'Sorting out?'

'Of you and Dad. Mainly Dad.'

And she burst into tears.

'Oh, my dear!' Mrs Cooper put an arm around her and shepherded her into the front room. 'Mrs Grayson, look who it is. It's Anna – Margaret's sister. Come and sit down, chuck. Margaret, you sit with her and I'll make us all a nice cup of tea.'

Anna sat on the sofa, sniffing and holding hands with Margaret. 'I'm sorry,' she said to Mrs Grayson. 'What must you think? A stranger turning up here and blubbing all over the place.'

'You aren't a stranger,' said Mrs Grayson. 'You're my penfriend. I'm Amanda Grayson.'

Anna gave her a watery smile. 'The cake lady.'

'I've been called worse things.'

Soon Mrs Cooper returned with the tea.

'I'm sorry,' Anna said again.

'You must be exhausted from your journey,' said Mrs Cooper.

'It's William,' said Anna. 'Our brother. I assume you know . . . ?'

'Yes, we do,' said Mrs Cooper.

'I'm so worried about him,' said Anna, 'and . . .' She made a visible effort to pull herself together. 'It's made me realise, Margaret, that this business between you and Dad has got to stop. It's been going on for far too long. Mum would never have let it happen, and if it had happened, she would have dealt with it pretty sharpish. She would never have let it drag on. That's why I'm here. I'm going to do what Mum would have done.'

Alison stood staring at Rachel. It was difficult to take in that she was here. But she was, as large as life and twice as beautiful. Her dress, yellow silk printed with white flowers, had buttons all the way from the V-shaped neckline to the hem. A white belt with a flower-shaped buckle emphasised her trim waist.

'Alison,' said Venetia, quickly recovering, 'what a surprise. I thought you were still in Leeds.' She glanced at Rachel.

Rachel's composure didn't falter. 'I could have sworn today was your final day at work and you'd be travelling back here tomorrow.'

She gave Alison the usual gracious smile. Alison didn't smile back. Her facial muscles seemed to have gone slack with shock. She felt completely wrong-footed.

'I swapped shifts so I could come home early,' she said – and why should she explain, anyway? Rachel wasn't her boss any more. She lifted her chin. 'I thought Joel was going to be here.'

'I'm expecting him shortly.' Venetia glanced out of the window and then stood up, looking at Alison. 'Where are my manners? It's lovely to see you again, Alison, and perfectly sweet of you to drop in.' Her gaze flicked archly from Alison to Rachel and back again. 'And I don't mind in the slightest that you're here to see Joel and not poor little me. Rather than sharing him with the two of us, why don't you let me put you in my own sitting room? Then you'll be able to see him alone. I'm sure you'd prefer that.'

Venetia looped her hand through Alison's arm, bore her to the rear of the hall and opened a door into a smaller room – smaller, but still quite a size compared to the house Alison had grown up in. It was a pretty room, rather chintzy-looking, with windows overlooking the gardens to the side and back of the house.

'Make yourself comfortable,' said Venetia, 'and I'll be back in a moment. I'll just organise some tea.'

She disappeared and Alison contemplated the best place to sit. In the armchair over there so Joel would see her the moment he opened the door? Or on the settee, so he could sit beside her? She opted for the armchair.

Venetia returned, closing the door behind her. 'Grace will bring a tray.' She sat down opposite Alison.

That was puzzling. 'Shouldn't you go back to Rachel?'

Venetia waved an elegant hand, dismissing the suggestion. 'In a minute. How clever of you to choose that chair. Or did you see my little bell on the table here beside this chair and know this must be where I sit?'

'I hadn't noticed.'

Venetia gave her a warm smile. 'Then you must be a mind reader, because you've left my favourite place free for me.' She looked round as the door opened. 'Ah, Grace. Put it down here and I'll pour. That'll be all, thank you.' As Grace left, Venetia reached for the teapot. 'I know I need to pour yours at once, because you like it weak.'

'You remember.'

'A good hostess remembers all her guests' preferences.'

'Thank you,' said Alison, taking the cup and saucer Venetia offered. 'I'm sorry to have arrived unannounced like this.'

Venetia arched an eyebrow. 'Sorry to have barged in on Rachel and me, you mean? It must have been a tad awkward for you.' She smiled as she spoke and gave a breathy little laugh that took the sting out of the words. 'I hope you don't mind, but Rachel mentioned to me that she was your superior in Leeds and that she'd gone to some trouble to provide you with an interesting timetable of work, only for you to think she'd done it because of Joel.'

Heat touched Alison's cheeks. She wished she'd kept her mouth shut over that suspicion.

'You're fond of Joel, aren't you?' Venetia went on. 'I'm sure he's fond of you too. In fact, I know he is, but you must see that it really won't do.'

There was a tiny *ting* as Alison returned her cup to its saucer. 'What do you mean?'

'My love, you're a dear girl, you truly are, but you should ask yourself if you are what Joel needs. Now I don't wish to hurt your feelings, I honestly don't, but will you permit me to speak frankly?'

Alison went cold right to the core of her being. No words would come. She nodded.

'Thank you,' said Venetia. 'And shall you be brave and listen closely to what I have to say? I know it won't be easy, but I also know I can trust you.'

'Trust me?' Alison asked in a croaky voice.

Venetia nodded. 'Absolutely, because I know you'll want what's best for Joel – won't you?'

'Of course.'

Venetia looked at her with warmth and approval. Alison half expected her to say, 'Good girl.'

As if considering what to say, Venetia tilted her head to one side. 'It's our family, you see. We aren't titled – though Father will probably be knighted one day – but we are a cut above. You know what I mean. Money. Influence. Private schools.'

'Finishing school,' Alison couldn't help adding.

'Exactly,' Venetia agreed, as if Alison had said something witty and perceptive. 'Now, I don't want to make us sound like dreadful old stick-in-the-muds, but we do have certain standards to maintain, all the more so with things changing because of the war. You know how it is. Some of the social boundaries are blurring and men are meeting girls whom they'd never have met in former times, or if they had met them, it wouldn't have led to anything serious. A young chap has to be allowed to have his fun, of course, but in the end he marries the right girl – a suitable girl.'

Something went *clunk* deep inside Alison. 'And I'm not a suitable girl.' She didn't make a question out of it.

'You're a darling girl,' cried Venetia. 'You're perfectly charming, but . . .' She hesitated, though with no sign of awkwardness. In fact, she was smiling. 'Joel is going to be an important consultant one day. He needs someone who can support him in his career, and that means a great deal more than someone who will put up with night shifts and weekend work. There's the whole social side of it too. Please don't think I'm talking down to you, but you don't know the ropes. It would be an awful struggle for you to cope, even if you took a crash course in one of the etiquette schools. Do those places still exist, or have they died out? It isn't just a case of being the perfect hostess. One has to be the perfect guest too, the perfect committee member and the perfect wife with—'

'The perfect background,' Alison finished.

Venetia's blue eyes were soft with sympathy. 'Precisely, darling. I knew you'd understand. Look, why don't I leave you to think it over? Have a bit of a weep, if you feel the need. I'll pop back in a while.'

Venetia rose quietly and left the room. Alison scarcely knew what to think. Was she truly not good enough for Joel? Venetia obviously thought so and presumably the rest of Joel's family would be of the same opinion. But Joel had never given any indication of thinking that way.

Alison felt shocked and hurt, but she had a stubborn streak too and it stirred into life now. She wasn't about to let Venetia tell her what to think or do – especially if it meant giving up Joel. That was for her and Joel to decide, no one else.

Standing up, she smoothed the skirt of her dress and picked up her handbag. She would go to the drawing room, say her goodbyes to Venetia and Rachel, very politely of course, and leave.

Opening the door to the hall, she was surprised to see Venetia. Why hadn't she gone back to join Rachel? A sarky remark about the perfect hostess started to form in Alison's mind, but she ignored it. She was all set to smile and say goodbye when she caught a flicker of something shifty in Venetia's expression, there and gone in an instant.

Why would Venetia . . . ? And why was she lurking in the hall? Without entirely knowing why she did it, just sensing it was the right thing to do, Alison walked smartly past her.

'Wait – no.' Venetia tried to catch Alison's arm, but she was too late.

Alison opened the door – and stopped dead.

Joel – Joel! – was sitting on the sofa with Rachel, each of them angled to face the other. Joel was holding one of Rachel's hands in both of his. The interruption made him look round and he jumped to his feet.

'Alison! What are you doing here? I can explain—'

It was too much. Alison had no idea what the merry heck was going on. She just knew she needed to escape.

'No, you can't,' she said quietly, and walked out of the house.

CHAPTER THIRTY-SEVEN

Margaret knew better than to try to talk her sister out of something when she got that determined look on her face, but she had serious doubts about what Anna intended to do now. Anna hadn't seen Dad in a long time. All she'd had to go by were his letters and Margaret doubted they had conveyed the full extent of the shame and contempt that Dad felt towards her. Back in Wilton Close, she had even wondered whether to let Anna tackle Dad on her own – but only for a moment. She wasn't going to hide from this. She had done enough hiding away after quitting Mrs McEvoy's house and leaving her job at Ingleby's and she had no desire to hide any more.

As the two sisters walked alongside Alexandra Park, Anna stopped to stare at its changed landscape.

'I knew it wouldn't be the same,' said Anna, 'but it's still a shock to see it.'

Margaret didn't say, 'Wait until you see our old house.' She just edged closer so they could hold hands as they carried on walking.

When their former home came into view, Anna let out a strangled cry and Margaret put her arms around her.

'Oh, Margaret,' said Anna. 'We were born in that house. All three of us were.'

All three of them. They held one another tighter, then Anna gently pushed Margaret from her.

'Come on. We've got a mission.'

An impossible one, in Margaret's opinion, but she didn't utter the words. Her main worry at this point was that by dramatically turning up and speaking out in Margaret's defence, Anna was in danger of having Dad turn against her too. That would be a devastating burden for her to carry back to Shropshire.

'What if he isn't in?' Margaret asked.

'He will be. I sent him a postcard to say I was coming.'

'Did you say you'd be bringing me?'

'Nope.'

They arrived outside Mrs McEvoy's house and Anna raised the lion's-head door knocker and tapped it a couple of times before giving Margaret an encouraging smile, as if what they were embarking on was something they were going to breeze through.

Mrs McEvoy opened the door. She was a faded woman who wouldn't see fifty again. Her hair was neatly drawn back from her face while across the front, from temple to temple, sat a row of small metal curlers wound so tight to her skull that Margaret felt a twinge of sympathy.

'Hello, Mrs McEvoy,' said Anna. 'Do you remember me? It's been a while. Anna Dixon – Anna Darrell-as-was. I've come to see my dad.'

Mrs McEvoy looked past her at Margaret. As the woman's eyes narrowed, Margaret experienced a return of the old fear and shame Mrs McEvoy had inspired in her when they lived under the same roof – yes, and the same loathing too.

Removing her gaze from Margaret, Mrs McEvoy bestowed a smile on Anna. 'You're welcome here any time, but that one isn't setting foot in my house.'

Anna gave Mrs McEvoy a dazzling smile. 'Fine. Then could you send my dad outside, please, because I don't go anywhere my sister isn't welcome.'

Taking Margaret's arm, Anna led her a short way along the pavement. When they looked back, Mrs McEvoy was glaring after them. With an exclamation of 'Well!', she shut the door.

'The old witch,' said Anna. 'I never liked her.'

'What if Dad doesn't come out?' asked Margaret.

'He'll come,' said Anna.

And he did. The door opened again and Dad appeared, pulling on his tweed jacket. He got one arm in, then Anna called 'Dad!' in a voice loaded with love and longing and he clean forgot about his other sleeve as he opened his arms for her to fly into. Seeing them cling together, Margaret felt as if she had received a punch in the gut. When had she last had a hug from Dad? Not since before Dunkirk.

Anna wriggled free, sniffing and wiping away a tear. She helped Dad put his jacket on properly. Margaret hadn't expected this. Anna had given her so much support that she had felt Anna was on her side, rational and compassionate in the face of Dad's unyielding distaste. Now she realised it wasn't that simple for her sister.

'It's so good to see you.' Dad gazed into Anna's face, his own expression glowing with tenderness.

'You too, Dad. You'll have to come to Shropshire to meet your grandchildren.'

'I never imagined my grandchildren growing up so far away.'

'I've brought Margaret with me.'

Anna stepped aside and Dad, tearing his gaze from her, looked at Margaret, and the expression that was soft with love for Anna changed, closed down. Pain filled the back of Margaret's throat.

'We need to talk about this, all of us,' said Anna. 'I suggest we don't do it in full view of Mrs McEvoy's parlour.'

'There's nothing to say,' said Dad.

'There's plenty to say,' Anna replied at once, 'and I've come a long way to say it.'

Margaret nodded across the road to the park. 'There are still benches in there.'

'Good,' said Anna. 'Then we can sit down.'

She marched across the road, leaving them to follow. For a moment, Margaret thought Dad wouldn't, but then he did.

They found a bench and sat down, Anna in the middle.

'Dad,' she said, 'I want to tell you how much I love and admire Margaret.'

'Admire her?' Dad repeated.

'Yes,' said Anna. 'She's got a good job, doing important war work. She's found a decent home, where she is looked after beautifully, and she's made a new life for herself with friends who care about her.'

'I bet they don't know about her shameful past.'

'No, they don't,' Margaret said.

'It's none of their business,' Anna said stoutly. 'They see her for what she is – a kind, clever, hard-working girl with a loving heart.'

'Oh aye, very loving,' said Dad. 'I expect the man who put her in the club thought so too.'

Anna surged to her feet and stood in front of Dad, leaning over and wagging her finger at him. 'How could you be so crude? Is that any way to talk in mixed company? You know what Mum would say. "Wash your mouth out." Only you'd never have said it in front of her.'

Dad huffed and puffed, then admitted, 'Maybe I went too far. A father shouldn't say such things in front of his daughters.'

Anna sat down again. 'As I was saying, I admire Margaret for the way she pulled her socks up and turned her life around. Yes, she made a bad mistake, and after that she ended up living with Mrs McEvoy, who was horrid to her.'

'And whose fault was that?' said Dad.

'Yours, partly,' Anna retorted. 'The way I understand it, no one would have been any the wiser about the miscarriage if you hadn't shouted it from the rooftops. You know what Mum used to say about folk washing their dirty linen in public.'

'Don't keep bringing your mother into this,' said Dad.

'Why not?' Anna asked. 'It's because she's not here that things have got so bad between the two of you. You know I'm right.' Without waiting for a response, she turned to Margaret. 'I want to tell you how much I love and admire Dad. He's not had it easy, what with losing Mum. Then the war came along and William volunteered, I was evacuated and all of a sudden it was just him and you rattling around in that house. You've both told me about the night of the miscarriage – and that was what you both focused on: the miscarriage. But, my God—'

Anna stopped. She shook her head and swallowed. When she spoke again, her voice was loaded with tears.

'A few minutes ago, I walked past what's left of our old house. All this time, I've known it must have been wrecked, but seeing it . . .' She had to stop again. 'Knowing something and then seeing it with your own eyes are such different things. It's made me realise something. That night, the night when Margaret lost her baby – for the two of you, the memory is all about the miscarriage, and I understand that, I really do, but it was a terrible night in other ways. You've only got to look at the damage and destruction up and down this road, *our* road. Margaret, Dad must have been frightened out of his wits when the house collapsed with you in the cellar.'

'Aye, I was,' said Dad. 'I ran like a mad thing to the park-keeper's house because I knew it was a first-aid post. I remember practically jumping up and down, trying to make them hurry.'

'And the reason you were so frightened,' Anna said quietly, 'is because you love Margaret. When she was eventually stretchered out, the relief must have been over-whelming.'

'I was trembling all over. I thought my knees were going to buckle, but then . . .'

'Then the ARP man or whoever it was told you about the baby, and the fear and relief and the shock must have clashed together and burst out of you. That's why you yelled about Margaret's predicament.'

To Margaret's surprise, and undoubtedly to Dad's as well, Anna joined hands with them both, linking the three of them together.

'Dad, I know you feel Margaret let you down,' Anna said urgently, 'but do you really mean to punish her for ever? Don't you think she's suffered enough? What would Mum say?' She lifted their two hands and pressed them against her face. 'It was so hard losing Mum. Now we might well have lost William too. Dad, are you really going to let yourself lose Margaret as well?'

CHAPTER THIRTY-EIGHT

Fighting tears, Alison marched down the road, past the grand houses with sundials and lily ponds in the middle of their wartime vegetable plots. To think that she had dreamed of surprising Joel. Well, she'd done that all right. She felt almost light-headed with disbelief. She had known, or at the very least strongly suspected, that Rachel had set her sights on getting back together with Joel, but even though she had found Rachel's conduct deeply upsetting, she had never thought that Joel would succumb to her charms.

Hearing running footsteps behind her, she moved aside so that whoever it was could get past, but the steps slowed and Joel appeared next to her. He placed a hand on her arm, stopping her and turning her to him.

'Alison, please, can we talk?' His cheeks were flushed, his blue eyes full of anxiety. For once, his face wasn't light-hearted and boyish. 'I need to explain. None of us knew you were home yet.'

'I think that was quite obvious.' Alison resumed walking.

Joel fell in step. 'I went to Venetia's to talk about organising the toys for children in hospital. That's all I was expecting, I swear. I had no idea Rachel was going to be there.'

'Her presence caught me by surprise too,' Alison said flippantly, 'though that was nothing compared to the surprise of catching you holding hands with her.'

'Alison, please.'

Joel guided her to a low garden wall and sat, pulling her down beside him. He put an arm around her shoulders as if he feared she might jump up and run away. Tempting as it was to remain in his embrace, Alison wriggled free, though she stayed on the wall.

'This isn't the homecoming I wanted for you,' said Joel. 'I'd planned – well, we'll come to that later, after we've talked about this afternoon. Venetia and I made our arrangement and apparently, at some point after that, Venetia had a letter from Rachel saying she was coming to Manchester and please could she invite herself over on the afternoon of Saturday the sixteenth, as she couldn't manage any other time.'

A chill rippled through Alison. 'I told her.' She looked at Joel. 'I told her you'd be at Venetia's.'

'Venetia never mentioned Rachel's visit to me. She – well, she always liked Rachel and had hopes for us. She thought that perhaps if we spent a little time together . . .'

'I don't need to hear the details, thank you,' Alison said crisply.

'I gather you arrived unexpectedly and a few moments later, Venetia saw me through the window.'

'So she bundled me off into another room,' said Alison. 'Yes, and then she stayed with me instead of going back to Rachel. I thought it was odd, but it was so that Rachel could be on her own with you and win you back.'

'She'd never be able to do that,' said Joel, but Alison was too busy feeling indignation rush through her at how she had been manipulated.

'That was why Venetia said she'd go and organise tea, instead of ringing for Grace. It was so she could let you in before you could ring the doorbell.'

Joel blew out a breath. 'I'll be having some serious words with my sister. I can promise you that.'

'Don't make out this is all her fault,' said Alison. 'You're the one who was holding hands with Rachel.'

'I was comforting her, trying to let her down gently. She said she'd never stopped having feelings for me and she'd do anything to win me back. It – it came as a bit of a shock to see her so vulnerable. She was important to me once and I hated having to hurt her, but I told her that I'm with you now and you're the only girl for me. When I took her hands – no, I'll tell you everything. She touched my face; she laid the palm of her hand against my cheek. She gazed at me, willing me to give in and say we could try again. Maybe I should have pushed her away or stood up, but I wanted to be kind. Perhaps that gave her the wrong impression. She leaned forwards and I think she intended to kiss me. That was when I removed her hand from my face and held it in both my own. Yes, I was holding her hand when you walked in, but I was rejecting her, kindly but firmly, and she knew it.'

Tension flowed out of Alison, sent on its way by relief and gratitude.

'Even if she didn't realise it before you came in,' said Joel, 'even if she was still clinging to hope, she certainly knew it from what I said before I left Venetia's house to run after you.' He took her hand. 'This is the only hand I want to hold.'

Alison smiled as she held up her other hand. 'Not this one?'

'I can stretch a point.' He reached for her free hand. 'I'm sorry it happened. I'm sorry Rachel turned up. I'm sorry Venetia was a prize chump. Above all, I'm sorry you were upset. Can we please put it behind us?'

'It seems we have a lot of putting behind us to do,' Alison said crisply. 'Margaret told me about you and her.'

'She did?'

'It came as quite a surprise, as you can imagine, but I'm not going to be silly about it.'

'It was a long time ago and—'

'You don't need to say anything. Believe me, if I had felt any lingering upset, it would have been dashed away the moment I saw you holding hands with Rachel.'

'Ouch,' said Joel.

'There's one more thing,' said Alison, 'and it's serious.'

'Tell me.'

'Venetia doesn't think I'm good enough for you. She tried to talk me into leaving you.'

This was obviously news to Joel. 'She what?'

'Apparently, you should only associate with girls who would be marvellous for your career – girls like Rachel, I assume.'

Joel thought for a moment. 'You know that my father is at the top of his profession.'

'Venetia says he'll be knighted one day.'

'That's the sort of career she wants for me, but listen to me, Alison Lambert. It isn't what I want for myself. You know that what I care about is paediatrics and, yes, I want to do well. I'll lose several years of my career to this war, but when I get back in the children's wards where I'm meant to be, I'll rise through the ranks and end up as a consultant. But I shan't be sitting on committees and writing papers or advising the powers that be, and you know why not? Because I'll be too busy working in the wards with the children, that's why not.'

Alison took a breath of pure satisfaction. She was so proud of him in that moment. 'I think that's wonderful.'

'I've tried to explain to Venetia, but she won't have it. Anyway, that's enough about my daft sister.'

Joel stood up, drawing her to her feet. They faced one another and the warmth in his eyes made joy unfurl inside her, every nerve ending tingling.

'I started to tell you earlier about something I'd planned,' said Joel.

'I had the impression it was to do with my return to Manchester.'

'Go to the top of the class,' said Joel.

Alison smiled at him. 'Go on. Tell me.'

'I'll do better than that. I'll show you. Come on.' But instead of setting off along the road, he stood very still, his gaze capturing hers. 'If this afternoon's debacle gave you any reason to doubt me, this will show you how much you mean to me. In fact, it'll prove it.'

In the kitchen, preparing Bob's snap tin for him to take to work, Joan put down the bread knife and reached round to press her hands into her lower back. She had been getting twinges all day, and last night too.

Coming into the house through the scullery with an armful of home-grown veg, Bob looked at her with concern. 'Feeling all right?'

'Achy.'

'I'm not surprised, with all that extra weight you're carrying around.' Dumping the produce on Sheila's kitchen table, he came to stand behind Joan. 'Let me. Is that the right place?'

'Lower – that's right.'

'Have a sit-down.'

'I'll get your snap finished first.'

She made his sandwich and took a couple of butter biscuits from the tin, though strictly speaking, they should be called Stork biscuits these days.

'I'll go and park myself in the rocking chair,' said Joan. 'It really has been a godsend. It's comfortable and gives me lots of support.' She gave her husband a cheeky smile. 'Like you.'

'I'll wash this veg and bring you a cup of tea.'

'Only because you want to see the saucer jump when I rest it on my bump.'

'It's nice to know my son and heir is going to be a footballer.'

'Maybe you'll have a daughter and heiress and she's going to join the chorus line.'

Going into the sitting room, she grasped the arms of the rocker to lower herself in, and rocked gently. Could the baby feel that?

Bob appeared with two teas.

'Thanks,' said Joan. 'Every time I sit down now, I wonder if I'll be able to get up again.'

'You might be stuck in that rocker until June.'

'The midwife thinks late May rather than early June.'

'Drat,' said Bob. 'I'd set my heart on this little 'un putting in an appearance on our first anniversary. Wouldn't that be champion?'

'It can't come soon enough for me,' said Joan. 'I felt wonderful earlier in the pregnancy, but now I just feel huge.'

'Are you sure about going out this evening?'

'If I can manage to do the shopping and walk Brizo,' Joan said wryly, 'I can manage to sit at a table. Besides, Persephone has insisted on taking us both ways by taxi. I do want to meet her father, so I can thank him personally. It's the least I can do after what he's done for us. I just wish you were coming too.'

'So do I,' said Bob. 'I'd like to shake his hand.'

'I don't remember Gran ever going out for a meal before. She never socialised. When we were growing up, she was on good terms with the neighbours, but it was all very formal. She never went round the shops with anyone and there was no popping in and out of one another's houses. She said it was important for us to keep to ourselves.'

'It must have been lonely for her,' Bob remarked.

'I don't think she saw it like that. I think she just accepted it as the way things had to be. You know what she's like. She would have seen feeling lonely as a sign of weakness.'

'And weakness was the one thing she could never afford to display,' said Bob. 'The secret – the real secret, not the one she fobbed you off with – must have hung over her the whole time.' He grimaced. 'Sorry. No pun intended.'

Joan spoke tentatively, searching for the right words to convey the new ideas that were forming. 'The business with Geoff Baldwin has made me start to see things differently. Here we are, you and me, suppressing the truth, hiding it away as if it had never happened. That's what Gran has had to do for years. I don't mean it was right for her to tell lies about my mother, but . . . I'm going to lie about my parents for the rest of my life. You are too. We're going to lie to our children about them. They're never going to know that their grandfather killed their grandmother. We're never going to tell them he was hanged. We shan't make up nasty lies like Gran did, but we still face a lifetime of concealing the truth – and I'll be glad to do it, because I don't want my children to have any sort of cloud hanging over them. So I shall tell the lies and smile as I do it, because it's the right thing to do.'

'You seem to be more sympathetic towards Mrs Foster.'

'I honestly don't know the answer to that. I'll never believe she was right to say Estelle ran away with her lover, leaving Daddy to die of a broken heart – never. But what we had to live through before Persephone's father dealt with it, the fear, the shame, the pounding heart and the bad dreams – all that has given me a glimpse of how it was for Gran after . . . after my father did what he did. There's something else too. It's made me see how she had to face everything alone. She came here with two tiny children to start again, with nobody to lean on, no one to talk to. That must have been hard. It makes me even more grateful to have you.'

Bob left his seat, took her cup and saucer and placed them on the table. Then he knelt beside her, taking her hand. 'You'll always have me. Whatever happens, we'll face it together.'

'I think this has hit Gran hard,' said Joan. 'I've never felt sorry for her before, but I do now, because I've got a better understanding of everything she's gone through. To us, this is new. We didn't know about the murder until last year, but Gran has lived with it for more than twenty years.'

'That's my girl,' Bob said tenderly.

'What?'

'You,' he said. 'Your kind heart. Mrs Foster told you horrible lies about your mother, and I know how deeply that hurt you . . .'

'And angered me,' Joan added.

'That too,' said Bob. 'Yet here you are, showing compassion for Mrs Foster's troubles. You're a good person, Joan Hubble, and I'm proud to be your husband.'

Joan kissed his forehead. 'I never saw Gran looking frail before Geoff Baldwin descended on us. I didn't know she even knew the meaning of frailty. Now I wonder if she's felt frail inside all along.'

'D'you know what I think?' Bob asked. 'I think we should move in with her and split the house upstairs-downstairs just as she said, sharing the kitchen and the bathroom. We'll have the space and the privacy we've been hoping for – and you, my dear love, will have peace of mind. Yes,' he went on in answer to her puzzled look, 'peace of mind. You've started to worry about her and living upstairs from her will give you the chance – will give us both the chance – to keep an eye on her as she grows older, though I don't think we should say that to her, because she'll be annoyed at the very idea.'

Joan had to say it one more time. 'I'll never think she was right to lie about my mother.'

'I know. But I also know that if we don't live with her, you'll feel guilty for not giving her that support, especially after she brought you up. I'm not saying it'll always be an easy arrangement. I'm sure she'll annoy the heck out of us at times.' Bob grinned. 'But we'll probably annoy the heck out of her too, so it'll all even out in the end. What d'you think? Shall we give it a go?'

All Joel would say about what he wanted Alison to see was that it involved going to Victoria Station, yet when they arrived in town, he took her to the Claremont Hotel, escorting her up the steps, where the top-hatted doorman opened the door for them. They entered the pillared foyer, with its gleaming woodwork, handsome armchairs and beautiful flower arrangements.

'I thought we were going to Victoria,' said Alison.

'We are, but not yet. I need to speak to you about something important.'

Was he going to propose? *No.* She had spent far too long thinking like that when she was with Paul. In fact, the Claremont had been one of the venues, one of the many venues, at which she had eagerly anticipated his popping the question.

With one hand at her elbow, Joel guided her to an alcove with a pair of chairs and a circular table. He raised a finger to summon a waiter and ordered drinks.

'This should be private enough,' he said. 'I'm sorry, Alison, but this isn't going to be easy for you to hear.'

Good heavens, he wasn't about to give her the old heave-ho, was he? Had the ructions with Venetia and Rachel made him feel that girls were best avoided? No, she was being daft. Recalling what he had said after they had left Venetia's, Alison felt her confidence return. One thing Joel had always done for her was boost the self-esteem that had been crushed when Paul left her for another girl.

'It isn't easy for me to say, either,' said Joel, 'but I want to be honest with you.'

'It sounds serious,' Alison remarked quietly.

'It is and it doesn't show me in a good light, I'm afraid.' He stopped talking as the waiter brought their drinks. 'Thank you.' He lifted his glass as if to take a sip, then put it down again. 'I need to tell you about something that happened a long time ago with an old girlfriend of mine. One night we went to a party and people were drinking and we both had one too many. One thing led to another and . . . and she ended up pregnant.'

Dismay swooped through Alison. 'Oh my godfathers.' It was an expression she had picked up from Margaret. 'It wasn't Rachel, was it?'

'Rachel?' Joel exclaimed. 'No. It was someone else.'

She didn't think she could have borne it had it been Rachel. 'Are you telling me you have a child?'

Joel's eyes popped open. 'Certainly not. The girl lost the baby. She miscarried.'

'Before you could do the decent thing.'

'I know this has come as a shock,' said Joel, 'and all kinds of thoughts must be flying through your mind, but please stop trying to anticipate the story. I never knew about the pregnancy until long after the miscarriage. Our drunken encounter happened immediately before I went to Leeds and the shameful truth is that I was relieved to get away. I was fond of the girl, but I never intended – that is, I didn't have marriage in mind. There,' he added. 'I told you it didn't show me in a good light.'

'So how did you hear about her losing the baby?' Alison asked.

'We met again a long time later. The poor love had spent all that time thinking I'd set out to seduce her and then, having had my wicked way, that I'd taken to my heels, but I swear to you it wasn't like that. I – I hope you can believe me.'

'Yes, I do, though I don't altogether understand why you're telling me this.'

'Because I don't want to have secrets from you. You've had one boyfriend and it was a long-term relationship for you. Me, I've had a number of girlfriends, but that's all behind me now. You're the only girl I want.'

CHAPTER THIRTY-NINE

Margaret went early to Victoria for her fire-watching. She was dressed in slacks, a blouse and the jumper Anna had knitted for her, which might be a bit on the warm side just now, but she knew she would be glad of it overnight. She wouldn't go on duty until ten o'clock, but Dot had worked today and was due to finish work around half seven and Margaret wanted to see her, so she could tell her that she had cleared the air with Joel. She knew Dot well enough to know Dot wouldn't expect an update, but Margaret wanted to tell her anyway. She felt Dot deserved it for being so supportive and kind, as well as for having had the imagination to see Margaret's problem in a different way to the way Margaret and Joan had. They had agonised over whether she should talk to Alison, but Dot had come up with a fresh new suggestion – and thank goodness she had. Otherwise Margaret would never have heard Joel's side of the story.

Margaret hovered on the concourse, waiting for Dot to emerge through the barrier with her loaded flatbed trolley. Dot smiled at the sight of her.

'Can I see you for a few minutes before you go home?' Margaret asked.

'Of course you can, chick, if you don't mind waiting. I've got to unload this little lot and make sure everything is in the right place for the next leg of its journey.'

'I'll wait for you in the buffet, shall I?'

'You do that, love.'

About half an hour later, Dot entered the buffet, wearing her coat over her uniform and her hat instead of her peaked cap. Margaret had bagged a small table in the corner. When Dot sat down opposite her, she shunted her chair round so they were side by side and could speak softly together.

'I want to thank you for advising me to speak to Joel.'

'Have you done it, then?'

Margaret smiled. 'I believe you're saying to yourself "About time too", aren't you?'

She related all that Joel had told her. Dot listened without interrupting.

'And how do you feel about that?' Dot asked when Margaret had finished.

'I'm not sure, to be honest,' Margaret confessed. 'Nothing will ever reduce the impact of the fear and shame I went through, or of the miscarriage, which frankly was appallingly painful, not to mention frightening, but I wasn't wilfully seduced and abandoned after all and that's something . . .' She wasn't sure how to finish that thought.

'Something to be grateful for?' Dot suggested.

'No, "grateful" isn't the right word. I'm just glad to know I didn't fall in love with a rat, that's all.'

'And do you feel confident now that Alison is safe with Joel?'

'Yes. I do. And I'm grateful that it got sorted out without her having to be told about me.'

'The road I see it,' said Dot, 'is you've been a good friend to her. Plenty in your position would have kept their secret and left her to sink or swim.'

'I did keep my secret,' Margaret pointed out.

'Aye, but only after a whole lot of heart-searching and because you found a different way to tackle the situation.'

'Thanks to you,' said Margaret.

'We all find ourselves in a pickle at some time. You can always come to me. You're one of my daughters for the duration, and don't you forget it.'

Margaret's heart filled with gratitude. Imagine being such good friends with a lady of Dot's age. It would never have happened before the war.

'Things seem to be sorted out with my dad as well. My sister did the sorting out.' Margaret laughed. 'I think she's a Dot in the making.'

'Nay, lass, I bet she's just like your mum. What did she do?'

Margaret explained about Anna coming all the way from Shropshire to have words with Dad.

'Though she didn't exactly have words with him. She talked about all kinds of things Dad had lost sight of. I'd lost sight of some of them too,' Margaret admitted. 'And then . . .' It was a moment before she could continue. 'She told Dad we might have lost William and did he really want to lose me as well? Dad sort of crumpled at the mention of William and the next moment, we were all crying and hugging one another.'

'I take it there's still no news,' Dot said gently.

Margaret's throat thickened. She shook her head. She didn't want there to be any news, because the chances were . . .

'He's in my prayers,' said Dot. 'Now that's enough on that subject. Did you pike all the way to Victoria just to see me?'

Margaret cleared her throat. 'I'm fire-watching tonight, so I thought I'd come early and catch you.'

'What about your sister?' asked Dot. 'You've never come out early, leaving her at home.'

'She's fine,' Margaret assured her. 'She and Mrs Grayson are getting on like a house on fire. Did I tell you Mrs

383

Grayson knitted cardigans for the twins? Anna sent a thank-you letter, only it was more than that, because Anna writes chatty letters, so then Mrs Grayson wrote back with a cake recipe. Anna made the cake and it was a success. In fact, it was a big success, because a couple of the ladies she cleans for asked her to make it for them, using their ingredients, of course, and they paid her for her trouble. So now Anna has a nice little sideline going. I left her and Mrs Grayson looking at recipes together. Mrs Grayson is so kind.'

'Aye, she is,' Dot agreed, 'but don't kid yourself that Anna is the one on the receiving end of all the kindness. This is every bit as good for Mrs Grayson as it is for her. Mrs Grayson used to have a miserable old life before our Mabel moved in with her and got to know her. I'll tell you summat, chick. That no-good, two-timing husband of Mrs Grayson's demanding to have the matrimonial home back so he could shack up with Floozy was the best thing that could have happened to Mrs G, because that was when we moved her in with Mrs Cooper and her life started to blossom.'

'We all help one another, don't we?' said Margaret. She looked at the clock on the buffet's mantelpiece. 'You'd best be getting home now. You've had a long day.'

'Aye, that's true enough.'

'Thanks for listening,' said Margaret.

When they pushed their chairs back and stood up, Dot gave her a hug.

'You carry my best hopes for your William with you,' Dot whispered in Margaret's ear, and gave her a kiss.

Alison was quiet on the way to Victoria Station, not because she was punishing Joel but because she needed to absorb everything he had told her. He left her to her thoughts and she appreciated his consideration. Arriving at Victoria and walking in past the Great War memorial to the men of the Lancashire and Yorkshire Railway who had given their lives for their country made Alison's thoughts change track and switch over to Margaret's brother, who might have given his own life. How terrible for his family not to know for certain.

Alison and Joel walked onto the concourse, the long, elegant sweep of the wooden front of the line of ticket-office windows to their right, and the buffet and other interior buildings to their left.

'Miss Lambert! How nice to see you,' a voice called – a familiar voice, though it took Alison a moment to place it. She recognised it a second before she saw Miss Emery with some files in her arms.

'It's good to see you too,' Alison told her, smiling. Then she smiled more broadly as she added, 'I was about to introduce you two, but you've met before, if you recall, Miss Emery?'

'I do indeed.' Miss Emery laughed. 'It isn't every day I'm called upon to act as matchmaker.'

'I'm very glad you agreed to do it on that occasion,' said Joel.

'You're home again,' Miss Emery said to Alison. 'You must be pleased.'

'Delighted. Thrilled. Couldn't be happier.'

'Goodness,' said Miss Emery, 'I hope Leeds wasn't *that* bad.'

'Not at all,' said Alison. 'It was a bit tedious to begin with, but it picked up considerably once I started being given more varied work to do.'

Miss Emery frowned. 'I wasn't pleased when I wrote to Miss Chambers to ask how you were getting on and requiring a summary of the work you'd done so far, only for it to turn out that you were doing menial jobs – important, necessary jobs, of course, but not what I'd sent you there to do. I wrote back by return, stating that if she was unable to provide you with the type of experience that had been previously agreed, then she should send you back to Manchester forthwith. Miss Chambers replied that more suitable work would be found.'

'So it was *your* doing that I got the interesting jobs,' said Alison.

Not Rachel's because Alison had been punished enough for her lapse on the first day. Not Rachel's because she had taken Alison under her wing. And not Rachel's because of Joel. It had all been down to Miss Emery. Clever Rachel had kept that under her hat. Well, well, well.

'I won't keep you now,' said Miss Emery. 'Come and see me on Monday.'

Alison couldn't help releasing a short laugh at what she'd found out about Rachel.

'What's so funny?' asked Joel.

'Nothing,' she said. Rachel was the last person she wanted to talk about. Frankly, she never wanted that name to pass her lips again. 'Just glad to be here.'

'And glad to be with me, I hope.' Joel grinned. 'Sorry. I shouldn't fish for compliments, especially after the afternoon you've had.'

'Let's forget about that. Why have you brought me here?'

'You'll see. First of all, let me pop into the first-class restaurant and book a table.'

'The restaurant? Very swish.'

Linking arms, they went towards the cluster of small interior buildings with walls painted a soft yellow and there, standing at the bookstall, was Margaret, running her eye over the Penguin books. Alison felt a moment's embarrassment, but then she realised this was up to her. The way she behaved now would set the tone for the future.

Letting go of Joel's arm, she went to her friend. 'Margaret, what brings you here this early? It's ages until you go on duty.'

Margaret was looking over Alison's shoulder. Alison turned, extending her hand to Joel so she could draw him to her side.

'Let's not have any awkwardness,' she said. 'Just think. I met Joel on the Leeds-to-Manchester train. Miss Emery was instrumental in bringing us together, and we've just seen her. Then Mabel and you, Margaret, helped me see I should stop playing silly beggars and allow myself to like Joel – and here you are. All we need is Mabel and we've got the complete set.'

'Why are you here?' Margaret asked.

'Among other things,' said Alison, 'we're going to have something to eat. What about you?'

'I wanted to have a word with Dot,' said Margaret, 'and now I'm about to get my clobber and go up on the roof.'

Alison consulted her wristwatch. 'It's only half eight.'

Margaret shrugged. 'It's a good place to be when you need to think.'

Of course: William. Alison gave her a sympathetic look.

'Nice seeing you.' Margaret nodded at them and went on her way.

In the restaurant, Joel booked a table and then took Alison to, of all places, Left Luggage. He removed his wallet from an inside pocket and handed over a ticket, in return for which he was given a valise that had a label pasted to it with his name written on it.

Alison was puzzled. 'Are you going somewhere?'

'Not any more,' said Joel. 'I was intending to go away this evening. Look, I bought the ticket in advance.' He took it from his wallet. 'I'd planned to go to Leeds and stay overnight so that I could travel home with you tomorrow. It was going to be a surprise.'

'And meanwhile I was planning to surprise you by coming home early.'

'I wanted you to see my luggage and the train ticket, so that if there is any lingering question in your mind about Rachel, this should dispel it. An overnight bag and a train ticket might not seem like much, but they show what you mean to me. Yes, I've had other girlfriends and I sincerely cared for them at the time, but here, now, I'm with the only girl I want, the only girl I'll ever want for the rest of my life.'

CHAPTER FORTY

In spite of all her hopes, the twinges Joan had been experiencing hadn't worn off, but she was determined not to make a fuss. She didn't want to spoil this evening for anybody, including herself. Persephone had collected her in a taxi, which had then travelled all the way down Barlow Moor Road to Chorlton, where Gran had been ready, wearing her faithful brown coat and her Sunday hat.

When they arrived at Victoria, Persephone shepherded Joan and Gran towards the restaurant and saw them settled at their linen-covered table.

'Who knows,' said Persephone, 'this could be the very tablecloth your wedding cake was displayed on. Let's sort you out with drinks and then I'll go and find Pa. He and his entourage are staying somewhere outside Manchester tonight before going on elsewhere in the morning. I've no idea where. It's all hush-hush. The point is, he should be here already. He said I'd find him with the stationmaster. Toodle-pip.'

'I never expected to have a meal in here,' said Gran, looking round.

Oh no, not polite small talk. Joan said quickly, 'While it's just the two of us, I've got something to tell you – to ask you, I should say. Can Bob and I move in?'

The flicker of pleasure in Gran's eyes was immediately replaced by a wary look. 'Into my house? Do you mean it?'

'Yes. Yes, please. But I want to make a rule.'

Joan waited. She knew exactly what Gran would have said in the old days about someone else laying the law down in her house.

But Gran asked stiffly, 'And what's that?'

'You're never to say a word against my mother, not to me, not to Bob, and more than anything, not to my child. We're going to tell our children that Mummy's parents died a long time ago in a train crash, and that's the story you'll tell them too. If you can't do that, then we can't move in – and we do very much want to move in.'

After a moment, Gran nodded. 'I hate being on my own. The lodger doesn't count. You need family around you, especially as you grow old. You can have as much privacy as you want. I'm not one to intrude, but I'll like knowing that you're upstairs.'

'Good,' said Joan. 'That's settled.'

Any other grandmother and granddaughter might have been weeping buckets in one another's arms at this point, but Gran wasn't that way inclined. She was stern and self-controlled – controlling too. Had she always been like that, or had the past twenty years done it to her?

Joan sat up straight, stretching her back. 'Here's Persephone.'

With Persephone was a tall, distinguished gentleman in uniform who carried himself with the upright confidence of a military man.

Persephone performed the introductions.

'This is my father, General Trehearn-Hobbs. Pa, may I present my good friends, Mrs Foster and her granddaughter, Mrs Hubble.'

The moment the handshakes were over, Gran started to say, 'Thank you very much—'

'Not at all,' replied the General. 'I won't hear a word of thanks. Men like Baldwin should be locked up and the key

390

thrown away. I'm glad to have provided assistance to you, madam.'

Joan had expected there to be at least some conversation about Geoff Baldwin. Now that General Trehearn-Hobbs had swept aside that possibility, what on earth were they going to talk about? The war, presumably. The General was in the War Office, after all. He looked like he expected to be listened to when he spoke.

She couldn't have been more wrong. General Trehearn-Hobbs was every bit as gracious and well mannered as his daughter and he led the conversation in all sorts of directions: summer holidays before the war, dogs, books, roses, brass-band music, not to mention laughing through all the *ITMA* catchphrases.

'Look who's walked in,' said Persephone. 'Alison and Joel.'

She waved to attract their attention. They came to the table and there were more introductions.

'Are you just back from Leeds?' Joan asked Alison.

'No, I came back yesterday,' said Alison. 'Joel has brought me here for a meal.'

'What you might call a busman's holiday,' said Joel. 'Excuse us. Our table is ready.'

As they walked away, the General turned to Joan. 'I gather you and Mr Hubble had the chance to move into Darley Court.'

'That's right, sir, but my husband wouldn't have felt comfortable living there. Anyway, we're going to move in with my gran now.'

'Splendid,' said the General. 'I imagine you'll be a great support to one another.'

'That's wonderful news,' said Persephone, but Joan could see the puzzled look in her eyes. It was no secret among Joan's friends that she and Gran had fallen out badly.

Joan gave Persephone a smile. 'It's the right thing all round.' Then her smile froze in position and she went cold with dismay as she experienced a gushing sensation between her legs. *Oh no, not here, not now . . .* Leaning towards Gran, she lowered her voice. 'Gran, I think my waters have broken.'

Gran turned to her, her eyes expressing the horror that came from her Victorian upbringing, but before she could utter a word, there started up, through the sounds of the voices in the restaurant, the rising and falling wail of the air-raid siren.

At the sound of the siren, Alison and Joel pushed back their chairs and stood up, both of them trained to respond in this situation.

'We must help get everyone to safety,' said Alison.

'Joan will need support,' said Joel.

Alison looked across at the table where Joan and Persephone were seated. Why weren't they getting up? Everyone seemed to be leaning towards Joan.

Alison and Joel hurried between the other tables.

'Thank heaven,' said Persephone. 'Just what we need. A doctor. Joan says the baby's coming.'

Panic raced through Alison, but it was instantly dispelled when Joel smiled reassuringly at Joan.

'It won't be the first to be born during a raid,' he said, sounding perfectly calm. 'How are you feeling? We need to get you down to the cellars.' He turned to Persephone. 'Alert First Aid, will you?'

Before Persephone could move, Joan uttered a cry that she tried to suppress but couldn't. Her hand flailed around her and Mrs Foster caught hold of it and grasped it tightly.

'Do something,' Mrs Foster demanded, looking at Joel.

'I need to examine you,' he said to Joan. 'If at all possible, we'll get you down to the basement. Otherwise,' and he looked around, 'you may be having your baby under the bar.' He smiled. 'At least there won't be a problem wetting the baby's head. Let's get you over there now, shall we? Then we can have some privacy while I examine you.' He looked at the others. 'I need towels, linen, hot water, cushions if you can find them, and a sharp knife as well. We'll need those wherever the birth takes place.'

Alison helped him and Mrs Foster get Joan to the bar and settle her beneath it. As Alison moved away, a prolonged vibration passed through the restaurant and there were cries of alarm from the retreating diners and people outside. Alison hovered anxiously by the door, awaiting the return of Persephone and her father with supplies.

A short while later, Joel stood up and walked across to Alison, Persephone and the General, leaving Mrs Foster with Joan behind the bar.

'There's no chance of moving her. This baby's in a hurry.'

A distant crunch was followed by a faint shaking within the room that brought flakes of plaster floating down from the ceiling and made dust rise from the floor. Quickly issuing instructions, Joel returned to Joan.

Alison caught hold of Persephone's arm. 'Margaret's on the roof on her own. You do what's needed down here. I'll go up and be with Margaret.'

She ran from the restaurant and across the concourse, which was alive with passengers scurrying to safety, shepherded by staff. So determined was she to support Margaret that Alison realised only belatedly that she wasn't sure how to get up onto the roof, but before she could ask a member of staff, she ran into Margaret, who was hurrying along carrying a scoop and hoe together with a Redhill container, which had triangular sides and a door in the front. Scoop, hoe and container meant one thing: incendiaries.

'I have to get onto the canopy,' said Margaret. 'I was on the roof and I could see incendiaries coming down. The fire engines are there, but the hoses can't reach the whole canopy. I have to get up there and help.'

'I'm going with you,' said Alison.

'You're not exactly dressed for it.'

'Who cares? Joan's giving birth right now in the restaurant.'

Margaret's eyes widened, then an air of resolve settled on her. 'Right. We're going to keep this canopy up while Joan has her baby, even if we have to stand underneath it and hold it up with our bare hands. Are you with me?'

'Try and stop me,' Alison said grimly.

'We need a ladder,' said Margaret and she darted away, her incendiary-fighting equipment bumping against her side.

Although she knew a ladder couldn't possibly get them as high as the canopy, Alison didn't ask questions. There was something fixed and determined in Margaret's expression that said she knew what she was doing. Alison ran after her, catching up with her as she stopped, panting, near the stores. Putting down her things, Margaret wrenched at the door but it didn't budge. She slammed the flats of her hands against it in frustration.

Margaret swung round in a circle on the spot. 'There!'

A ladder stood against the wall under a lamp. Margaret ran to it, Alison behind her. Together, they pulled the ladder away from the wall, lowering it so that the two of them could carry it between them. Alison's shoulder pulled in its socket: the ladder was heavier than she had expected.

'Where are we going?' she asked.

'Parcels office.' Margaret looked at the incendiary-fighting equipment she had dumped. 'We'll have to come back for that.'

It took all Alison's energy to keep up with Margaret's pace. At the parcels office, Margaret headed round the side and they set the ladder against the wall, then dashed back for the other things before returning to the ladder.

'You do realise that the roof up there is nowhere near as high as the canopy?' asked Alison.

'If I can get the container up there,' said Margaret, 'can you bring the scoop and hoe?'

Grasping the handle of the Redhill container in one hand and holding on to the ladder with the other, she started to climb. At the top, she heaved the container onto the roof before pulling herself after it. Then she leaned over to give Alison the thumbs up. Alison followed with the scoop and hoe, trying hard to ignore the swooping sensation in her stomach. She didn't like heights at the best of times. At the top, Margaret helped her from the ladder.

'Now we have to pull it up after us,' said Margaret.

Alison looked down at the ladder. 'We can't.'

'We must. We have to do it for Joan. Come on. Put your back into it.'

Together, they heaved the ladder up after them, the pair of them falling over backwards as the foot of the ladder arrived on the flat roof.

Margaret pointed to a window up above. 'If we can climb through there, we can reach a part of the main roof that will give us access to the canopy.'

'Is this the way you climb up to do your fire-watching every time?' Alison asked in disbelief. 'There must be an easier way up.'

'There is, but it won't take us where we need to be. This isn't the official way up, but I made it my business to find as many ways up and down as I could – just in case. And this is the "just in case". Come on.'

Alison gulped down her breaths, trying to keep her fear contained, but Margaret seemed immune to fear. With Alison's help, she set the ladder against the wall, testing the bottom rung with her foot before she started to climb. The ladder bounced gently as Alison held its sides. At the top, Margaret let go and fiddled with the window to open it, then descended to collect the Redhill container, which she carried up, pushing it through the window and then following it. After a moment, she appeared at the window, grasping hold of the top of the ladder to hold it steady for Alison. Not letting herself think about it, Alison climbed up, keeping her eyes fixed on the rungs in front of her, not daring to look down.

Margaret helped her through the window and she emerged onto a tiled section of roof. Even though it wasn't yet dark, there were enemy planes overhead. Alison watched in fearful fascination as lines of incendiaries were dropped, whistling their way down through the air, before her gaze was torn away by the sight of planes with RAF roundels on the wings coming to see off the Luftwaffe.

Margaret tugged at her arm and they scrambled up the tiles, grasping hold of the ridge tiles at the top. It took Alison a moment to get her balance – then she looked ahead and her breath caught at the beauty and sheer scale of what lay before her. The station's iron and glass canopy was magnificent, a truly inspiring piece of architecture and engineering.

And incendiaries were landing on it.

Firemen on vast ladders attached to the backs of fire engines were training their hoses on the canopy, but they couldn't reach the incendiaries furthest from them – the ones closest now to Margaret and Alison. Seeing Margaret take firm hold of the Redhill container, Alison did the same with the scoop and hoe. Then, following Margaret's lead, she let herself down gingerly onto the edge of the canopy. Lying down to spread their weight on the glass, the two girls rolled and wriggled towards the nearest incendiary. They had to smother each one as swiftly as possible to prevent fires breaking out.

From her prone position, Margaret reached behind her and Alison passed her the scoop and hoe. Margaret tried to pull the incendiary into the scoop using the hoe, but ended up having to rise into a crouching position. Alison held her breath, terrified that the canopy would crack open, sending them both plunging through.

'The Redhill!' Margaret called.

Alison wriggled nearer, raising the container's door. Margaret carefully swung the scoop towards it, placing the incendiary inside, whereupon Alison pushed the door shut on it.

They moved on to the next one, repeating the process. Other fire-watchers appeared, having gained access by a different route. Alison had a moment of giddy relief, because there were way too many incendiaries for her and Margaret to deal with.

Only when all the incendiaries were accounted for did Alison realise that the skies had cleared because the boys in air-force blue had seen off Jerry.

A fire-watcher called across to her and Margaret. 'How did you get up that way?' he asked, and when Margaret pointed vaguely, his face creased in a frown. 'I don't know how the heck you managed that, but it's a good thing you did. If you can find your way over to this part, you can come down with us. Don't walk on the canopy.'

'We'll make our way through the guttering,' Margaret said to Alison. 'Are you up for that?'

'Rather that than go back the way we came up,' said Alison. She looked down at herself. 'I'm afraid Mabel's dress may never be the same again.'

She followed Margaret through the lines of gutter, concentrating so hard on keeping her footing and not turning her ankle that she almost forgot to be scared of heights – almost.

As they waited to go through a trapdoor and down a set of steep steps, she remarked, 'This looks easier than the way you brought us. That isn't a criticism, by the way.'

'From where I was on the roof earlier, I could see where the incendiaries were landing and it looked too far over for the usual ways up onto the canopy, so we had to come up the hard way.'

'Well done,' said Alison. 'What we did was all thanks to you.'

'I couldn't have managed without you,' said Margaret.

'Yes, you could.' It seemed to Alison that Margaret had been determined enough to do anything.

Margaret looked at her. 'Maybe, maybe not – but I wouldn't have wanted to do it without you.'

Another pain built up inside Joan, threatening to break her apart. Pulling in a prolonged, ragged breath, she squeezed Gran's hand for all she was worth. Gran squeezed back, brushing sweat-streaked hair away from Joan's face with her other hand.

'Steady breaths, please, Joan,' came Joel's voice. 'Good girl. You're doing well.'

She felt like throttling him. Doing well? What was 'well' about it? She'd known being in labour would hurt, but she'd fully expected it to happen in her own bed, with the security of knowing that Bob was pacing up and down the hall, anxious for it to be over. All along, she had set her sights on that, on Bob being nearby, ready to welcome their child into the world.

This – this – giving birth under a wooden counter in the middle of Victoria Station during an air raid was terrifying. She had never felt more scared or vulnerable in her whole life. She clung to Gran's hand. Gran was strong. For years Joan had thought Gran had the wrong kind of strength, the kind that came from being stern, critical and judgemental, but right now none of that mattered. Joan was prepared to hang on to any kind of strength and draw something from it.

She heard herself making grunting sounds like an animal as the contractions came closer together.

'You're doing well,' Joel said again, damn him. 'It'll soon be over. Tell me when you need to push.'

The midwife had told Joan about contractions. 'You have to ride them, *r-i-i-i-de* them,' she'd said, as if they constituted some kind of sporting activity. If Joan ever got her hands on that midwife . . . The vengeful feeling dissipated as a dark pain intensified.

'Breathe,' ordered Gran.

When Joan made it out of the other side of the contraction, gasping and feeling spent, Joel examined her, feeling her stomach.

'I can feel the baby's shape. It's in position. When it's time to push, tuck in your chin and heave with all your might.'

A new sensation took possession of Joan, bringing her lurching upright.

'I need to push,' she gasped.

'Deep breath,' said Joel, 'and push.'

Joan didn't need telling. She had no choice in the matter. Her body had taken over and knew what to do. She strained. At the end of the push, she expelled a loud half gasp, half gurgle, appalled by the level of pain and dreading the next one. She lay back, but whatever they had provided for her to lean against had slid sideways and she exclaimed at the sensation of falling back too far.

'Here,' said Gran. 'Shift a fraction and I'll wedge myself behind you so you can lean on me. That'll be better for you.'

After more contractions, Joel said, 'I can see its head. Next time you need to push, make it the biggest one ever.'

In amongst all the pain, Joan felt a flicker of excitement. Her baby was about to be born. Her wartime baby, born under a counter during an air raid. That would be quite some story to tell him or her one day.

Then the pain rose up again and roared through her. Joan threw her remaining strength into the push. It was like having to poo a sack of potatoes. The pain was never going to end. Then there was a sort of gushing sensation.

'It's a boy,' said Joel. 'You have a beautiful son. Here we are, little fella. Hold still while . . . I . . . cut . . . the cord.' He held up the child by its feet and smacked its bottom, bringing forth an indignant cry. 'There we go. Let's wrap you in this towel and . . . here you are, Mum. Congratulations.'

Before she could catch up with what was happening, Joan had her baby, *her* baby, in her arms. Tears poured freely down her face, tears of pure happiness. Her baby.

'Look, Gran.' She moved so Gran could wriggle out from behind her.

'He doesn't look very big,' said Gran and Joan didn't miss the note of concern.

'Probably six pounds or so,' said Joel. 'Nothing to worry about.'

'So he's all right, even though he's a bit early?' asked Gran.

'Looks like it,' said Joel.

Gazing at her son, Joan could feel Gran gazing at him too. It gave her the oddest feeling of a connection between the three of them. Family.

'For someone so small,' said Joel, 'he's certainly caused the maximum of trouble.'

And Joan knew. She just *knew*.

'Max,' she said. 'Welcome to your family, Max Hubble.'

CHAPTER FORTY-ONE

On Sunday afternoon, Mabel, Mrs Cooper and Mrs Grayson went over to Withington to see the new baby. It was a big event in Mrs Grayson's life, making an unfamiliar journey, especially one that involved public transport, but she was determined to see baby Max. Mabel and Mrs Cooper linked arms with her and they went on their way in good spirits. Margaret waved them off, then went into the front room, where Alison was mooching around, looking preoccupied.

'We were lucky to see Max yesterday evening,' said Margaret, taking a seat.

'Yes, we were,' Alison agreed. 'But poor Joan – fancy having him in the restaurant like that.'

'I know.' Margaret hesitated before confiding, 'I feel rather honoured to have been one of the first to see him. It's made me remember how I didn't get to see Tommy and Anne-Marie when they were babies.'

'It can't have been easy for your sister, having them so far away from home and family.'

'Anna's a sensible girl. I'm sure she made the best of it.'

'Wartime calls for an awful lot of being sensible,' said Alison.

She didn't seem very engaged by the conversation and Margaret half expected her to leave the room, but instead she came and sat down. Margaret felt a stirring of unease. Alison's eyes were serious; more than just serious – worried.

'Can I tell you something?' asked Alison. 'It's about Joel and it's got me rattled.'

Margaret's muscles squeezed. What was coming next?

Alison pressed her lips together hard, then she burst out with, 'He got a girl in the family way and I know . . .'

Dread rolled through Margaret, slowing her heartbeat. *I know who she was.* Was that how the sentence ended? *I know it was you.* Dear heaven, had Joel caved in and told?

'Well, don't just sit there staring at me,' Alison exclaimed. 'Say something!'

Margaret drew a breath and cold air rushed into her lungs. 'How did you find out?' she whispered.

'Joel told me. He wanted to be honest.' Alison gave a short, bitter laugh. 'That's one piece of honesty I could have done without.'

Margaret leaned towards her. She didn't quite have the nerve to go to her and put her arms around her, but at least she could lean closer. 'I'm so very sorry. I know how much it must hurt.'

'And astonish,' said Alison. 'I knew he'd had girlfriends before me, but I'd had no idea anything had gone that far.'

'People sometimes get carried away,' said Margaret.

'I don't know what to think,' said Alison. 'After he told me, he made such an issue out of how much I mean to him that it didn't sink in. I was too busy lapping up the adoration and the reassurance – and then there was the air raid. But I've had time to think since then, and I . . .' She shook her head. 'When he told me, I was so relieved that the pregnant girl wasn't Rachel—'

'Rachel?' It came out almost as a squeak.

'I worked with her in Leeds – worked for her, I should say. She's Joel's old girlfriend and she's spent the past few weeks trying to get him back – including yesterday afternoon, as it happens, but never mind that now. The point is,

I was so grateful that she wasn't the pregnant girl, I didn't think any further.'

'But you've thought about it now.' Margaret fought to keep her voice steady. Surely if Joel had mentioned her by name, Alison would have flung the information in her face by now. Or maybe Alison had worked it out for herself, without Joel having to say a word.

'I've thought of nothing else all night.' Alison closed her eyes for a moment. When she opened them again, Margaret quaked at what might be coming next, but Alison asked, 'Am I wrong to be upset?'

'Of course not. It's a shock.'

'With bells on.' Alison looked directly at her. 'Aren't you going to ask what became of the baby?'

Margaret looked away, unable to hold Alison's gaze. Then she made herself look back. Alison was troubled and conflicted and she had turned to Margaret for help. This was Margaret's chance to be the friend that Alison deserved.

'I don't need to ask,' Margaret said in a calm voice that gave no sign of the thoughts and feelings seething around inside her.

'What? Why not?'

All at once, Margaret felt composed. 'Because I know Joel and I know what a decent person he is. I know that if he had been told about the pregnancy, he would have married the girl at once. And that means . . . it means the girl must have lost the baby before she could tell him.'

It was another half-truth. Another! But at the same time, it was the full and profound truth of the man Joel was. He would indeed have married Margaret, had he known – and then the miscarriage would have been a different sort of tragedy, because how long would it have taken her to realise that the man she adored didn't exactly view her as the love of his life?

But here, now, this moment wasn't about her. It was about Alison, and more than anything, Margaret wanted to be the best friend she could be to Alison in her turmoil.

Margaret left her seat and went to kneel in front of Alison, taking her hands. 'Joel is a good man. That's what you have to remember. I know this has upset you, but it doesn't change the fact that Joel is a decent man with strength of character and a conscience.' She dared to smile. 'And a past.'

Alison laughed, a short sound, quickly cut off. 'You can say that again. I suppose I have a past too – in a different kind of way. I was with Paul for years and it was very serious. I thought we were going to get married – that kind of serious. I honestly believed we were destined to spend our whole lives together.' She squeezed the hands that held hers. 'I've thought before about Joel's and my different sorts of past. It never really bothered me that he'd had several girlfriends. The fact there were several made me think that, even though he was fond of them at the time, they couldn't have meant all that much to him. I thought it must be harder for him knowing that I'd only ever been with Paul, who was the sun, the moon and the stars to me at the time. I never worried about Joel's . . .'

'String of girlfriends?' Margaret suggested.

'Until Rachel came along, and then I felt threatened.' A hard note had entered Alison's voice, but she shook her head as if refusing to let it take over. When she spoke again, her voice was softer. 'Maybe hearing about the pregnant girl wouldn't have been so much of a shock if I hadn't already been wound up over Rachel.'

'Are you still worried about her?' asked Margaret.

'No. Joel has made it very clear that I'm the one he wants.'

'You're lucky.'

405

The corners of Alison's lips twitched as if she was trying to contain a smile. 'Yes, I am. Mind you, I'd still like to give Rachel a custard pie in the face.'

'It sounds like she deserves it.'

A new light appeared in Alison's eyes, a glow of happiness and peace. 'It's all about accepting the past for what it is and not letting it spoil the present. I've had two boyfriends who've done things the opposite way round to one another. With Paul, it was a long relationship, but then he left me high and dry to go off with another girl. Then along comes Joel and he's had various relationships in the past – but that's exactly where they are, in the past, so there's no need for me to worry. He makes me feel as if I'm the only girl in the world.'

Margaret nodded. 'Yesterday I saw the way he looked at you.'

Alison smiled. 'I feel better. It's now that matters. Isn't that what we all keep saying? We don't know what wartime will bring, so we have to make the most of every moment.'

'Yes,' said Margaret. 'We do.'

CHAPTER FORTY-TWO

Early the following week, when Margaret was leaving Victoria Station at the end of her day's work, she was about to walk past the war memorial when she saw Dot and Cordelia standing there, gazing at it. It was a handsome and imaginative design, and well worth stopping to look at, taking up as it did a section of wall that was separate from the rest of the station. The entire top half was laid out as a mosaic map of the old Lancashire and Yorkshire Railway, while underneath stretched the line of panels bearing the names of the fallen. Margaret could hardly bear to look at it these days, though at the same time she felt compelled to be near it, contemplating it.

Was that what Dot and Cordelia were doing? Sharing a moment of silent contemplation? Margaret hesitated. Part of her felt a strong urge to walk past. She didn't want to think about all the names on the wall. She didn't want to imagine William's name one day appearing on a memorial. But how could she walk by? She owed it to those men and their families to pause and reflect. One day, others might owe the same to William, her funny, football-mad, teasing, annoying, unutterably dear brother.

As if sensing her presence, Cordelia glanced round, which alerted Dot. Cordelia nodded in Margaret's direction and Dot looked at her.

'Margaret.' Dot came over to her and linked arms, drawing her a few steps away. 'Can I have a quick word?' They stood side by side, with Dot speaking quietly into Margaret's ear. 'It's to do with what you told me about Joel and how he tried to get in touch with you while he was in Leeds. I hope you don't mind, but I've done a bit of digging and I don't know the details of the exact dates or anything, but I do know that in the summer of 1940, a mail train was hit by incendiaries one night between Leeds and Manchester.'

Margaret swung her face round to stare straight at Dot. She felt hot and cold all over.

'All I know is a lot of letters were destroyed. It doesn't prove anything,' said Dot, 'but I thought it might make you feel better to know.'

'It does,' Margaret whispered.

She wasn't sure how it happened, but a moment later she found herself in between Dot and Cordelia, the three of them linked together, facing the memorial.

'My mam fetched us up to say our prayers every night,' Dot told her, 'and I still do it. I pray for my lads, for them to come home safe, and I'm praying for your William an' all, and for his family, because not knowing is a hard thing to endure.'

'I'd rather not know,' Margaret said fiercely, 'because the chances are . . . and if that's the case, then it's better not to know, because . . .'

'Because while you don't know,' Cordelia finished for her, 'you can tell yourself he's still alive. He's still out there somewhere.'

Margaret nodded.

'I know, chick, I know.' Dot pressed Margaret's arm to her side. 'Now, there's summat me and Cordelia want to talk to you about and it won't be easy for you to hear, but it's important you think about it.'

'It's your change of name,' said Cordelia. 'I know you put it off when the news came about William, and that was understandable, but now Dot and I want you to think seriously about going ahead.'

Margaret didn't need to answer in words. The movement she made said precisely what she thought of that idea.

'Hold your horses,' said Dot. 'Just hear us out, eh?'

'If you don't change your name now,' said Cordelia, 'then when shall you? Suppose the worst happens and William is declared dead, you won't feel able to do it then, will you? It might seem disrespectful, you marking a special change in your life when . . . well, you understand my point.'

'And what if you never know for certain about him?' asked Dot. 'Some families don't. They get a "missing presumed dead" notice and that puts them in a terrible limbo. If that happened to your family, well, it's like Cordelia said. How do you set that kind of sorrow aside and give yourself your new start?'

'My dear Margaret,' said Cordelia, 'please consider it. Go ahead with your change of name. Do it soon and do it for the very special reason of honouring your mother.'

'Aye,' Dot added, 'and do it with a heart full of hope for your William.'

Margaret gave a lot of thought to what Cordelia and Dot had suggested. Having cancelled her appointment with Mr Hughes because William was missing, at what point would it become appropriate to make a new appointment – if ever? As hard as it would be to do it now, while not knowing about William, it would be a hundred times harder to face it if he . . . She shut her eyes, trying to blot out the thought. Not that she could ever rid herself of it. It was with her night and day, a cold, hard lump of fear and misery lodged inside her chest.

She talked it over with Mabel.

'I understand what it's like when someone is missing,' said Mabel, 'because Harry was missing for a short time last year. It wasn't anything like as bad for me as it is for you, because Harry was missing for a day – but that was the longest day of my life, so I do have some understanding of what you're going through. For what it's worth, I think Dot and Cordelia are right. This is wartime and you have to grab your chances when you get them. You aren't changing your name on a whim. You're doing it because it's important to you.'

The breath caught in Margaret's chest.

'It's like when Alison didn't know whether to go out with Joel, and you and I encouraged her,' said Mabel, which made Margaret stare at her in shock. 'No, let me finish. I know it isn't a bit like that, really, but it's also exactly like it, because it's about doing what feels right even when there's a risk attached, even when the circumstances aren't perfect. It's about being strong and having hope; it's about building a future even though we're at war. It's about living our lives.'

It's about living our lives. Yes, it was. With those words, something in Margaret's heart opened up and accepted that doing this for herself wouldn't be a betrayal of William. It would be, as it had been all along, a means of honouring their dear mum and also of signalling her own fresh start. After everything she had gone through, all the torment caused by the shame and humiliation, she had finally come to feel right and comfortable just being herself. And the self she wanted to be, the self she had become, was Margaret Thomas.

'Does that smile mean I've said the right thing?' asked Mabel.

'It means,' Margaret answered, 'that I wish I could have three witnesses instead of two.'

*

'It will be difficult to fit in a party,' said Mrs Cooper. 'It's Whit Sunday this week, so this weekend and all next week, Miss Persephone and Mrs Green will be doing extra shifts.'

'You wouldn't think folk would want to take holidays in wartime,' said Mrs Grayson.

'This is the week when a lot of parents go to see their evacuated children,' said Margaret.

She imagined going to stay with Anna and the twins. Much as she would love to go down there, she couldn't take time off again so soon. Besides, more trains running during Whit week meant more locos in need of cleaning, so she would be working longer shifts all next week as well.

'If Mr Hughes can't fit me in this week,' she said, 'it'll have to wait until June and I don't want to steal the thunder of Joan and Bob's first anniversary.'

'That's sweet of you,' said Mrs Cooper, 'but with the new baby and moving house, they've got far too much on their plates to worry about you doing that.'

'And they wouldn't mind even if you did do your name change on their anniversary,' Mrs Grayson added. 'They'd see it as just another reason to celebrate.'

'Could you toddle along to Mr Hughes's office, Mrs C?' Margaret asked. 'If he could fit me in on Friday afternoon, I know I can swap my shifts around and come home at midday – as long as Friday afternoon is all right for you and Joan.'

'Of course it is,' said Mrs Cooper. 'Mrs Wadden can do my Friday-afternoon job and Joan says she'll fit in with whatever suits you.'

'I'm going to look after baby Max,' said Mrs Grayson, her satisfaction at doing this every bit as great as Mrs Cooper's pride in being asked to be one of Margaret's witnesses.

'It's such an honour to be a witness,' breathed Mrs Cooper, looking quite starry-eyed. 'I'm going to have a shampoo and set for the occasion. What are you going to wear, Margaret dear?'

'My lilac dress,' said Margaret.

'Anyone would think it was a wedding,' Mrs Grayson commented.

'It's just as important in its own way,' said Mrs Cooper. 'Something to be celebrated. I still think it's a shame we won't be able to have everyone here for a party.'

'You gave me a lovely birthday tea,' said Margaret, 'and that's quite enough.'

It was too. Much as she enjoyed the little parties her friends held to mark their special occasions, she didn't need a party for this. What she needed was to have two of her dear friends by her side to act as her witnesses. What she needed was a sense of the seriousness of the occasion. A sense of hope. A sense of her own completeness as a person, which was something she had lacked for a long time until now.

Margaret was delighted to come home from work the next day to hear that Mr Hughes had got a space free in his appointment diary for Friday afternoon and Mrs Cooper had booked it for her. Before that there was something it felt important to do.

She went into Alison's room at bedtime for a chat.

'I want you to know I'm happy for you.'

Alison looked surprised. 'You mean about Joel?'

'Yes.' Margaret knew that Alison hadn't a clue about the significance of this conversation, but it was important to say it all the same. 'I'm feeling better about life in general too – aside from William, I mean. Dot, Cordelia and Mabel between them made me see that you have to grab the good things while you can.'

'That sounds familiar,' said Alison with a smile. 'Isn't that what you and Mabel advised me?'

'More or less.'

'Well, I'm very happy to be home and to be seeing Joel,' said Alison.

'So that counts as a happy ending for us both.'

'I know that changing your name is important,' said Alison, 'but it takes more than that to make a happy ending, surely?'

'I don't know about that.' Margaret laughed, or tried to.

'You know what I'm saying. I'd love you to find a boyfriend. I'd like you to have the chance to be as happy as I am.'

'I've had other things to worry about for quite a long time.'

'Like being estranged from your father. That must have been beastly.'

'But now . . . well, maybe I'm in a better frame of mind. I feel happier inside myself, happier *about* myself, if you know what I mean. So maybe I can stop being so inward-looking.'

Alison smiled. 'If you're ready to look outwards, you'll see there are plenty of men and maybe one of them will be the right one for you. You deserve it,' she added fervently. 'Any chap would be lucky to have you. I mean it. You were kind and encouraging to me before Christmas when I was in a pickle over Joel, and you were so brave the night of the air raid. The moment you knew Joan's baby was on the way, you turned into a lioness, determined to keep her safe. I can't tell you how much I admired you for that. I'm glad we live in the same billet. I want us to get to know one another better.'

'Me too,' said Margaret, and meant it.

'Congratulations, Miss Thomas,' said Mr Hughes. 'You have now officially changed your name.'

Seated on either side of Margaret, Joan and Mrs Cooper both leaned towards her to squeeze her arms. Margaret leaned towards each of them in turn to exchange kisses. It would have been much easier had they all been standing up, but the deed poll was simply a matter of paperwork, which was done sitting down.

'If you wish,' said Mr Hughes, 'you can enrol your deed poll with the court, in which case I would apply to the King's Bench Division on your behalf, but I must stress that this isn't by any means a legal necessity. More a question of belt and braces, you might say. If you wish to do that, come back and see me another time. There's no need to think about it now. Just be assured that your change of name has now been made legal.'

Margaret, Joan and Mrs Cooper left the building, spontaneously laughing as they emerged into the street, probably because of the release of tension after the proceedings, which, in spite of being simple and straightforward, had felt formal, just as Margaret had wanted.

To her surprise, she seemed to have walked into a miniature snowstorm.

'Congratulations,' called Mabel. 'Three cheers for the new Miss Thomas.'

'Mabel, you idiot,' laughed Joan. 'What's all this?' She brushed at the little white bits that had landed on her sleeve.

'You know the tiny circles of paper you're left with after you use the hole puncher?' said Mabel. 'They make wonderful wartime confetti. Cordelia got Emily to gather up as many as she could from the offices of Wardle, Grace and Masters, and – ta-da!' Raising her arm, she threw a few more into the air over Margaret's head.

'I thought you were at work,' said Margaret.

'I swapped shifts specially so I could be here to chuck bits of paper all over you.'

'Let's go home,' said Mrs Cooper. 'I expect Joan wants to get back to Max.'

'Bagsy the first cuddle,' said Mabel.

'You'll have to wait your turn, Miss Bradshaw,' teased Joan. 'The first cuddle goes to me, because – well, you'll understand when you're a new mum. And the second goes to Margaret, because this is her special day.'

'Assuming we can wrest him out of Mrs Grayson's arms,' Margaret added.

They made their way to Wilton Close, where Joan, modestly draping a shawl over her shoulder and across her front, fed her little son. Margaret watched the glow of happiness in her friend's face and thought of the child she had briefly carried. But her pregnancy, whether it had lasted three months or nine, would never have had a happy ending.

'Margaret,' said Mabel, 'we've got a little present for you, a keepsake. It's from all of us.'

She produced a small packet, wrapped in a hanky. Margaret unwrapped it and found a tiny silver W on a chain.

'The jeweller didn't have an M,' said Mabel, 'so then we asked for a T and he didn't have one of those either. Then Persephone thought of this.' She caught her lower lip under her teeth. 'I hope – we all hope . . .'

Margaret gazed at the dainty W. 'For William,' she said, deeply moved. 'It's perfect.'

It made him part of today; not just because he was in her thoughts constantly, but because her friends had thought of him too and recognised her love for him.

'Turn round,' said Mabel, 'and I'll fasten it for you. There we are.'

Margaret turned back. 'How does it look?'

'Lovely,' said Mrs Cooper.

'Thank you,' said Margaret. 'All of you.' She laughed. 'Including the ones who aren't here.'

Joan had finished feeding Max and had adjusted her clothing beneath the shawl, which she then draped over the arm of the sofa. She held her baby against her shoulder, patting his back until he burped, which Mrs Cooper and Mrs Grayson treated as if it was a great achievement.

'It's your turn for a cuddle,' Joan told Margaret.

Margaret sat beside her and Joan gave her the baby and showed her how to hold him. Mabel, Mrs Cooper and Mrs Grayson started a conversation with one another, leaving Joan and Margaret to spend a little time together.

'What does Brizo think of Max?' Margaret asked.

'He adores him,' Joan said happily. 'Max is his new favourite person.' Leaning forward and speaking in a quieter voice, she said, 'I've got something to ask you. Bob and I would like you to be Max's godmother.'

Margaret raised her gaze from the baby to stare at Joan. 'Really?'

'Really.' Joan smiled.

'I'd love to. I'd be honoured.' Margaret looked down at Max again. 'Maxwell Robert Hubble. My godson.'

'Actually, he isn't just Maxwell Robert. Me and Bob have added a third first name, because of how he was born.'

'Oh yes?' Margaret kept looking at the baby. Of course. Joel. Babies were sometimes named after the person who delivered them.

She could feel Joan's eyes on her as Joan said, 'Maxwell Robert Thomas Hubble.'

Margaret found herself staring at her friend again. 'Thomas?'

'Because of what you did the night of the air raid; how you worked to save the canopy.'

'It wasn't just me. Plenty of fire-watchers ended up on the roof. Alison was there too.'

'If you think we're going to call our son Maxwell Robert Alison . . .'

'But . . .' Margaret was overwhelmed. Did she deserve such an honour?

'It's a good thing you went through with the name change,' Joan said lightly. 'Maxwell Robert Darrell Hubble doesn't have anything like the same ring to it. As for Alison, she's made it clear to all and sundry that you were the resourceful one. All she did was follow your lead. I've heard exactly what you did that night, the way you climbed up by a dangerous route because you knew the water from the hoses couldn't reach that part of the canopy. You did an amazing thing, Margaret, and I know you'd have done it anyway, but I feel as if you did it for me and Max, to keep us safe.' She blinked away a tear or two. 'So stop opening and closing your mouth like a goldfish and say "Thank you. I'd love him to be called Thomas." Yes?'

'Thank you,' Margaret whispered. 'I'd love it. I really would. And I'll be the best godmother ever. Hello, Maxwell Robert Thomas Hubble.'

The doorbell rang and Mabel got up to answer it. After a few moments, she came back in, looking serious.

'Margaret, your father's here.'

Dad walked in. 'I'm sorry, ladies. Pardon the intrusion, but I couldn't wait . . . I thought I'd take a chance on finding Margaret at home . . .'

Joan took Max out of Margaret's arms, freeing her to stand up, though her legs felt shaky.

'What is it, Dad?'

She knew what it was. Her heartbeat slowed right down, as if to spin out the time of not knowing . . . of William being alive somewhere . . .

'He's all right.' The words burst out of Dad. 'William's alive. He's in a field hospital, but he's all right. Well, he isn't all right, he's injured, but it isn't life-threatening. He's going to be all right.' The next words came out in a jumble of emotion and were unintelligible. Then came, 'I hardly dare believe it. My boy is safe. My William . . .'

Mabel jumped up and hugged Margaret. 'That's marvellous news. Congratulations. What a relief for you.'

'A relief for all of us.' Mrs Cooper brushed away a tear.

'Mr Darrell, thank you for coming,' said Mrs Grayson. 'We're so pleased for you.'

Dad nodded, his throat bobbing up and down.

'Tea,' said Mrs Grayson. 'I think we could all do with a cup, especially you, Mr Darrell.'

'I couldn't—' he began.

'Of course you can,' said Mrs Grayson. 'Sit down. I won't be a jiffy.'

Soon they were all drinking tea – well, the others might have been, but Margaret was trembling with relief and had to put her cup down. Dad glugged his drink down and stood up.

'I'd best be on my way. I just came to . . . that's all.'

'If you're sure,' Mrs Cooper began.

Margaret pulled herself together. 'I'll see you out.'

In the hall, Dad turned to her. He looked exhausted, but his eyes were bright. Margaret thought she probably looked the same.

'There's one more thing,' said Dad. 'I want you to know.' He stopped.

'What is it?' Margaret asked.

'I've decided to leave Mrs McEvoy's,' Dad told her. 'I can't be doing with someone who has no time for my daughter. It's high time I found another billet.' He shuffled, looking embarrassed. 'I just wanted you to know.'

'Oh, Dad.'

'I hope – I mean, after what Anna said, I hope . . .'

'So do I,' Margaret exclaimed, warmth pouring through her and tears welling up. 'I so want us to be friends again.'

'Not friends, Margaret. Father and daughter, the way we're meant to be.'

'Yes, please,' Margaret whispered.

Dad fiddled with his sleeves and glanced away for a moment. Then he looked back at her. 'Have you . . . have you got a hug for your old dad?'

'Oh, yes,' said Margaret, tears spilling over with joy as she walked into his arms.

Welcome to

Penny Street

where your favourite authors and stories live.

Meet casts of characters you'll never forget,
create memories you'll treasure forever,
and discover places that will stay with
you long after the last page.

Step into the home of

MAISIE THOMAS

and discover more about

The Railway Girls...

Dear Readers,

In the world of publishing, everything happens months in advance. Take this letter. *Hope for the Railway Girls* will be published in April 2022, but as I sit here writing to you, it is October 2021 and the evenings are drawing in. I am in the middle of working on the copy-edits for *Hope for the Railway Girls* at the same time as preparing for publication of *Christmas with the Railway Girls* in November and planning the sixth book in the series, which will be called *A Christmas Miracle for the Railway Girls*. No wonder I sometimes have to stop and remind myself which book is which!

As well as writing, editing and publishing my books simultaneously, I'm always chatting to my lovely readers on Facebook. If you haven't visited my page yet, I do hope you'll join me at www.facebook.com/MaisieThomasAuthor for news about the series, a peek into the publication process and to find out more about the research that goes into creating the background detail for the stories. You'll also find, among other things, photos of beautiful Llandudno in North Wales, where I live.

During the Second World War, many civil servants were relocated from London to Llandudno, where they and their families occupied several hundred buildings. The Grand Hotel became the new headquarters for Companies House and the Imperial Hotel was filled with people from the Inland Revenue. You may remember that in the story, Mr and Mrs Morgan, who own the house in Wilton Close, have moved to North Wales for the duration, because that is where their son, an Inland Revenue official, has been sent. As well as being a new home and place of work to all these civil servants, Llandudno also had a radar station and an artillery school on the Great Orme.

For me, living by the sea in Llandudno is a dream come true. Growing up in Manchester, my family came every year to Llandudno for holidays and I always knew that I would live here one day. I can honestly say that the magical 'Wow! We really live here' feeling is something that never fades away.

I am lucky to have two places that are dear to me, because Manchester, where my family has lived for generations, will always be close to my heart too. I love setting my stories there and dropping in local details. When I embarked upon writing *The Railway Girls* series, there was no question at all in my mind where I'd set it. It couldn't be anywhere but Manchester.

Hope for the Railway Girls sees Alison being uprooted and sent across the Pennines to Leeds just when she most wants to be at home building her new relationship with Joel. Joan also has some serious thinking to do about the meaning of home and family. And I am delighted to welcome Margaret as a new viewpoint character for you to get to know. I have a soft spot for Margaret, and I hope you'll love her too.

Much love,

Maisie xx

BRIZO, THE RAILWAY DOG

I expect you've heard the old joke, 'How many plumbers/teachers/solicitors does it take to change a lightbulb?' In *Hope for the Railway Girls*, the question is: how many dogs does it take to create a fictional railway dog? And the answer is three.

LADDIE

The idea for Brizo working as a fundraising dog in Victoria Station came from the work done by a dog called Laddie, who collected money on behalf of the London & South Western Railway for their orphanage. Laddie was an Airedale terrier and he wore a collecting-box on his back, just like Brizo in this story. Laddie worked at Waterloo Station for seven years, from the late 1940s to the mid-50s.

If you would like to find out more about Laddie, search 'Laddie railway dog' online.

MO

Mo was my mum's family's dog from part way through the Second World War. A few weeks after my grandfather died, the family decided to get a dog. Apparently, for some years afterwards, the family joke was 'Pop died, so we got a dog instead.' Mo was a black Manchester terrier and she had two claims to fame: one was that when the family went for a walk, she used to run around them, wanting to make sure they all stayed together; and the other was that if someone said 'Mo-Mo-Mo-Mo-Mo', she would throw back her head and howl. I have borrowed both these characteristics for my Brizo.

BRIZO

I wanted either Persephone or Cordelia to choose what to call the dog, naming him after something they had seen in London before the war – an item in an exhibition, a character in a play, that sort of thing. My go-to person for information about London is Catherine Boardman, who runs the Catherine's Cultural Wednesdays website, which is filled with information about exhibitions, museums, houses open to the public, gardens, art… you name it. If it's in London, Catherine knows about it.

I sent her a message to ask if she could suggest a suitable name for the dog in the book, thinking she would take a day or two to get back to me, but no – her reply came back less than a minute later with the suggestion of Brizo. 'Brizo, a Shepherd's Dog' is a painting by Rosa Bonheur and it is in the Wallace Collection. Catherine's article about the Wallace Collection can be found at www.culturalwednesday.co.uk/wallace-collection/

I hope you'll do an online search for 'Brizo shepherd's dog' so you can see for yourself why Jimmy and Joan fall in love with Brizo in the book. And if you live in or near London or are going there for a visit, you can find Catherine's website at: www.culturalwednesday.co.uk/

THE JOY OF BEING READ TO...

When I was an infant school teacher, I made a practice of reading to the children every single day, whether it was a complete story in one go or the continuing story of what the children called a 'chapter book'. Every morning and afternoon ended with a story and the children adored being read to. I remember the near-hysteria that was occasioned time and again by John Prater's *Once Upon a Time*, as the young audience glimpsed the fairy tale characters strolling one by one onto the pages; and all those favourites that were loved by class after class, such as 'Gobbolino', 'The Witch's Cat', 'Red Herring' and 'The Kitnapping of Mittens'.

Perhaps my favourite memory is of finishing reading Dick King-Smith's wonderful *Lady Daisy* to a Year 2 class. There was a moment of breathless silence at the sheer perfection of the ending and then the children burst into spontaneous applause. (Those children will be leaving university this summer!)

Frankly, I think that being read to is one of life's joys and I believe that the pleasure of being read to is something we never grow out of. Personally, I always have two books on the go – the book I am reading and the one I'm listening to. As well as having favourite authors I also have favourite narrators, and there have been times when I have chosen an audiobook written by an author I have never read, simply because I know I will enjoy the narrator's performance. Yes, narrating an audiobook is a performance – a proper acting job – and to do it effectively takes considerable specialist skill and talent.

The narrator is required to tell the story in a way that conveys character and atmosphere, but without their reading being intrusive. The listener should be absorbed by the story itself and, other than enjoying listening to it, shouldn't be especially aware of the reader's voice at the time.

As a keen audiobook listener, I'm thrilled to bits to think of my books being recorded and enjoyed by a listening audience. I was curious as to which actor would be chosen to read The Railway Girls series. Anxious, too. What if I wasn't keen on their narration? In the event, Julia Franklin was invited to do the job – and I couldn't have been happier. She has been up there among my favourite narrators for years and I am enormously proud to have her as 'my' narrator. Her performances are engaging and unforced, with an intuitive sense of timing, character and atmosphere. I don't know whether authors are supposed to listen to their own audiobooks, but I've loved listening to mine and am delighted that Julia has added an extra dimension to my stories.

Turn the page for an exclusive
extract from my new novel

*A Christmas Miracle
for the
Railway Girls*

COMING OCTOBER 2022
Available to pre-order now

CHAPTER ONE

June, 1942

With their tools over their shoulders, Mabel and the other members of her gang of lengthmen walked from the station to their allocated length of the line. Finding their starting place, they dumped their knapsacks and got going. Bernice wasn't the sort to allow slacking. The first job was to hoe out the weeds from the railway tracks, then they set to in pairs, getting on with the real task of the lengthman, which was to level the railway bed on which the permanent way was laid. While one of each pair used a crowbar or a pickaxe to raise a sleeper, the other had to shovel the ballast back underneath – and in due course, the same length of track would need exactly the same work to be done again because the ballast shifted every time a train travelled along the line.

It wasn't long before Bette took off the old jacket she wore for work and dropped it on top of her knapsack. 'Lots of folk hate working outdoors in the winter because of the cold. Me, I don't mind, because this job keeps us warm. It's the summer when I'm not so keen.'

'I don't care how hot it gets,' said Mabel. 'I shan't be stripping off. I'm not going to fall for that one again.'

'You were unlucky, that's all,' said Bernice.

'Unlucky with bells on,' Mabel answered.

'Ah, but you met your Harry as a result,' said Bette.

Mabel couldn't suppress a smile. 'That's true.'

She'd had a tough time two years ago, during her first summer on the permanent way. Working in a sleeveless blouse, she had ended up with badly sunburned arms, which had blistered. She hadn't thought anything of it when some of the blisters burst, but after that she'd become unwell and eventually collapsed, waking up to find herself in hospital, where she was told that soot and dirt had got into her bloodstream via the open blisters and she'd gone down with blood poisoning. It had been a truly ghastly experience, but – and it was a very big but, as Bette had pointed out – it was when she was laid up in hospital that she had caught Harry Knatchbull's eye. Harry, her very own cheeky blighter.

'How long have you two being seeing one another now?' asked Louise. 'It must be coming up for two years.'

'It's about time you made it official.' Bernice said as she stopped working for a moment to wipe the back of her hand across her fore-head. 'Look at our Joan: married a whole year as of the beginning of this month, and with a gorgeous new baby. He'll be a month old next week, bless him.'

That made Bette laugh. 'Everything comes back to Max, doesn't it, B? I swear that if I said "Pass the salt", you'd find a reason to say what a good baby he is.'

Mabel laughed too. 'And why not? Max Hubble is the most ador-able baby ever, as any of his honorary aunties will tell you.'

The four of them worked on, stopping mid-morning to take off their thick gloves and sit beside the tracks for a drink from their flasks. Later, when Bernice announced it was time for dinner, they walked to the nearest lengthmen's hut. This was constructed from railway sleep-ers standing up like planks of wood. Inside, more sleepers had been stacked to create makeshift benches, but there was no need to take shel-ter indoors today – not like they had to in the winter. The real reason for coming here was to have a hot drink, freshly prepared. Bette shook the old iron kettle to ensure it contained sufficient water before she placed it on the brazier.

Once the tea was made, they sat outside to eat their barm cakes and sandwiches. There was fish paste in Mabel's barm cake and she wouldn't have been surprised if the others had paste as well. There wasn't that much choice these days. A picture sprang into her mind of Mumsy's pre-war picnics, with dainty finger sandwiches, delicious meat pies, salads and summer fruits, complete with a jug of cream. Oh yes, and bottles of wine and homemade cordial standing in wine cool-ers packed with ice.

And here she was with fish paste! Mind you, one of the advantages of having a billet in 1 Wilton Close was that Mrs Grayson was a wizard in the kitchen. She was a fellow lodger who had assumed responsibility for all the cooking and baking while Mrs Cooper, their landlady, took care of the house as well as working as a cleaner.

There was also a slice of walnut cake in Mabel's snap-tin today. When she took it out, she caught Louise looking at it and immediately held it out to her.

'Here, have a taste. Go on. It's de-lish. According to Mrs Grayson, it's eggless and fatless, but I swear you'd never know.'

Louise took a tiny bite and closed her eyes for a moment in appreciation. 'Lovely. Thanks. My mum's a good baker an' all, but she gives the boys the lion's share.'

'More fool her,' Bernice said bluntly. 'Sorry, Lou. I know I shouldn't speak against your ma, but the whole point of rationing is that we all get the same.'

Louise shrugged.

Bernice tilted her head back to drain the last drop from her mug. 'C'mon, girls. Back to work.'

Mabel replaced the lid on her snap-tin and put it back into her knapsack along with her mug, easing them in beside her bottle of hand lotion – another thing you couldn't get for love nor money these days, but there were recipes in abundance in women's magazines and this one smelled faintly of roses. Also in her knapsack was the most essential of all items: toilet paper. There was a toilet, if you could call it that, built onto the side of this particular lengthmen's hut – a tiny add-on containing a bucket, which was smelly and profoundly unpleasant to use. It was a toss-up as to which was better: using the bucket or nipping behind a bush.

They walked back to their section of permanent way. The sky was azure-blue, almost cloudless.

'A perfect summer sky,' said Bette. 'Mind you, the war has taught us a clear sky isn't necessarily something to be appreciated.'

'Will we ever look at a sky like this again without fearing a clear night for the Luftwaffe to come calling?' asked Bernice. 'I know the raids have dwindled to practically nothing these days, but I still wonder.'

Mabel nodded. The most recent air raid over Manchester had been in May, the night Max was born, and the previous one had taken place as long ago as January but, even so, she wasn't taking anything for granted. Manchester had suffered heavy air raids throughout the second half of 1940 and it hadn't been until the autumn of 1941, less than a year ago, that the attacks had started to tail off.

'My younger brothers loved the air raids,' said Louise. 'They thought it great sport to identify the planes and collect pieces of shrapnel.'

'I hope the war will be over long before Max is old enough to do any of that,' said Bernice and, for once, the others didn't tease her about bringing her precious grandson into the conversation.

As they arrived at the place where they'd left off earlier, they stood to watch a train go by on the furthest track away. Two locomotives pulled a long line of goods wagons that took ages to pass by. Every time Mabel saw a pair of locos working together, she wondered whether there was more to it than simply hauling a heavy load. Was it in part because these were locos that in peacetime would have been retired before now? Many older locos were still at work because of the war.

It was the same for people. Numerous old folk had come out of retirement to step into the places of men who had been called up. And not just old folk – women too. Housewives and mothers who, before the war, would have spent their lives inside the home now did long hours of war work before going home to cook and clean and put the children to bed. Girls who, pre-war, would have worked only until they got married now carried on working, doing their bit for the war effort. That was what everyone did, everyone in the entire kingdom: their bit.

'You and me will work together until tea-break,' Bernice said to Bette, 'and Mabel and Lou.'

Some gangs of lengthmen always worked in the same pairs, but Bernice preferred to chop and change about. Mabel liked that. She felt it strengthened them as a group. Not that you had much breath left over for chatting when you were hefting a sleeper or shovelling ballast, but swapping the pairs made you feel you all knew one another.

Bernice was the sensible, no-nonsense sort, which made her an effective boss, but she was kind-hearted too and her heart had positively turned to mush ever since the arrival of her baby grandson. Bette (with her double-T-E, just like Bette Davies) had copper-coloured hair that peeped out at the front of her turban and hour-glass curves. She had been a barmaid before the war but had taken to working as a lengthman as if she'd been born to it. That left Louise. Though she was careful not to let it show, Mabel had always felt rather sorry for her. At the start of the war, she'd looked thin and under-nourished, though like so many who had grown up in deprived circumstances, she had benefited from wartime rationing. She would always be as slim as a reed because she had that sort of build, but she didn't look underfed any longer.

Yet that wasn't the main reason Mabel felt sorry for her. Lou came from a pretty rough background. Her father, who by all accounts had been a violent man, had abandoned his family before the war, whereupon Louise's older brother Rob had stepped in and taken up where he'd left off, fists an' all. Then, early last year, Mabel and her chums had worked together to catch a thief who was helping himself from a secret store of food. It turned out there was not one thief but two: one of whom they had caught, and the other who had escaped and disappeared for good – Rob Wadden.

Hoping that her thoughts hadn't shown in her face, Mabel cleared her mind and applied herself to lifting the next sleeper. Although her muscles were strong and her body was now honed after more than two years of hard physical labour, it was still an effort. She was proud to have a tough physical task to perform rather than, say, something clerical. Pops might be a rich factory owner, but Grandad had been a humble wheel-tapper. Mabel had loved him dearly and she still missed him. Working as a lengthman made her feel they were connected.

'What are you smiling at?' Louise asked.

'I'm remembering my grandad.'

'The wheel-tapper? It takes real skill to do that. You have to be able to hear the tiniest fault.'

Mabel knew Louise's praise was for wheel-tappers in general, not for Grandad personally, but she felt chuffed all the same. She hid it beneath a laugh. 'Not like us, eh? Shovelling ballast.'

Louise laughed too. 'Ah, but this is precision-shovelling to put exactly the right amount under the sleeper, and you've got to keep it level.'

She stopped talking as she matched the action to the words. When she had finished, Mabel lowered the sleeper back into place, then stretched her spine.

'One more,' said Louise. 'Then we'll change over and you can shovel and pack.'

'Deal,' agreed Mabel.

The women carried on until Bernice called a halt for their tea break. They walked across the tracks, lifting their feet clear with each step, and settled themselves at the side. The ground was hard and bumpy, the grass thin and coarse, but who cared so long as it was dry? Out came the flasks. The tea that had been poured in early that morning had cooled somewhat by this time, but again, who cared? It might be cooling and wartime-weak, but it was tea and that was what counted.

Finishing hers, Bette lit up a cigarette and lay on her back, blowing smoke into the air. Mabel tilted her face towards the sun, closing her eyes in pleasure at the feel of the warmth on her skin.

'How's your mum getting on with her cleaning job, Lou?' Bette asked.

Mabel poured a thousand blessings on Bette's head. It was a question she would have liked to ask, but she always felt constrained from doing so. As the person who had arranged for Mrs Wadden to lend a hand when needed in Mrs Cooper's little cleaning business, Magic Mop, she didn't feel she could ask in case Louise thought she was lording it. She could be a bit spiky about personal matters.

'Fine, thanks.' Louise took out the remaining half of the cigarette she had started at dinnertime. 'She likes the work and the money helps. Things were rather tight after Rob went.'

'Aye,' said Bernice. 'I expect they were.'

After Rob went? Mabel looked at Bette and Bernice, neither of whom batted an eyelid. Mabel had to glance away for fear of her own eyelids batting like crazy. *After Rob went!* Louise said it as casually as if he had gone off to join the army. The man was a wartime criminal, and a violent brother to boot. For all Mabel knew, he was a violent son to his mother, too. To hear Louise now, you'd never imagine he had given her a serious beating before he disappeared. After he went, indeed!

'And with your Clifford leaving school this summer,' Bernice added, 'that'll be a bit more money coming in. He won't earn much at fourteen, but it all adds up.'

Soon it was time to return to work for the final stint. A length was the space from one set of joints in the track to the next, and each gang was required to do a certain number of lengths every day, hence being called lengthmen.

When they had finished, they walked back to the station, where they'd arrived this morning, and waited for the next train to Manchester Victoria. It came chuffing along the track, white clouds puffing from its funnel. Chuffing and puffing both ceased as the train coasted alongside the platform. The brakes squealed and the train slowed, then there was a loud clunk as it halted, doors already banging open and passengers emerging.

Those waiting on the platform pressed forward. There was a feeling of urgency these days when boarding a train. So many passenger trains were full to bursting even before they started off and there was always the worry you wouldn't get aboard.

'Think slim, girls!' Bette said and the four of them squeezed on.

They had to 'think slim' all the way to Victoria, where Mabel's heart lifted as it always did when the half-spicy, half-sweet scents of steam and smoke crept into her nostrils. This was the smell of the railway and she loved it. To her, the railway meant Grandad.

Passengers surged up the platform towards the barrier. On the adjacent platform, a guard was walking the length of the train, slamming doors and checking those already closed were secure as he prepared the train for the off. Mabel and the others joined the crowd working its way past the ticket collector and onto the concourse that stretched out beneath the overarching metal and glass canopy. Opposite the platform was the long line of ticket office windows contained within an elegant sweep of wood panelling, and over at one end were the buffet and the restaurant, the exterior walls of which were tiled in pale yellow, as was the bookstall. The restaurant boasted a glass dome on its roof as befitted a first-class facility.

Bernice must have caught Mabel looking, because she said, 'I can't look at that dome now without shuddering. Just imagine if it had fallen in when our Joan was in there having Max. As if giving birth in an air raid wasn't bad enough.'

They went to the Ladies', each of them using the supposedly 'out of order' cubicle that meant they didn't have to queue up with members of the public.

Louise stood beside Mabel at the mirror above the basins. 'Are you meeting your friends in the buffet before you go home?'

Before Mabel could answer, Bette thrust her face in between theirs, her eyes twinkling in the reflection.

'Of course she isn't, you daft ha'p'orth. She'll be heading home at a run to get ready for darling Harry, won't you, Mabel?'

Mabel laughed, too excited to feel embarrassed. 'Since you mention it …'

She wasn't just seeing him tonight. She was going to be with him tomorrow evening too, at a dance that Cordelia had invited all her friends to. Mabel felt tingly with happiness all the way home. She loved living there in Wilton Close. To begin with, she'd shared a bedroom with Joan and the two of them had become good friends. These days, Mabel shared with Margaret while Alison bunked down in the small bedroom at the end of the landing that in former times had been the boxroom.

When Mabel opened the front gate and entered the garden, Mrs Cooper and Mrs Grayson were sitting on kitchen chairs in the sunshine, shelling peas into a large cream-coloured bowl.

'Hello, Mabel dear,' said Mrs Cooper. 'Have you had a good day?'

Mabel joined them on the lawn, sitting at their feet. Before the war, she would have thought nothing of helping herself to a few juicy peas from the bowl, but no one did things like that now. Food was precious and you didn't fritter it away.

They chatted for a few minutes, then Mabel stood up.

'I'll go and get changed.'

She ran upstairs to take off her work clobber and put on a skirt and scoop-necked top before carrying her corduroy trousers and old shirt outside to give them a good whack against the wall, jumping backwards so the day's dust didn't settle all over her. She hated feeling dirty. Mind you, no matter how grimy or sweaty her own job was, it was nothing compared to Margaret's work as an engine cleaner.

Soon Alison and Margaret arrived home and it wasn't long before the girls were setting the table while Mrs Grayson and Mrs Cooper finished off in the kitchen.

When they sat down, Mrs Cooper said grace.

'Thank you for our meal and thank you for Lord Woolton, and please bless the brave men of the merchant navy. Amen.'

'And thank you for Mrs Grayson and her magic wooden spoon,' Mabel added.

Mrs Cooper looked flustered. 'I'm not sure you should say thank you for something that doesn't really exist.'

They tucked into tomato macaroni followed by stewed apple. Afterwards, Margaret rose from her place. Her hazel eyes had sometimes looked strained earlier in the year, but now they were warm and serene.

'I'll wash up and put the kettle on,' she said. 'I imagine you two are dying to linger over a cup of tea, aren't you?' She looked at Mabel and Alison.

'Very funny,' said Mabel as she stood up, Alison following suit. She addressed Mrs Cooper. 'Excuse us dashing from the table, Mrs C, but you know how it is.'

'I think I can guess.' Mrs Cooper smiled.

'You're welcome to come out with us, if you like', Alison told Margaret.

'Thanks for the offer, but I'm going to the flicks with Persephone. We're going to see *The Maltese Falcon*.'

'Ooh, I like Humphrey Bogart,' said Alison.

Margaret nudged her. 'You're not supposed to go all dreamy over another man when you're about to go out with Joel.'

Mabel and Alison went upstairs to get ready. Mabel changed into the apple-green dress she had worn last summer as one of Joan's bridesmaids. They had all worn something pretty and they'd had matching lacy boleros and also knitted white flowers attached to their hats so that, even though their dresses were all different, they still had a similar appearance.

Mabel brushed her dark brown hair, securing it away from her face with a pair of diamanté clips and letting it hang loose down her back. Then she went along the landing to Alison's room, where she found Alison fastening her pale yellow dress.

Alison laughed. 'Look at us. A pair of bridesmaids.'

Mabel helped Alison do her hair – and just in time too, because the doorbell rang and Mrs Grayson called up the stairs.

'Harry's here.'

Mabel darted back into her room to pick up her beaded evening bag, then ran downstairs to greet Harry with a quick kiss before standing back, feeling a little breathless as she drank in the sight of his dark eyes, generous mouth and broad forehead. He had taken off his cap, showing his slicked-back short back and sides and the slight widow's peak at his temples. He was so handsome that her heart drummed in her chest, but it wasn't just that he was good-looking. It was also because he was in uniform. Mabel had a thing about men in uniform. They looked so much more attractive than fellows in civies. The combination of Harry's looks and his RAF blue was enough to make her bones melt.

Harry escorted the girls into town, where they were to meet Joel outside the Ritz ballroom on Whitworth Street. Joel would be coming straight from work, having got ready at the end of his hospital shift. Mabel felt like an old married woman as she smiled in pleasure at the sight of Alison's sparkling eyes and pink cheeks when Joel appeared.

He was good-looking, but he wasn't in Harry's league.

It was always a delight to be at the Ritz, with its graceful pillars, art deco features, and balcony above, from where you could sit at the tables and look down onto the dancers and the famous revolving stage, if you felt so inclined. Personally, Mabel was far more interested in being on the dancefloor.

They chose a table before taking to the floor for a waltz followed by a quickstep. Mabel felt weightless as she whirled around in Harry's arms. How she loved him! Early in their relationship, she had been distraught to discover that his original interest in her had stemmed from finding out about her father's money, but he had worked hard to convince her that, since then he had truly fallen in love with her. From then on, their love had deepened and he meant the world to her – just as she knew she meant the world to him.

'Shall we sit this one out?' Harry suggested.

He escorted her to their table, holding the chair for her as she sat down, then he went to buy drinks. When he returned, he pulled his chair closer to hers. Oh, the temptation to snuggle against him! Plenty of other couples these days showed their feelings in public in a way that would have been unthinkable before the war but Mabel, although she was happy to show affection, had never – much as she had been tempted – quite shaken off the influence of Mumsy and her etiquette book. Nobody was better acquainted with the rules of social behaviour than Esme Bradshaw. It came from being new money and a determination not to make any blunders.

'I've got something to tell you,' said Harry.

His dark eyes were serious and alarm flickered into life inside Mabel.

'What is it?' she asked.

'Don't panic. You'll think it's good.'

'But you don't?' Mabel asked at once. 'Sorry. Tell me what it is and I won't interrupt.'

'Last year, the Air Council put a two-hundred-hour maximum on any single tour of duty. What's meant to happen now is that you do your tour of duty, then you're rotated for six months before your next tour. It's normal to spend the six months working in the OTU – that's the Operational Training Unit – training up the next batch of pilots and so forth.'

'Or bomb aimers, in your case,' said Mabel, making sure she kept her voice steady as she said the words.

'And my tour of duty is coming to an end,' said Harry.

'I understand if you feel disappointed to be grounded, but obviously it'll be a relief to me.' And how! Being the bomb aimer was said to be the most dangerous position.

'There's something else,' Harry went on. 'RAF Burtonwood is going to become an American air base. I'll be leaving there.'

Mabel's breath caught in her throat. Having Harry close to Manchester had always been something to be grateful for.

'Where will you be sent?' This time, there was no keeping the tremor out of her voice.

'I don't know yet,' said Harry. 'It could be anywhere...'

Stories You'll Love to Share

SIGN UP TO OUR NEW SAGA NEWSLETTER

Penny Street

The home of heart-warming reads

Penny Street is a newsletter bringing you the latest book deals, competitions and alerts of new saga series releases.

Read about the research behind your favourite books, try our monthly wordsearch and download your very own Penny Street reading map.

Join today by visiting
www.penguin.co.uk/pennystreet

Follow us on Facebook
www.facebook.com/welcometopennystreet/